PANGOLIN

PANGOLIN

Peter Driscoll

J. B. Lippincott Company | Philadelphia and New York

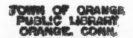

U.S. Library of Congress Cataloging in Publication Data

Driscoll, Peter, birth date
Pangolin.

I. Title.
PZ4.D7816 Pan [PR6054.R53]   823'.9'14   79-471
ISBN-0-397-01070-2

For Stephanie Townsend

Outline of a Memorandum
on the Project

Objectives: To abduct an employee of the United States Government, code-named Pangolin. To hold him prisoner until the ransom demanded of his employers has been paid.

Personnel required: Four.

Procedure: See Memorandum attached.

Observations: Kidnapping is generally an unsuccessful crime because it has two inherent weaknesses:
1. At some stage the kidnapper must expose himself in order to collect the ransom;
2. Unless he is executed, the victim can usually identify the kidnapper after release.

In this Project, no rendezvous will be necessary; and Pangolin will never know who his abductors were.

Budgeted expenditure: Twelve thousand dollars (Hong Kong).

Anticipated profits: Ten million dollars (U.S.).

Prologue

The March morning was cloudy and cool, but with a hint of the soggy humidity of summer already in the air, dampening Kao Ling's shirt under the armpits as he walked up the steep incline of the Wanchai Gap Road. At this point it was no more than a narrow paved footpath running straight up the side of Victoria Peak, leaving the traffic and crowds and noise of Wanchai far below. To the right there was low forest, dense and impenetrable. On the left, squatter shacks had been built in the gully beside the road, flimsy tiers of planking and tin that looked likely to be swept away by the next typhoon.

He was growing short of breath but he went on climbing at the same steady pace until, well above the squatter camp, he reached the intersection with Bowen Road. Another footpath pretending to be a road, this, but running level across the hillside and giving a sweeping view of the harbour, the concrete slabs of Kowloon on the other side and, almost lost in haze, the distant purple mountains of China. Panting, feeling his face lightly filmed with sweat, Kao Ling rested for a minute. He ignored the view and stared back along the deserted footpath, clearly visible all the way down to where it met up with Kennedy Road. No one could have followed him up there without making himself obvious. He had no reason to believe he had been followed, but it was as well to be sure.

When he had recovered his breath he set off along Bowen Road to the west. On this weekday morning he had the path to himself. He rounded a bend and the skyscrapers of Central District came into view —a spectacular sight, if not exactly beautiful. Now he could see, too, the place where Bowen Road ceased to be a footpath and actually became a road. There was a viewing point here, a clearing that backed onto a hollow in the hillside, with benches scattered round it and a few parking spaces, only one of which was taken.

The car was a pale green Plymouth. Two men sat in it, a Chinese chauffeur in the front and a Westerner in the rear, watching him approach. Kao Ling got a fleeting impression of ginger-blonde hair edged with grey, blue eyes, a tawny complexion. He stopped in the centre of the clearing and turned to stare out across the deep blue of the harbour. A hundred junks and lighters and sampans and ferryboats plied across it, all seemingly set on collision courses. He stood there for a minute while the men in the car took stock of him. Then he heard a door open and footsteps approaching, steel-tipped heels crunching the gravel. They stopped behind him and slightly to his left. A lighter snapped. Kao smelt the smoke of a toasted cigarette.

He took a deep breath. "A remarkable view," he said. "They say it is one of the world's great sights."

"Personally," said the American, "I think San Francisco Bay has the edge."

"I wouldn't know about that."

There was an awkward silence, as if, with the artificial preliminaries out of the way, they were searching for a real opening to the conversation. Both of them were nervous.

Finally Kao said, "You are the one to whom he addressed the letter?"

"Yes."

"You were supposed to come alone."

"That wasn't possible. Benjy is only my driver; he's paid not to be interested."

"All the same—"

"Listen," the American snapped, "I've broken enough of my own rules coming up here, meeting you like this." He paused. "Who are you, anyway?"

"My name is Kao Ling."

"Ah." Recognition came into the American's tone. "New China News Agency, right?"

"I work in the bureau here."

"But what are you to him?"

"A friend."

"A good one?"

"Taking such a risk for him, I would hope so." Kao Ling suddenly felt exposed and vulnerable, the protection of anonymity stripped away. He turned to face the American. "Let us walk a little way, please."

The other man drew on his cigarette, thinking about that, and then nodded. Close to, his appearance was rather boyish: smooth tanned skin and clear blue eyes belying the grey hairs and the weight of his influ-

10

ence. An android, Ch'ien had once called him, a man who took decisions without reference to human feelings, with the indecent detachment of a computer calculating megadeaths. A powerful and well-protected android, all the same.

They turned together and began to stroll along the footpath, back in the direction Kao had come from. The chauffeur, who was clearly also a bodyguard, got out of the car and followed them at a discreet distance.

"I gather you smuggled the letter out of Peking and posted it here in Hong Kong. It was addressed to me in person. Why?"

"Because he knew you. He trusts your discretion. He wants to deal with you personally."

"That would be very irregular. How did he know I was stationed here, anyway?"

"As an alternate member of the Party's Central Committee he sees intelligence reports, I imagine. Your presence here would hardly have escaped the notice of our secret service."

"The letter was subjected to analysis, naturally. The handwriting compares well with the samples we have on file. However . . ."

He was good at this, Kao thought. He would state his reservations obliquely, keeping face for both of them.

"I'm sure you'll understand how hard it is for us to accept this for what it appears to be. To start with, we must ask ourselves whether it is a forgery. And if we decide that it is not, we must ask whether it was written under duress."

"I was with him when he wrote it," Kao said simply. "There was no coercion."

The American gave a polite nod. "Then there is the question of motives—his own, and perhaps other people's." He was choosing his words carefully. "The biggest question of all is: Why? A man using you as a courier sends a message to us. This man is not only your country's leading expert in his field but a member of the Central Committee, and he wants to come over to us. Why, Mr. Kao?"

"He lived in your country once," Kao said. "That is part of the reason."

"He was hounded out of it by the McCarthyites."

"He does not believe that era will be repeated. He has faith in the present generation. He remembers you, as a young officer assigned to his case, telling him things would soon get better, trying to persuade him to stay. He admires you for your foresight."

11

If the American felt flattered he showed nothing. "My motives were simple," he said. "I would rather have had him designing rockets at Pasadena than Lop Nor."

"His background is part of the trouble. Because of the years he spent away, he has never been fully trusted. He brought barbarian ways back with him. We can be a xenophobic people, you know." Kao Ling allowed himself a small smile. "But his fears are more fundamental. He has always been a moderate—too moderate for the radicals who may well regain control of the Party soon. He will lose his seat on the Committee and perhaps disappear from public view. Political oblivion can easily lead to total oblivion. He fears, frankly, for his life."

"A man that valuable? That's preposterous!"

"During the Cultural Revolution," Kao said mildly, "a man named Liu Shih-kun, one of the country's most talented pianists, was seized by the Red Guards. They objected to his playing bourgeois music. They broke his fingers, one by one. He has been unable to play since. That was preposterous, but it happened. Political line is everything."

They walked on for a minute without speaking. Beside the path, mynah birds chuckled and squabbled over the contents of litter bins. The man in the chauffeur's uniform kept twenty yards behind.

"What does he expect of us?" the American asked at last.

"Asylum. He is watched. He must choose the time and place of departure for himself. It may be a year, even two years, before the opportunity comes. Meanwhile he wants an assurance that he will be welcomed."

"How can we contact him?"

"Only through me. I am in Peking once every month."

The American stopped walking and faced the other man squarely. "Mr. Kao, I do not like to say this. In this trade it is too easy to believe the things that we want to believe, and there are always people eager to tell us such things. We learn to be sceptical. When someone offers me the defection of Ch'ien Hsue-shen, the head of the Chinese missile programme, then I have to be very sceptical indeed."

"Perhaps," said Kao with dignity, "others might be less so."

"The Soviets? The British? I doubt it. I am willing to believe, Mr. Kao, and you say Ch'ien is willing to trust me. Have him send me proof."

"What proof?"

"Something more than a letter. Something whose authenticity we

12

can check. Information." The American watched Kao carefully. "Information connected, shall we say, with his work."

Kao felt a thrill of apprehension. "You are asking him to commit espionage?"

"If he crosses over he'll be doing that anyway. That's always the bargain—asylum in exchange for information. He will have to give us everything. Where is the difference in giving a small part now?"

"He will not agree," Kao said. "His loyalty may not be to the Party, but it is to China."

"And yours, Mr. Kao?"

"Something of the same."

"Yet you would help him get out?"

"Because he is a *friend,*" Kao said vehemently.

The American offered him his pack of Lucky Strikes. Kao shook his head. The American lit one for himself. "You took a risk bringing that letter out, another risk meeting me here. Obviously you thought they were worth taking, for his sake. The risk would be no greater if, next time you went to Peking, you brought back some documents. Something of his choice, anything he could copy without undue risk. I could arrange a safe means of delivery. It would not be necessary for you to see me again."

Kao stared at him in horror. "It is out of the question."

"I must have that proof."

"Then you must get it another way."

"I can't force you," the American said, "but if the only access to Ch'ien is through you . . . can't I ask you to think it over?"

"It is no use. I refuse absolutely."

"There is no other way, Mr. Kao. At least speak to him. Put my suggestion to him."

Kao swung away and began to walk again. The American sidled along a few paces behind. Within a minute they had reached the junction of the Wanchai Gap Road, where Kao stopped, glanced down the pathway and faced the American again.

"I shall speak to him, nothing more. I shall give his answer to you next month. To you personally; it is out of the question that I deal with anyone else."

He turned away and began to walk down the path. "Wait!" the American called.

He had taken out a small notebook and was scribbling in it. He tore out the sheet and handed it to the Chinese.

"Call me when you're ready, but not through the consulate switchboard. That's a secure number, unlisted, unbugged. Memorize it and destroy the paper. And by the way, don't use my real name. Ask for Pangolin."

PART ONE

1

The Project was born on the day of the picnic; of that there was never any doubt. But its conception, so to speak, had occurred through one of those coincidences that can later be seen to have set a whole train of events in motion. Two things happened to Alan Pritchard on Tuesday, the twenty-fifth of July: he received a fateful summons to the office of the general manager of the *Cathay Star,* and he bumped into Ailsa.

It was one of the regrets of Pritchard's life that he had not, all that time ago, plucked up the courage to kill off his failing marriage and make an honest woman of Ailsa. Things might have been different for him if he had. There had never seemed any likelihood that they would meet up again, but there it was—six years later, a thousand miles from Saigon, he found himself staring at her across the lobby of the Mandarin Hotel.

The beginning had been earlier. He had arrived at work, as usual, at seven forty that morning. The *Star* had its premises in Kennedy Town, two miles and a far cry from the smart modern office blocks of Central District. Here, in one of the oldest parts of Hong Kong, the buildings were lowlier and shabbier, and the dark shopfronts of herbalists and pawnbrokers, jade dealers and snake merchants, lurked in shadow along the colonnaded sidewalks. Tourists thought it picturesque; to Pritchard it sometimes brought an unsettling sense of alienation. Take away the taxis and the neon signs and you might have been in one of the old China Treaty Ports in the days before the *gwai-los,* the foreign devils, had made their presence felt.

Kennedy Town and the *Cathay Star* suited each other. It was the oldest of Hong Kong's English-language newspapers. Once an influential voice in the colony's affairs—in the 1890s it had campaigned against the abolition of the opium trade—it had been running at a loss for several years now, and rumours of imminent closure surfaced from time to time. Even the takeover from its old European management by a powerful Chinese publishing syndicate, ruthless in their cost-cutting,

17

had failed to stop the slide. In the Quill Club they said, privately and sometimes not so privately, that you couldn't do much worse than work for the *Star*. Pritchard never took up the argument. They probably said that he and the *Star* suited each other too, a pair of old Far East hands looking grumblingly back on better days.

The building was an uninspiring place to work, a four-storeyed tenement converted into what was basically a factory. There was little concession to its partial role as an office block and none at all to style. The front door opened into a tiny lobby; straight through from there was the machine room. Up a flight of stairs was a combined switchboard and reception desk, where a sullen Cantonese girl spent most of her day painting her fingernails with green varnish. Beyond that were the editorial offices, small, cramped and awkwardly partitioned with dark wood and glass, like cubicles in a Victorian public house.

Pritchard went through the newsroom to the sub-editors' office. Corless, the new young chief sub, was in already, frowning over a dummy page layout. He'd been through the overnight agency tapes and there was a pile of stories in his basket. Pritchard said hello and Corless looked significantly at his watch. This had happened most mornings lately, ever since a month ago when Corless, exercising a precarious authority over a man nearly twice his age, had reprimanded him for coming in late. For the sake of his self-respect, Pritchard had taken to arriving ten minutes late every morning. Corless had never quite plucked up the courage to reproach him again, but always made his displeasure known. It was a small test of wills that usually got the day off to a bad start.

"Take this Filipino kidnapping story first, would you, Alan? We may have to lead the first edition with it if nothing better turns up."

Deliberately, Pritchard took off his jacket, hung it over the back of his chair and rolled up his sleeves before approaching the desk to collect the story. Then he started work.

Six days a week for almost three years, his job had been the same. He would work for nine and a half hours, with a break for lunch and a couple of beers at a cooked-food stall round the corner. He would cut and rewrite copy, mark it up for the typesetter, and compose headlines. For a man of his experience it was mind-bending work; one day, he thought, someone would invent a machine that did it more efficiently. He spent much of his time looking forward to the high point of the day, at five o'clock, when the final edition of the *Star* had been put to bed and he would catch a tram to the Quill for his first drink of the evening.

18

His day was entirely predictable and rarely varied. He was surprised, then, five minutes after his arrival, when the switchboard girl came in and accosted him.

"Mr. So want to see you."

"Mr. So? You mean now?"

"Now. Right now," she said with a hint of indignation, as though no summons from Mr. So, the general manager, could be construed as anything but immediate. At least it was unusual. Mr. So usually sent for people just as they were leaving for home, thereby avoiding the loss of working time. And he summoned rarely to praise, often to blame.

Pritchard was still working on the kidnapping story. He turned to Corless.

"Seems I'm wanted on high."

"Make it as quick as you can, Alan."

He put his jacket back on—that was the form for a visit to Mr. So—and trudged with vague apprehension up to the general manager's office on the third floor, trying to recall some story he had handled recently that might have led to a complaint. Usually there would be a pompous letter from some Chinese lawyer: *Our attention has been called to a headline in your issue of* . . .

Mr. So—you could only call him that; none of the European staff knew his other names—had been installed by the new owners last year. He was a very small, narrow-framed Cantonese of indefinite age with a gaze made impenetrable by thick, oval-framed glasses. Sitting in the large swivel chair behind his desk he looked like some unsmiling Chinese version of a Charlie McCarthy puppet—knees drawn together, legs dangling, hands held loose by his sides, a tiny mandarin who took most of the important decisions over the head of the *Star*'s editor, an aging Australian who was nowadays more interested in safeguarding his pension. He waved Pritchard to a seat and sent the *foki,* his personal messenger, to fetch tea. While they waited he made small talk, in his excellent but convoluted English, about the headlines in the morning papers. When the tea came they drank a small cupful each and Mr. So refilled Pritchard's from the pot. Then he said, "How long have you been here now?"

"Nearly three years. Three in September."

"Longer than myself. It must have been quite a change, after your years as a foreign correspondent."

"Yes." Pritchard shrugged. "I've got used to it."

"All the same," Mr. So persisted gently, "for a man of your

background, with an international reputation, this—working down-table on what is, after all, a small colonial newspaper ... you can't view it as a permanent career, surely?"

"Right now it's the only one I've got."

"Of course." Mr. So looked troubled. "It was the Federated Press you were with, wasn't it? I suppose you did a lot of travelling, lived in many different places."

"I joined them in Singapore. That was nearly twenty years ago. Then I was based in Kuala Lumpur for a while, and Bangkok and Saigon. There was a lot of hopping to and fro, of course; there always is, in those wire-service jobs."

"Unfortunately we're not able to offer you the same benefits here. You earned an American salary, I imagine?"

"Yes."

"And fringe benefits? Expenses? Free housing?"

Pritchard nodded.

"Don't you hanker after that life?"

"Sometimes." From the blankness of Mr. So's face it was impossible to guess where the discussion was leading. "Sometimes it's more than a hankering, to be honest. But those days are over. I've put it all behind me."

"I would not blame you, though, for wanting to get back to it. In your position I would keep a sharp lookout for opportunities." He paused. "You can be quite frank, Mr. Pritchard. Do you have your eye on some other job?"

Pritchard smiled and drank some tea. Either Mr. So was naive or he was being too Chinese-subtle to make sense. "No," he said. "I won't pretend I haven't looked around. Reuters, AP, UPI, France Presse, I've tried them all. And the newspapers, British, American, Australian, you name it. They're looking for bright young kids with degrees in Chinese these days. I'm forty years old. Besides, I have a history. There's a funny thing about journalism. You can be a promising young man for quite a long time and then one bright morning you wake up and find you're a has-been. Particularly if you wake up in a hospital bed suffering from alcoholic poisoning. You've heard the story, of course. Probably you've heard one of the more lurid exaggerations."

Mr. So stared into his teacup. Perhaps he was trying to save Pritchard's face, since the Englishman clearly had no regard for it himself. He must surely know the story of the spectacular crack-up that had cost Pritchard his job with Federated.

20

"The reason I ask," said Mr. So, raising his eyes to watch Pritchard carefully through the thick lenses, "is that I have a problem. You know we have been cutting costs?"

"Yes."

"We have tried to get our staff down to a more manageable size, financially."

That was a euphemism. In the tradition of the sweatshop, the new management had dramatically improved efficiency by paring the staff to the minimum.

"One more job has to go, Mr. Pritchard."

"Which job?"

"That's why I wondered if you had something else lined up."

Belatedly, Pritchard began to get the meaning of this tortuous discussion. "Just a minute. Are you telling me that . . . ?"

"You've worked very competently here. Nobody is sorrier than I."

"For Christ's sake, what are you saying?" Pritchard demanded, standing up to tower threateningly over Mr. So.

"We have thought carefully. We decided, in fairness to men with families, men a bit younger than yourself . . ."

"Look, are you firing me or aren't you?"

"Firing?" Mr. So raised two offended palms. "No, there is no question of that. You will be made redundant, quite a different thing. You will leave under no cloud whatever, with an excellent testimonial. In fact it can be arranged for you to volunteer for redundancy."

"And what happens if I don't feel like volunteering?"

"That would be less agreeable to everyone, don't you think? Remember, the terms of your appointment do not include compensation for redundancy."

"Well?"

"We do not have to keep to the letter of those terms, provided we can settle things amicably."

"You're saying if I go without a fuss you'll give me some kind of golden handshake?"

Mr. So could not bring himself to acknowledge this. He spread his hands and said, "It would be best to keep things friendly, that is all."

"Listen," Pritchard said, placing both hands on the desk and thrusting his face close to the little man's. "Before I took a nose dive three years ago I was right at the peak of this profession. I was one of the top agency men in the East. I could have wiped the floor with anyone on this rag. I've still got some pride left; don't expect me to trade it for charity."

Unmoved, Mr. So adjusted his glasses. "You came here with a reputation behind you, of course. All the same, you took the job . . ."

"Because it was the only one I could get," Pritchard said, drawing back, the flicker of defiance going out in him.

". . . and you accepted the conditions. One of them is one month's notice of termination of employment. I do not intend to be so arbitrary. What I propose is this: leave at any time you like within the next three months. We will pay your salary up to the departure date and also, in recognition of your three years' service, we will pay you an amount equivalent to two months' salary. I don't think you can say that is not generous. A flexible departure date will also allow you to seize any opportunity that comes up."

"I'm sure offers will come flooding in," Pritchard said bitterly.

Mr. So joined his palms and parted them, a Buddhistic gesture of helplessness. Then he stood up, indicating that the interview was over.

2

The tram that took Pritchard back to Central at five that evening was more crowded than usual and consequently hotter, a clanking sardine can packed with steaming Asian flesh, an invitation to claustrophobia if ever there was one. There'd been times in the past few years when everything around him, the whole encompassment of his life, seemed to pen him in just as these inescapable hordes of Chinese did. There was no opening in it, no vision of the future. Even the dream that English expatriates in the tropics cling to—the retirement home in green, gentle countryside, Sunday-morning drinks in the village pub, walks in the autumn woods—was alien to his experience and struck no chord in him.

The sense of desolation had increased, not diminished, in the three years since he had, quite simply, broken down under the weight of events. Too much had happened too quickly not to have done something permanently destructive to him—the divorce, the death of his son, the strain of the work he had been doing in Vietnam, then the crack-up that had nearly killed him. Now this—not that it rated very high on the melodrama scale, but he had discovered that you could, after all, do worse than work for the *Cathay Star;* you could get fired from it.

Pritchard had been born in Johore, the son of an English rubber-estate manager, and, apart from a four-year period of evacuation with his mother in Australia during World War Two, had spent all his life in Asia. His father died in a Japanese internment camp in Singapore. His mother, returning to Malaya after the war to salvage what was left of her home and go back to England, instead met and married a colonial police officer. He drank a bottle of whisky a day and frequently assaulted her. What was left of his pay after his mess bills had been met was not enough to send Alan to a boarding school in England. He went —depending on where his stepfather was posted—to various day schools in Kuala Lumpur, Penang and Singapore, run by religious orders and attended mostly by the ambitious sons of middle-class Chinese merchants. He left school, and home, as early as possible and got a job at seventeen as a trainee journalist on the *Straits Times.*

When the newspaper had served its purpose as a training ground he landed a job in the Singapore bureau of the Federated Press, the American wire-service agency. At the age of twenty-five he became head of their bureau in Kuala Lumpur; it was there that he met and married Wendy, the daughter of a former colonial civil servant who had stayed on as an adviser to the government of independent Malaysia. In 1966 their son, Gary, was born.

Already, though, the cracks in their marriage had begun to show, as if reflecting inwardly the disruption that was all around them, the disintegration of what passed for an old order in Southeast Asia. American involvement in Vietnam was approaching its deepest level; Cambodia, Laos, and Thailand were being sucked increasingly into the maelstrom. Malaysia was experiencing its second Communist insurrection in twenty years; in Borneo the British were fighting the Indonesians. Among these conflicts Pritchard was building a reputation as a correspondent of international standing, but at considerable cost to his personal life. More often than not he was away from home; when he was there he was preoccupied with work and his schedule was unpredictable. Wendy, who had had a leisured colonial upbringing and liked to send out invitations to her dinner parties two weeks in advance, never did reconcile herself to the demands of his job.

That, of course, was a symptom and not the cause of what was

23

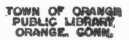

going wrong between them, a malignancy that festered for years without coming to a head, draining them both emotionally. They told themselves, and sometimes each other, that they were staying together for the child's sake. In fact that would not have prevented their parting if they had actually grown to hate or even strongly dislike each other. Instead of love there was only a debilitating indifference that kept either of them from making a positive move.

After Kuala Lumpur there were three years in Bangkok. Then came his last posting: Saigon, the eye of the storm, for which in a sense everything else seemed to have been a preparation. It was no place to take a family. He sent Wendy and Gary on an extended holiday to her parents, now retired and living in Hampshire, a holiday from which they never returned. After four years she asked him for a divorce and for custody of the boy. In the meantime Ailsa had entered, and then left, his life.

His time in Vietnam had been relentlessly demanding. After years on the periphery of the war he had discovered a commitment to it which amounted almost to an obsession. The Americans were pulling out by the time he arrived, and he was appalled at the legacy of destruction, waste and despair that was left behind. Driven by a need to expose the continuing horror and futility of the war in a way that few journalists any longer bothered to do, he concentrated on probing the corruption and inefficiency of the regime and the uselessness of the "Vietnamization" programme. He derided the South Vietnamese armed forces and, in one memorable special-feature article, went so far as to predict, eighteen months before it happened, their total collapse in the face of an all-out onslaught from the North.

Reporting of this nature endeared him neither to the American establishment in Saigon—the collection of earnest diplomats, snappish colonels, cold-eyed CIA officers, and fulsome public-relations men who inhabited the U.S. Mission—nor, at times, to his American-based employers. The story on the South Vietnamese army never went out on the wires; instead he received a curt cable from New York advising him to cease writing "opinionated" reports. He gained a reputation for being left-wing or, because of his tenuously British background, anti-American. In fact his only real prejudice arose from his identification with Asia. What made Vietnam important to him was that he had turned its torture into his own.

Meanwhile he was working himself—literally, in his doctor's opinion—half to death, seven days a week for anything up to eighteen hours

24

a day, chasing the agency man's perpetual deadline, living on whisky, adrenalin and nerves. Something had to give sooner or later, and it happened at a climactic moment—for Vietnam as well as for himself. On March 29, 1975, as the Communist tanks raced down Highway One from Hue to Da Nang and the ARVN divisions disintegrated in front of them and the country began its rapid slide into chaos, Pritchard received the cable from England that snapped his own fragile hold on himself.

Getting off the tram in Des Voeux Road, he walked through the rush-hour crowds to Gloucester Building and took the lift up to the Quill Club on the sixth floor. The Quill was a sort of poor relation to the fashionable Foreign Correspondents' Club, across in Sutherland House. It was where journalists went who could not afford the Foreign Correspondents' Club fees, and it offered none of the same amenities. It offered nothing, in fact, but a horseshoe-shaped bar counter, twenty rickety bamboo barstools and a couple of adjacent tables. It had been the fate of the Quill to grow old without becoming venerable. One of its few claims to distinction was that once a visiting American novelist, well-known in his own time, had spent fourteen hours drinking at the bar and then hanged himself on the chain in the men's lavatory. To some of the members it seemed ominously appropriate for the Quill to have witnessed the end of a career rather than the beginning.

Still, the drinks were cheap and you could get them on credit, though there came an unpleasant moment at the end of each month when the club manager would bow at Pritchard and present him with his accumulated chits in a fat little envelope resting on a saucer. He enjoyed the atmosphere, too. There were always people he knew there, journalists from the *Cathay Star* and the *South China Morning Post,* talking shop and exchanging gossip. Another reason he spent so much time there was that he hated going home to his empty flat.

It wasn't that he was lonely—or so he told himself. It was just that he was, somehow, uneasy in his own company, as if in spite of having lived alone for much of his life he had never quite grown used to the idea.

It was the usual sort of evening at the Quill. Although founded as a club for journalists, it could not afford to restrict its membership to them, and from five till about seven it was usually crowded with Europeans from the middle and lower rungs of the business community and the civil service. Pritchard found himself standing at the bar beside Ed Baxter.

"Wotcher, Alan? Get you a drink? What's in the news today, then?"

"Nothing very exciting."

"Get on, that's what you fellows always say. Scotch, is it? Still Life!" Baxter bellowed suddenly over the din of the crowd, thumping on the counter. It was one of the ruder nicknames for one of the club's two barmen, an ancient, stolid Shantungese who had been at the Quill thirty years and sublimated his hatred of the members into an infuriating sluggishness at serving them.

"Still Life, get Mr. Pritchard here a whisky-soda, plenty of ice. And another gin sling for me. Chop-chop!" he added as Still Life moved away, nodding and muttering to himself. He did not understand the nickname; or if he did it made him move all the slower.

"Dear me, this is the only club, the *only* one I know, that would put up with him," Baxter said with a sigh. He might have added, as Pritchard thought with secret amusement, that it was also the only club that would tolerate *him,* since it was widely rumoured that he'd been blackballed by both the Jockey and Royal Yacht clubs. He was in investment management, and when he had blown in from East Malaysia a couple of years ago he had brought with him a whiff of financial scandal; in Hong Kong it was a scent easily detected.

Baxter claimed to be Welsh, though his accent suggested Liverpool. He had also claimed at various times to be related to David Lloyd George, but closer inquiries into this relationship were met by a smokescreen of evasion. He was in his early thirties but had the look as well as the manner of an older man: his jawline self-indulgently blurred, his middle thickening against the waistband of a creased tropical suit. At one time his features had been framed by a scrubby black beard; since he had shaved it off, his face had seemed oddly formless, distinguished only by a pair of protuberant blue eyes that fixed you with an insistent, slightly manic stare. An excitable, devious, worrisome man, he was beset by minor obsessions and managed somehow to be at the same time engaging and irritating, assertive and craven, boastful yet strangely humble. Loosely speaking, Pritchard and he were friends; that was to say, they had not yet quarrelled. Baxter had fallen out with almost everyone in the Quill at one time or another, usually in the course of some trivial disagreement that he would inflate into a major issue. Pritchard rarely bothered to argue with him; they drank together and made no demands of each other.

"What's the inside story on this drug raid, then?" Baxter asked, fixing his eager blue gaze on Pritchard's face. He often spoke to journalists about "inside stories," crediting them with omniscience.

"I don't know any more about it than you do."

"Ah, get on!" Baxter chided. "I know you blokes—always telling the public what you think is good for them. Bloody great junk comes in from a rendezvous at sea, gets stopped by a marine police boat, and all they find is eight kilos of morphine. Eight kilos! The big boys don't operate in piddling amounts like that, I can tell you. They've got a deal with the police, haven't they? The cops knock off a few small shipments every year and let the big ones through. Why, I wouldn't mind getting into that business myself: take the boat out, meet up with one of those freighters from Bangkok and load up with three, maybe four tons of the stuff. And who's going to suspect a *gwai-lo* of running drugs?"

Pritchard said nothing. There was no contradicting Baxter once he was launched on one of his themes; the best thing was to let him go on until he suddenly switched course.

When Still Life arrived with their drinks Baxter signed the chit and then, seizing the copy of the *Cathay Star* that Pritchard had put down on the bar counter, ran his eye over the front-page headlines. "This kidnapping, then: what d'you reckon's behind it?"

"Kidnapping?"

"In the Philippines. I reckon their motives are dodgy—especially if old Abu Bakr Salim's got anything to do with it."

"Cheers," Pritchard said, taking a grateful pull at his drink. He had the newspaperman's habit of clearing his mind of today's events in anticipation of tomorrow's, but he remembered the story he had subbed and headlined. There was some government official who had been abducted in the southern Philippines. His kidnappers, members of the Muslim underground movement who were fighting for regional independence, had demanded a ransom of money as well as the release of some of their imprisoned members.

"Who do you say, Abu . . .?"

"Abu Bakr Salim. He's not mentioned in the story. Never is. He's the Chief Minister of Simpang State in East Malaysia; he's the guy who gives the Moro guerrillas in the Philippines most of their support—material as well as moral. The Brotherhood of Islam, all that crap. I knew him fairly well when I lived down there. Crafty old sod—made a mint out of getting into politics at the right time. Anyway, I'll bet this lot, the Muslim guerrillas, will end up settling for the money. Know why? Because that's probably what they wanted in the first place, not

27

their beloved bloody comrades back. The Filipinos will negotiate with them and hand over a million pesos or whatever they're asking for and heave a sigh of relief because they didn't have to free the prisoners. Hell, anyone can call himself a political movement these days and get away with murder. Literally, murder. Governments fall over backwards to do their bidding. And why? Because this is what they think: They're fanatics, unstable, unpredictable. They'll kill themselves as well as their hostages if they have to. They're not like ordinary villains, whose main interest is always Number One. And so they get the soft-pedal treatment."

"If you want to save lives," Pritchard said absently, "then it seems sensible to humour them."

"Oh, sure, but that's what they're trading on. Most of them are not actually fanatical enough to kill themselves. It's the threat that works, not carrying it out. I mean, look at kidnapping," Baxter said excitedly. "You don't even have to *do* it these days to turn a profit on it. When I lived in Simpang I knew this bloke: American, oil-company executive. He'd lived in Venezuela and he told me his company were quietly paying the local revolutionaries an annual retainer *not* to kidnap him. It was a straight protection racket. It was easier for them; it cost the company less than kidnap insurance and much less than the ransom would have been. He said any number of other firms were doing the same, all over Latin America. Anything for a quiet life, that's the attitude. . . ."

Pritchard's mind began to drift. He decided he would not tell Baxter about losing his job. He hadn't told anyone yet, not even his colleagues on the *Star,* though it was only a matter of time before the news leaked down to them from the third floor. Soon he'd have to put out feelers for another job—that is, if he decided to stay in Hong Kong at all. But where else was there? He couldn't afford to fly off anywhere on spec. He had no savings. The two months' salary he would get when he left the *Star* wasn't much of a golden handshake—a lousy twelve thousand Hong Kong dollars, about twelve hundred pounds, or less than twenty-five hundred U.S. dollars; what could you do with that? Perhaps he should have a quiet word with Scully over at the *Morning Post. . . .*

He was brought sharply back to earth. Baxter had asked a question.

"Sorry," he said.

"I said don't you think we could do it ourselves?"

28

"What?"

"Set up a kidnapping, of course. Right here in Hong Kong. Grab some rich Chink, call ourselves the Happy Valley Liberation Front or something, and demand a million bucks from his family and a plane from the government. Take him to Algeria or Libya; you've got to have a bolt hole arranged beforehand, of course."

Pritchard snorted. "You make it sound simple."

"It *is* simple, Alan. The political angle would make it seem legitimate, you see. It puts a government, any government, under an obligation at least to try to negotiate with you. Once you're negotiating you've won half the battle."

"What's your interest in kidnapping?"

"It's my perfect-crime daydream. Some people want to commit the perfect murder. I want to carry out a flawless kidnapping. Everybody has fantasies like that. Your glass is empty, old son. Still Life!"

"It's my round," Pritchard said, and to change the subject he added, "You're still running your junk, I gather."

"The good old *Lady Belinda*—oh, yes. Liz and I get out on her most weekends, lose ourselves among the islands. It's the only way to stay sane in this bloody place. Why don't you come out with us again one of these days?"

"I wasn't angling for an invitation. . . ."

"You're not doing anything this Sunday, are you?"

"Well, no, but—"

"Join us on the *Lady B,* then. Do you good to get out in the open, in the sun, do some swimming. Lunch and booze all laid on. We'll pick you up at your place. Around ten?"

"Well, all right, Bax. Thanks." His reluctance had stemmed from his one previous experience of an outing with the Baxters, when Liz— a petulant bitch, in his private opinion—had been unwelcoming and Baxter's company, undiluted, had proved slightly oppressive. But he was right; Sundays could be desolate times, and just now he could use a diversion.

They had a few more drinks together and then Baxter left. After a while Pritchard got talking to Corless, the *Star*'s chief sub-editor. Corless was fresh off a weekly paper in Lancashire, keen as mustard and eager in his enjoyment of the novelty of Asia. Pritchard found himself responding to an urge to prick that enthusiasm—he couldn't have explained why, beyond the fact that a streak of unpleasantness, usually expressed as sarcasm, came out in him when he'd had a few drinks.

Perhaps it came down to envy. Corless could pack his bags tomorrow and head off to anywhere that beckoned; it was a lot easier to be penniless at twenty than forty.

Goaded by some remark, Corless said, "Well, I'm sorry to hear about your job."

"It's got about, has it?"

"Unofficially."

Pritchard grunted and finished his drink. "You win a few, lose a few. I'd better go."

"What will you do, Alan?"

"I don't know."

"Good luck, anyway."

Pritchard left, taking the lift down to street level and stepping out into the clinging heat of the July evening. He was angry with Corless because he had recognized a condescension in his tone that he himself had once had for older men. Suddenly he could see himself through the kid's eyes: a caricature of a cynical middle-aged journalist appeasing his failures in booze. Everybody knew Pritchard's story; the ones who laughed loudest at it were those who sensed the potential for failure in themselves.

3

Pritchard set off on the twenty-minute walk home. He usually walked, avoiding another crowded tram and begrudging the taxi fare. He no longer owned a car. He'd bought one when he first came to Hong Kong but sold it within three months. The kind of flat he could afford didn't come with parking space, and parking garages' rates were astronomical.

He had walked a block before he realized he needed a pee. In his irritation with Corless he'd forgotten to go before he left the club. Rather than go back there he walked down Ice House Street and across Chater Road and entered the elegant marbled lobby of the Mandarin Hotel. He went through the Chinnery Bar, where the polite laughter of well-heeled tourists and businessmen competed with the cocktail-hour Muzak, to the toilet. When he came out into the lobby he saw Ailsa.

She was standing on her own beside one of the marble pillars,

30

looking towards the entrance so that he saw her face in profile. Oddly, the first thing that registered in him was not surprise but an awareness of some change that had come over her. It was nothing physical: there was the same deep Australian tan, accentuated by the white sleeveless pants suit she was wearing, the same straw-blond hair, the same tall, flat, rangy figure with shoulders as square as a man's. The difference was in the set of her features: there was a serious, withdrawn expression that he had never seen before. How old was she now, thirty-three, thirty-four? He stood watching her with an odd detachment for ten or fifteen seconds, before confusion set in. To approach her or not? To renew an acquaintanceship painfully broken or to sidle quietly away? The decision was made for him. She glanced with an irritated gesture at her watch, looked up and turned, facing him directly. The shock started into her face.

"Alan!"

"Hello, Ailsa." It sounded lame, but it seemed the only thing to say.

"Alan!" she repeated. Involuntarily she started towards him, puzzled, starting to smile. "You've been standing there, watching me. . . ."

"I'm just as surprised as you are."

"Well! You're the last person. . . . What are you doing here?"

He had moved towards her as well and they stopped, appraising each other, a couple of feet apart.

"I live here now. In Hong Kong, I mean, not the Mandarin."

She shook her head, smiling, still getting over the surprise. Her eyes, cornflower-blue, were full of curiosity. "I'm living here too. We, that is."

"You're looking well."

"Thank you." She seemed on the verge of returning the compliment, but she had never been able to lie easily. She could hardly have helped noticing that he had aged and put on some weight.

"My husband was transferred here, just after Christmas." She hesitated and then, choosing to personalize, said, "Rod. You know I married him?"

"You wrote and told me."

He had not replied to the letter, he recalled, which had been postmarked Washington, D.C. Instead he'd drunk a secret, sarcastic toast to them on his own on the terrace of the Continental Hotel in Saigon, convincing himself that the marriage wouldn't last. It seemed that it had, in spite of the pins he had mentally stuck into effigies of them both. There'd been times when he had thought he actually hated her, especially if he'd drunk too much and was feeling sorry for himself. In more honest moments he might admit that, since he no longer knew her, what he hated was the idea of her, of what she might have made of herself since the day they had parted, her patience in the waiting role of a married man's mistress finally at an end. The truth was that he'd used her as a focus for resentment, even as an excuse for his own failure.

"I'm meeting him here," she said, perhaps giving Pritchard a tactful hint. "At least I was supposed to meet him, twenty minutes ago." She looked at her watch again. "He's taking me to a once-in-a-blue-moon dinner, if and when he gets away from his precious office."

"Still doing the same job? Throwing sand in the eyes of the Big Red Dragon? Making Asia safe for democracy and peanut-butter sandwiches?"

He knew as he said it that it wasn't funny, but couldn't stop himself. He saw a dangerous glitter come into Ailsa's eyes and then subside. "He still works for the United States Government," she said shortly, "if that's what you mean."

"Sorry. Just being my old sarcastic self. Look, since you're waiting, why not let me buy you a drink?"

"Well. . . ." She glanced uncertainly down at her hands, clasping a sequinned evening bag across her middle. There was a sudden awkwardness between them, a mutual reminder of past intimacy. Then she looked at him resolutely. "Well, why not? I hate hanging about places like this on my own."

They went through to the Chinnery Bar and sat at the counter. Ailsa asked for a Campari-soda; Pritchard had a Scotch. They cost the earth, after the Quill.

"We had two years in Washington right after we got married. I hated that. Then two in Taipei; that was pretty good. Then a short stint in Bangkok, and now here."

"And how about here?"

"The worst of the lot. Nothing to do with the place. Just the circumstances."

"Where do you live?"

"Quarry Hill, on the Kowloon side. An apartment complex owned by the State Department. I don't like spending my days among a lot of other consulate wives, but there's no choice nowadays. It's what they call secure. For our husbands."

32

"You mean guarded?"

"Discreetly. But it's like living in an open prison. Rod is classified as ultra-sensitive, you see."

"But you're not a prisoner. You must have things that take you out. Shopping? Running kids to school?" He hesitated, sensing that he might have said the wrong thing. "Do you have children?"

"No." Ailsa took a deliberate sip of her drink. "He never wanted any. He said the demands of his work wouldn't give him time to be a proper father to them. He's right, I might add."

Pritchard nodded appreciatively. "Your Mr. Kiley must be very important these days."

"I wouldn't know," she said brusquely. "I'm not supposed to know that sort of thing, Alan." There was the same expression on her face that he had caught out in the lobby, a heavy seriousness that had again descended suddenly on her. Then she brightened. "Tell me about yourself. Did Federated send you here?"

"No. I'm working for the *Cathay Star.*"

"That—" She stopped herself.

Pritchard grinned. "Go on, call it a small-town rag. Call it whatever you like, it doesn't bother me. I'll only be with them a couple more months anyway."

"And then?"

He shrugged. "Something will turn up. I've been given the shove —or, as my boss prefers, made redundant. The job is hardly worth fighting for. I'm a hack down-table sub, nothing more."

"But that's terrible, Alan." She looked truly perturbed. "You're a good journalist. You should be doing better."

"I turned forty this year, Ailsa. If you haven't reached somewhere near the top by then, you never will."

"But you had a good career with Federated. What made you leave?"

"They did. Don't tell me you haven't heard the story?"

"I haven't."

"They've been dining out on it in every press club in Asia ever since. In a phrase, I went crazy. I went on the biggest international bender of all time. It started in Saigon, three and a half years ago, just as the war was reaching its climax. The workload was incredible. The pressures had been building up for years. Then I got this cable from Wendy. We're divorced now; she's been living in England for a while. It said Gary—my son, you remember?—had been killed by a hit-and-run driver. It happened in Winchester, outside his prep school. The cable took three days to reach me. It was too late even to go to the funeral."

"Jesus," Ailsa breathed, her eyes closed in anguish. "I'm sorry."

"He was nine. They never got the bastard who did it. If they found him I swear I'd go over there, even to this day, and personally. . . . Anyway, that was what pushed me over the top, not the work. I can't remember what I thought; probably I didn't think at all, my mind just cracked open. I started drinking. I'd been hitting the sauce quite hard as it was, just to keep going, but now I went into the big league. First and only time I've ever done it. I drank a bottle of Scotch that afternoon and decided to get out of Saigon. Just dropped everything and went. I bummed a ride through the American Public Affairs Office on a C-One-Thirty carrying embassy dependants to Guam. From there I went on to Hawaii; I remember that far, then everything becomes a blur. I was drunk all the time. When we pieced it together afterwards it seemed I'd been on ten plane trips in the course of a fortnight. I doubled back to Singapore, then flew to Djakarta and went island-hopping all over Indonesia. I flew first class, on Federated's credit cards. I stayed in the best hotels and spent money like a sailor—their money. I'd flipped my lid and I didn't care who knew it. Federated had six people out hunting for me, all over Asia. But they'd never have caught up with me if I hadn't got myself physically immobilized. I came to Hong Kong and got acute alcoholic poisoning. Bloody nearly killed me." He gave a harsh laugh. "Police picked me up, passed out, in Statue Square at four in the morning, using an empty gin bottle as a pillow.

"I came back to earth two days later, in Central Hospital. The police still hadn't identified me; they assumed I was a hobo or a seaman off some ship. Then I sent them to fetch my baggage—from the best suite at the Hilton!"

Ailsa was shaking her head in wonder.

"The results weren't so funny, physically. I had pneumonia, portal hypertension and the DTs. Then I got a bad dose of hepatitis. I was laid up for nearly four months."

"And Federated fired you?"

"They did better than that. They wanted the firing to go down in company history, a lesson never to be forgotten. They flew the managing editor, the personnel director and a lawyer from New York to my bedside, here in Hong Kong, to fire me. I was lucky they didn't sue me as well. It was the money that bothered them, you see, more than the dereliction of duty. They'd seen journalists go off on binges before. No, my real crime was that I'd made what this lawyer called 'unauthorized disbursements on an excessive scale.' What he meant was that I'd blown twelve thousand dollars of their money."

"In two weeks?" Ailsa said incredulously.

"It isn't hard, if you really try. And I was trying. Starting with hotel suites at two hundred a night and vintage champagne at forty a bottle. Not to mention some fairly expensive female company along the way. To this day I'm not sure why I chose that way of doing it, but I guess I was getting back at them for all the stories they'd spiked—them, and in a wider sense the whole of America. To save a country they had destroyed it, and now they refused to read the truth about it. Perhaps that sounds crazy to you; I *was* crazy at the time. I was hitting them in the only place where it hurt—their pockets. That's what put the kiss of death on me. Who'd employ a correspondent who might just pop his cork again and repeat the whole performance? It has its funny side."

A pageboy came wandering towards them, holding a message board. Ailsa winced at the sight of her name, picked out in plastic letters on the felt backing: MRS KILEY.

"God damn! I know what that means. He's delayed again. It's the telephone, is it?" she asked the boy.

"Yes, missy."

"I'll be right back," she said to Pritchard, who sat and watched her walk out to the lobby. She moved a little self-consciously but the swing of her hips was natural, exaggerated only by the tight fit of the cotton pants. Her figure was still perfect, and the sudden memory of her naked body brought a thin flicker of desire, like the glimpse of a far-off lightning flash: the small breasts, the flat belly, the thighs long and lithe. There were always two pale bands left by her bikini, standing out against the rich tan that she kept up by sunning herself beside the pool at the Cercle Sportif at weekends, and when they made love—usually in the late afternoons, on the shuttered porch of her small bungalow across from the Botanical Gardens—he would tease her about her lily-white breasts and buttocks. Christ, he thought, how long since he'd had a woman he hadn't paid for? There'd been a brief, distasteful affair with a married secretary on the *Star;* then there was the Canadian girl he had picked up one Sunday lunchtime in the coffee shop of the Imperial Hotel, who turned out to be bombed out of her skull most of the time on Chinese heroin pills. Eventually she'd stolen five hundred dollars off him before flying to Bali with the lead guitarist of a touring pop group. That must have been eighteen months ago. Since then he'd settled for a visit once a month or so to the Evergreen Music Parlour, where, foregoing the ritual of tea-drinking and fox-trotting followed by the regular clientele of Chinese businessmen, he would simply pay Mama-san Julie the going rate to take one of her taxi dancers home for the night.

He signalled to the barman for another Scotch. He'd been happy in Saigon, he thought, as happy as he could have been in the middle of a war with the growing knowledge of a failed marriage. The compensation had been his job and Ailsa. She'd been—what, twenty-six?—when he met her, at a cocktail party thrown by the Australian Ambassador, an embassy secretary newly arrived from Canberra. Three days later he made love to her. It had gone on for two years, well beyond some indefinable sticking point at which it had ceased to develop, a point where what had been pleasurable for her became furtive and without a future. In spite of that, he had thought they had things going for them: a common sense of humour, a fundamental liking for each other that seemed to transcend their quarrels and incompatibilities. Then Kiley had turned up. On reflection, he couldn't blame her for having chosen Kiley, but irrationally he blamed the man for being what he was: a bachelor, untrammelled, handsome, with a certain cool, if synthetic, charm and a big future ahead of him. Also, he was American.

She came back from the lobby, and he could tell by her walk that she'd been right about the phone call. She moved like an angry lioness, stalking purposefully to the bar with her strong mouth set in a grim little line. She got back on the stool and took a deep swallow of Campari, staring straight ahead at the rows of bottles on the opposite wall.

"Bad news?" he inquired gently.

"Bad enough. He's not going to make it at all."

"I'm sorry." He thought that lacked conviction and added, "He must have a good reason."

"How the hell would I know?" she snapped. "There's only ever one excuse, one word: work. I'd like to have a dollar for every time this has happened, every dinner party that's been spoiled, every meal at home that's been ruined."

Pritchard weighed a remark and decided to chance it. "I don't want to say I warned you," he said. "But I did."

"Did what?" she said defensively.

"Tell you that you would become a Company widow. That a whole area of his life, a whole chunk of his personality, would be closed to you. It's inevitable in that business."

"He does important work. I have to accept that."

"Sure. Right now he's standing you up to save us all from a nuclear holocaust that's about to be launched by a bunch of slit-eyed dinks."

"Oh, shut up, Alan," she said easily. Familiar once again with his sarcasm, she had no trouble putting it down. "Anyway, the wives of foreign correspondents don't have it any easier. I recall that yours didn't."

"No. That's true." Pritchard had warmed to Ailsa in her annoyance, sympathizing with her in a way, he suddenly realized, that he had never done for Wendy. Which only proved that he had been a selfish bastard. Encouraged by her relaxed tone, he said, "Wendy had a hard time, I'll admit. But at least she knew the reasons for all the stand-ups. It was there in the next morning's headlines. What about you? The whole thing is a big nothing, isn't it? I'll bet I know how you spend your days up in that enclave on Quarry Hill: coffee mornings and tennis and Tupperware parties with those other nice little homemakers, none of you ever daring to discuss the work your husbands are doing. That doesn't sound like you, Ailsa."

This time she didn't take him up. She drained her glass in silence.

"Another one?"

"No, thanks. I'll head for home now."

"Would it help," he asked hesitantly, "if I offered to take you to dinner instead? I mean here you are, all togged up for a night out. If it doesn't seem odd to you. . . ."

Ailsa laughed. "It's a sweet thought, Alan, and I appreciate it. But I'm not in the mood for going anywhere now."

"Another time, then? What about next week?"

She gave him a long look of cool, faintly amused appraisal. "That isn't a very proper invitation to a married lady, is it?"

"Hell, I'm sorry," he said, genuinely confused. "I didn't mean it to sound like that. It's just that . . . well, I'm glad to see you again. I'd like to talk to you some more, about the Saigon days. I've lost contact with most of the friends I had there."

"Me too." She paused. "I suppose you and I are old friends, aren't we?"

"Yes, we are. Look, next week, why don't you come to dinner with me? You and your husband, I mean."

"I don't think Rod would like that," she said quickly, and then elaborated. "First of all, he probably wouldn't make it. And then he's —well, a tiny bit New England-prudish."

"You mean he knows about you and me?"

"He had to know. Only he'd rather not know. He'd like to pretend you didn't exist, that there were never any men in my life before you came along. I'd like to leave now, Alan."

They left the bar together and walked to the front door of the hotel. She must, Pritchard thought, be as aware as he was of the irony of their situation, the mirror image of what it had once been—she, now, trapped in a marriage that was clearly unhappy, and he a single man. If she'd been prepared to wait longer, for the divorce that had been inevitable, or if he'd had the guts to kill it off quickly. . . . But where was the sense of wondering what might have been?

At the front entrance, the Sikh doorman flagged down a taxi to take Ailsa home. When she said good-bye, her eyes seemed to linger on Pritchard's for just a fraction longer than they needed to—with affection, regret, nostalgia? He couldn't be sure. She got into the taxi. Holding the door open, he said, "Am I going to see you again, Ailsa?"

"Well," she said, smiling suddenly, "I suppose *I* could take you up on that dinner invitation."

"Won't he mind that?"

"After standing me up tonight, he'll be in no position to object."

"Any night will suit me. Can I call you?"

"No. Let me phone you, at the newspaper."

The cab drove off, heading for the Cross-Harbour Tunnel to Kowloon, leaving Pritchard to resume his interrupted walk home. Where Queen's Road met up with Hennessy he took the right fork and entered the first of the string of Chinese residential districts east of Central. The streets teemed; people overflowed from the shabby, crowded apartment blocks and flooded the baking sidewalks like a liquid mass seeking its own level. All the shops were still open, their signs picked out in gaudy red neon. So were the cooked-food stalls selling pressed duck and congee, the pawnbrokers locked in their steel-barred cages, the tailors who ran up suits in twenty-four hours, the fish restaurants with bubbling tanks in their windows, full of croakers and crabs, goatfish and carp. Pritchard, immunized to the sights and sounds and smells by having lived too long among them, made his way stolidly through the crowds to Happy Valley.

His flat was on the third floor of an eight storey block built in the forties and now showing considerable signs of wear. Often the lift did not work, and on the walls of the lobby and the stairwell there were black stains where damp had got in during successive rainy seasons. Pritchard had a comfortably furnished living room, a kitchen, a bathroom, and a bedroom in which he had installed an air-conditioning unit. There were the usual boxlike amah's quarters on the staircase at the rear, but the only domestic help he needed—or could afford—was a bossy old shrew who came in once a week to clean and launder for him. His bedroom looked across Yiu Wa Street into the stockroom of a department store, but from the living room he had a partial view of the Peak and a glimpse of Happy Valley racecourse. He was the only European in the building. The walls were thin, and through them he could hear the constant discordant music of the crowded lives all around him: the high-pitched voices, the clacking of chopsticks, the TV soap operas and the shuffling of mah-jong tiles would go on till two or three in the morning. He had got used to it; privacy was an expensive commodity in Hong Kong.

Once home, he pulled off his jacket and loosened his tie. Then he poured himself a Scotch, went through to the bedroom with it and turned on the air conditioner. He lay down with his hands behind his head, the drink balanced on his chest, staring at the ceiling and thinking about his encounter with Ailsa. What did he feel about her? Regret, yes —but whenever he'd thought of her over the past few years the regret had expressed itself as a sort of sour irony. That and a dull anger at Rod Kiley, the anger of hurt pride.

He remembered the last time they had seen each other, that afternoon on the porch of her little bungalow, with late sunshine streaming in thin bands through the shutter slats. She got home from the embassy just before five; he could usually manage to get an hour or so off work at the same time. That morning he had got back from a gruelling week-long trip through the central and northern provinces of the country; in spite of his tiredness he ached with desire for her. But she was nervous, ill at ease as she greeted him. He tried to kiss her; she turned her face quickly so that his lips glanced off her cheek. He put his arms round her; her body was tense and unresponsive.

"What's the matter, darling?"

"Alan, I have something to tell you."

He drew back, holding her arms, trying to look into her eyes.

"Tell me the worst. It's the curse."

"No."

"It's the Colgate commercial getting through to you, then. You've finally steeled yourself to tell me I ought to see my dentist about bad breath."

"Don't be facetious, for Christ's sake!" She pulled herself free of his hands and stood facing him, wide-shouldered, flat-chested, hands on hips. "While you've been away, Alan, I've been seeing somebody else."

"What do you mean, seeing?"

"What do you think I mean?"

He was silent for several seconds. Then he said, "Ailsa, are you trying to tell me you've had an affair?"

"An affair!" She gave a sudden harsh, deprecating laugh. "Is that what you'd call it? I thought that's what *we* were having, Alan, you and I, a perpetual affair. I mean we aren't exactly married, are we?" Flushing, half regretting her own sarcasm, she brushed the fair hair nervously off her face. She tried to light a cigarette, fumbled, made a mess of it. She said, "All right, let's call it that, Alan. I'm having an affair. I'm having an affair with an American. A diplomat. What's more, he wants to marry me."

He stood rooted to the spot, feeling his mind fill with confusion, anger, even a slight sense of the ludicrous. Then he subsided onto the couch on which they had made love so often. "He wants *what?*"

"You heard. I'm sorry, but this thing has just gone on too long. I've got a life to lead."

"*I* want to marry you, Ailsa. Have you forgotten that?"

"Perhaps I have, Alan, you've been saying it for so long. For two years you've been talking about getting a divorce, and what have you done about it? Nothing!"

"I've had Gary to think about. . . ."

"You've had me to think about too. Don't I count?" She tried lighting the cigarette again. This time it worked, but her hands were shaking badly. "Look, I'm sorry I had to break the news this way but I'm glad I've done it, do you understand? I hate lying. I'm no good at it. I want you to know exactly what happened—no, I want that, it's only fair. I met this guy at a reception in the U.S. Embassy. He asked me out and—well, I went. He's never been married. He's in his early forties. He's going back to Washington soon and he wants me to go with him. I . . . I'm thinking seriously about it, Alan."

Pritchard sighed wearily and rubbed his eyes, his tiredness returning. "So you're off to the Big PX, are you? May I ask the name of this paragon?"

"Roderick Kiley."

"That son of a bitch!"

"Calling him names won't make him go away."

"I've called him worse names before now," Pritchard said with a weary laugh. "Do you want to know something, Ailsa? That guy is no more a diplomat than I am. In my job you get to learn about these people. He's a Company Joe—an officer of the Central Intelligence Agency, working under diplomatic cover. Quite a rising star, I gather: he's even been tipped to become Director one day. Here in Saigon he's rumoured to be Superspook, head of the CIA station. As a matter of fact I had the distinct impression he was already married—to his job."

"Very funny," Ailsa said. "I know he's not an ordinary diplomat, that his work comes first—"

"It comes first, second and third, believe me. Is that what you want, to be a Company widow in the coast-to-coast Consumerama?"

"Just because you don't like Americans . . ."

"I don't dislike them. I think what they've done to this country is insane, that's all, and Kiley is the concentrated essence of the insanity. He sits there in his stainless-steel office with his stainless-steel mind, feeding loyalty ratings and kill ratios into his computers, just like all the others before him. They've never learned. They're still trying to buy the support they've never known how to earn. They drop CARE packages on villages one day and napalm the next, and they call it pacification!"

"And you?" she snapped. "What do you contribute? You can't do anything but sneer, Alan; you've got worse at it since I've known you. What are you, anyway, when you're not pretending to be armchair Viet Cong? A colonial with a hankering for the good old days, a bit of imperial flotsam left behind by the tide."

He hit her then. In an upsurge of jealousy and rage he stood up and slapped her face hard, once, with the back of his hand, knocking her to the floor, where she lay with her arms protectively raised. They remained that way for half a minute, Pritchard standing over her, breathing hard, she staring up at him with the fear in her eyes quickening to contempt. Then he turned and walked out of the bungalow. They had not seen each other since.

Pritchard got off the bed, went to fetch another Scotch and then lay down again in the cool. He had never been angry with Ailsa, he thought, not even in that impulsive moment of violence. It had been Kiley he had been hitting out at, not her, because it was easier to believe in the American as a cuckolding son of a bitch than to see himself as too inadequate to hold onto his woman.

Kiley: a shadowy figure, familiar to some of the Saigon press corps in those days, though only the veterans like himself had picked up enough hints to guess at what his real role was. Pritchard had spoken to him only once, back in late 1971 when the U.S. Mission were still holding those daily press briefings on the progress of the war that had come to be called the Five O'Clock Follies. Spook playing diplomat, Kiley did not put himself on show on these occasions, but that evening he accosted Pritchard in a corridor of the Public Affairs Office. He was holding a tearsheet from a newspaper.

"Mr. Pritchard, did you write this?"

He pointed to the paper. It was the front page of yesterday morning's *Los Angeles Times;* an agency piece on the Vietnamization programme was run as a strong single-column story on one side. Pritchard glanced at it and said, "Since it carries my by-line, the question is a little superfluous."

"This is a highly irresponsible piece of journalism, Mr. Pritchard."

"Because it tells an unpleasant truth, you mean? Because it says the South Vietnamese army is a corrupt and undisciplined force, incapable of paying and supplying its own men properly, let alone fighting off an invasion?"

"I repeat, it is irresponsible." Kiley was the kind of man who never got angry; the anger was sublimated into coldness, a steady cold stare from his pale blue eyes. "You may not be American yourself, but you are working for an American agency. You have a duty to the public over there, not to raise alarm by malicious reports like this."

"Are you disputing the facts I set out?"

"Certainly. You've suggested that this country is soon going to be left almost defenceless. The fact is that by the time the last American troops pull out there will be half a million South Vietnamese under arms, an army of eleven divisions, as many men as we had even at the height of our involvement."

"I'm sure you know the figures better than I do, Mr. Kiley. I'm sure they look very good on your computer printouts. It's a pity you can't feed a few X factors into those computers, though: factors of morale and motivation, money and supplies. If the biggest and best-paid and best-fed army in the world can't beat a bunch of skinny dinks, who else do you think is going to do it for you?"

His last words came in a shout, as Kiley turned and marched away from him down the corridor, crumpling up the piece of newspaper and flinging it aside.

It was Kiley he had been angry at when Ailsa left him, he realized, and the anger was still there, buried like grit in an oyster, swollen by layers of protective covering to a shiny pearl of malice. He fell asleep with his clothes on, a half-empty glass beside him and the air conditioner racketing away.

4

There were seven people, including the Baxters' child and their amah, in the picnic party that Sunday. They met at eleven o'clock on the jetty at Hebe Haven and got the boatboy to row them out to the *Lady Belinda,* a seagoing pleasure junk, at her mooring in the bay. At midday they reached Shelter Island to find the beach deserted—"and that," as Ed Baxter boasted to the others, "is quite an achievement in Hong Kong on a Sunday. *Quite* a bloody achievement!"

They dropped anchor and rowed themselves and their provisions ashore in the rubber dinghy. They went for a swim to cool off, and then the men opened cans of beer and bottles of wine from the portable ice chest and got the charcoal burning under the barbecue grill. The women spread rush mats on the sand, got the plates and cutlery out, and prepared salads and fruit, bread and butter. Baxter took charge of grilling the steak and sausages.

Beneath the uneventful flow of the day's events, however, there were currents of tension. Liz Baxter, like many Western women in Asia, had grown lazy and bored, snappish and mildly neurotic. She hated the climate and disliked the Chinese. Today she was in a quiet fury at her husband—apparently because, without consulting her, he had invited a young man called Fong, formerly a barman at the Quill Club, to join the party. Fong had brought along his current girl friend, an expressionless Cantonese who had even less to say for herself than Liz and annoyed everyone by playing shrill Chinese pop music on a transistor radio. Worse still, she had a superb, tightly muscled figure, not at all underplayed by a provocative string bikini, and after a few drinks Baxter began ogling her unashamedly.

After lunch they all drifted apart, as though with the meal out of the way there was nothing to hold them together. Fong and the girl, perhaps made uncomfortable by Liz's tacit hostility, went for a walk along the beach, holding hands, and disappeared among some rocks at the far end. Liz went to join her child, a rather glum little boy of five, down at the water's edge, where the old amah was trying to coax him to play with his bucket and spade. Pritchard could never remember his name; Baxter referred to him only as "the kid." Baxter and Pritchard stayed by the fire among the picnic debris, lounging contentedly in their camp chairs, the booze close at hand. Even their own relationship, away from its usual setting in the Quill, had been slightly strained at first; but both of them now felt more relaxed.

The junk rode at anchor twenty yards offshore, high and square in the stern, slim in the bows, gracefully silhouetted against the dazzle of sunshine reflected off the sea. Baxter shaded his eyes against the glare and gazed out at her.

"Lovely, isn't she? You know, they've been making those things to exactly the same design for a thousand years."

"Have you ever run her under sail?"

"I've got the sails—big red batwing jobs with bamboo battens— but they're too much work for one man to handle. So I stick to the engines: couple of big Lister Blackstone diesels. She's good for twelve knots and she can take just about anything the weather throws at her." He paused and looked at Pritchard. "You wouldn't be interested in taking a half share in her, I suppose? Twenty-five thousand Hong Kong would cover it. We could use her on alternate weekends, and sometimes perhaps get together like this. . . ."

Pritchard was laughing, shaking his head. "What makes you think I've got that sort of money?"

"Just thought I'd ask, old son. I've got to go halves with someone and I'd rather it was someone I knew. It's either that or sell her outright. It may yet come to that."

"But why, for God's sake?"

"Between you and me, business hasn't been too hot for me lately. I've got what's known as a short-term liquidity problem, which is another way of saying I have to raise some cash, pretty sharpish. Something has to go."

Privately, Pritchard was not altogether surprised. Baxter had come here from Simpang to set himself up as an investment broker, his role basically being to advise rich Chinese what to do with their money. He had rented a lavish office in Central and an expensive flat on the

44

Peak and had bought the *Lady Belinda* with the object of entertaining —and, of course, impressing—his clients. In Hong Kong, perhaps more than anywhere else in the world, it was necessary to be seen to be successful. Pritchard had suspected that, beneath the show of extravagance, Baxter had financial problems. He seemed always on the verge of pulling off some big deal which he never quite accomplished. The investment market wasn't good, and rich Chinese on the whole did not need advice—or if they did, they did not want it from a *gwai-lo*.

"I'm sorry to hear that," Pritchard said. "But you're talking to the wrong man."

"Never mind. I didn't really expect you to be interested." Baxter suddenly straightened up, looking past Pritchard along the beach. "You know, I do believe Fong is getting his end away down there."

Pritchard followed his gaze towards the rocks, perhaps a hundred yards off at the edge of the small bay. Fong and the girl had been out of sight for about fifteen minutes.

"Randy little bastard. Lucky, too," Baxter said enviously, with a furtive glance to where Liz still sat at the water's edge. "That chick could piss in my ear any time, I'll tell you. And next week he'll have another one in tow. Living on his reputation from the movie stuntman days."

"I suppose so," Pritchard said. "What's he doing now?"

"Working in some Chinese gag-stand in Kowloon. His uncle gave him the job, apparently; there was nothing else going for him, after what happened."

Pritchard nodded. Everyone at the Quill knew Fong's story. At one time he had had a big name in the Kung Fu movie business: crashing cars, falling off roofs, standing in in the dangerous sequences for stars like Bruce Lee. In money terms it was almost as good as being a star, and Fong lived high for a couple of years, with all the girls and booze he wanted. Then the Kung Fu fashion faded, the bottom dropped out of the market and Fong found himself in need of a job. He got one at the Quill, as a trainee barman, though his meagre earnings there could not possibly support the expensive life-style to which he was accustomed. He was popular with the members—cheerful and personable where Still Life was churlish—so it was widely lamented when he was arrested on a charge of dealing in Red Chicken heroin pills and sentenced to two years in Stanley Prison.

"Came out just a few months ago," Baxter said, reaching for the bottle of Australian wine that stood beside the icebox and refilling both their glasses. "I bumped into him in Kowloon on Friday and invited him along here, just on the spur of the moment. Felt sorry for the bugger, really. Still pulls the birds, though, which I suppose is some consolation."

"Yes," Pritchard said absently. He had suddenly been struck by the coincidence that all three of them, all the men on that beach, had hit bad times, had found their own routes to a common failure. Pathetically they protected their dignity, pretended to be what they weren't. Pritchard had still not had the courage to tell Baxter about losing his job; nor was he expected to guess that Baxter's "liquidity problem" probably meant he was deeply in debt. Fong, he could imagine, still told the girls he was in the movies. There was some vague comfort for Pritchard in the feeling that he was not alone in his despondency.

Perhaps Baxter sensed something of what he was thinking. He looked at Pritchard uneasily for a moment and then, characteristically, changed the subject.

"I see that kidnapping in the Philippines turned into a shambles. Remember, we were talking about it?"

Pritchard's mind went back to the stories in that morning's papers. The Philippines National Bureau of Investigation had somehow stumbled on the hideout—in a slum on the outskirts of Pagadian town— where the captured government official was being held. A typically frenzied Filipino shootout had followed, in which the hostage, his four Muslim kidnappers, six policemen, and two innocent bystanders had been killed.

"They could have avoided all that mayhem," Baxter said. "In the first place they should never have kept him near a town. You need somewhere right out in the wilds, away from nosy neighbours, where even if the victim tries to escape he won't get anywhere. Matter of fact, if I were to kidnap someone here in Hong Kong, I'd know exactly where to take him."

"You would?"

"A spot I discovered last year, out sailing the junk, over that way." He gestured vaguely at the horizon: the line of the South China Sea lost in heat haze, the bare brown humps of islands.

Pritchard leaned forward to top up Baxter's glass. In the corner of his eye he had seen Fong and the girl emerge from among the rocks. "Indulging your fantasies again?" he asked.

"Oh, I'll admit I've got a weakness for daydreaming about it. The perfect kidnapping—quite a challenge, I can tell you. It's a difficult

46

crime to get away with at the best of times. Sure, anybody can grab a millionaire's kid off the street. . . ."

"Better to grab the millionaire, surely? It would cause less public revulsion, hence less pressure on the police to track you down."

"That's the easy part," Baxter said testily. This was his hobby-horse and he didn't want anyone else riding it. "The easy part is lifting the victim. Collecting the ransom without getting caught is the real challenge. And then afterwards, of course, staying out of the hands of John Law. Don't tell me you haven't had the same sort of pipe dream."

Pritchard nodded. "I wanted to rob a bank. When I was about twenty, I decided that if I hadn't made a lot of money by the time I was forty, I would stick up a bank."

"How old are you now?"

"Forty."

Baxter chuckled. "Mine started even younger, when I was at school. What's more, I actually took one thing beyond the idea stage, turned the fantasy into reality. I worked out a way of turning pennies silver, by electrolysis, and passing them off as half-crowns. How about that—a three thousand per cent profit!"

"Did it work?"

"They turned green instead," Baxter said ruefully. "I've never worked out why."

"Get the formula right and it might solve your liquidity problem."

"Sure would. I still think it's a better idea than robbing a bank. Pritchard wants to rob a bank," Baxter said to Fong, who had approached to within a few yards of them. He and the girl had separated; she was down by the water's edge trying to make friends with the unresponsive child.

"And he wants to kidnap a millionaire," Pritchard said. "Which would you go for?"

Fong thought for a moment, mock-serious, a slight frown creasing the brow of his flat, handsome, mooncake face. "A difficult choice, Mr. Pritchard. . . ."

"Call me Alan. You're not serving me drinks any longer."

"Alan, then. Kidnapping is an old Chinese profession, you know. Only I would not choose a Chinese millionaire, because his family may be too stingy to pay the ransom. There was a famous case of a man in Macau whose son was kidnapped a few years ago. He refused to pay. He said he had enough sons as it was."

As they laughed, Pritchard noticed a damp patch on the front of

47

Fong's bathing suit, over the bulge of the genitals. So Baxter had been right.

"Okay, no rich Chinese, then," Baxter said, drinking some wine. "A foreign devil. A diplomat."

"They don't run very big here," Pritchard said. "There's no one with higher rank than consul general. What price could you ask for the Nicaraguan consul?"

"Whoever the victim is," Fong said, "he should not know who you are. Kidnappers always get caught afterwards, usually because the victim can identify them."

"But not in political cases," Baxter said firmly. "That's my idea, you see, to give it a political flavour. It puts you a cut above the common criminal, and it makes people sit up and listen. I bet there are people right here in Hong Kong who would make perfect targets for a terrorist kidnapping—people working for companies, or governments, that would pay plenty to get them back."

"Why not go the whole hog," said Pritchard, "and kidnap the bloody Governor?"

"You'd need too many people for that," Baxter replied promptly; it sounded as though he had given the matter some thought. "Besides, the Governor doesn't represent anything that any political movement wants to destroy. They choose symbols: capitalist fat cats in Germany, agents of American imperialism in South America. In the Philippines the Muslim rebels go for officials of the Christian government—"

"I know somebody like that," Pritchard said suddenly.

The others turned to him. He had not thought the remark had any significance. It would not have had, as he came to realize later, were it not for a curious fact: without any of them being aware of it, the discussion had passed some invisible point at which it had ceased to be mere idle banter. It was actually serious.

"What was that, old son?" Baxter asked uneasily.

"I know somebody," he repeated. "Somebody who might just make the perfect victim. The perfect symbol as well. An important man —only nobody's supposed to know he's important."

"Then how do you know it?"

"As a foreign correspondent you get to learn a few things that ordinary mortals don't. You get to see behind some of the doors that lead off those corridors of power. I knew this man six or seven years ago. He was big then and he's bigger now."

"Big in what way?"

"He's a senior intelligence officer, working under diplomatic cover."

"Oh, get on!" Baxter said, waving a disparaging hand. "I can see that some rival outfit might want to bump off somebody like that, but whoever heard of kidnapping one?"

"His job is highly sensitive. He's a custodian of a great deal of secret information. He's worth a lot to his employers, not just as their functionary but for the value of the knowledge he carries round in his head." Pritchard spoke bemusedly now, as if to himself, working things out as he went along. "None of that knowledge could possibly be allowed to reach a potential enemy. If he should vanish and end up in the hands of the Russians, say, or the Chinese, voluntarily or otherwise, it would be an intelligence disaster at least on the scale of the Philby defection."

"We were talking about doing it for money, Alan, not—"

"Well? You could practically name your own price. What's more, they'd fall over themselves to pay it. They don't want to make waves, they—"

"Daddy!" Baxter's little boy had run up the beach and thrust himself dramatically into the circle of men. "There's a dog, Daddy, a dead dog!"

"Where?"

"Down there, in the sea!"

"It's disgusting," called Liz, following the child across the sand, wearing a grimace of distaste. "You can't get away from it anywhere in this place: the filth, the pollution. Why can't these people—?" She checked herself, but too late, remembering the presence of Fong and the girl. "It's awful. Won't you go and try to do something?"

The men dutifully walked down to the water. The dog had been a mangy chow. It was a bloated, stinking carcass, nibbled by fish and humming with flies, now beached a few yards from where the boy had been playing. It was impossible to ignore. Baxter got an oar from the dinghy and shoved the thing into the water. A minute later it drifted back on the sand. Several more times he pushed the body out, but each time the tide returned it gently to the beach. Suddenly overwhelmed by the stink, Baxter turned aside and vomited.

It was Fong, eventually, who took one of the big plastic bags in which they had brought their provisions and eased the dog's carcass into it. He found a heavy rock, forced it in on top of the body and tied the neck of the bag with a strip of rope cut from the painter of the dinghy. Then he rowed out into deep water and dumped the package overboard.

After that no one felt like swimming. They didn't even talk much. The incident seemed to have cast a mood of uncertainty over them, exposing the incompatibilities among them that the conviviality of the picnic had covered over. They left earlier than they needed to.

On the way back, as the *Lady Belinda* nosed her way into the harbour at Hebe Haven, Pritchard joined Baxter at the wheel of the junk.

"Pity we got interrupted," he said.

"Interrupted?"

"Remember what we were talking about, before the dog turned up?"

"Oh, that!" Baxter gave him an uneasy sidelong glance. "Alan, you didn't take any of that crap seriously, did you?"

"Didn't you?"

"Hell, no! I was daydreaming, fantasizing. I do it all the time."

"I had a feeling it had become something more than a daydream for a moment. It gave me an idea."

"What idea?"

"Maybe we'll talk about it another time. Perhaps I could use your help."

"Now *you're* fantasizing," Baxter said.

5

On Tuesday Ailsa phoned him at the office. They talked inconsequentially for a while, then he repeated his invitation to dinner. She said she was free that evening and they arranged to meet in the Lee Gardens bar.

"I'll be on time," he said. "I've seen what happens when a man stands you up: you go out with someone else. Are you sure your husband won't mind?"

"He won't know," she said lightly. "See you at eight, Alan."

A thrill of anticipation ran through him as he put down the receiver, and for the rest of the day the call lightened his mood. It had come at the right time: an hour earlier he'd heard from Scully of the *Morning Post.* Scully was sorry to say there were no editorial vacancies at present, but of course the application he'd put in would be kept on file. . . .

The future was a blank again, a purgatory without promise of redemption. A few years ago he wouldn't have wiped his arse with the *Morning Post,* much less gone crawling to them for a job. But the job was only part of it. He would never starve. Something would turn up sooner or later, but not something that would rescue him from the empty evenings at the Quill and the clatter of chopsticks through the walls. He wasn't alone in his resentment and self-pity, of course; the shrinks had been going on for years about the mid-life crisis, the male menopause, all that crap. They said the way to snap out of it was to make a radical change in your life: easily said, not so easily done when stuck in a tropical backwater at forty. Yet, for the past two days, that part of his mind that he had not needed to concentrate on work had slid obsessively back to the idea that had occurred to him during the picnic at Shelter Island.

An idea: a random, momentary clash of brain cells, nothing more, a fantasy talked out in half-drunken drivel on the beach. It sounded foolish in retrospect, even embarrassing—like Baxter's attempt to turn pennies into half-crowns. Yet Baxter, at least, had had the courage to try. There would be no harm in taking the idea one stage further, by doing a little research.

After work, instead of going to the Quill, he headed for Sutherland House and the Foreign Correspondents' Club on the fourteenth floor. He wasn't a member, but nobody would query his presence unless he tried to buy a drink. He ignored the bar and turned off the lobby into the club's small reading room and reference library.

The library contained files of Hong Kong and foreign newspapers and periodicals such as *Time, Newsweek* and the *Far Eastern Economic Review,* as well as a row of shelves filled with the sort of reference works and yearbooks that journalists found useful. Pritchard made his way straight to the shelves and ran his eye along the familiar titles: *Keesing's Contemporary Archives, Whittaker's Almanac,* the Jane's yearbooks, *Who's Who in America* and a few dozen more. At the end of a row he found what he was looking for: the American State Department's *Biographic Register* for 1976. That was the last year it had been made publicly available; subsequent editions were on the classified list. The reason for this was simple. As many journalists had always known, it was quite possible, by studying the register of State Department employees in foreign postings, to pick out those who were actually under-

51

cover CIA officers. When radical and "underground" newspapers in America and Europe began using this information to expose the CIA's operatives abroad—leading, in at least one case, to the murder of a Chief of Station—State had clamped down. The register was no longer available outside the Department.

However, 1976 had not been that long ago. To anyone who knew what to look for, the alphabetical entries on diplomats and their careers, together with cross-references to the embassies or consulates in which they were currently serving, could be informative even if they were now out of date. The things to watch for were the absence of a detailed biography for an officer, and blank spaces in his career. Pritchard had learned to use the register to good advantage in Saigon. Among the endless Mission statements, briefings, press conferences and inspired leaks it was often useful to know whose line of crap was being peddled —the State Department's, the Military Assistance Command's, the CIA's or somebody else's. Identifying the peddler was as good a start as any.

The entry that he looked up now read:

KILEY, Roderick Neill. b. 2/4/30. Vientiane R/off 3/60. Bangkok R/off 7/64. Saigon R Coms off 12/68. Taipei R/off 7/74, 3 Sec 11/75. Bangkok R/off 3/76.

That took his career as far as the currency of the register—which, far from maintaining the fiction that he was a diplomat, actually revealed more about him than Pritchard had expected. Firstly, the postings made it clear that he was an Asian specialist. Then there was the frequency of the telltale letter R, standing for Reserve. If these details were to be believed, Kiley had spent almost his entire career, apart from a brief stint as third secretary at the U.S. Embassy in Taipei, as a reserve officer with no full-time posting—thankless treatment which, Pritchard knew, no career diplomat would have tolerated. There was no biography, and there was a significant gap: those two years in Washington that Ailsa had mentioned, right after their marriage and his tour of duty in Saigon, were not recorded here. Which meant, almost certainly, that he had been assigned for that period to the CIA's headquarters at Langley, Virginia. There would seem little point in pulling a specialist like Kiley out of the field in mid-career unless it was to familiarize him with headquarters work, possibly with the prospect of a big job sometime in the future.

A rising star, indeed, and made for the job; in spite of that gap

52

where his biography should have been you could practically hear the upper-class ring of his New England credentials: Groton and Harvard, probably, plus good connections in the Administration and that steel-trap mind. Yet already he seemed to belong to an older and less irreverent era in the history of the organization he served: the Cold War years and the sixties, a freebooting period of clandestine glamour, mystery and dash. It was no secret that the CIA these days was demoralized by public exposure of its activities, the scrutiny of Congress and even the revelations of some of its former employees. It had become defensive and inward-looking. Like a recluse afraid to venture out on the streets, it walled itself in with its computer banks and satellite tracking gear. Little wonder that Kiley was forced to live in what Ailsa had described as something like an open prison.

Pritchard searched further along the bookshelves until he found a copy of the U.S. Government's *Foreign Service List,* also for 1976. This State Department publication, though more innocuous than the register, had ceased to publish at the same time and for the same reason. Since it listed the diplomatic staff of every American embassy and major consulate in the world, it was a relatively simple matter—by comparing the entries here and in the *Register*—to get some idea of how many people in any one diplomatic mission were not diplomats at all.

He took both books and went to one of the reading-room tables. He sat down, opened the *Foreign Service List* at the entry for the Hong Kong Consulate General and glanced through the names. It was a long list. Nobody pretended that that sprawling complex of steel and glass buildings up in Garden Road, the size of a major embassy, performed merely the duties of an ordinary consulate. It was recognized as America's key listening post in the Far East; apart from the regular consular staff it employed a small army of analysts, translators, cryptographers, radio monitors and, of course, intelligence men like Kiley. Most were "China watchers," specializing in one field or another.

It took him over an hour to work through all the names, comparing them with their biographical entries in the other book as he went along and making notes on the pad of copy paper he had brought with him. Kiley's name was not on the Hong Kong list for 1976, of course, and certainly a number of those who had been working here then would have left by now. That wasn't important. What mattered to Pritchard was the kind of information that allowed him to draw inferences and make informed guesses, to build up a picture of a particular kind. At the end, the picture made sense.

He stood up and returned the books to their respective places on the shelves. He felt pleased with himself. There could not be many people in Hong Kong who knew what he knew: between forty-three and fifty employees of the Central Intelligence Agency were working under diplomatic cover in the Consulate General. On the basis of age, seniority and experience Roderick Kiley simply had to be on top of the pile, the Chief of Station. And that made him, masquerading as a vice-consul, probably the most powerful single intelligence operative in the East.

Pritchard glanced at his watch. Seven o'clock: there was ample time to get home, shower, change and make it to the Lee Gardens by eight. In time to begin the second stage of his research.

"Married people should be companions. Friends. Don't you think?"

"Sure," Pritchard agreed.

"And it's difficult enough to sustain a friendship when you never see each other, let alone a marriage. Right?"

"Right."

"Here's to friendship, then. And good marriages."

Ailsa, by now rather tipsy, raised her glass and drank some brandy. She was clearly enjoying her night out. They sat at a table in the Japanese Okahan Restaurant of the Lee Gardens Hotel, in air conditioning cold enough to chill a side of the beer-fed Matsuzaka beef on which they had dined. Pritchard had winced inwardly at the bill, even though he had decided earlier that a show of lavishness would be to his advantage. Ailsa, who had met him in the bar, had taken some trouble to look good; she was dressed in a stunning belted pants suit of pale blue Indian cheesecloth. They had drunk a good deal of warm sake with the meal and now, after the custard-egg dessert, were finishing their brandies.

"Don't get me wrong," Ailsa said. "I have a very nice husband. I admire him: his application, his intelligence. But how would you like to be married to someone who goes to work at eight in the morning and gets home at ten at night? And that's on a good night. Weekends, too: as often as not it's a full Saturday in the Annex. And part of Sunday, sometimes. It's the paperwork, he says, always threatening to overwhelm him. I actually feel sorry for him, you know: he's a victim of the American high-pressure work machine. You prove your worth by putting in more hours than anyone else. At least, that's my guess. What

54

I resent is that there's so little left of him for me."

Pritchard creased his brow, slightly embarrassed by these confidences while he absorbed every word. "The Annex, you said? What's that?"

"Oh, it's the building where he works, beside the main consulate. But I'm not even supposed to know that. There you are: all I know is that a car arrives for him at eight every morning and he disappears from my life until Uncle is finished with him. Our lives hardly seem to touch; we're like two lodgers sharing a front-door key to the same boarding-house. I don't meet anyone, apart from those inane women up there. It's not that I want to be in on the diplomatic cocktail circuit, like in Saigon, it's just that, well—" She turned quickly away, and he realized that tears had started into her eyes. He pulled a handkerchief from his top pocket and offered it to her but she shook her head, took a Kleenex from her bag and blew her nose. Then she wiped her eyes and faced him again, eyes watery, mascara slightly smudged.

"All I'd like," she said, sniffing, "is just occasionally to get out with him for an evening like . . . well, like this."

Pritchard smiled at her over the rim of his glass. "I'm no substitute, I know. But I'm glad you've enjoyed it."

"Don't knock yourself, Alan. I've enjoyed it. No reservations."

"Let's do it again, then."

She blew her nose once more and composed herself. "That's very generous of you. But next time let me treat you. I saw the prices on that menu."

"I wouldn't hear of it. Look, it's none of my business," he added, "but in case there should be any comeback, where did you tell him you'd be tonight?"

"Having dinner with a girl friend."

He glanced at his watch. "You'll want to be going soon, then."

"There's no great rush."

"I wish I could offer you a lift home. I don't have a car."

"I'll take a taxi."

"If you've got the time, we can walk down to the Wanchai ferry and save you a fare through the tunnel."

"I'd like that, yes."

She went to the powder room to repair her makeup and came back smelling of fresh scent. When they got outside, the heat was like a slap in the face. Buildings and paving-stones were still giving back the warmth of the day. The streets were crowded. They strolled, decorously arm-in-arm, through the side streets off Leighton Road, Ailsa enjoying the novelty of the markets, the food stalls, the hawkers and the haggling customers. Pritchard chose a route that brought them close, but not too obviously close, to his flat.

In Canal Road they stopped to watch a Buddhist funeral ceremony, a symbolic pyre burning fiercely in a vast iron drum, stoked by sweating attendants who also fed into it gifts to comfort the deceased in the afterlife: brightly wrapped boxes, a papier-mâché doll's house and a perfect scale model of a Lincoln Continental, symbols of an unfulfilled capitalist dream. The mourners in their fearsome white robes stood in a row beside it, their faces grotesquely swathed in bandages, like victims of burning or a skin disease. Ailsa suddenly shivered and clung to him tightly.

"Goose walk over your grave?"

"Yes."

"Are we friends, Ailsa?"

"Yes, we're good friends."

She did not resist his kiss. Her face turned up to his and her lips parted gently. In the darkness just outside the ring of garish, flickering light their bodies moved together with a sudden rush of yearning.

It happened more smoothly than he could possibly have hoped. They reached his flat in five minutes. They went straight to the bedroom, where he drew the curtains and turned on the air conditioner. They undressed calmly, without haste or self-consciousness, as if after the gap of six years they had fallen at once back into the rhythm of each other's appetites. All she said, hesitating as she unzipped her slacks, was, "You'll think I've got fat."

"I know you haven't."

She hadn't. She wriggled out of her trousers and then her panties, exposing the same long brown legs he remembered, the same pale, firm buttocks he had once teased her about, the wispy triangle of fine hair. He was burning for her now. She folded the slacks deliberately across a chair before unbuttoning and shrugging off the top of her trouser suit to reveal the small white pods of her breasts.

He was undressed now too. He walked to her, kissed her, crushed her body against his, his hands running up and down the warm, smooth skin of her back, wanting her with an urgent ache that pushed all his calculations out of his mind. He lowered his head to run his lips down her body, dotting kisses on the throat, the hardened nipples, the navel. She moaned gently, taking his hand and stroking the inside of her

56

thighs with it. Then, gripping the hand tightly, she led him to the bed.

She was as strong, passionate and considerate a lover as she had always been. At the height of her excitement she gave a stifled little cry. Then they rolled apart, panting, and with the roar of passion no longer in their ears they could hear, over the hum of the air conditioner, the small sounds of Chinese life through the thin walls: teacups clinking, a radio blaring. Ailsa laughed gently. "Do you think they heard us?"

"I don't know. Don't care, really."

"Used to it, are they? I suppose you have lots of women in here."

"Not exactly." Was there a hint of instant jealousy? She got up and walked to the bathroom, making a slender, long-legged silhouette as she paused against the light in the doorway. Pritchard lay back and composed his thoughts. When she returned and came to lie with her head on his shoulder he said, "What about you?"

She raised her head and stared into his face. "What about me?"

"Have you had other affairs?"

"What difference would it make if I had?"

"None. I just . . . well, it's nothing to do with me, but the way you've talked about your husband . . ."

She lay back and stared at the ceiling. "This is the first time. He hasn't made love to me for months now. It's a final insult, a kind of metaphor for how totally the Company has taken him over. It's been like watching him, slowly but steadily, fall in love with another woman. Anyway," she added abruptly, "I don't want to talk about him."

"All right." He'd been meaning to lead her onto the subject of Kiley with the sort of considerate embarrassment that one reserves for people one has betrayed. This was different. He said, "When can I see you again?"

"I don't know. I'll phone you, Alan."

"Couldn't I call you? It would be safe during the day, wouldn't it?"

"The number is ex-directory, supposed to be secret . . ."

"For God's sake!"

". . . and I've never been quite sure that the calls aren't being monitored in the Annex. I used a call box to phone you today. After all, it's at least possible that they take an occasional interest in me. If they knew where I'd been tonight I'd go all the way to the top of their security-risk ladder."

"Good God!" he said, sitting up in alarm. "I never thought. . . . You think they might be keeping you under surveillance or something?"

"I doubt it. They gave me a clean bill of health a long time ago. I took a few precautions all the same, before I left home." She faced him with a mischievous smile. "I have a little secret of my own. A joke. I laugh about it sometimes, to myself. You won't think it's very funny."

"Try me."

"It's a name I made up for our apartment. You know the way people give their houses those awful coy names like The Nest and The Eyrie? Well, I call ours The Burrow. That's because of Rod's code name. They all have to have these code names, for when they speak on open telephone lines, and they're all called after little animals. There's Civet and Mongoose, Foxbat and Porcupine. You should hear them talking to each other, they sound like . . . like children playing a zoo game. Anyway, his is very appropriate. It's"—she gave a sudden splutter of laughter—"it's Pangolin."

"Pangolin," he echoed blankly.

"It's another name for the Chinese Scaly Anteater. Pangolins, so my encyclopaedia tells me, are solitary, nocturnal, secretive creatures. They roll themselves up in a ball when they're threatened. And they live in burrows." She lay shaking with quiet laughter. "It's ridiculous!"

"Real *Boys' Own Paper* stuff, eh?"

"Oh, but they take it all very seriously. Poor old Rod: he and I don't have the same sense of humour. The Company has got so paranoiac that they practise secrecy for its own sake. Nobody is supposed to know who he is or what he's doing here. And of course he's guarded, twenty-four hours a day. They're all obsessed by what happened to the Chief of Station in Athens a couple of years back: shot dead by terrorists because he'd been identified in a newspaper. It's all very discreet, but there's never a man with a gun far away: in the grounds of the apartment block, in the car that takes him to and from work. And, of course, in the Annex."

"Pangolin," Pritchard repeated thoughtfully.

"I started out saying I wasn't going to talk about him. Let's make the most of our time, Alan."

Their bodies moved together again and her mouth went down hungrily onto his.

6

The next morning, at work, he had some unexpected luck.

For several days now he had been wanting to do some research among the files in the *Cathay Star*'s reference library. The problem was Mrs. Naicker, the bossy and inquisitive Anglo-Indian lady who ran the library with an iron hand. Mrs. Naicker would never allow Pritchard to hunt through the files for himself. She would accost him at the counter, which served also as a barrier to her sanctum, and ask him what information he needed and why. She would then part grudgingly with one or two folders of cuttings in exchange for his signature in the file-removal book.

He did not want that. He was searching for ideas as well as facts, and he needed to be able to browse at will. Besides, he knew that even at this early stage it was important to leave no traces behind him.

On Wednesday morning he learned that Mrs. Naicker had gone down with one of her periodic attacks of gout. She would be away till the weekend, at least. At lunchtime Pritchard went to see her assistant, an easygoing Chinese youth. He explained that he wanted to research a series of articles on crime—a subject sufficiently vague to give him access to almost any file in the library without raising questions. The young man, already overworked, readily fell in with Pritchard's suggestion that he be allowed behind the counter to find the material for himself.

He started at five o'clock, forsaking an early drink in the Quill once his work in the subs' room was over. The librarian gave him a spare table to work at, and to it he carried a methodically chosen heap of files: everything under the heading CRIME: KIDNAPPING, diluted with a few others on CRIME: MURDER, RAPE, and so on, which he spread about the table to avoid any hint that he was actually concentrating on a somewhat narrower subject. Then he began to read.

If there was one good thing to be said about the *Cathay Star,* it was its collection of library cuttings. For over seventy years the best of the British and American newspapers had been culled, as well as all the local ones, and there were twenty brittle envelopes stuffed full of contemporary reports of kidnapping cases. They ranged from early stories about the shanghaiing of foreign sailors in China ports—still quite a common occurrence in the early part of the century—through such infamous cases as the Lindbergh baby and the Loeb and Leopold abduction in America, the Peugeot child in France, the McKay and Black Panther affairs in Britain, to the more recent phenomenon of quasi-political kidnapping, particularly in Europe and Latin America. Pritchard began reading through them in chronological order. From time to time he made notes on a pad of copy paper, initially to mark out cross-references to the more prominent cases, which were filed in greater detail under the names of the victims and/or perpetrators. He was about halfway through the material when he was startled by the Chinese assistant, who had silently approached the table.

"It is six o'clock. Time for me to go."

"Oh." Pritchard began gathering up the files, trying hastily to disguise what he had been reading by shoving a few of the extraneous ones on top of the pile.

"There is no need for you to leave. You can lock up behind you and give the key to the watchman."

"All right, I'll put in another hour or so."

The boy nodded and left. Six o'clock and he hadn't had a drink yet, Pritchard thought: must be years since that had happened but he wasn't missing it, the need for alcohol displaced by his absorption in what he was reading.

He finished the kidnapping files and put them back in their cabinets, along with the unread folders on other crimes. He would return to them tomorrow evening, to make further notes. From what he had read tonight he had already been able mentally to devise a mode of classifying them into two groups: the successful and the unsuccessful. There were few that could be defined as totally successful—those, that was to say, that met all the criteria of success: effecting the crime without leaving damaging clues, securing the ransom without being detected, releasing the victim unharmed and evading arrest afterwards. But further analysis could wait. He needed information on another subject.

He went to a different cabinet, one of a row in which information was filed by country, and thumbed through the folders suspended on runners in the drawers—THE PHILIPPINES: AGRICULTURE: THE PHILIPPINES: ECONOMY, GOVERNMENT, INDUSTRY; and so on, until he came to REBELLION AND SEPARATIST MOVEMENTS. He took this file from its folder and returned to his table. He extracted the cuttings, noticing at once that they were all recent, none older than six years. That was about as long as the Muslim separatist movement in the southern Philippines had been operating actively against the Manila government.

His interest in the Moro National Liberation Front, as it was officially known, had of course been spurred by Baxter's talk about the story of the disastrous kidnapping last week. The connection with Roderick Kiley had been made in Pritchard's mind like a spark between two electrodes brought suddenly into dangerous proximity. A man like Kiley, he had realized, lived permanently in danger of murder or kidnapping. That, if for no other reason, was why he worked under diplomatic cover. And that was the reason for the armed guards. The exposure that he feared would not be to rival secret services—the KGB and its Chinese equivalent, the T'e Wu, had probably had him fingered for years, after all, just as the CIA probably knew who most of their opposite numbers were. The danger came from those groups of left-wing terrorists who had little to thank the CIA for and even less to lose. The nearest of such groups were the Moros.

For six years they had been waging what the counter-insurgency experts liked to call a "low-intensity war" against the central government and its forces. Most of the action took place on the southern island of Mindanao and in the Sulu archipelago just to the southwest of it. It was never important enough to enjoy regular attention from the media; it was highlighted just occasionally when a Western correspondent spent a few days there, filed a couple of reports and flew out again. Manila was getting help from the CIA, in the way of counter-insurgency expertise and possibly money—or so at least the Moros claimed. They, in turn, seemed to have support surreptitiously from the Communist Chinese and, much more openly, from the small East Malaysian state of Simpang, formerly part of British North Borneo, where the Muslim-dominated state government had been providing them with arms and training facilities.

It was a small war, remote, sporadic and largely self-contained. It was the kind of war Pritchard was looking for.

The Chief Minister of Simpang and the main source of aid and comfort to the Moros was Dato Abu Bakr Salim. Politically well-entrenched but little known outside Malaysia, Salim was viewed with disfavour by the federal government in Kuala Lumpur, not only for his support of the rebels in the Philippines but because of his reputation as an opportunist and—not to put too fine a point on it—a crook. He was also a friend of Baxter's, which made a certain amount of sense.

Pritchard sighed and closed the file. The idea—or at least the fantasy—had been Baxter's in the first place. It was he, Pritchard, who was busy translating it into reality. But Baxter, he had already decided, was going to have to be part of the Project whether he liked it or not.

It was the first time he had thought of it that way—as the Project, with an upper-case P.

Baxter was still at the bar of the Quill when Pritchard got there a little before eight. He was drinking gin slings on his own and toying with a plate of the club's samoosa pastries.

"Dry as a bone," he complained as Pritchard hoisted himself onto the stool beside him. "Been in the oven for days, by the look of them. What can I get you, old son? Still Life!"

"Not going home for dinner?"

"Not tonight. Case of a small domestic squabble. Phone call: cash a cheque on the way home. The amah is due for a rise this month. I say she'll have to find it out of the housekeeping. Says she's not getting enough housekeeping as it is. Anyway, if I would spend less money drinking in the Quill . . . and so on, and on." Baxter gave an exaggerated sigh. "You single fellows don't realize how lucky you are."

"I don't know about that."

"Get on. You can play the field with the chicks. You've got no responsibilities, no one to answer to. And no extra mouths to feed. It's the money side of it that's the worst worry. When you're short of it you're so tied down. You . . . you could take off for wherever you wanted tomorrow."

Pritchard shook his head. "It might look like that to you. But after a certain age you lack the courage." Still Life shuffled over to take their order: Scotch and another gin sling. Pritchard said, "Made any plans to sell the junk yet?"

"I'll probably start advertising next week. I've been hanging on, hoping to save a half-share, but it looks as if the whole thing will have to go. There's a Chink creditor leaning on me and—"

"Do me a favour, will you? Before you make any firm plans, take me out on her one more time."

"Sure. We'll be going out on Sunday again, I expect."

"I was thinking of just you and me, Bax, not your family. One weekday, perhaps. Can you spare the time?"

"Probably, but—"

"There's something I want to discuss with you."

62

Baxter gave him his big blue loony stare and wiped some flakes of samoosa off his mouth.

"You need a trip on the *Lady Belinda,* just for a discussion?"

"Not entirely. I thought we might do a little exploring. Perhaps visit that spot you were talking about at the picnic on Sunday."

"What spot was that?"

"You said you'd discovered a place last year, out among the islands. Very remote, away from nosy people, I think you told me. Could you find it again?"

"Sure. But why . . . ?"

"I'd like to see it. How would Tuesday suit you?"

7

He had several things to do before Tuesday. First there was the completion of his notes from the *Cathay Star* files. He stayed late at work again on both Thursday and Friday, immersing himself totally in the folders at his table in the library. He drew up a chart on which he broke down the facts on each case of kidnapping—or, at least, those on which sufficient facts were available—under several headings. They included the name, age and sex of the victim or victims; the motive, whether political or purely mercenary; brief notes on the modus operandi of the kidnappers and the circumstances in which the victim was held; and, finally, whether the crime had been successful or not, and in either case why.

It was almost ten o'clock on Friday night by the time he had finished. He locked the library and gave the key to the nightwatchman, and on the way out of the building he decided, for once, to skip the Quill and go straight home. Funny. It seemed suddenly as though all that time and money spent propping up the club bar from five thirty onwards had been a compensation for something else, a compelling interest in something outside the daily, grinding monotony of his life. Some men went home from their dull jobs to tend their gardens, to build model planes or to play squash. He understood, then, that he had made the Project into his hobby.

He had also to prepare the ground for two days' absence from work. On Saturday afternoon he began to complain of abdominal pains and told Corless he thought he had one of his bouts of amoebic dysentery coming on. He had caught this disease many years ago in Bangkok and once every couple of years it recurred, though the attacks had grown progressively milder. The treatment was routine: a few days in bed and a course of emetine injections. He left work early, warning the chief sub that he probably would not be back before the middle of next week.

Usually the *Star*'s management insisted that anyone taking even a couple of days' sick leave produce a medical certificate. In the circumstances of his impending departure he did not think Mr. So would bother to ask for one. It was a calculated risk.

Sunday was given over mostly to typing up the notes on his research and analysing them. But first he phoned a garage in Leighton Road which he knew ran a car-hire service and asked if he could rent a self-drive car for twenty-four hours. He picked it up that evening, a two-year-old Volkswagen Polo, after handing over a down payment of two hundred Hong Kong dollars. It was the first money he had laid out on the Project.

He drove the car straight to a private multi-storey car park round the corner from his flat and left it there for the night. He was up at six the next morning and collected the car half an hour later. With him he had brought an elderly pair of Zeiss 8 x 30 binoculars that had once belonged to his stepfather.

He drove to the entrance of the Cross-Harbour Tunnel in Causeway Bay and crossed over to the Kowloon side. Weaving his way through the complicated flyover system, he emerged on Chatham Road, heading north. Shortly before the turnoff to Kai Tak Airport, on the right, he swung left onto a narrow road that ran steeply uphill. Within a minute the congestion and noise of Kowloon were left behind. This was Quarry Hill, still largely covered in tropical scrub because it was too steep for intensive building, and giving an impression of well-heeled suburban tranquillity. Low-rise apartment blocks were spaced out across the hillside and the roads were lined with tamarind trees. From the oblique references Ailsa had made to it, he thought he could pinpoint where she lived.

Near the summit he spotted a lay-by with a footpath leading off it. He parked there and got out, carrying the binoculars. He followed the path as it led him further uphill, through head-high bracken and ilex, until he reached a small level outcrop of rock where the undergrowth fell away sufficiently to give him a clear view of the whole eastern slope of the hill, all the way down to the Kowloon shoreline and the airport runway, sticking out into the bay like an admonitory finger. He sat on the rock, brought the binoculars to his eyes, focused them and began to search the hillside, traversing methodically from left to right and back again.

Within three minutes he had found the State Department complex. At a glance it was like any one of the several dozen residential developments on Quarry Hill, three rows each of four duplex apartments built in pale grey brick and set on a grassed-over patch of levelled ground about four hundred yards down the slope. It was a panhandle site, approached by a fifty-yard drive from the road, from which it would barely be visible. The giveaway was the barbed wire, a ten-foot fence snaking across the wooded hillside behind the buildings to surround them on three sides. The fourth, parallel to the road, doubtless had some more discreet form of protection. Then there were the outbuildings. What appeared to be a porter's lodge at the head of the drive might just be doubling as a control post; and the large janitor's lodgings adjacent to the garage might serve equally well as quarters for security men.

What would look to an outsider, down at that level, merely as a desire for privacy was visible from up here as a tightly controlled security system.

He kept the binoculars trained on the complex for twenty minutes. Nobody was about at that time of the morning—nobody but the guards. He saw two of them in that period. One left the control post to walk to the security hut and returned a minute later; shortly afterwards a second man came out of the hut and walked all the way round the perimeter fence, presumably carrying out a routine morning check. There was no sign of weapons, but they were probably carrying hand guns under the flaps of their khaki uniform tunics.

At seven thirty Pritchard put the binoculars away. Time to check on something else. He slithered down the path to the car and drove back in the direction he had come from, down Quarry Hill Road until he reached the entrance of the driveway that led to the complex. Diagonally opposite was a small shopping centre containing a supermarket, a post office and a branch of the First National City Bank of New York. He reversed into a parking bay in front of it and cut the engine. Then he waited.

The apartment complex was screened by a row of fan palms. That didn't matter; he didn't want to get any closer to the place, at least for

65

now. Behind him the shops were not yet open, and the only people about were amahs in black pyjamas, on their way to work. Once every couple of minutes a car drove by on its way into town.

At exactly five minutes to eight a pale green Plymouth Valiant driven by a Chinese chauffeur slowed down and swung in through the gateway to the complex. Two minutes later it came out again, pausing for a few seconds between the gateposts, the driver checking for other traffic, before it slid out into Quarry Hill Road.

The pause was long enough for Pritchard to recognize the passenger in the back seat, his head bent forward over something he was reading. It was Kiley.

Pritchard started the Volkswagen and moved out into the road behind him.

An hour later he was sitting on a bench at the edge of Boundary Path, a narrow paved lane running up the scrub-covered slope that overlooked Central District on Hong Kong Island, staring through the binoculars again. Casual passersby, he guessed, would take him for a tourist admiring the view of the harbour. In fact the binoculars were focused on something rather nearer.

The United States Consulate General was housed in a modern L-shaped building occupying what was, in effect, a large traffic island at the junction of Garden Road and Lower Albert Road, a short way above Central and overlooking the harbour. It was not this building that interested him, however, but another one tucked away behind the long leg of the L. It was squat and square, three storeys of bronze-tinted one-way glass, looking like some cheap new classroom block in the grounds of a distinguished school. You would hardly notice it from Garden Road; if you did, you might think of it as a mundane functional adjunct to the consulate: the trade commissioner's offices, perhaps.

The view from above exposed a flat, felted roof bristling with low-profile radio antennae. It also showed a basement garage entrance that could not be seen from below, the approach to it dug out of the hillside to the south and connecting with the main traffic entrance from the consulate.

At twenty-one minutes past eight the steel door to the garage had been briefly raised from within to admit the Plymouth bringing Kiley to work. Pritchard, following at a discreet distance in the Volkswagen, had shot past the entrance and carried on up the hill.

The building was the Annex, headquarters of the CIA in the Far

East. It housed one of the biggest concentrations of Company operatives outside the United States, and Kiley was bang on top of them.

Pritchard lowered the binoculars and stood up. The sun was hot now, beating down on him in his exposed position on the hillside. He would learn nothing more by continuing to stare at the inert bronze mass of the Annex. What he had found out so far, he thought as he began to walk down Boundary Path towards where his car was parked, was useful enough. Kiley was guarded round the clock; he moved from his home to his office as if between two fortresses, both of them fairly impregnable.

The fact that he was so closely protected did not dismay Pritchard. It was a challenge. It also confirmed what he had believed from the start —that Kiley was a very worthwhile target indeed.

8

Baxter collected him early on Tuesday. They drove through the tunnel and out of Kowloon to Pak Sha Wan village in the rural New Territories. From there it was a short drive down a bumpy track to the shore of the small sheltered bay of Hebe Haven, where the *Lady Belinda* rode at her mooring. They got out of the car with their bags of provisions and called to the boatboy, who was working on the deck of another junk. He was a "look-see" man whose wages were paid jointly by the owners of the moorings to look after the boats and carry out small repairs. He climbed into his sampan and paddled it swiftly, with the single oar that was lashed to the stern, across to the jetty.

"All well, Ah Leung?" Baxter asked, heaving his cold-bag full of beer and sandwiches into the small boat. "No opium hangover today?"

"Opium?" Ah Leung turned an expressionless face up to him.

"Get on, you know what I'm talking about. Chasing the Dragon. Monday is his day off," Baxter explained to Pritchard. "Every Monday he spends in a divan in the Walled City, smoking himself stupid. Still, that's his only vice. As long as it doesn't interfere with his work we turn a blind eye, don't we, Ah Leung?"

The boatboy said nothing. Pritchard, clambering into the sampan behind Baxter, said, "What happens if you want to get out to your boat on a Monday?"

"Yeah, what *does* happen, Ah Leung?"

"Mondays I leave sampan here," he said. "You use."

He paddled them out to the *Lady Belinda*. As soon as they were aboard, Baxter started the two diesel engines, which both coughed satisfyingly to life. Pritchard unlocked the double doors leading down to the big saloon and stowed their provisions away. Baxter used the boathook to pull the mooring buoy inboard and cast off the line. Returning to the cockpit, he pushed the throttle levers down to half speed, brought the junk round to face the narrow mouth of the bay and headed her out to sea.

They travelled southeastwards for about five miles, passing between Tiu Chung Chau and Shelter Island, where the picnic had been nine days ago, into the open sea. Then Baxter brought the junk round 90 degrees to port, heading for the channel that would bring her out on the seaward side of Basalt Island.

Away from the mainland there was a breeze, making the water choppy and occasionally, as the slender prow dipped into a wave, flinging a handful of spray over the top of the deckhouse. Pritchard, exhilarated, stood in the cockpit beside Baxter, drinking beer and looking round appreciatively at the seascape, the grey-brown islands standing like ghostly hills above the haze. Most of them were uninhabited, for lack of fresh water if nothing else. Even the larger ones had only one or two villages sited in sheltered coves where fishing boats could be drawn up on the beaches.

It was just after midday when they headed in towards the rocky east coast of Basalt, another uninhabited mound, featureless and stark, dominated by a peak that rose steeply on the north side to five or six hundred feet and then fell away more gently to a broken coastline on the south. A couple of hundred yards offshore, Baxter turned the junk to run parallel to the coast. In a few minutes he had found what he was looking for: a small bay with a low, rocky promontory jutting out to sea at its southern end. At the centre of the inlet was a beach, a sliver of pale sand fifty yards wide at the foot of a steep, brush-covered hillside —a place that would be easy to miss from further out at sea.

Baxter nosed the junk towards it. About thirty yards short of the beach he put the engines in neutral, ran forward and dropped the stockless anchor into the pale green water. It got a good grounding at once, the chain tautening as the *Lady Belinda* strained against it and came round into the wind.

While Baxter went aft to cut the engines, Pritchard gazed round him, impressed by the breadth of the view. He could see all the way from the northeast tip of the mainland to what he guessed was Tung Lung Island at the entrance to the main harbour of Hong Kong. In all that expanse there was not another vessel in sight; they were alone in the world.

They lowered the swimming steps over the side, stripped to their shorts and dived into the clear, blood-warm water. As they scrambled out on the beach Baxter said, "Now look around you, Alan. Notice anything unusual?"

Pritchard studied his surroundings carefully—the scrubby grey hillside, the sickle curve of the bay. Then he looked further afield, out to sea, trying to define the horizon through the haze.

"Not a thing."

"Closer in," Baxter said, enjoying Pritchard's puzzlement. "It's really very close." Neither of them had yet mentioned the subject of the discussion Pritchard had promised. Baxter seemed to sense that it would be delicate.

Pritchard dutifully gazed around him again. Then suddenly he felt his eye drawn back to the jumble of rocks at the base of the promontory, just twenty yards away, focusing on some unnatural regularity of form. There was a flat rock there, or rather a low shape that seemed too flat and square to be a rock even though it shared the colour and texture of the dark volcanic boulders around it.

He glanced at Baxter, who nodded, smiling. Then he plodded across the sand towards the thing. Stopping a few yards short of it he made the flat surface out to be a roof, supported by low walls nestling among the rocks. A sloping flat boulder formed the rear wall; the other three, all facing out to sea, had narrow horizontal slits in them. Now, too, he made out the rectangular doorway, screened by the shadow of a flat overhanging rock, and recognized the structure for what it was: an army pillbox, long abandoned. Weathering over the years to dark grey, its thick reinforced-concrete walls had acquired a perfect natural camouflage.

"I stumbled on it last year," Baxter said from just behind him. "And I mean stumbled—there's no other way you'd know it was there. Go on in."

Pritchard, feeling a slight, irrational trepidation, stood for a moment by the doorway. It had been hacked roughly out of the rock to the right of the pillbox and a few feet above it, and the entry tunnel to which it gave access went down two steps before turning left. He entered the tunnel, took the turn, and then another one. He went down three more steps in the gloom and then he was inside the pillbox. It was trapezium-shaped, about twenty feet by twelve, and between the concrete roof and the sandy floor, set well below ground, there was a bare six feet of headroom.

There was a dank smell about the place and a coolness that felt sticky, somehow, in spite of the relief it gave from the midday sun. Pritchard stood in the centre of the floor and looked around. On the wall to the left, a line of cursive Japanese characters had been traced in the concrete before it had set. The date beneath them was in Arabic numerals: 11/4/1942.

"That was three years before the Japanese surrender," said Baxter, who had followed him in and seen him staring at the writing. "The Japs spent a fair bit of time strengthening the defences in the first year or so of the occupation. This place is no different to what it was in 'forty-five: completely forgotten now, probably. That was mine." He pointed to a rusty San Miguel beer can lying in one corner. "Nobody's been here since me. There are no KILROYS on the walls, no shit on the floor. I bet nobody even knows it exists."

Pritchard nodded slowly, imagining how the Japanese machine-gun crews must have felt, manning this wretched outpost probably for months at a time; waiting for a boat once a week, perhaps, with water and rations from the garrison stores in Hong Kong; waiting for an enemy who never came.

The post had been sited here for the view it commanded. Its field of fire covered the whole of the northeastern approach to Hong Kong. It was settled in among the rocks as though it had always been there; only from the air—and from pretty directly above, at that—would the regular shape of the roof be likely to give it away.

A strange excitement filled Pritchard. It wasn't just the knowledge that this place was ideal for his purpose; it went deeper than that, satisfying some strong instinct of the human animal to make its own lair. He remembered a similar sensation from his boyhood in Malaya, at a time when his stepfather had been in charge of a rural police station in Penang. On an overgrown hillside behind the police kampong young Alan had discovered a bunker—a trench three feet deep, with corrugated iron laid over it and that in turn covered with earth—which apparently had been used by Chinese guerrillas during the war, as a food or ammunition dump. He made it his own den, a place where he could hide from the world and indulge in his fantasies. It was there—

and the memory sliced through his mood like a knife through a nerve
—it was there that he had planned to murder his stepfather.

All at once the inside of the pillbox seemed gloomy, cold, menacing. "Let's go," he said to Baxter, and they turned and climbed out into
the sunshine.

When they had swum back to the junk they opened their packets
of sandwiches and some more beers and had a leisurely lunch at the
table in the saloon. When he had finished eating, Baxter wiped his
fingers up his bare thighs and said, "You've got something to discuss
with me, Alan."

"Yes."

"You brought me out here for two reasons: to talk, and to have
me show you this place. All right, I've done my part."

"Then let's talk. I think you've got some idea why I wanted to see
this spot."

"I've got an idea you're going peculiar, if you really want to
know."

"Why?"

"Well," Baxter said uncomfortably, "the only time I mentioned
this place to you . . . it was in a pretty crazy context."

"We were having a conversation about kidnapping. You said you
knew an ideal place to hide the victim. Now that I've seen it I have to
agree: it's perfect."

"Conversation, you call it! It was all bullshit!"

"I wouldn't agree."

"Jesus, you're so serious! I wasn't being serious."

"Don't back down on me, Bax."

"Back down? What the hell from?"

"From an idea you put into my head at that picnic. I've been
thinking about it ever since. In fact I've been working on it. And I've
begun to think I can make it really happen. I've taken your fantasy,
Bax, and begun to turn it into reality—like you said, about that experi-
ment when you were a kid, turning pennies into half-crowns. Only I
don't intend to come up with green pennies."

"Neither did I, Alan."

"You got the formula wrong. I think I've got it right."

Baxter rolled his eyes to the pine-panelled ceiling of the saloon.
"Just what the hell are we talking about?"

"I think you've already guessed, up to a point. But let me spell it
out bluntly: I want to kidnap somebody, Bax, and bring him out here

to this place of yours. And I need your co-operation."

"Jesus Christ!" Baxter shifted on his seat and puffed out his plump cheeks in distress. "Jesus Christ, listen to him!"

"If I can convince you that we can make it work, will you go along? If I can't, then, okay, we'll forget about the whole thing. The point is, it can't work without you."

"A kidnapping, for God's sake! Alan, what's got into you?"

"Call it desperation, if you like. Let's level with each other, chum. How badly are you strapped for money?"

"Badly." Baxter lifted his shoulders in a shrug and nodded several times, staring down at the table. "Pretty badly. I got screwed right at the start, by a Chinese banker and a smart team of lawyers. He staked me the money to set myself up here, in exchange for every cent's worth of collateral I would ever have, now and in the hereafter. The business just didn't work as well as I expected, that's all. And then the overheads —Christ, the money you have to spend just to try and prove to people that you've *got* money! I told you I'd probably have to sell the junk. Well, that's just the beginning. If I sold her and everything else I owned, down to the kid's tricycle, I'd still be in the hole for two hundred thousand Hong Kong. Maybe a quarter of a million. Look, you'll keep this to yourself, Alan, won't you? Nobody knows quite how bad it is, not even Liz. Just me and the banker, and he's started to make nasty noises about sending me into liquidation. That's just for the fifty thou I owe him on the initial stake. But once he makes a move the other sharks will get the scent—the backlog I owe on rent, for instance. Quite frankly," he said, raising his eyes to look squarely at Pritchard, "I've been thinking of doing another bunk."

"The way you did from Simpang?"

"It wasn't half as bad down there. It wasn't even my fault. There was this offshore investment-trust outfit I was involved in that went bang. There was a threat of prosecution against two or three of us, the directors, for misapplying trust funds. Luckily we had the Chief Minister on our side, old Salim—I may have mentioned his name to you. Frankly, he'd been getting a kickback for arranging permission to operate there in the first place, and he gave us timely warning to leave before things got too sticky. For him as well as us, you see, because he couldn't afford to have his connection aired. Anyway—"

"I want to talk to you about Salim later," Pritchard interrupted, opening another can of San Mig. "Meanwhile, I said I'd level with you. I'll tell you this: I've lost my job. I have no prospects of finding another

72

one—or if I do it'll be the same sort of grinding piss-willy nonsense job I've had until now. I'm in a hole just as much as you are, Bax, and I want out. I think I know a way of getting out, if you'll go along with it."

Baxter gave him a long, level look. "You're really serious, aren't you?"

"I am. You come in with me and you can write off those two hundred grand's worth of debts and still have enough left over to live like a king. I'll tell you why I need you, Bax. I want three things from you. I want the use of this place of yours, the pillbox out here. I want the use of your junk. And I want your connection with this man Salim. Are you still on good terms with him?"

Baxter shrugged. "I haven't been in touch with him since I left Simpang, but we parted cordially."

"Could you get back in there? Arrange a meeting with him?"

"I suppose so, if he gave me the okay. But what—?"

"Just listen. In a few days' time I'll have the whole story ready to unwrap. And then I hope I can convince you that it'll work."

"Is it just you and me who are in on this?"

"We'll need two more. I want Fong to be one of them."

"Fong!"

"He was in on the original discussion, remember? Leaving him out would be a security risk. Just as it happens, he has a talent that we can use."

"You think you'll be able to persuade him to come in?"

"He needs money as badly as we do, doesn't he? The way I see it, though, you and I are the senior partners. You supply the three things I mentioned; I supply everything else—including the victim."

"Including weapons perhaps?"

"Just one gun."

"Where do you find a gun in Hong Kong? They're worth their weight in gold."

"That problem is already solved. Look."

Pritchard delved into the bag on the seat beside him and took a heavy package from the bottom of it, something wrapped in a square of oilskin and tied with string. He set it down on the table between them, untied the knot and unwrapped the oilskin, and took out the biggest revolver Baxter had ever seen.

"Webley .455," Pritchard said proudly. "Service job. Obsolete now, of course, but it'd still blow the head off an ox."

73

"Where in Christ's name did you get a thing like that?"

"I've had it for thirty years. And never once fired it." Pritchard hefted the gun in his hand—a massive weapon, a foot long and two and a half pounds in weight, unloaded. "One of the biggest hand guns made this century, or so my stepfather used to say. He was a collector, in a small way. He liberated this from a Japanese prison-camp guard at the surrender of Singapore. The Jap had taken it from a Royal Navy petty officer four years earlier, so it was untraceable."

"And your stepfather passed it on to you?"

"Not exactly. I nicked it from him, together with fifty rounds of ammunition. I was going to kill him, you see."

Baxter's blue eyes were bright with wonder. "You're full of surprises today, Mr. P."

"It was in Penang. I was ten years old. I hated the bastard and I was going to wait for an opportunity to shoot him in his sleep. I knew he had it illegally so he wouldn't be able to report the loss. All he did was beat up the houseboy and the cook. It turned out, when I tried a target practice in a rubber plantation, that I didn't have the strength to pull the trigger, let alone hold the bloody thing straight enough to aim. So I hid it away. It was difficult to get rid of. One way and another I've had it ever since. It's as good as new, really. I've kept it oiled and cleaned."

"But never fired it?"

"I thought I might remedy that now. Besides, I must try out the ammo."

"After thirty years it'll be dud, surely?"

"It's been kept dry. There's no reason why it should have deteriorated much. Come on, let's try her out. Bring some beer cans."

Pritchard collected the ammunition and followed Baxter up the companionway to the afterdeck. He broke the huge revolver open and shoved six of the squat nickel-nosed cartridges into their chambers in the cylinder. He closed the gun and locked the antiquated stirrup-and-barrel catch. He tossed one of the empty San Miguel cans overboard, watching it bob on the slight swell for a few seconds before he slipped the safety catch, raised the gun, took careful aim, and fired.

The recoil knocked his arm up and sent him staggering back a pace. The shot was deafening; the bullet went hopelessly high, pocking the water twenty yards beyond the can. He swore, then knelt down and rested his aiming hand on the rail of the junk. He fired again. The shot went high once more but was nearer its target. For the third attempt,

74

he clamped his left hand over his right wrist to steady it and got within six feet of the can. It was drifting out of effective range now; he threw another one in.

"The old grouping needs a bit of polish," said Baxter helpfully, at his elbow.

"We'll see how well *you* get on in a minute."

Between them they fired twenty-four rounds. By then their hands were too shaky with the weight of the gun to make any more practice worthwhile. But Pritchard, once he had got the feel of the revolver, had emerged clearly as the better shot. In the last six attempts he had got within a foot of the target every time, and overall he had actually hit the can twice. More important, every round had fired; the ammunition was still good. While Baxter weighed anchor and got the engines going, Pritchard carefully pulled through the barrel of the revolver, oiled it and wrapped it up, with the remaining cartridges, in its oilskin package.

On the way back, Baxter stood silent at the wheel of the junk for a long time, looking troubled. Finally he said, "Okay, Alan, you've got your gun, that's a start. But have you really thought this whole thing through? Kidnapping is a violent crime—"

"It doesn't have to be, if it's handled right."

"These things have a way of getting out of hand. I know that; I follow them in the papers."

"I've done my homework too," Pritchard said, "and I probably know more about it now than you do. The ones that work are the ones that have been carefully and intelligently planned, all the way through. If everyone does exactly what he's supposed to do, nothing can go wrong. Besides, I intend to keep a whip hand over the action. I'll be the only one armed."

"That sounds okay, Alan. I . . . well, I just find it hard to imagine people like you and me doing a thing like that. Look at us." He let go of the wheel for a moment to make a half-shrugging gesture that encompassed them both. "What are we? Respectable, peaceable, middle-class men. I don't know about you, but I've never done anything you could call violent in my life. I run away from violence. That's the difference between us and professional criminals—bank robbers, say. They have the temperament for that sort of thing. They've got nerve. Have we got the sheer bloody nerve to go through with something like this?"

"No soldier, left to himself, would have the nerve to go into battle," Pritchard said. "That's a well-known fact. It's what drilling,

75

training, square-bashing are all about: reducing individuality and the imagination that goes with it. Replacing it with a corporate identity that doesn't think beyond the next order. That's what we'll be doing, Bax: rehearsing, training, drilling, till we've got it perfect, so that when the moment comes for pulling it off the idea of failure won't even occur to you. All the same, I intend to stiffen the team with a professional—or at least someone who can fight his way out of a tough corner."

Baxter nodded thoughtfully. "That might be wise. There's one other implication that may not have occurred to you. The threat that a kidnapper holds over his victim is death. If something goes wrong, if the ransom isn't paid or can't be collected . . ."

"In this case that won't happen."

"Let's say for a moment it did. Would you be able—you're the one with the gun, remember—would you be able to put that gun to the victim's head, in cold blood, and pull the trigger?"

Pritchard turned to face him, giving him a long, intense stare. "When I stole that gun, at the age of ten, I wasn't playing a game. I was serious. If I'd been able to pull the trigger I would have. I knew it then, Bax, and I know it now. I'm capable of killing."

9

It was four-thirty by the time they had moored the *Lady Belinda* at Hebe Haven, got the boatboy to row them ashore and set off for town: up the steep incline of Razor Hill, then down the long, gently winding slope that led onto the Kowloon Peninsula; past Kai Tak Airport on the left and the festering slum known as the Walled City on the right, then into the racing traffic of Chatham Road. Before they reached the tunnel entrance Pritchard asked Baxter to drop him off. He caught a Number Five bus to the Star Ferry terminus and from there walked several hundred yards up Nathan Road, past the junk-jewellery shops and denim boutiques, the shirtmakers and silk merchants, the girlie bars and massage parlours. This was Tsimshatsui, part down-market business district, part tourist trap, where Japanese visitors bought Japanese watches cheaper than they could get them at home, where European kids who'd come east for a good time shared bug-ridden guest-house dormitories and bowls of noodles, where American sailors' dollars would buy them anything from a woman to a fix of heroin.

On the ground floor of a building to the right was a vast arcade full of shops and cooked-food stalls. The stalls were tiny places packed with pots rattling and steaming on gas rings, their tables crowded with Chinese snacking on noodles and chow fan and congee. Pritchard, following Baxter's directions, made for the one where Fong now worked.

He saw him from the rear, standing at a tiny table beside the stove and dunking rice bowls in a plastic basin full of greasy water. The cook was cramming fresh greens from a saucepan onto a plate with his hands, and on the floor between two tables a man in shorts and T-shirt, with a cigarette clamped in his mouth, was cutting chunks off a boiled pig's head and feeding them into a stockpot.

"Hello, Fong."

The young man turned to Pritchard, startled. He wasn't used to hearing English in here. Then the mooncake face broke into a smile.

"Mr. Pritchard! Hello!"

"It's Alan, remember?"

"Alan. How are you?"

"Well enough. You?"

"All right, I guess." Fong shrugged, then pulled his hands out of the soapsuds and wiped them on the dirty apron he was wearing. He looked tired and his complexion was unhealthy from the heat and steam in which he worked. His uncle—probably the one who was cutting up the pig's head—had given him the job, but that was as far as family favouritism went. He worked six days a week, fourteen hours a day, and it wasn't the kind of work that his year at Hong Kong University or his glamorous career in the Kung Fu business had cut him out for.

"Did Mr. Baxter tell you where I was?"

"Yes."

"You wanted to see me?"

"I came for some food. But we might have a chat, if you can spare the time."

Fong called in Cantonese to the man squatting on the floor, who was now delicately severing the pig's cheek from the bone, cutting out with a small, sharp knife every available scrap of flesh. He got a grunted reply, then eagerly undid the apron and steered Pritchard towards a vacant table.

"Come. You sit down. What can I get you, something special?"

"Anything that's good. I'll have a San Mig to go on with."

The young man sat him down, bustled away and conversed with the cook. Fong—his other names were something unpronounceable, never used by Europeans—was a slightly built Cantonese who had been brought as a baby to Hong Kong, on the flood tide of refugees fleeing the civil war on the mainland, and had grown up in the Kowloon slums. Hard work and high intelligence had helped him overcome the disadvantages of his background, but a fondness for easy money had run counter to these attributes. While fighting his way through the intensely competitive Hong Kong secondary school system, he had helped support himself by getting part-time work as a film extra. One day somebody asked him to try his hand at stunt work, and he proved to have a natural aptitude for it. By the time he had finished his first year at university he was earning so much money on the side that there seemed little point in pursuing an unprofitable academic career. Fong had known both poverty and a degree of wealth, and there could be no doubt which he preferred. Money fever was a recurring disease, to no one more so than a Chinese. That was what Pritchard was counting on.

Fong returned to the table, clutching a large bottle of San Miguel and a glass, and placed them in front of Pritchard.

"Have some yourself."

"Thank you, no," Fong said hurriedly, with a glance at his uncle. He was gouging out one of the pig's eyes.

"Don't worry, I'm buying."

Fong smiled slightly and went to fetch another glass, then sat down opposite him. He poured the beer carefully into both glasses.

"You and I didn't get a chance to talk," Pritchard said, "that day of the picnic. I meant to ask you what plans you've got."

"At the moment, none."

"You're going to stay here forever?"

"I have no choice, Mr.—Alan." The use of the surname was habit, not deference. "Do you know how hard it is for a man out of jail to find *any* sort of job? If I had finished my education, then perhaps—"

"Education didn't count when you were a stuntman, did it?"

"There's no more work of that kind around. The Chinese movie business has gone serious: operas, love stories, folk tales."

"There might be *some* sort of opening for you, mightn't there?"

"Show me, I'll take it."

Pritchard glanced round the room, at the bubbling pots, the few early diners wolfing down noodles. The concrete floor beneath his shoes was tacky with grease. He watched the uncle toss another piece of pork into the boiling water and said, "Does he know any English?"

"No."

"Then I can talk freely. I have an idea, Fong. An idea that could make us both a lot of money."

The young man took a long, thoughtful drink of beer. "What is involved?"

"I can't go into details yet."

"Why do you come to me?"

"I want a stunt rider. Someone who can do some fancy work with a motorbike or scooter. Interested?"

"You will have to tell me more first."

"All I can say now is that it's worth a lot of money."

"Just for riding a motorbike?"

"That's the main part, the crucial part, for you."

"Well, I don't know."

The first course of Pritchard's dinner arrived. He had seen the cook swirling it round in a chafing dish over the gas fire: a succulent blend of braised goose, bean curd and noodles. He prodded at it with his bamboo chopsticks.

"Look," he said, "I know what you're thinking. You're thinking, 'This *gwai-lo,* this crazy foreign devil, is trying to talk me into doing something stupid. Something that will turn out to be illegal. Why else won't he tell me about it?' Isn't that right, Fong? Well, all I'm saying is trust me for the moment. Do you trust me?"

It was an unfair question, one to which almost nobody was capable of saying no. Fong said, "Well, sure, but—"

"Then just tell me whether you're interested, that's all. It doesn't have to go any further yet. And there'll still be time to back out."

Fong watched him eat for a while. The goose was delicious.

"Look, Mr.—Alan," Fong said hesitantly. "You are an honest man. I wonder if you have got yourself involved in something that even you do not know much about? Whoever the other people are, I should stay away from them. I would not want to see you get into trouble."

Pritchard smiled. "You don't need to save face for me, Fong. This is all my idea. I'm putting together a team to do a job, and I want you in it."

"A criminal job?"

"Not to mince words, yes."

"You are not the right person for that."

"This isn't a crime in the conventional sense. Nobody is going to

79

get hurt. It's all a matter of brains, planning. Stick to the rules and it can't fail."

"I have heard other men say that," Fong observed wryly. "They ended up in Stanley all the same. I won't do anything that will put me back in Stanley."

The cook came to the table and took away Pritchard's empty bowl. He replaced it with one filled with fried prawns, black beans and green peppers. He brought small saucers of soya beans, sweet pickles and spring onions, and sauces to dip them in.

Fong sat staring at the tabletop—troubled, Pritchard guessed, by his Asian politeness, the inability to say no directly.

"Listen," Pritchard said urgently, dropping his voice almost to a whisper. "I won't even ask you to say yes or no—not yet. I'll give you a few days to think it over. There's time to spare, nothing is final. I need one more man as well as you."

"What sort of man?"

"He'll have to be muscle, basically, but it would help if he had enough brains to tell the time of day. I was wondering whether you might know someone."

"Could be," Fong said thoughtfully, "if you would take an American."

Pritchard made a face. "I had a tough Chinese in mind. Or an Asian, anyway."

"This one is tough. And he needs money. He's a sailor, jumped ship two, maybe three months ago. He lives with a Chinese girl."

"A deserter? Jesus, no! He'll be hotter than hell."

"I don't think the police are looking too hard for him."

"Even so," Pritchard said doubtfully. "How do you know him?"

"When I was dealing in Red Chicken, and he was on shore leave, he would come to me sometimes."

"A junkie, to boot?"

"No. Oh, maybe he used a bit himself, but basically he wanted stuff to sell on his ship. He dealt with several wholesalers: he'd take pills, White Dragon Pearl, anything he could get. He came to see me again soon after I left Stanley; I told him I was out of that business now. But I introduced him to Canny—that's the girl, an ex-girl friend of mine. Soon after that he jumped ship and went to live with her. If you want muscle, he's your man."

"I don't much like the sound of him," Pritchard said. On the other hand he could see the advantages of using another Westerner, communication being the most obvious one. The sort of Chinese heavy he'd had in mind—the kind who probably made a living "debt collecting" from reluctant shopkeepers on behalf of the Triad Societies—would be unlikely to speak English. "Could you arrange for me to look him over?" Fong nodded. "No commitment, mind, not a hint of what's in the offing."

"All right, Mr.—"

"Alan."

As he opened the door to his flat the telephone began to ring. For a nervous moment he thought it must be the office, inquiring about his illness, and wondered how many times they might have called already. He stumbled through the dark to the hall table, lifted the receiver, and did his best to sound enfeebled.

"Yes? Pritchard here."

"Alan!"

It was Ailsa. Relief mingled with pleasure at the sound of her voice.

"Alan, I must have tried your number six times. I called your office. They said you were sick."

"Yes, well. . . ."

"What's the matter?"

"A touch of my old complaint, dysentery. It was nothing much," he added hastily, then hesitated. "You didn't call them back, did you, to say I wasn't at home?"

"Of course not. I was worried, that's all."

"Nothing to worry about," he said, the tension draining out of him. "Yes, I was sick for a couple of days. I'm fine now. Today I've been malingering, frankly. What can I do for you?"

"You can see me, that's what. I'm free the rest of this week."

"You mean he—"

"He's on a trip to home base."

"I see." Something seemed to fall pleasurably into the pit of his stomach. "Well, when?"

"What's wrong with your place? In half an hour?"

"Hell, I can't offer you dinner or anything. . . ."

"Who said anything about eating?" she said, and put the phone down.

10

The bed gave a final long creak and Ailsa gasped. They separated and then lay holding hands for a time in the dark. Finally she shivered in the chill of the air conditioning, stood up and slung Pritchard's shapeless old silk dressing-gown over her wide square shoulders. She walked across to the table by the window where they had left the drinks they had brought to the room. She took a swallow of hers and then turned resolutely to face him.

"There's something you'd better know, Alan. I'm going back to Sydney next week."

He sat up in the bed, puzzled, faintly alarmed. "What do you mean?"

"I don't know how long I'll be away. Ostensibly I'm going on a visit to my mother. In fact it's going to be a trial separation. That's the fashionable term, isn't it?"

"Jesus," he muttered, taken aback. "You're finally thinking of leaving him?"

"It's been heading that way for a long time. The point has come to try it out, see if I can manage on my own."

Suddenly there was an edge of resentment in his surprise. "You've been thinking about this since before we met up the other day?"

"For a lot longer than that."

"What about me, then?"

"What about you, Alan?" She was watching him steadily. "You had your chance with me once. You didn't take it."

"You mean you think of all this"—he gestured at the bed, the room—"as a pleasant diversion, something to use up the time while you plan your departure? What am I, just the handiest non-Company cock you could find to be going on with?"

"Don't be crude, Alan. Don't be sarcastic, either; that's in even worse taste."

"Well? You tell me what this little dalliance has been all about."

"About you and me, of course. I always liked you, Alan, you know that. It's just . . . I don't know . . . you get into a position like this, you want reassurance." She shivered again. "You want to know whether it's something to do with you, whether you've lost whatever it takes to keep a man. I wanted to know whether we still had anything going."

"And do we?"

"In bed, yes. Beyond that I don't know. I want to get away for a while and think."

Pritchard fell back on his pillow and gave a bitter laugh. "You know, I think I've heard this conversation before. When Wendy left me it was, and I quote, 'to visit her parents.' Tacitly, that was a trial separation, except we didn't have the phrase then. She had to 'get away for a while and think,' too. I think she got the words out of some lousy romantic novel."

"Well, I didn't!" she said angrily. "You don't break up six years of marriage that easily. Anyway, what is it to you?"

"I've always liked you too, Ailsa. In fact I think I've been half in love with you all this time, without even realizing it. Sometimes I told myself it was actually hate: that's the sort of trick your mind plays on you. It rationalizes. Since I couldn't have you, I convinced myself that I didn't want you."

Ailsa watched him warily for a minute. Then she began to pace back and forth across the small room, hugging the gown around herself. "I'm booked to leave next Wednesday—that's a couple of days after he gets back from Washington. Probably he'll hardly notice I've gone."

"You mean you're just walking out on him?"

"Oh, no. I'm going to tell him he'll have to choose, once and for all, between his lousy job and me. And he's going to get his chance at the end of the month. He has two weeks' vacation coming up. He can choose whether he spends it with me in Sydney or cancels it *yet again.*"

"You can't settle your future on the basis of two weeks' holiday."

"At least, if he comes, it'll be a sign of something. That he cares just enough not to lose me. I've told him—how many times?—that I'm not out to ruin his career with the Company, just to strike some sort of bloody balance!" She sounded close to tears then, but stifled them and said firmly, "Things are coming to a head, anyway."

"Listen to me, Ailsa," Pritchard said seriously, sitting up again. "If he doesn't join you in Australia, if you decide it really is all over, will you think about coming back to me? And trying again?"

She stopped pacing and smiled at him. "What makes you think it would work the second time?"

"Things would be different," he said urgently. "We'd both be unattached, for a start. And we're both older and wiser now. We wouldn't have to stay in the tropics. I could take you to Australia, or anywhere else you liked. I can always make a living. In fact I might do better than just earn a living, you wait and see. I'm not asking you to commit yourself. Just promise me you'll think about it."

"All right, Alan. I'll think about it." She slipped out of the gown and began to get dressed.

When she had gone, seen off at the door with a kiss, he went back to the bedroom and finished his whisky. He put on the gown himself, the animal scent of her body still clinging to it faintly, then went through to the kitchen and poured himself another drink. There was a tight knot of nervous anticipation in his stomach, and his whole body seemed to tingle. Ailsa, without knowing it, had just added a whole new dimension to the Project. She had also unwittingly set the timetable for it.

He carried his glass through to the small desk that occupied one corner of his living room. There was a desk calendar on the blotter, which he consulted carefully. Kiley's vacation began at the end of the month, Ailsa had said—say the thirty-first, which was a Thursday. It wasn't certain that he would take the leave that was due to him, but the risk that he might was one that Pritchard, for more than one reason, couldn't countenance. She'd be leaving for Sydney next Wednesday: that was the sixteenth. The gap of fifteen days, with her absent from Hong Kong but Kiley still here, provided the ideal period in which to do the deed. Since it had to be done on a Monday, there was only one possible date: Monday, the 21st, thirteen days from now. Was it conceivable that he could get everything organized in so little time?

He had known from the start that his affair with Ailsa carried the risk of compromising him. It was at least possible—in fact, knowing how bad a liar she was, it seemed probable—that she would admit to it in the first round of police questioning once the Project was under way. That, in turn, meant that he would be drawn into the investigation and was going to need a watertight alibi. Her absence in Australia would provide just the breathing space he needed to set one up. Monday the 21st it would have to be.

He sat for a minute staring at a small damp patch on the wall in front of him. What an exquisite irony it would be if Ailsa were to leave Kiley and come back to him, the very man who—unknown to either of them—had initiated the Project against her husband! It was a revenge so sweet as almost to be worth waiting six years for. Funny, he thought, how Ailsa had turned the tables on him. He had deliberately engineered her seduction so as to learn what he could about Kiley; since then she had made him want her again as badly as he ever had.

What, he suddenly wondered, if the Project were to affect her decision? What if a sense of shared suffering should draw her back to Kiley, bring a new appreciation of each other?

He recollected himself. Tomorrow would be a busy day, the next day even more so. A call to the office, first thing, to say his dysentery was still troubling him. He set up his small portable typewriter on the desk. He put a sheet of plain copy paper into the roller and typed a heading:

Outline of a Memorandum on the Project.

11

Seymour Quinn woke up to the tinny rattle of a cheap alarm clock. Six thirty on a Thursday morning in August, and the air was already like a goddam steam bath. When he had shut off the clock he lay blinking into the morning light for a few seconds, gathering his thoughts, trying to remember why he had set the thing. Then it came to him: Fong and the man called Pritchard, the rendezvous at seven thirty.

Quinn's head was slightly thick from the fumes of White Dragon Pearl he had smoked last night. He yawned, sat up in bed and looked around the apartment. Canny called it an apartment, anyway; to him it had never been more than a room full of junky Chinese furniture, with a tiny bathroom off the entrance hall and a pair of gas rings in the alcove that served as a kitchen. Usually he didn't give much of a goddam about his surroundings, but lately this place had begun to get to him. He guessed, though, that he ought to be grateful he and Canny had it to themselves. In this same building there were families of eight and ten living in rooms this size, not to mention the other fifty people, and their ducks, up on the roof. Goddam Chinese enjoyed living like cage hens, he sometimes thought.

His gaze went to the girl lying naked beside him, her skin smooth and honey-coloured against the white sheet, her pose as she slept curiously formal: the arms half folded across her small breasts, the broad Cantonese face perfectly composed. She hadn't stirred yet; would sleep through a fucking air raid. Last night they had got high together before making it, and the memory brought a pleasurable quickening to his loins; it would be easy to forget about Fong and this other freak and just stay in bed, and later he and Canny could screw the way they did most mornings before she left for work. But he had promised Pritchard. Besides, it was too hot to go back to sleep. Sweat had already gathered in the hair on his chest and was trickling down the line of his backbone. Reluctantly, Quinn heaved himself out of bed and yawned his way to the bathroom. He didn't like early mornings; he'd seen too many of them in the Navy.

Standing in the bathtub, he took a long leak down the plughole. Then he stuck the detachable shower head in its socket on the wall, drew the plastic curtain and turned on the water. The cool, sharp needles braced him up, gradually clearing his head of the fumes of the heroin. Quinn, in fact, never used that word, preferring one of the Chinese euphemisms like Red Chicken or White Dragon Pearl, but not because he was an addict or even afraid of becoming one. Provided you used the stuff carefully, smoking it and not mainlining, and provided you stuck to Number Three and avoided graduating to Number Four —the difference being a 45 per cent concentration of diacetyl morphine against 95 per cent; oh, he knew all the facts and figures—well, then it was no worse than shooting amphetamines or dropping acid, no more serious than getting drunk occasionally. If the dumb mothers who bought the stuff off him couldn't handle it, that was their problem.

It was nearly three months now since Seymour Quinn, Gunner's Mate Third Class, had been posted as a deserter from the United States Navy. He was twenty-six years old and powerfully built: big-boned, wide-shouldered and heavily muscled. At six feet two and a hundred and ninety pounds his shape was almost as good as it had been three years ago, when he'd fought for the heavyweight boxing championship of the Seventh Fleet. The fact that he hadn't won—had been, in fact, knocked bowlegged by a nigger ten pounds lighter and four inches shorter than himself—said something about Quinn that he half recognized for himself: he hadn't been trying. He'd had the strength, the speed, even the heart—but winning just wasn't that important to him. He was unambitious and, well, okay, lazy. He asked little more out of life than enough money at any given moment to buy himself a good time.

Quinn was third-generation Irish-American, from the Roxbury section of South Boston, and he had joined the service right after dropping out of high school. The war in 'Nam had been on at the time, and the draft, and it seemed to make sense to volunteer for the Navy instead of—as he told his friends—getting his ass shot full of holes in

86

some stinking rice paddy. Besides, he liked the idea of shore liberties in foreign ports, with money to spend and chicks to ball. For a few years it was pretty cool. There was grass on the scene to relieve the monotony of life at sea, and if you needed a bigger charge there was harder stuff easily available out East: opium and smack. It wasn't long before he had set up some contacts in Hong Kong and was running a profitable little sideline selling the stuff around the USS *Kitty Hawk.* But gradually the spells at sea seemed to get longer and the ports of call lost their appeal. One whore got to be pretty much like the last and one clip joint was much the same as another. On his last liberty in Hong Kong he had met Canny and said what the hell, jumped ship and moved in with her.

He hadn't done it for her sake, though she liked to believe he had. She was no hustler, which was exactly the reason he had chosen to shack up with her. The cathouses were the first places the shore patrol would have gone looking for him. Canny—Miss Chan Chuk-yan, to give her the full Chinese treatment—was a receptionist in a respectable doctor's office, where she'd taken to popping barbiturates a few years back. Canny was no whore, but she sometimes betrayed the same kind of tough commercial streak as those hard little bitches down in Wan-chai. She had marriage on her mind, he figured—not because Gunner's Mate Third Seymour Quinn was the most eligible bachelor on earth, but because he could be a ticket to the World, Stateside. She had been a child refugee from Red China and had a passport that wasn't worth forty sheets of shitpaper when it came to travelling anyplace useful— at least, not without a stamp in it that would give her residence rights as the wife of a paid-up U.S. citizen. Canny had often urged him to turn himself in, serve his time in the brig and take his discharge. She'd wait for him, she said. Canny wanted the books balanced before she took him over, but Seymour Quinn had plans going for his own little thing, and Canny didn't figure in them.

He turned off the shower and went back naked, towelling himself down, to the main room. She was half awake, blinking her big almond eyes at him.

"You up early," she muttered.

"I have to go someplace. Meet a guy."

"What guy?"

"Just a guy. Friend of Fong's. He may have a deal for me."

She turned over and went straight back to sleep. Quinn parted the drapes briefly and looked out over the chaotic sprawl of Causeway Bay, the squatter shacks perched on the roofs of apartment buildings, the

87

sampans crowded with people in the typhoon shelter. Things were beginning to stir; traders in the Canal Road market had started setting up their fruit carts and food stalls, and the first streetcars were clanking down Hennessy Road toward North Point. The sky was clear, steely-grey turning to blue. It would be another bitch of a day.

As he turned away from the window Canny murmured in her sleep and twisted her body round to expose the breasts that had been half hidden by her arms. It was an unconsciously provocative gesture and made him hot for her as he always was in the mornings. He was tempted to forget Fong and this Pritchard after all, but . . . no. Pritchard might be crazy, but it wasn't every day that somebody offered him a chance to make real money. Easy money, Pritchard had said, and that was how Quinn liked it. He chose a clean T-shirt and a pair of jeans and began to get dressed.

He left the apartment at seven o'clock, opening and then locking behind him the heavy steel trellis that guarded the door. Every apartment in the building had this mugger-proofing, making the place feel like a prison. He took the elevator nine floors down to street level, and in Hennessy Road he hailed a cab and told the driver to take him to the Wanchai ferry pier. He moved about pretty freely now, having got over the early fear of recognition which had kept him penned up in the apartment for days at a time. The fact was—a fact he'd known all along but was unwilling to put to the test—that since the draft had ended there were very few deserters, and the Navy didn't put much effort into trying to find them. In a foreign port all they could do was notify the consul and the local police, who in their turn didn't exactly knock themselves out. They figured that sooner or later the fugitive would be caught trying to leave, or turn himself in, or get flushed out in the course of some routine raid on a whorehouse, and that in the meantime he wasn't doing much harm.

But Quinn knew better than to push his luck. There must be a picture of him on file someplace, and there was always the danger of being recognized by some zealous limey cop—even from behind the shades he always wore outdoors and the dark sideboards and Zapata moustache he had grown. He never frequented places where Westerners didn't normally go, and out on the streets he passed for a tourist or for just one more of the forty thousand or so Europeans, Americans and Australians who lived and worked in the colony.

The taxi dropped him in less than five minutes. Soon after that he was standing at the rail of a ferryboat chugging across the harbour to

Hung Hom on the Kowloon side. There'd been a time when he'd liked this place better than anywhere else out East, but now he'd had enough of it. It hadn't occurred to him when he jumped ship that he was going to be stuck here. Unlike most ports, Hong Kong had no hinterland to escape to. That long stretch of highway that ran up through Lion Rock Tunnel into the New Territories travelled just fifteen miles to the China border and stopped dead. The only way out—to anyplace—was by scheduled sea and air services, and it was surer than hell that Seymour Quinn's name was on the stop-list that those cold little Chinese immigration officers would consult through their gold-rimmed eyeglasses before letting you out.

Eventually he had figured a way round the problem. He'd kept himself going with a little discreet dealing of Number Three around the cheap hotels and eating houses of Tsimshatsui, where the English and American kids hung out. They trusted him the way they wouldn't trust a Chinese pusher, who might be anything from a Triad Society squeeze artist to a narcotics cop. From one of the kids, who had been here several months, he had learned the procedure for applying for a Hong Kong resident's identity card. After that it had been easy. In a few days' time he would have the card in his hands and be ready to light out. He wouldn't tell Canny he was going, just up and split. Canny was possessive enough to make trouble for him.

The problem was, Quinn couldn't get the measure of this Pritchard creep: his strange, mocking manner, his barbs of sarcasm. All he knew about Pritchard was that he was a limey and claimed to have been some big-deal foreign correspondent, which didn't explain what he had been doing last night eating in a pesthole like Fong's uncle's place. Whatever deal he was working on, he hadn't been ready to talk about it then. He had started in, once they were settled at a table together with Fong bustling around them, by asking him where he intended to go once he got out of Hong Kong.

"With this ID I'm getting, I can reach Macau. From there I figure I can buy my way onto the crew of a freighter. You can buy pretty well anything in Macau, I hear. If I can get to Thailand, say, or the Philippines, and pick up seaman's papers, I can go almost anywhere. I guess in the end I'll wind up back in Boston."

"God's Own Country, eh?" Pritchard said derisively.

"Dunno about that, but I like it well enough," Quinn said testily. He wasn't specially patriotic, but it riled him to hear foreigners dumping on his country.

"Oh, yes," Pritchard said with a faint smile. "You Yanks are all the same. One word of criticism and you're out there waving the Stars and Stripes in people's faces. And you know why? Because you're all rednecks at heart."

"Is that right, now?" Quinn asked, matching the other man's tone but unable to find a telling response.

"You suffer from the colonial disease—an inferiority complex. What do you expect, after a hundred and fifty years of backwoods politics? All that time you pretended the rest of the world didn't exist; then you came out and tried to take it over. No wonder you made the sort of fuck-ups I've seen in Vietnam."

"Listen, mister, I don't have to take that shit!" Quinn had risen menacingly from his chair, balling his fists. All Pritchard did was smile, the lines at the edges of his brown eyes wrinkling with a strange amusement.

"I like it, Quinn, I like it. Aggression—that's what I'm looking for. Now sit down, meatball, and let's talk about earning yourself some money."

Even at the end of the conversation, Quinn wasn't sure whether Pritchard had meant any of the provocative things he had said or was merely testing his temper. One thing he was sure about was that he didn't like the prick. Yet here he was, at seven twenty in the morning, joining the surge of passengers off the ferry at Hung Hom, going to meet with him. The money was the lure.

He spotted Fong, lounging against a newspaper stand at the edge of the car concourse in front of the terminal, and went up to him.

"No sign of Pritchard yet? Listen, what did he tell you about all this?"

"Not much. Just it's a job, that's all. He wants me to do some trick work with a motorbike."

"He figuring on knocking over an armoured truck or something? If he is, he can count me out."

"Ask him yourself. Here he is."

A brown Range Rover was slowing to a stop at the kerb beside them. Pritchard was in the front passenger seat. The driver was another European, a stout black-haired man in a floral sport shirt. Pritchard's face was framed in the door window as the car halted—a lean, seamed face, paler in daylight than it had looked in the harsh glare of electric bulbs last night. He said, "Hop in. I want you to drive, Fong. Quinn, you'll sit in the rear with Bax, here."

90

Orders already, the American thought, opening the back door in silence and climbing in behind Pritchard. The man called Bax joined him in the rear, and Fong slid into the vacant driver's seat.

"Head for Chatham Road," Pritchard told him. "I'll direct you from there."

The Chinese shifted gears and swung out into the traffic. A minute went by in silence as the car moved between squatters' encampments and apartments festooned with washing. Quinn could feel himself being surreptitiously looked over by the man called Bax.

"Where are we going?" he asked Pritchard.

"You'll know soon enough. This is Bax's car, by the way, but it looks more natural for the only Chinese among us to act as chauffeur. Between now and when the job goes operational, two or more of us will be travelling the same route—but in different cars, at different times of day."

"Now just a minute," Quinn said. "I didn't agree to anything. I don't know what all this is about. Neither does Fong."

"Turn right here," Pritchard said to Fong, ignoring the American, "and head for Quarry Hill."

They drove on for a while in silence. The Chinese, following instructions, turned left off Chatham Road and up a steeply wooded hillside. The road was a quiet, winding, residential backwater and there was little traffic on it yet. At a point about halfway up the hill Pritchard told Fong to stop and reverse into a gap in the steep embankment on the right. The opening, partly screened by a recent growth of ilex, puzzled Quinn for a moment until he saw the concrete pipe that ran along the ground to disappear under the road. A nullah, a seasonal stream, had once run down this little gorge; probably it had flooded the road in the torrential rains of successive typhoon seasons and so had been diverted into a conduit. What it had left was a dry, U-shaped ravine lying diagonally off the road, just wide enough to admit a car and just at a sharp enough angle to make the car invisible to passing traffic. Fong backed up until Pritchard told him to cut the engine.

"Great," said Quinn. "Now what?"

"Get out and I'll show you."

They all climbed out of the car and Pritchard led them scrambling up the rocky bank to the right. It was perhaps twelve feet high, with a fringe of bush at the top through which the road could be seen meandering down the hill, perhaps for a hundred and fifty yards. There were a few small apartment blocks scattered on either side of it. Pritchard stopped them when they were high enough to see over the ridge without exposing themselves above it. He checked his watch.

"It's now five to eight," he said. "At two or three minutes past, a car will come down that road that I will identify to you. We'll drive out of the nullah and follow it. It will contain a Chinese chauffeur and a passenger. You don't know the man. You don't know where he's coming from, where he's going to. You won't know anything more about him, any of you, until I decide the time is right for telling you."

"A mystery tour, yet," Quinn muttered. Then suddenly Pritchard, squatting to his right on the bank, thrust his face forward, close to the American's, the eyes glittering small and sharp and brown.

"Listen, Quinn. I'm offering you a job. If you want it, you're going to do it my way. I'm the brains and you're the muscle. The muscle is not going to be paid for thinking."

"Okay," Quinn said coolly, and turned to the other two, on his left. "If he's the brains, what about you two guys? You know any more about this than I do?"

Bax looked uneasy, his belly sagging as he held himself on all fours on the slope. "I've been in with Alan on this from the start," he said. It was the first time he'd spoken; his accent was some sort of English regional. "But I don't know much more about it than you, honestly."

"You, Fong?"

"No, nothing."

"Well, then," Quinn said triumphantly, turning back to Pritchard, "how about letting us in on this deal of yours, seeing as how none of us know what the hell it's all about? I may be what you call muscle, but I like to think I have something between my ears too, you know? And what my brain is telling me right now is that you're planning some kind of hit against that unknown party you mentioned, and that just isn't my bag, thank you."

Pritchard gave him a weary look. "Why can't you just wait to hear? Half an hour? An hour?"

"No, sir." They all watched Quinn as he stood up and ran down the bank. At the bottom he paused and turned. "It just occurred to me. Maybe you owe me a little attendance fee for my trouble. I mean, if I was to call the cops and say, Look, there's this freak Pritchard, and he's fixing to waste some guy out at Quarry Hill. . . . Okay, I don't know any more than that, but it would spoil your game, right? How much is it worth to you, Pritchard?"

The three men on the bank watched him silently, a frozen tableau. Eventually Pritchard stirred. "All right, Quinn, we'll count you out. Go on home."

"Not so easy. What are you offering me?"

Pritchard hesitated for a second, then glanced at Fong and Bax. "Stay here," he said. "Watch for a light-green Plymouth."

He slid down the slope and stopped a couple of yards short of Quinn, his brow creased by a worried frown.

"Okay, you've got me over a barrel. Take five hundred and forget that any of this happened."

"Make it a thousand."

Pritchard mouthed something silently. He turned and walked round to the nearside front door of the Range Rover. He leaned in through the window, opened the glove compartment and took something out. Then, unbelievingly, Quinn was staring across the roof of the car into the muzzle of a huge revolver. Behind the compelling stare of that single black eye he was aware of Pritchard's face, the glint of anger in his gaze turning slowly to amusement.

"Hey, look, put that goddam thing down. I . . ."

Pritchard cocked the revolver, grinning at him now. "You really are a dumb bastard, Quinn. You haven't got the brains you were born with."

"Okay, okay," the American said, feeling a quake in his stomach. "Call me anything you like. Forget about the money. Just don't let *that* go off."

"You're so bloody dumb, sailor, that you're wrong on every single count. You're not going to call the cops, and I'll tell you why. Number one, nobody is going to get killed, except maybe you if you do something stupid. Number two, you haven't a clue what this business is all about. Number three, if anybody goes to the law it'll be me, to report the whereabouts of a U.S. Navy deserter who's been peddling drugs for a living. Fong was kind enough to give me the address of the bint that you're shacking up with."

Quinn glanced uncertainly up the slope to where the other two were perched, half turned, watching the scene below.

"Okay. Seems like you got the hook into me. Just let me walk away and we'll call it quits."

"But I still want you in on this proposition, sailor. Muscle is easy enough to come by but it takes time. I'm in a hurry. Just answer one question: Do you want to make yourself a million dollars or don't you?"

Quinn stared past the gun into the Englishman's face. It wore that infuriating, mocking grin again.

"Don't put me on, Pritchard."

"I'm not."

"One million Hong Kong, for me? You've got to be shitting me."

"Who mentioned Hong Kong? I'm talking about good old United States greenbacks."

Whatever it was that had briefly suspended Quinn's disbelief suddenly collapsed. "A million bucks? Come on, Pritchard, you're talking horse shit." Getting no response, he turned and called to Fong, "He give you the same shit?"

"He told me nothing," Fong said.

"A million for him, too," said Pritchard.

"Man, are you ever in fairyland!" Quinn's laugh was half nervous, half derisory. "What sort of a trip are you on? What do you figure on making for yourself?"

"Baxter and I will split three million between us," Pritchard said calmly. "We get a bigger cut because I'm putting up the capital and he's supplying some equipment and some contacts. You and Fong are the hired help."

"That's five million in cold green between us?"

"After another five has been deducted for other participants. Our sleeping partners. The job is worth ten million in all, if I read the market right."

"It's a bank job," Quinn said. "It has to be a bank job."

"It's not," Pritchard said. He lowered the gun suddenly, pointed it at the ground and eased the hammer forward to uncock it. "And now, if you want to walk away, go. I want you in on it. But I want you with a good will or not at all."

"Jesus, I don't know." Quinn was genuinely in a quandary. "I hate to go into anything blind. . . ."

"Fong knows no more about it than you do. Bax knows a little more, but not much. They're willing to take me on trust."

Fong made a sudden sharp movement at the top of the slope. "It's your car!" he called, and he and Baxter came sliding down.

"Let's go!" Pritchard said urgently. He opened the car door beside him and looked swiftly back at Quinn. "Well?"

The American said nothing. He jerked the rear door open and swung himself inside. The others piled in after him, slamming doors.

They caught a glimpse of the green Plymouth flashing across the gap just as Fong started the engine.

"Get behind him," Pritchard ordered, replacing the big revolver in the glove compartment, "but not too close."

The Range Rover bumped out onto the road and accelerated. The Plymouth by now had disappeared round a bend fifty yards to their left, heading for Chatham Road and Kowloon. Suddenly there was an atmosphere of almost tangible tension in the car.

When they reached the junction with Chatham Road the Plymouth was still out of sight. "Turn right," Pritchard said. "We'll catch him up soon." He glanced at his watch. "Five past eight exactly. You can set your watch by the bugger."

Quinn glanced at him with interest. "You been setting this thing up for a while, right?"

"Right."

"That guy in the car—you've been figuring out some way to hit him. You say nobody's going to get wasted, that can only mean one of two other things. Either he carries ten million dollars in his pants pocket or you figure on snatching him."

Pritchard, concentrating on the view ahead, did not reply. The traffic moved fast in both directions along Chatham Road—private cars, taxis and minibuses, ferrying early-bird commuters into the concrete wasteland of Kowloon. They spotted the Plymouth after another minute, a hundred yards ahead, left-side flashers going as the driver filtered onto the Cross-Harbour Tunnel approach road.

"Stick with him," Pritchard told Fong. "Get as close as you like now."

On the flyover scything across the Kowloon–Canton railway line and the Hung Hom marshalling yards, they got within two cars of the Plymouth. Then, when the traffic fanned out to form two separate queues at the toll gates of the tunnel, Fong stopped right behind it. The driver and passenger were visible through the rear window as a pair of dim silhouettes. Pritchard handed him a five-dollar bill to pay the toll.

"Take a good look at that car, all of you. Looks just like another company sedan taking a business executive to work. It isn't. It has bulletproof windows and puncture-proof tyres. The way it's down on its suspension suggests there's armour plating in the bodywork, too. The chauffeur is almost certainly also a trained bodyguard, and armed."

Quinn whistled softly. "So who's the big news?"

"See the little radio aerial on the roof?" Pritchard said, ignoring the question. It was a stiff, chrome-plated pylon no more than eighteen inches long. "That's not for listening to music. It's two-way VHF. The driver is constantly in touch with a control centre, and we must assume that they have some sort of hot line to the police. However, the system does have one weakness."

They watched the Plymouth move slowly forward to take its turn at the toll booth. The driver's window came down, a dark-sleeved arm was extended and five dollars was handed to the attendant. The car began to roll down the ramp into the square, concrete maw of the tunnel.

Fong stopped beside the toll booth. He thrust his money into the attendant's hand and gunned the Range Rover forward.

"Listen," Pritchard said, and turned on the car's radio.

The high-pitched, piping tones of a Cantonese commercial came to them and then, almost immediately, as the car accelerated into the dark mouth of the tunnel, it faded and blanked out to a soft buzz.

Pritchard pressed each of the selector buttons in turn. "It's the same on all channels. And that VHF transceiver in the Plymouth has the same problem down here."

The tunnel sucked them in like a hungry mouth. It was cavernous and harshly floodlit, and its concrete walls and roof threw the roar of engines back into their ears. The Plymouth was fifty yards ahead, in the left-hand lane of this southbound carriageway, moving at the regulation thirty miles an hour. The lanes were divided by a continuous double white line which it was forbidden to cross.

"Ever been through here before?" Pritchard said to Quinn, over the din. The American shook his head.

"All very modern. There are TV cameras up on those gantries, monitoring the traffic every inch of the way. They have people spotting for lane jumpers: cross those white lines and you can get stopped at the other end and spot-fined. Also, of course, they know the instant an accident has happened."

The tunnel was a mile long. It took two minutes and a few seconds before they emerged into daylight on the Hong Kong side, still tailing the Plymouth. Up the ramp, just as they were about to follow the other car into the spaghetti-like convolutions of the Causeway Bay interchange, Pritchard suddenly said, "Left here. We've seen enough."

Fong swung the Range Rover sharply onto a filter that brought

96

them out a few seconds later on Waterfront Road, heading east past the massed junks and sampans of the Causeway Bay typhoon shelter. The Plymouth had vanished in the opposite direction.

Quinn felt a vague sense of anticlimax. Apparently he wasn't the only one. Baxter leaned forward and said, "Well, what was all that about, Alan?"

"That was what they call, I think, a familiarization exercise. Fong, pull off the road anywhere you can manage along here. I want to take over."

There was some excavation work going on along the waterfront off the road to the left. The bulldozers had left a bare patch of ground there and had also, in the course of moving on and off the site, broken down the kerbstones at the edge of the road, making it possible for a car to cross them. As always in Hong Kong, motorists had taken advantage of the temporary free parking space; there were a couple of dozen cars and vans standing haphazardly about. Fong swung in among them, stopped, and cut the engine.

"Well," Pritchard said, twisting in his seat, "you've looked it over. That's where it's all going to happen."

"All what?" Quinn demanded. "All I know is we tailed a couple of guys in a car for a while and then quit before we found out where they were going."

"*I* know where they were going," Pritchard said, "and for the moment it's my business. The point was to set the scene for you. You used the word snatch, earlier on. That's what I plan to do—snatch that man, the passenger in the Plymouth—and do it in the tunnel."

"Jee-sus," Quinn breathed incredulously. "And just how do you figure to do that?"

"By arranging a small accident. That's where Fong comes in."

"An accident, sure—watched by about a hundred TV cameras."

"We can use those cameras to our advantage. I want you to imagine a crash in that southbound carriageway of the tunnel, close to this end. You've seen how it works: the slow traffic sticks to the left, the faster stuff is on the right, and they can't switch lanes. Sometimes you get something on the right that isn't moving fast enough, that runs neck-and-neck with a car on the left, and between them they block up everything behind. There's this impatient somebody in the rear, on a motorbike, who's willing to risk a fine and is narrow enough to squeeze between the two cars along the double white lines. Unfortunately he bumps into one or both of them, goes sprawling, him and his bike, along the road ahead, and stops both lines of traffic. That's you, Fong. Think you could manage something like that? Without getting hurt?"

Fong looked thoughtful for a moment, then nodded. "With some practice, I could get it right."

"You'll get the practice." Pritchard turned to the others. "Still imagining? Fong and his motorbike are spread out all over the road. He could be dead, or badly hurt anyway. One of the cars he collided with was the Plymouth. The driver gets out and runs towards him."

"How do you know?" Baxter demanded.

"It's instinctive. He feels involved. He wants to know that Fong is okay. He has no reason to think this is anything but a chance accident. He forgets, for a few critical seconds, that he's driving a VIP in a bulletproof car, and that his radio is out of action."

"Okay," Quinn said. "Then what?"

Pritchard explained what would follow, carefully and deliberately. When he finished they were all silent for several seconds.

"Well, old son," said Baxter eventually, the nervous agitation of his tone suggesting something of what they all felt. "Well, you've told us the how. What about the why?"

"We'll come to that. Anybody want to pull out now?"

Pritchard studied them each in turn once again. Fong and Baxter shook their heads slowly. Quinn said, "Now or never, that it?"

"That's it."

"A million bucks for me?"

"Guaranteed."

"Then lay it on me."

Pritchard turned to open the glove compartment. From beneath the weight of the big revolver he slid a quarto-sized envelope and shook out from it three sets of typed papers, each set stapled together at the top left corner. He handed one to each of them.

"Read those," he said. "Read them while I drive. Commit every single fact to memory. When we stop I'm taking them back and destroying them. There are no other copies. There will be no written record of this undertaking, no evidence to leave behind. Until it happens, it will exist only in our minds."

He got out of the car and walked round to the driver's side. Fong shifted across to the passenger seat. Seymour Quinn looked down at the title page of the document Pritchard had given him. It read: *Memorandum on the Project.*

12

Pritchard drove them to the south side of the island, through the chaotic little fishing port of Aberdeen and then on along the winding coast road. In the car park of the Repulse Bay Hotel he took back the copies of the memorandum, set fire to them and dropped the ashes in a litter bin. Then they went into the hotel for breakfast.

They sat at a table secluded at one end of the long, shady veranda that overlooked the bay. No one else was in earshot. As soon as the waiter had taken their order and left, Seymour Quinn said, "What I want to know is, why pick on him? Why not an easy target like a fat Chinese millionaire?"

"Because he's perfect," Pritchard said. "He's not only a legitimate political target, but also a highly sensitive one. In the wrong hands he could be an incredibly dangerous weapon. He knows about major decisions that are being made in Washington this minute. Even more important, he knows about every CIA intelligence operation mounted in this region—past, present, and future. He knows the politicians and civil servants who are in the Company's pocket, the clandestine groups they are arming or financing, the laundered money that's being spent on projects. Why do you think he works under diplomatic cover? In the hands of an enemy intelligence agency, interrogating him with truth drugs, he could be worth more than they could earn for years of eager-beavering. And that's exactly what our friends in Garden Road are going to think. They'll come running with their ten million, and they'll think they're getting him back cheap at the price."

"They're going to figure these Moro dudes are that dangerous?" Quinn asked.

"Not in themselves. It's who their friends might be. For all the Americans know, they might sell him to the highest bidder—or simply hand him over to their patrons, the Chinese. All this is going to work to our advantage."

"A hell of a lot depends on getting the Moros to co-operate," Baxter said. "You're presuming rather a lot, considering you haven't even approached them yet."

Pritchard studied Baxter's face for a few seconds. It was looking worried this morning, he thought; the reality of the business was getting to him. "Bax," he said, "if someone came to you offering you five million dollars for doing nothing, for simply lending your name to go on the label of a product, what would you do?"

"I'd be suspicious—at first, anyway."

"But once you were convinced that there really were no strings attached, you'd start thinking you could use five million as well as the next man—especially if you were trying to fight a guerrilla war on a shoestring budget. That's going to be your job, Bax—to convince them."

"I'll try," Baxter said, rather unhappily. "This trip to Simpang: how will I explain it to Liz?"

"Business. What else does she need to know? You'll have to find excuses for a lot more absences between now and the twenty-first. The Project is a full-time job from now on. That shouldn't be any problem for you, Quinn. As for me, I'm leaving the paper to-morrow. Fong, can you tell your uncle you're quitting? If you're short of cash I'll lend—"

He was interrupted by the return of the waiter, bringing orange juice, bacon and eggs, toast and hot rolls, tea and coffee. Pritchard had a quiet word with him before he went away, then they all tucked in hungrily.

"That list of equipment we're gonna need," said Quinn, through a mouthful of egg. "Where does it all come from?"

"We find it between us. The vehicles we use on the day will be stolen. What we need for practice will be bought or hired. I'm putting up the capital but there's a limit to it: twelve thousand Hong Kong, my redundancy pay. That's every penny I own."

"One item on that list I didn't much like," the American said. "One hand gun. Why only one, and who gets to carry it?"

"I do. I don't want any accidents. The way I've planned it, one will be enough."

"I hope you're right. Personally, I'd like to have more hardware than the opposition. What if this Kiley or his bodyguard puts up a fight?"

"That's why you're there, sailor. You're the muscle, remember? Carry a gun and you're tempted to use it. Kiley is worth nothing to us if he's dead."

They ate in silence for half a minute. Then Baxter, who had been uncharacteristically quiet all morning, laid his knife and fork down and said, "There's one thing you haven't mentioned in that memorandum, Alan. What about the reaction from Kiley's employers? Okay, they'll

100

want him back—but they won't necessarily just sit up and beg for him. Do you know what you're up against? You're taking on an organization with a billion-dollar budget, with agents and resources you know nothing about. How do you know you won't be catching a tiger by the tail?"

Pritchard paused before answering. The other two were silent, awaiting his reply. If there was one thing he would not do, it was let an initiative pass into Baxter's hands. Baxter was showing signs of being the balkiest of the three.

"The CIA is like any other bureaucracy," Pritchard said. "It knows what's on its file cards and in its computer memory banks. When it's faced with a problem on which it has no data, it's as helpless as anyone else to solve it. We're going to play on their preconceptions. As soon as Kiley is lifted, they'll assume it's a political kidnapping. It's something they are psychologically geared to expect. It'll make sense to the computers. The computers don't know about us."

"They don't know about me," said Baxter quietly, "and I dare say they don't know about Fong or Quinn. What about you? Another thing you haven't told us is where you got all this stuff on Kiley in the first place."

Pritchard was prepared for the question. A degree of frankness was necessary. "I knew him, who he was, when I was a correspondent, back in Saigon. A couple of weeks ago I found out he was here. It's that simple. I bumped into his wife. She and I used to be . . . rather good friends."

"That your prissy-ass way of saying you were fucking her?" the American asked bluntly. Pritchard felt himself redden.

"You know what you can do, Quinn? You can start minding your own bloody business."

"But it's all our business, Alan," said Baxter. "If Kiley can identify you—"

"He won't get the chance. Did you read that memorandum or didn't you? Kiley won't see any of our faces, before, during, or after the event. The connection with me will probably come out, yes, but I'm going to have a cast-iron alibi—and you're going to provide it, Bax."

The waiter returned, bearing an ice bucket and a bottle of champagne. Pritchard smiled at the surprise on the faces of the others.

"Today the Project is officially launched," he said. "The moment shouldn't pass without a small celebration—unless any of you objects to drinking at breakfast time?"

None of them did. The champagne was Ayala sixty-nine. When he had tasted and approved of it and the waiter had poured it and left, Pritchard raised his glass.

"Here's to the Project," he said. "To the political swindle of the century!"

13

From the air, Simpang town, capital of the East Malaysian state of Simpang, looked like a thousand other places in tropical Asia: a huddle of tall modern buildings—banks, government offices, hotels—standing isolated in a sea of rusted iron roofs and colourless, single-storeyed wooden shacks. The sprawl had been limited on one side by the curving shoreline of the bay, on the other by the steep foothills of the Crocker Mountains, and so the town had spread in both directions along the narrow coastal plain until it petered out on the fringes of the pineapple and rubber plantations. The place to live if you could afford it—and there were a number who could, for oil, timber and rubber had made Simpang prosperous—was just out of town, on the lush slopes of Bukit Longnawan, where the air was always cooler than at sea level. The peak of the mountain on this Friday morning was obscured by cloud, but through a porthole of the descending Malaysia Airways Viscount, Baxter could see the terraces on the lower and middle levels where the state's most successful businessmen and politicians had built their villas. Dato Abu Bakr Salim, successful at both occupations, had one of the most sumptuous of them.

Baxter and his family had left Simpang in something of a hurry three years ago, and he had been unhappy at the idea of returning ever since Pritchard had mentioned it. It wasn't that he had anything very obvious to fear; after all, the prosecution that at one time had been pending against him and two other directors of Simpang Investment Services had subsequently been dropped. If he had been open to arrest he would never have agreed to come; what he was anxious about was the sort of unpleasantness that might happen if word of his return got about among certain people: those, for instance, who had lost a fair proportion of their savings by entrusting them to Simpang Investment Services in the months before its collapse. Baxter had vowed to keep a low profile.

102

In the airport terminal he had a moment's anxiety when he saw that the kiosk from which car-hire firms once used to operate had vanished. Then he spotted a Chinese youth holding a slip of cardboard with MR. BAXTER printed in large letters on it. It was the *foki* from the Avis office; he led Baxter outside to a newish-looking Datsun parked in the forecourt.

He threw his jacket and his overnight bag into the back seat and set off on the short drive to town. The car was not an extravagance but a necessary precaution which he had suggested and Pritchard had agreed to. He wanted as few people as possible to know of his meeting with Salim. One sure way to start tongues wagging in a place like Simpang was to summon a taxi and ask to be taken to the Chief Minister's residence.

The road into town ran along the coast, parallel to the pipeline from the oil terminal. Among the fishermen's shacks, new, ugly, but prosperous-looking brick bungalows had sprung up. Simpang was still doing well for itself; the fourteenth state of the Malaysian Federation and the last to have joined, it had done so for reasons of security rather than geographical logic or compelling economic need. In the mid-sixties its gigantic neighbour, Indonesia, had had hungry eyes on it, together with the adjoining territories of Sabah, Sarawak and Brunei. Simpang, like Brunei, was an independent sultanate which had been under British protection for the best part of a century. Two battalions of Gurkhas were garrisoned there as a deterrent to the Indonesians, but they could not remain forever. As it became clear that the statelet would soon have to accept semi-autonomy within Malaysia and that a form of democracy must replace the benevolent despotism of the sultan, ambitious would-be politicians began jockeying for position. The most ambitious, and possibly even the most able, had been a lawyer and businessman named Abu Bakr Salim. He had won the first state election in 1966 and had never lost one since.

The town hadn't changed much. The Borneo was still the best hotel but Baxter had booked a room at the Royal, an old colonial-style place where cockroaches were rather more prevalent but where he was less likely to be recognized. It was close to lunchtime when he parked the Datsun in the banyan-shaded car park and checked in.

Upstairs in his room he unpacked his grip, got undressed, and opened the bottle of lemon gin he had bought duty-free at Kai Tak. He had two drinks while he showered and changed into a lightweight cream suit and silk shirt and tie, then another with the ham sandwich he ordered from room service. After that he cleaned his teeth to get the alcohol off his breath and inspected himself in the wardrobe mirror. The image was just about right, he thought: the freewheeling Far East businessman with a piece of some action to offer, brash and successful, confident enough to offer it right at the top. The drinks had set him up nicely for the interview, too.

His appointment, made on the telephone with a flunky yesterday, was for two o'clock. Baxter felt encouraged at having been able to arrange the meeting at such short notice—and on the vaguest of pretexts—as well as by the fact that Salim had chosen to see him at home rather than in his office at Government House. Each man had the measure of the other, he thought; there should not be too much need to talk around the subject.

He left the hotel at one forty-five, driving out through the Chinese and Indian commercial quarters towards the mountain and the houses dotted at well-spaced intervals on its slopes. Simpang had never been a beautiful town; what grace it possessed it owed to its setting and the elegance of its remaining Islamic architecture. Up here on Bukit Long-nawan, however, there was something of the atmosphere of an Indian hill station: sumptuous bungalows half hidden behind cascades of bougainvillea or shaded by nipa palms, and signposts pointing to the Polo Club, the library and the British military graveyard.

At the top of the hill the twisting road ended abruptly in a circle of asphalt wide enough to allow a car to make a U-turn. Across from this were the high, iron-barred gates of the Chief Minister's residence, with a small gate-lodge beside them. A Malay policeman in khaki shorts and shirt came to the car, asked Baxter his name, inspected his passport and went back to the lodge to make a phone call. Then he opened the gates and waved him through.

Driving up the smoothly macadamed driveway, Baxter glimpsed through a screen of bauhinia trees a couple of acres of unblemished lawn dotted with beds of orchids. Just as he reached the top of the rise and came within sight of the house, he had a sudden attack of nervous anxiety.

Backing onto the hillside and looking out over the gardens, the town and the bay, the Chief Minister's residence, like most colonial dwellings, was white and long and low. But there the similarity ended; its style was pure middle-Islamic, with a colonnade of onion-shaped arches along the front in place of the usual open veranda, and a balcony on the floor above with matching smaller archways and decorative

104

grilles. At each corner was a small minaret with a domed roof. It was like a two-tiered, over-elaborate wedding cake; you might almost expect to find plaster models of the bride and groom lurking coyly within the colonnade. In front of it was a flat grassy terrace with a flagpole at either end; one had the Malaysian and one the Simpang State flag hanging from it.

Baxter parked in the shade of some casuarinas at the edge of the driveway, got out and walked along a flagged pathway towards the front entrance. To the right, behind the house, he caught a glimpse of a row of carports; among the six or seven vehicles parked in their shade were the gleaming grilles of two Rolls-Royces. The black one was the official limousine, no doubt, and the white one a private car, but Baxter found himself wondering, absurdly, why anyone needed two Rolls-Royces. The question gave him some understanding of the sudden anxiety that afflicted him. Salim had unquestionably reached the top in every way that was possible in Simpang; had he, perhaps, ceased to need anything more? Could Baxter offer something that was wanted, or would he be met with indignant refusal, expulsion, even arrest? As he hurried along the pathway towards the steps leading up to the portico, he felt smaller and more vulnerable than when he'd surveyed himself in the mirror under the fortifying influence of three gins.

A thin Malay in a dazzling Hawaiian shirt came tripping down the steps to meet him. "Mr. Baxter? We spoke on the phone. I am Osman Khan, the Chief Minister's personal assistant. Welcome to Simpang."

Osman Khan had a professional smile and small, sharp eyes: one of Salim's numerous young business acolytes, at a guess, given a leg up onto the political bandwagon. He waved Baxter theatrically up the stairs. "Dato Salim awaits you."

Dato Salim, in fact, appeared on the shaded portico just as Baxter reached the top step. He was casually dressed in cotton slacks, sandals and an embroidered cream *barong tagalog,* the loose-fitting traditional shirt improbably made of pineapple fibre. Between him and Osman Khan, who followed close behind him, Baxter felt immediately over-dressed.

The Chief Minister beamed at him, black eyes twinkling behind his delicate gold-rimmed glasses. Baxter could not remember him ever looking much different. The range of expression on that ageless, cherubically plump face with its smooth caramel skin was confined to variations on the theme of the smile. It was a big smile when he felt pleased, amused or benevolent; it was a little smile when he did not.

105

Baxter earned a big smile and a handshake; Salim's small brown paw, when squeezed, felt like a damp sponge.

"Mr. Baxter! What a pleasure!"

"A pleasure to see you again, Chief Minister."

"Hong Kong must suit you. You're looking prosperous."

"Some people use that word to mean fat."

"My dear fellow, I can't afford such innuendos! I should lose some weight myself. How long now since you left us? Eighteen months? Two years?"

"A little over three, actually."

Baxter had no doubt that Salim knew the right answer; when Simpang Investment Services had gone bang they had also ceased paying the monthly sum of three thousand Malaysian dollars by way of a kickback into a company bank account across the border in Brunei— an account to which Salim was the signatory. He had asked the question out of habit, the mischievous habit of tricking people, trapping them in small and even unnecessary lies, which he had learned when he'd practised law at the Simpang bar, along with expressions like "my dear fellow."

"It was that year we were nearly struck by the freak typhoon, remember?" Baxter said. "In fact I was afraid my plane would be grounded and I'd be arrested."

Salim laughed and snapped his fingers. "Of course! Well, there's no danger of that this time. Come through and have a drink."

They turned and walked together through one of the wide archways into the gigantic drawing room, followed at a respectful distance by Osman Khan. In another age, Abu Bakr Salim might have been the caliph of a Muslim palace-city, an amiable but fickle autocrat, capriciously dispensing favours and punishments. But this was today and he had made the democratic cap fit him. He had been born not here but on one of the neighbouring Sulu islands, predominantly Muslim yet contentiously ruled by successive, always Christian, Filipino governments. Since the days of Spanish rule there had been a separatist movement among the Moros, and as a young man in the 1930s Salim had been an active participant in it. Arrested—so the story went—for masterminding a series of politically motivated bank robberies, he had bribed a guard, escaped from police custody and fled into exile in Simpang. There, during the Japanese occupation, he had become a leader of the resistance movement.

It was hard to reconcile this adventurous past with the blandly

106

smiling face and the tubby, compact, sixty-year-old figure of today. Age had made him comfortable in mind as well as body, but his devotion to the cause of Moro separatism and his animosity towards the American-sponsored Commonwealth—later Republic—of the Philippines had never left him. It was precisely this contradiction between cynicism and conviction that Baxter hoped to exploit.

The cynical phase had probably begun after he had been rewarded for his anti-Japanese exploits with a scholarship to study law at a minor British university. Returning to Simpang, he had become the sultanate's first "native" barrister and divided his energies between law, business and politics, soon learning that these three activities could be rewardingly complementary. He became the leader of the Simpang People's Party, which drew most of the state's Muslim support; by the early sixties it had emerged as the largest single political force. It also had the blessing of the British, who by then were preparing to pack their colonial bags, arrange for the decent abdication and retirement of the sultan and his eight wives, and woo a stable, pro-Western government into the Malaysian federation.

About this time, too, offshore oil was discovered. The Franco-British consortium which won the concession to exploit it were not slow to court Salim, offering financial inducements in return for the extension of their own guarantees.

Since 1966, when Salim had won his first election, he had been consolidating himself both politically and financially. He benefited not only from his personal stake in the state's oil business but from rubber plantations, cheaply bought in the mid-sixties slump in that commodity, and from the timber concessions that his government had generously awarded to himself and his hangers-on. In spite of the chronic rumours of corruption, he retained the support of his Muslim following. In spite of the Kuala Lumpur government's disapproval, they depended on him for his oil and the support of his party in the federal parliament. When the heat from KL became particularly strong he threatened secession, and the threat was not an empty one. Simpang was perhaps the only state in Malaysia which could go it alone economically, and now that the threat of invasion from Indonesia was over, the need for collective security was no longer important.

Salim *was* the caliph, immensely rich, an autocratic ruler in all but name, yet careful to keep his democratic halo shiny. He waved Baxter into a chair—hand-carved teak, with a rattan back and seat to allow circulation of air. He lowered himself into a similar chair opposite, across a glass-topped coffee table, his smiling eyes shrewdly observant behind the non-reflecting lenses.

"What will you drink, Mr. Baxter?"

"Oh, I don't know. . . ."

"This is a Muslim household, but you need not be embarrassed about asking for alcohol."

"I'm not embarrassed," Baxter said, but suddenly realized he was. He had been trying to be polite.

"Come, come, we are used to catering for Western guests. Beer, whisky, gin?"

"A gin sling then, if you don't mind," Baxter mumbled.

"Excellent." The smile was still broad and there was a conspiratorial twinkle in the eyes. "As a matter of fact, between you and me, I indulge occasionally myself. Religious laws must learn to change with the times, don't you think? Otherwise, like the dinosaurs, they become extinct."

Salim spoke swiftly in Malay to Osman Khan, who had stationed himself beside a tall mahogany cabinet. He opened it and busied himself with bottles and glasses. Baxter sat in silence, unable to escape the impression that the Chief Minister, in some obscure way of his own, was sending him up.

The drinks arrived, in tall glasses wrapped in paper napkins, on an inlaid brass tray. Salim's looked like a whisky and soda. Without further instructions, Osman Khan left the room.

"Good to see you, my dear fellow," said Salim, sipping at his drink. "Your very good health."

"And yours, Chief Minister."

"You're back in the investment management business, I gather."

"That's right."

"And you have some project that you think might interest me?"

Baxter took a bracing gulp of gin. "Yes. It's rather an unusual one."

"Tell me about it."

"It's based in Hong Kong, but it has some international aspects—"

"One moment," Salim said, raising a finger. "What makes you come all this way to me? Can't the equity be raised in Hong Kong?"

"It's not a question of equity, Chief Minister. I know you as a businessman who can recognize potential, who's willing to stake a lot on a high short-term yield."

108

If Salim felt flattered he did not show it. In fact the smile dimmed. "Mr. Baxter, if I may say so, your record as an investment broker is not a happy one. Simpang Investment Services specialized in buying high-yield portfolios, and what happened to them? They collapsed like a house of cards. There could easily have been political embarrassment to me."

"With respect, Chief Minister, we've had a similar conversation before. On the day I left Simpang, remember? I got out to avoid prosecution, of course, but in doing so I also spared you the possible embarrassment of having your connection mentioned in court. The company was badly managed, I'll admit. We didn't get enough corporate funds on our books; we were top-heavy with small investors—employees of the oil company, Chinese shopkeepers, civil servants, all with a couple of thousand dollars or so going spare. They were amateurs—greedy, panicky amateurs. When the high yields didn't materialize as quickly as we had hoped, they took fright and pulled out. And of course there wasn't enough money to go round. This is something quite different. It's a project I'm involved with myself, not just as a fund manager. We— that is, my associates and I—think it's assured of success if we can persuade you to come in on it. May I take it that we are speaking in confidence?"

Salim waved a hand carelessly, as if the question could not be in doubt. "What magical quality would my percentage of the shares possess?"

"There is no share issue, Chief Minister. We don't want your money. We want your position, your political influence—"

"Ah, the name on the company stationery." Salim's smile was back at full glow. "The problem is that when the company fails, the well-known names are the first to get dragged through the mud. But this sounds as though it would involve rather more than that."

"Yes. And it won't fail. As I was saying, position and political influence are the important factors. Let's start with the influence—and I mean the influence you have over the Moro National Liberation Front in the Philippines."

The smile became distinctly puzzled. "What on earth have they to do with it?"

"Nothing, as yet." Baxter had rehearsed his argument and he moved into it smoothly. "I don't think you'll deny, Chief Minister, that you and your state government have been the chief outside supporters, moral and material, of the Moros' cause. Correct me if I'm wrong, but the newspapers have said that you've supplied them with money and arms, you've given refuge here to their guerrillas, and even—according to some reports—established secret training bases for them in Simpang. I'm not concerned with the rights or wrongs of these actions, just setting out the facts as I understand them."

Salim sipped his drink noncommittally. Baxter continued.

"The Moro movement began as a reaction to the land-grabbing activities of Christians, which the Spanish rulers of the Philippines positively encouraged and the Americans, later, didn't do much to stop. Nowadays the Moros' main demand is to rule themselves in a separate Muslim state in the south. To achieve this aim they use the standard tactics of guerrilla forces. They attack isolated government outposts, ambush military convoys and sabotage state property. In general they try to tie down large numbers of security forces and gradually wear down resistance.

"They have also, from time to time, used the lives of civilians as bargaining counters. Two years ago they hijacked an airliner. There was a shootout at Zamboanga airport, the plane caught fire and ten hostages and three hijackers were killed. Only a fortnight ago they kidnapped a government official in Pagadian and demanded seventy-five thousand pesos and the release of some political prisoners as a ransom. That ended in another holocaust. You have not condemned these events or dissociated yourself from the tactics of the Moros. From that I deduce that you approve of them."

There was still a faint smile on Salim's face, but his manner was uneasy. He shifted in his seat and studied the drink in his hand. He said, "What happened at Zamboanga and Pagadian was entirely the fault of the trigger-happy Filipinos."

"Nevertheless, the deaths would not have happened if there had not been a hijacking and a kidnapping in the first place. Do you think such things are justified?"

"The Moros' cause is a just one," the Chief Minister said, looking up at him. "Desperate situations require desperate measures. And now let me ask you a question, my dear fellow: What is all this leading up to?"

"Discussion of a hypothesis." Baxter was well into his stride, now, and much more at ease. He drank some gin. "Let me put it to you this way. Until now the Moros have confined their activities to their own territory, the Philippine Islands. If they suddenly chose to go international—to do what the Palestinians do and carry out an operation on

110

foreign soil, with the object of attracting world-wide attention to their cause—would you go along with that?"

Salim thought for a moment. "It would depend," he said, the politician in him gaining the upper hand. "It would depend on the operation and what it was trying to achieve."

"Shall we say the holding of a hostage against a large ransom? An operation guaranteed to cause no loss of life, and to enhance the Moro cause both morally and financially."

"You know of such an operation?" Salim asked sceptically.

"This is a hypothesis, remember. If they were planning something like that I'm sure you'd know about it sooner than I would. They would need your approval. After all, to internationalize the conflict would put a new dimension on it. It might embarrass their chief benefactor. On the other hand, if you had been fully briefed beforehand—or if, to carry it further, you had a whiphand over the entire thing, with any financial gain depending on your consent and co-operation—wouldn't that win your agreement?"

"No, for one good reason: the embarrassment you mention. Gaddafi of Libya can get away with virtually open support of Palestinian guerrilla operations. He is the dictatorial ruler of a country; I am merely the leader of one small state in a larger polity—a democratic one, at that. There is a line beyond which I cannot tread."

"But there might not need to be any embarrassment, Chief Minister. This is where we move from the question of influence to that of position. What if you were to adopt a different role in public to the one you were playing in private? What if, instead of tacitly supporting the rebels by remaining silent, you were to come out with some mild condemnation of this particular action *and offer to act as mediator?* Think of it. Far from being embarrassing, it would enhance your prestige enormously! It would put you in the world limelight as a humanitarian, as a leader who is trusted by the Moros but who can make an equal claim to the trust of the other side. The Moros accept you as a go-between; the others have no choice but to do the same. You negotiate a settlement; you take the credit for securing the safe release of the hostage. And all the while you are laughing up your sleeve, because the whole thing was arranged in advance between you and the Moros."

Salim was leaning back in his chair, smiling up at the ceiling. He was enjoying the idea, Baxter could tell: the idea of the headlines, the political kudos, a blow struck for the Moros. As things stood now he might quietly accumulate his millions and grow into a bigger and bigger

111

fish in the small Simpang pond; here was a chance to move briefly to a larger one. Watching him, waiting for a response, Baxter knew with excitement that Pritchard's instinct had been right: Salim was their man.

The Chief Minister came out of his reverie and faced Baxter. He put his empty glass down on the tray. Then he laughed, a brief explosive guffaw. "People come to me with many mad schemes, but I have never heard a crazier one than this. My dear fellow, what you haven't told me is where you—and your associates—come into it. After all, you haven't come all this way simply to give me the benefit of your madcap idea."

"Certainly not. We take fifty per cent of the ransom. In exchange for that we supply the victim and we carry out the kidnapping. We do everything, in fact, except claim responsibility. The other fifty per cent is yours to split between you and the Moros in any way you care to arrange."

Salim shook his head, still caught between pleasure and incredulity. "And who, may I ask, is the victim?"

"To tell you that would be to give away my trump card, Chief Minister. You'll find out just as soon as I've secured agreement in principle from both you and the Moros. I can say this, though: he is worth ten million American dollars, and we're snatching him on Monday week."

The smile was etched onto Salim's face, but the merry little eyes were still, intense, watchful. "Mr. Baxter," he said at length, "you surprise me more and more."

"Well, what do you think?"

"Give me a minute. We both need another drink."

The Chief Minister stood up and walked to one of the arched doorways. He spoke around the edge of it and Baxter, hearing a chair scrape on the tiled floor, realized with dismay that Osman Khan had been there all along, almost certainly listening. He got up, angrily, and walked towards Salim where he stood plumply in the doorway, arms folded, staring out across the town and the bay. Osman Khan slid past him into the room, towards the drinks cabinet.

Baxter spoke to the Chief Minister's back. "We were supposed to be speaking confidentially."

"My dear fellow," said Salim equably, turning to face him. "Of course we were. Osman is my most trusted confidant. He also happens to be the chief liaison officer between me and the Moros. Since you are

112

going to have to sell this idea to them as well as to me, you will find him useful, perhaps invaluable."

"I won't deal through third parties."

"You won't have to. A man named Mustapha Diaz is head of the military wing of the Moro National Liberation Front. You will deal with him direct—on his own ground, in the Philippines. After all, if you're going to pretend to be Moros, it would help to learn at first hand a little about who and what they are, don't you think? Diaz has had a price of two hundred thousand pesos put on his head by the Philippines Government: you surely don't imagine you can fly into Manila and call him up on the telephone, do you? Osman here can arrange a meeting."

Osman Khan had sidled up between them, with two fresh drinks on the brass tray. He smiled a voluptuous Malay smile at Baxter before backing away.

"Well now," said Abu Bakr Salim, turning back into the drawing room, "let's get down to discussing this business in detail, shall we?"

14

The conversation between Pritchard and Mr. So that afternoon was brief.

"I heard you had not been well."

"It was dysentery. It hits me from time to time."

"I am sorry. What can I do for you?"

"I want to take you up on your offer. I'll take the redundancy cheque."

"You mean now?"

"Right now. I want to quit."

Mr. So never looked surprised, but for once he seemed unsure of himself. "You've found another job?"

"No. Well, that is, there are some prospects. The point is, I'd like to leave now."

"Are you sure you are being wise?"

"Fairly sure."

"As you wish, then," said Mr. So, with a neat little shrug.

Twenty minutes later Pritchard left the *Cathay Star* office with a cheque for fifteen thousand Hong Kong in his pocket: half a month's salary and the two months' redundancy pay he'd been promised. Apart from the fact that he was now devoting himself full-time to the Project, he needed the money. There'd been Baxter's air ticket to Simpang to pay for, and there now would be several more hefty inroads to be made into his budget.

He took a tram straight to Central, deposited the cheque just before closing time in his account at the main branch of the Hong Kong and Shanghai Bank, and immediately withdrew five thousand dollars in cash. He rode another tram back in the direction he had come from, getting off halfway down Des Voeux Road and climbing the hundred or more steps up a narrow pedestrian lane that led to Upper Lascar Row, better known as Cat Street, the thieves' market of Hong Kong.

Most of the shops and stalls that faced each other across the crowded little street sold bad jade and fake antiques to tourists, who went home thinking they'd picked up bargains shadily acquired. But there were also shops that the tourists didn't enter; the junk in their windows looked like junk. To the owner of one of these, specializing in secondhand radio and television equipment, Pritchard had yesterday been introduced by Fong. Fong had known him in Stanley, where he'd been serving two years for dealing in stolen property. You could trust him to be discreet, Fong said; he was also one of the few people capable of providing the sort of equipment Pritchard wanted without raising such awkward questions as whether he had a radio transmitting licence and a frequency allocation from the post office. He had simply nodded and asked him to come back in twenty-four hours.

He greeted Pritchard at the door of the shop and led him through to a tiny workshop in the rear. The item stood on a bench in one corner: a brand-new Pye Pocketfone walkie-talkie system, base unit and three portable transceivers, all with built-in scramblers, just unpacked from their protective polystyrene. Pritchard looked up at the shopkeeper with a grin.

"Looks pretty professional. You reckon it'll do the job?"

"It will work fine, if you place it and use it properly. It's a frequency modulation system. Its range is limited from the point of transmission to the horizon; where the horizon is depends on the height of the aerial. You can take it pretty high?"

"I think so," Pritchard said, and for the next twenty minutes they discussed the installation of the set. Most people's ideas of a walkie-

114

talkie came from seeing television detectives talking to each other into neat little battery-powered units the size of small transistor radios. That was less than half the story. The hand-held transceivers were useless without a mains-powered base unit to receive, amplify and rebroadcast their messages. This one was the size of a whisky crate and weighed fifty pounds. Manned by an operator, it could be used to direct or co-ordinate a police or small-scale army operation; unmanned, it could be switched over to patch the mobile units through to each other.

"Where do you get stuff like this?" Pritchard asked.

"Contacts in the import business. It's not normally sold to anyone but police and such people. You'll be pirating a frequency, of course; you must expect the post office to notice you—but if, as you say, you will not be using it for more than a few minutes every day, and at different times, they will not be able to trace the source of transmissions."

"Fine," said Pritchard. He paid the man forty-five hundred dollars in cash and left, staggering to the door under the weight of the set and calling a taxi. They did not know each other's names. They hadn't asked.

Back at his flat, he dumped the set in his living room and then, re-locking the door behind him, trudged up the stairs to the top of the building. The lift was out of order again. From the eighth floor there was a steel stairway leading to the roof. He went up it, opened the door and stepped out into the muggy evening air.

The roof commanded a reasonable view of the harbour. Until recently, the owner of the building had had a useful supplement to his income in the form of a refugee family whom he had permitted to build a shanty of wood and corrugated iron up here. Officials of the Housing Authority, learning of this illegal arrangement just a few weeks ago, had ordered the removal of the family but the shack still stood, a square little hovel tackily partitioned into two rooms. There was no running water but there was a power outlet, provided by the simple expedient of running an extension off the main electricity supply from the floor below. There was also a television aerial, which could be used to mask the monopole aerial of the radio. Pritchard nodded in silent approval; it would make an excellent home for the base unit.

Baxter did not leave the Chief Minister's house until six that evening. Driving down the hill back to Simpang town he felt elated and exhausted. At the back of his mind there had always been some doubt that the Project could be pulled off; now he knew that it could and would. After withholding his uncertainty from Pritchard for all this time, he would be delighted to report back on the success of his meeting with Salim.

He parked the car and entered the lobby of the Royal Hotel. As he walked past the reception desk the Chinese clerk called out to him.

"Mr. Baxter? There's someone to see you."

"Someone . . . ?"

"A gentleman. He said he'd wait in the bar."

Blankly, Baxter walked to the door that led into the bar. There was only one customer inside, a heavily built man in shorts and a sweaty T-shirt, perched on a stool and hunched over the counter. Baxter approached him slowly; the man looked up when he stopped a few feet short of him.

"You want to see me?"

"Yes. That I do." The man was studying his features carefully, an aggressive look on his lobster-red face. He sounded English. "That I bloody do, mate. You've shaved the beard off, but you're the son of a bitch, all right."

Baxter recognized him now with a dawning horror. He was one of the oil-rig workers who had lost money on Simpang Investment Services. He backed off a pace. "Now wait a minute," he said. "You start calling me names, you—"

"I'm going to do more than that, you shithouse. I've been waiting three years to plant you one in the eye, you cheap bloody crook! I spotted you driving away from here this afternoon, and I came in and waited. I've waited over four hours and I'm going to make every minute of it worthwhile!"

He hopped off the stool suddenly and strode towards Baxter, who turned in sheer blind panic and ran. He raced out of the bar and swung into the lobby, hearing the thump of the Englishman's footfalls on the stone floor behind him. Halfway across the lobby he felt a hand on his shoulder, and he was half lifted and flung against the wall. He saw a blur of fist and meaty forearm and felt a blow on the side of his head that sent his senses reeling.

The oilman stood in front of him, fists clenched, grinning. Vaguely Baxter was aware of the reception clerk and a couple of guests staring in a stupor of surprise.

"Don't hit me!" he shrieked desperately. "I'm a friend of the Chief Minister's! I'll—"

116

The fist seemed to come from nowhere again, slamming into his mouth, snapping his head back against the wall.

"Get the police!" Baxter called to the desk clerk. "He's going to kill me, can't you see? The Chief Minister—"

Then the breath was driven out of him by a piledriver blow in the solar plexus. The oilman followed it through with another swing to his head that lifted him clear off his feet and dropped him on the floor.

He must have blacked out for a minute. The next thing he knew the clerk was bending solicitously over him. Someone had undone his shirt collar, and someone else was taking his pulse. "Regrettable incident, most regrettable . . ." the clerk kept saying. ". . . hope you will accept our profoundest apologies. . . ."

"Where is . . . ?" Baxter croaked. He could taste blood in his mouth and felt his lips beginning to swell.

"He walked out, sir. Don't worry, the police will find him."

Baxter struggled to sit up. "Look, that really won't be necessary. I thought he was going to kill me. I don't need the police."

"They've already been called, sir. Can I help you to your room?"

By the time the police inspector knocked on his door twenty minutes later, he had washed his cut lips, taken two aspirins, drunk two lemon gins and regained some of his equilibrium. Through no fault of his own he had attracted attention to himself. Getting involved in police inquiries would only make matters worse, and at all costs he must keep the reason for his visit secret. As an old Simpang hand, Baxter knew that there was only one solution to such problems.

The inspector was a thoughtful young Malay who listened in silence to his story about an old grudge, a score now settled, a feud best forgotten. Finally he said, "Then I take it you do not wish to press charges?"

"That's correct."

"But assault is a serious matter, Mr. Baxter. We could go ahead and prosecute, and insist on your co-operation. That might mean impounding your passport and holding you here to be a witness at the trial."

"That would be very awkward," said Baxter in agitation.

"Indeed. On the other hand, trials are expensive, and we have a duty to our taxpayers to avoid spending their money frivolously. Even a simple police call-out like this costs a certain amount, after all."

The signal was up, the moment had arrived. Baxter took an envelope embossed with the hotel's crest from his jacket pocket and handed it over. "I trust that will compensate your taxpayers," he said.

The policeman lifted the flap of the envelope and thumbed through the three one-hundred Malaysian dollar bills. Then he nodded, thrust the envelope into his tunic pocket and stood up.

"That should cover it," he said. "Incidentally, the clerk downstairs told me you said something about being a friend of the Chief Minister's."

"He misheard me," Baxter said. "Please don't give it another thought."

"Of course." The policeman bowed to him and left the room.

15

The sound of the toilet flushing woke Seymour Quinn the next morning. Then he heard Canny's bare feet padding across the floor back to the bed. He watched her surreptitiously through half-closed eyes, the morning light giving her skin a golden glow and outlining the movement of her thigh muscles as she walked. Her figure was boyish, flat and lithe, no tits to speak of but a good handful of ass. Quinn realized he had woken with a hard-on. When Canny had slipped into the bed and lay with her back to him, he put a hand on her butt and slid it down into her crotch. She murmured a protest. He got his fingers to work on her but she pulled away, clamping her thighs together.

"Not now, Seymour."

"Why not?"

"Just no, that's all."

"C'mon, I'll persuade you."

He moved in close beside her, till his rampant rod was thrust against her buttocks. He put an arm across her waist and ran his fingers down through the coarse pubic hair.

"No, Seymour!"

She squirmed uncomfortably, trying to break free of his powerful grip, but the wriggling of her butt only excited him further. If there was one thing that really turned him on, it was a chick acting like she didn't want it. He pushed her on her front and then rolled on top of her, pinning her to the bed. He shoved a knee between her clamped thighs, parting them easily.

118

"Please!"

"Can it!"

He took her from behind, entering forcefully and thrusting hard into her tight, dry sex. She had given up struggling and lay tensely beneath him like a trapped bird, uttering only a small gasp as he shot his load.

He rolled off her, panting. "You got it together now, baby? When I want it, best thing to do is lay back and enjoy it."

She said nothing and he looked at her again—her eyes closed and her rich black hair in disarray—and saw on her cheek that very rare thing, a tear. It took a lot to make a Chinese woman cry.

"Hey," he said. "What's the matter?"

She shook her head and buried her face in the pillow.

The silence annoyed him. He said, "Listen, you don't want to get laid, you shouldn't be shacking up with me. Quinn likes to get his rocks off pretty regular, or haven't you noticed? Christ, women! You put out when you're trying to get a man, and when you've got him you start holding back. Well, not with me you don't."

He swung himself out of bed and stamped angrily off to the bathroom. He didn't know what it was about Canny that was pissing him off these days. It wasn't just that she seemed to be losing interest in sex, her whole attitude to him was like a silent reproach. You'd think she had found out something about him that she could not bring herself to mention, like a wife silently enduring her husband's screwing around. Could she, he wondered as he stood under the shower, have found out about his escape plan? No, that was impossible. Nobody knew about that but himself and the little English prick he had made the deal with. The prick was now safely home in London, and this morning Quinn would collect his passport back to the World.

So what was Canny's hang-up? He didn't know, but he was happy with the thought that he wouldn't have to put up with it for much longer. Next Monday, the day the Project took off, he would vanish quietly from her life. Which reminded him that he was meeting Pritchard this morning. Shit, he didn't even know what the time was.

He turned off the shower, wrapped a towel round his waist, and returned to the room. Canny was sitting up with the sheet pulled over her breasts, pale and composed, watching him like a cat. He sat down on his side of the bed and strapped his wristwatch on. Three minutes past eight, it said; Pritchard would be downstairs, waiting. He stood up, went to the cramped little closet and took out a clean pair of jockey shorts, T-shirt and jeans. As he was pulling the jeans on Canny spoke.

"Are you going to leave me, Seymour?"

The question caught him with one leg raised to fit into his pants leg. He stumbled and grabbed at the end of the bed for support. Had she guessed? Did she know something?

"Leave you?" He managed a hollow laugh. "Hell, no. What makes you ask that?"

"It's the way you've been acting lately. You're restless."

"Who wouldn't be, living in this goddam broom closet?"

"It's the way you treat me, too. It's different from what it used to be. You think I'm just a convenience."

He stood up straight and got his jeans on properly, did up the zipper and buckled the belt. The little bitch shouldn't be underestimated, he thought—but then the thought was submerged by anger.

"Convenience? What's so convenient about screwing a corpse?"

"You enjoyed yourself. What more do you want?"

"Maybe just a little participation, know what I mean?"

"My period is due today." There was resentment in the almond eyes now. "I was sore. I didn't want to."

"Well, why the fuck didn't you say so?" He sat down and pulled on his sneakers, defensive suddenly but needing to disguise it. "All you had to do was say you had the flags up. I'd have left you alone."

"Why do I have to say? Why couldn't you guess?"

"How do I know what time of month it is? It's *your* goddam plumbing."

"That's not all." She watched him warily as he pulled the T-shirt over his head and wriggled into it. "I've been straight with you, Seymour, I wish you'd be straight with me. What are you fixing to do?"

"About what?"

"Getting out of Hong Kong. You've got to leave sometime."

"Oh, I don't know. I ain't doing badly here."

"What at? Dealing White Dragon Pearl?" She gave a contemptuous toss of her head. "It's only a matter of time before they get you. Then where are you? Not in the Navy brig but in prison. Three years, maybe five. What sort of future is that?"

"You'd prefer me in the brig, that right?"

"At least you'd come out with a clean sheet. It would be six months, not three years, not five. How long do you think you can go on living like this?"

120

"It's my life, okay? I—"

There came a sharp, peremptory rap on the door. Quinn started and backed instinctively away. Canny sat rigidly upright in the bed, dropping the sheet that she'd been clutching to her chest. They waited a few seconds and the knock came again. Quinn made frantic signals to her.

"Who's there?" she called, her tone high with anxiety.

"I want Quinn," said a man's voice.

Canny gave him a questioning glance. Recognizing the voice, he shouted angrily, "What the hell are you doing up here?"

"I haven't got all day to wait. You were due downstairs ten minutes ago."

Quinn went to the door and opened it. He unlocked the steel trellis and let Pritchard in. He was wearing worn cotton slacks and a sport shirt. He stepped into the room and nodded at Canny, who had drawn up the sheet to cover her breasts again. She stared with hostility at the newcomer and Quinn in turn.

"This is Canny," Quinn said affably. "Canny, this is Alan, a new buddy of mine."

"If you're coming with me then let's go."

"Alan is taking me on a little joyride," Quinn said. Pritchard shot him a warning look.

"What time will you be back?" the girl asked, without much interest.

"How the hell do I know?"

The two men left the apartment and rode down in silence in the elevator. When they stepped out onto the street Pritchard stopped him and said, "You're a bloody meatball, Quinn." He turned to look up into the American's face. His own was pinched with fury. "A bloody meatball, nothing more. You keep me waiting down here, force me to come looking for you. What the hell were you doing, anyway?"

Quinn checked his own surge of anger. "As a matter of fact, I was getting laid. You got the chance to get laid, you'd be late too."

He walked on. Pritchard followed him, hurling verbal abuse at the big man like a terrier worrying a wolfhound. "And then using my name, talking about joyrides, in front of that girl. Where's your bloody sense? We made a rule at the start of this thing that none of us would say *any*thing, to *any*body, that might be remembered later."

"Ah, Canny won't remember. Anyway, I had to tell her I was going *some*place."

"How deeply are you involved with her? Will she make trouble about your leaving?"

"She ain't gonna know I'm leaving. I don't want any heavy scenes."

They reached the car that Pritchard currently had on hire, a dark blue Volvo, parked on a meter in Great George Street, and climbed into it. "Now, Mr. Pritchard," Quinn said, "if you'll kindly pass the door of the Causeway Bay Magistracy on the way out, I have an errand to run."

"We're late already. Fong will be waiting."

"This'll take five minutes. And it can't wait. Today I get my new dog tags."

The Magistracy building, which housed courtrooms and government offices, was a couple of minutes' drive away, the other side of Victoria Park. Pritchard stopped outside and glanced up at the imposing entrance.

"This place is always crawling with cops. You'd better let me go in for you."

"Thanks, but it has to be done in person. No sweat—I've been here before."

Quinn left the car, mounted the steps and disappeared through the big glass doors. Pritchard couldn't escape the feeling that the sailor had grown overconfident during his months of freedom in Hong Kong. He was staying loose, as he put it himself, maybe too loose for his own good. Somewhere his name and description were filed away in a computer's memory bank, and possibly in the heads of a few sharp cops as well.

The five minutes turned into fifteen. Pritchard fretted with impatience; he was in an explosive mood again when Quinn came trotting down the steps and hopped into the car.

"Have you got no bloody conception of time at all?"

"I had to stand in line," the American said, unapologetically. "But it was worth waiting for. Take a look."

He flashed a card in front of Pritchard—cream-coloured with blue edging, sealed into plastic, about four inches by two and a half. The identity card of a Hong Kong resident. Technically, every adult who lived in the colony more than three months had to apply for one, though in practice many of the British, including Pritchard, had never bothered; they had the right of residence anyway. For Chinese refugees the document was vital, proving their right to stay and permitting them to travel.

Quinn's photograph was in the lower right-hand corner, his head pushed up against a height board and just tipping the six-foot-two mark. Next to that was typed a name: LINDSAY, Patrick Weir.

In spite of himself, Pritchard was impressed. "How did you manage that? The identity checks are pretty strict, aren't they?"

"They got a system, but there's a way of screwing it. I found out from one of the little skagheads I used to supply over in Tsimshat. A couple of them had done it before, made enough bread for themselves to fly home to England or wherever." He tucked the card into a pocket of his jeans as Pritchard started the car. "The way it works, you're supposed to apply for this card if you figure on staying more than three months, right? So I get this English creep, Lindsay, to go fill in the forms and they want to see his passport, birth certification, Christ knows what else. Then they give him this registration form that he has to go get stamped in another office. Then from there they send him down the corridor to get his prints and his picture taken. That's where we do the switch, in the corridor. Nobody goes with him, see, from one department to the next, so nobody knows that the guy who picks up the form here is the same guy who arrives with it there. So I get *my* picture and *my* prints taken. For an hour's work I stake this Lindsay to his air fare, three thousand Hong Kong, and the next day he lights out for England. Only problem is I had to wait three months for the card. Three *months,* for Christ's sake!"

"They've got a record of your fingerprints in there, then?"

"My prints, yeah, but another guy's identity. There's no way they could use them to trace me. Besides, the cops don't get to see them: some civil rights crap, it's all on the forms."

"I wouldn't be too sure about that," Pritchard said abstractedly. "Anyway, let's get down to business." He moved out of the parking bay, swung left, and headed for the Causeway Bay entrance to the Cross-Harbour Tunnel. "I want you to take note of some details as we go through here. Firstly, that the tunnel is really two quite separate tunnels, running north and south under the harbour. Secondly, that there are no toll barriers at this end. You pay on the Kowloon side whichever way you're going—which means they haven't got an instantly effective way of blocking traffic from leaving or entering on the Hong Kong side. That's important. Thirdly, most of their emergency

123

services and their central monitoring installations are on the other side as well. That means more delay, all working to our advantage.

"Now, think about these figures. The twin tunnels are used by fifty thousand vehicles a day, on average. That works out at seventeen entering in each direction every minute of every day—and the figure is higher in the morning peak period. But let's stick to seventeen. It takes two minutes to make the crossing, so at any given moment there'll be between thirty and forty vehicles inside each of those tubes."

They drove down the ramp, and the dark throat of the tunnel swallowed them. Pritchard stuck to the slow left-hand lane. He raised his voice against the roar of engines.

"So, imagine our little accident, occurring at this end of the southbound run. It'll be picked up immediately by the TV monitors, of course, but in the first moments the picture will be confused. It won't be till the cameras further behind pick up the tailback of halted traffic that they'll realize the southbound tunnel is totally blocked. The first thing they're going to do is cut off the vehicles entering from the Kowloon side, to save adding to the jam. By my reckoning we have two minutes from the moment of the crash till that happens."

"Then what?" Quinn asked.

"Well, by then we have something like sixty to eighty vehicles queueing up behind us. A few have probably banged into each other, adding to the confusion. The tunnel police know they have a full-scale emergency on their hands. They realize that the people on the Hong Kong side can't cope. They're going to have to get the tunnel company tow trucks and emergency tenders, perhaps even a fire engine, in there to sort out the mess. But those things are all at the *Kowloon* end. The only way to get them across is to close off the northbound tunnel as well, from the Hong Kong side. That takes more time, and it means more delay. It means, once they've sealed the northbound tunnel, waiting another two minutes for all the traffic to pass through it before they can send their trucks through in the opposite direction. What it boils down to is that we have exactly six minutes to work in. We have four minutes, from the moment of the crash, to grab Kiley, drive out on the Hong Kong side, switch vehicles and cut back over the interchange to get back into the northbound tunnel before they block it off. Two minutes after that we pay our five dollars at the Kowloon toll barrier and we're home and dry."

Quinn expelled a long breath. "Whoo-wee!" he said. "You're sure cutting things fine, man."

"Those are minimum time estimates. It could be we'll have an extra minute or two, but we must work on getting it right within those limits. With practice we can do it, I promise you. Oh—and one point about the practice: we won't be using Kiley's own car as a target again until the day."

"Why not?"

"Those TV cameras, Seymour, are feeding their pictures onto video tape. It's done to provide subsequent proof of traffic violations, mainly the crossing of the white lines—but the fact is that every car that goes through here gets its number recorded. The first thing the cops are going to do is run those tapes and check out every vehicle that has followed Kiley through the tunnel at his regular time each morning in the last week or so. Which is a very good reason not to follow him. We'll target on random cars at random times of day—and each day we'll be using a different hired car to do it with. They've only got the resources to work within certain limits, and they can't run a check on fifty thousand cars a day."

They boomed out of the tunnel at that moment into the glare of a Kowloon morning. As they slowed to approach the toll barrier, Quinn smiled and nodded appreciatively at Pritchard. "You got it all figured out, don't you? But do we have to take on all this TV shit, this tight schedule? Why not hit him somewhere easier?"

"Because nowhere else *is* easier, don't you see? The tunnel is practically the only place in Hong Kong where traffic flows smoothly and fast. It also knocks out Kiley's radio. But more important, what we do will put the police immediately onto a false lead. They'll think we stayed on the Hong Kong side; they'll never guess that after creating havoc in the tunnel we'll have had the audacity to go right back through it again. And by the time they find out it'll be too late."

They stopped at the barrier and Pritchard paid the toll. They filtered off the flyover onto Chatham Road, turned left into a side street after a quarter of a mile, and found Fong at the kerbside, straddling the secondhand 250cc Honda he had bought the day before with a deposit of two thousand five hundred Hong Kong provided by Pritchard. He was wearing jeans, a fancy leather motorbike jacket, and a crash helmet with a one-way visor of smoked perspex, which he raised when they stopped beside him.

"Hello, Mr.—Alan."

"All set, Fong?" Pritchard glanced up and down the street. It was at the edge of a high-rise resettlement estate; kids played on the pavements and old women gossiped in the doorways of shops. There was no sign of a policeman or anyone else who might take the slightest interest in them. He reached under the driver's seat, took out one of the Pye walkie-talkie transceivers with its short aerial and handed it through the window to Fong.

"Keep that out of sight, as far as possible. There are just three controls: on-off and volume, you push the button to transmit, otherwise you receive automatically; then there's the scrambler, which stays permanently on. Move down to the corner of Chatham. We're going further back to pick up a target."

Fong took the instrument and stuck it into the side pocket of his jacket. He lowered his black visor, pushed the Honda off its stand and started the engine. He gunned it to the corner, stopped and balanced the bike between his thighs. He took out the transceiver, switched it on and put his left wrist through the loop strapped to one of its corners and his left hand beneath the flap of his jacket, keeping it concealed from passersby. He sat waiting to hear from Pritchard.

It was exactly four minutes before the Englishman's voice came booming out at him, so loud and clear that he had to pull out the set hastily and turn down the volume. Luckily the roar of traffic from Chatham Road was loud enough to drown the sound in anyone else's ears.

"Unit One, Unit One," the voice said.

Fong pressed the transmitter button. "Unit Two receiving."

"Excellent. We have a subject, red Toyota taxi, number AK49203, registered on the Hong Kong side, which probably means he's taking the tunnel. You can pull out just as soon as you like."

Fong gunned the engine, hastily checked the traffic from the right and swung out to turn southwards down Chatham Road. Once he had straightened out he glanced in his wing mirror and caught sight almost at once of the taxi. He drifted into the left-hand lane and let it overtake him, then signalled right and got behind it. Glancing in the mirror again, he saw Pritchard's Volvo following him. The first dummy run had begun.

16

Pershing Plaza did not live up to the grandiloquence of its name—a rectangle of ramshackle one and two-storeyed buildings around a small formal garden, doing justice neither to General Pershing nor the concept of a city square—but it passed for the centre of Zamboanga. On its south side at nine fifteen on Sunday evening Baxter, following the instructions given by an anonymous voice on the telephone at his hotel, stood waiting to be met.

Perched on the southeastern tip of the Philippine island of Mindanao, Zamboanga was only four hundred island-hopping miles across the Sulu Sea from Simpang. But there was no direct air service, and Baxter had spent the best part of the weekend waiting for connections through Singapore and Manila. Since his arrival in the city, however, the boredom induced by air travel had quickly been replaced by uneasiness. It was a pleasant enough place, with its palm-lined streets and its view across the Basilan Straits to the Sulu Islands; the long, slender *vintas* of the Muslim fishermen lay at anchor off the terrace of the hotel, and the Moro children, agile as seals, dived for pesos tossed into the water by the guests. But there was also a tangible tension in the atmosphere. The city stood at the epicentre of the Moro revolution that was going on in the jungles around it. As in the eye of a typhoon, the calm that prevailed there was threatening. Thousands of refugees from the fighting on the outer islands had flooded in to pack the markets and docks; there were armed soldiers on foot patrol and troop carriers rumbling through the streets. The curiosity with which visitors, particularly white visitors, were regarded was not wholly a friendly one.

Baxter paced restlessly up and down the dimly lit side of the square. Even this early in the evening there were few pedestrians about, and fewer vehicles. There was a curfew starting at midnight; whoever was coming to meet him had better hurry it up.

He stopped in front of a lighted shop window, gazing unseeingly at the objects displayed: Moro brassware, trays, shells, bric-a-brac.

"Hey, Joe!"

Startled, he turned towards the voice, paper-thin but strident, that had accosted him from behind. He made out a small figure, half hidden in a dark doorway beside the shop: a barefoot urchin in shorts and

127

T-shirt. He thrust out a thin arm draped with a row of necklaces that rattled against each other.

"Whaddaya know, Joe! Coral. Look, you buy, special price!" He came forward into the light, extracting a string of coral from the tangle on his arm. "Twenty pesos, no shit! For your wife? Your sweetheart?"

Baxter smiled faintly and shook his head. The kid was ten or eleven and his argot was World War Two GI, passed on through a generation of touts and hucksters.

"Okay, Joe, you no buy. You gimme peso? Gimme Lucky?"

There was not much conviction in the appeal, Baxter thought, just as there was little percentage in begging these days. The Americans who had once probably dispensed dimes and chewing gum and cigarettes to the boy's father had been replaced by a more cautious breed: tourists walled up in their hotels and sightseeing buses, protected from the world outside their windows. Baxter reached into his pocket for some loose change and then realized that someone had moved up very close behind him. He swung round, feeling the sick clutch of terror in his bowels.

"Hello, Mr. Baxter," said Osman Khan quietly.

"For Christ's sake!" Baxter breathed, weak with relief. "Why'd you sneak up on me like that?"

"I was trying to be discreet."

"You nearly made me shit myself." He saw Khan make a small grimace of distaste. "What the hell are you doing here anyway? I thought—"

"Please," the Malay interrupted. "We cannot linger. You are conspicuous, and I cannot afford to become so. Let us go."

He turned back along the sidewalk. Baxter followed. At the kerbside a few yards up, strategically parked at the dim point between two street lights, was a jeepney—a mad and ubiquitous Filipino vehicle, basically an open-sided Willys station wagon with about half a ton of chrome-plated ornamentation clinging to it. In addition to the usual trim, this one was decorated all over its bodywork with stars and crescents and had twin sets of spotlights and klaxons. It looked like a pinball machine on wheels. There was a man sitting in the driver's seat, smoking.

"You expect to be inconspicuous in that?" Baxter asked, stopping beside it.

"They are a common sight," said Khan. "Besides, many operate as taxis. They attract no attention."

128

Baxter found that hard to believe, but he clambered awkwardly into one of the two long seats at the rear. Khan got in and sat facing him. The urchin, who had trotted after them down the street, hopped in beside the driver. Baxter gave Khan a questioning look.

"That is Tewfik. He made sure you were not followed to the rendezvous."

"Who did you think might follow me?"

"Who can tell? We cannot be too careful."

The driver started the jeepney. He was a narrow-headed man in a dark knitted shirt. The car pulled away from the kerb and moved round the square.

"Where are we going?" Baxter asked, nervous again.

"You'll see soon enough. If you want people like the Moro freedom fighters to trust you, you must learn not to ask too many questions, Mr. Baxter."

"And what do they do in return, to prove I can trust them?"

"I'm sure they will win your confidence, but security must be first priority. Take my case: if I were arrested here, there would be serious embarrassment for my chief."

"You mean you came in illegally?"

"It is possible that the police here know of my role as liaison officer between the Chief Minister and the Moros. I came by a route I have used before: by air to Sandakan, in Sabah, and then across the straits by fast boat. It takes less than thirty-six hours."

Baxter nodded. "I think I know those fast boats. They're run by smugglers bringing in contraband booze."

In the darkness, he could only sense the faint smile on Khan's hawkish features. "In a war you take all the allies you can get, smugglers or not. They are all Muslims; their sympathy is with the Moros."

They were out of the square now, heading up a long street that seemed to be leading them towards the northern outskirts of the town. The driver was careful, making sure he attracted no attention to his car. At the end of the street he stopped at a traffic light, where a policeman in the American-style uniform of the Philippines Constabulary lounged against a pillar. Baxter tensed, but it seemed Osman Khan had been right; the glance that the cop gave the bizarre vehicle was no more than casual.

The lights changed and they moved off. A turn to the right brought them out of the town, onto a road running parallel to the shore among fishermen's huts and clumps of palms. In the moonlight Baxter could see the silhouettes of *vintas* against the pearly sheen of the sea. Ahead he saw something else: a bulbous shape suspended above the horizon, a faintly glowing silver thing like a second, larger, moon. He watched it grow as they drew nearer, gradually making it out to be part of a structure that dominated a huddle of low, dimly lit buildings. Suddenly he had it: the dome of a mosque, sheathed in silver-painted metal, towering over the village that surrounded it.

A minute later the jeepney bumped off the road onto a potholed track leading into the settlement. Its centre was a patch of baked mud right in front of the mosque, and there the track ended. The village square, if that was the name for it, was surrounded by a jumble of clapboard huts; pale light—from candles or oil lamps—showed through windows and open doorways. The car stopped and immediately a dozen children converged on it, babbling excitedly in Chabakano. The boy, Tewfik, got out and slid familiarly between them to vanish into the night.

"I wasn't expecting red-carpet treatment," Baxter said.

"This village is totally Moro," said Khan. "A ghetto. Very little that happens inside it can be hidden. On the other hand, nothing gets out."

"I'd like to believe that."

He climbed out over the tailboard to be surrounded by a sea of children, bobbing and laughing and pulling at the hem of his jacket as he stood waiting for Osman Khan to leave the car. Nervous and suddenly enraged, he turned and swung a clumsy fist at the nearest boy, who ducked easily away from the blow and laughed. Suddenly there came a word of command from the darkness at the edge of the square, a man's voice, not harsh, but even and penetrating with authority. The children stopped moving, quietened, and began to melt away. Within a few seconds they had scattered into the shadows like cockroaches scared off by a light. By then Osman Khan had joined Baxter and they could make out the black silhouette of the man who had given the order, standing between two of the huts. The figure stepped forward into the light, a tall, dark-skinned man wearing nothing but faded jeans and cradling an American M3 submachine gun across his bare chest.

"You follow, please," he said in English, and turned and disappeared into the dark again. Baxter and Khan moved cautiously down the path between the shacks. Baxter began to realize that the village overlapped some inlet of the sea, perhaps a tidal river estuary. Apart from the mosque, almost every building stood on stilts above the water,

130

and the path they were following led at once onto a precarious walkway of planks, unprotected by handrails and turning unpredictably every few yards in a new direction between the formless sprawl of hovels. The man in front moved with swift, surefooted strides; the other two picked their way cautiously across the planking, forcing their guide to stop and wait every half minute or so, impatience in the rigidity of his bearing. The place smelt of low tide and spiced cooking. They saw no one else, but there was a strong impression of their progress being watched from behind the dimly lit openings on all sides of them. Some bloody security, Baxter thought bitterly. He had a deep wish to be back in the Quill or at home with Liz and the kid. The euphoria he had felt after leaving Salim on Friday had been worn off by two days of travel and uncertainty. He wished he had never heard of the Project.

Eventually he was aware that the man with the submachine gun had stopped again, this time opposite the door of a hut. Like most of the others, it had clapboard walls and a window without glass, but with light showing through a square of sacking that served as a curtain. The man knocked on the door and said something in Chabakano. It opened and he showed them through with a wave of his gun.

The light inside was much stronger. It came from a gas pressure lamp which stood hissing on a shelf at head height in one corner, with a myriad insects flying, crawling, or lying dead within the glare immediately around it. Beyond that the glow was dimmer, just about reaching into the other three corners of the single-room shack. There was another door leading onto a porch that looked out over the sea. There was a potbellied stove with the remains of a meal of rice standing on it in a shallow saucepan. There was an old brass bedstead, five plain chairs made of bamboo and sea grass, and a low rectangular table. It was the five men in the room, rather than the furniture, which made the place seem crowded. One stood in the doorway to the porch, another in the opposite corner; they were the guards, both armed with submachine guns.

The Military High Command of the Moro National Liberation Front sat behind the table. On the left was a very thin, middle-aged Chinese in a high-buttoned cotton drill suit, his narrow face set off by big protruding ears and high, prominent cheekbones, giving him the look of a cadaverous rodent. On the right was a young Malay with a squint. In the centre, wearing a faded blue singlet, white denims and rubber sandals, sat the military leader of the movement, Mustapha Diaz. His face was handsome in a predatory way, middle thirties, still youthful, but with marks of premature aging superimposed on it as if by a rubber stamp: the crow's feet at the corners of his eyes, the beginnings of bags beneath them. The eyes were very brown, burning with intensity. They warmed briefly to a smile for Osman Khan, then turned to Baxter. There was interest in them, but no welcome.

"As salam alaikum," said Khan, and hesitated. "This is Mr. Baxter."

"We have looked forward to meeting Mr. Baxter," Diaz answered, still watching him. His face was tilted back, his narrow body slumped comfortably in the chair. "Some risk has been involved for us in arranging the occasion. Let us hope it will not be a waste of time. Please sit down, gentlemen."

They pulled the two spare chairs up to the table and sat facing the three men across it.

"We have only two hours before the curfew," Diaz said, "and all of us must be well away from here by then. Let us, then, go straight to business. This scheme of yours, Mr. Baxter." He made a gesture of perplexity. "I have heard it in outline from my friend Khan here; I will hear it in detail from you. But let me say this at once: it has a flaw. In its present form it is not acceptable to us."

"Not acceptable!" Baxter thought he had misheard. It was the one possibility he had never even considered. He stared stupidly into Diaz's face.

"Not the way it is now," the Moro said.

"You mean you'd turn down a chance of making five million dollars, for doing practically nothing?"

"It is not that simple."

"Salim finds it acceptable. Doesn't he?" Baxter appealed to Osman Khan, who nodded. "If the Chief Minister, your main supporter and a very smart operator to boot, thinks it's a good idea, then why shouldn't you?"

"The Chief Minister is an admirable man," said Diaz, "but he does not have my experience—or, if I may say so, my responsibilities."

"This flaw you're talking about—"

"We will come to that shortly. We will see whether you are willing to amend your plans to our requirements. Are you empowered to speak on behalf of your colleagues?"

"Yes. But they'd have to agree to any changes."

"It would help us, to begin with, if we knew who these mysterious colleagues of yours are."

132

Baxter had regained some of his composure. After all, he told himself, he was a businessman; he had come here with a pretty impressive offer and there was no reason why he should let himself be bullied by a ragged revolutionary like Diaz.

"Suppose we start with your own little committee here," he said. "You haven't introduced me."

Diaz shrugged and gestured, right and left. "Mohammed Tariq is head of our political department. Major Wen is an adviser from the Chinese People's Liberation Army."

Tariq nodded and squinted at Baxter. Major Wen smiled briefly, showing long rodent teeth. Baxter narrowed his eyes at him suspiciously and turned back to Diaz.

"Adviser? How much of his advice do you take?"

"As much as I need. He is an acknowledged expert on guerrilla tactics."

"And how much of what goes on here gets reported back to Peking? I don't want any third parties getting in on this act."

"I don't think you need worry. The People's Republic has no interest in influencing our policies or our actions. They help us on fraternal grounds, as fellow-strugglers against imperialism."

"I take that to mean they're long on brotherly love and short on hard cash. The money comes mostly from Salim, right? But never enough of it. I don't know much about guerrilla warfare, Diaz, but I guess that like any other kind of war it's expensive. Guns, munitions, food, medicines all cost money, and I suspect you can't dun much of it from your supporters. Look at yourselves, old son," he said, warming to his theme, waving an expansive hand from the trio facing him to the two guards slouching in their corners. "What are those guns they're carrying? World War Two American surplus, I'll bet. If you want to win this fight of yours, you're going to need better equipment than that, better everything.

"Another thing. Publicity. Among all the organizations like yours —guerrilla movements, freedom fighters, terrorists, the labels make no difference to me—the ones who make the running these days are the ones who carry out spectacular operations right out there in the public eye, who get themselves worldwide attention. The kidnappings, the hijackings, the bombings: I'd hardly heard of your outfit, frankly, until that kidnapping up at Padagian last month. You may not win much sympathy outside with that kind of thing, but you don't need that anyway. The only goodwill you want is from your own supporters,

133

because without it you're nothing. So, in a nutshell, these are the things you need: goodwill, publicity and money. I'm here to offer you all three, Diaz, on a plate, and for free. Now what the hell is your objection to that?"

In the seconds that followed, the hissing of the gas lamp could be heard again, and the whirring and thumping of insects. Occasionally there was a soft crackling noise as one of them incinerated itself over the flame. Eventually Mustapha Diaz sighed.

"Now, Baxter, you listen to me. You came here tonight, representing yourself and your group of friends. You came, in effect, offering a contract—a neatly packaged deal for you to kidnap someone and let us take the credit for it. Or, as it might turn out, the blame."

"There'll be no blame. I tried to tell you—"

"Wait!" Diaz said, and there was a sudden menace in the hot brown eyes. "Listen to me. We came to this village, and you were brought here to see us, because it is a safe place to meet. We are the law here. Places like this are our strength as well as our sanctuary. Time is on our side, but there is another factor: success. To convince our supporters of the inevitability of final victory, a series of small successes is far more important than one brief and spectacular one. On the other hand, a brief, spectacular failure could set back our cause by five years."

Baxter waited till he was sure Diaz had finished. Then he spoke. "It won't fail. Why should you think it will?"

"I don't say it will, only that it might. We can't afford another failure. There was the plane hijack in 'seventy-six, the unsuccessful kidnapping you mentioned last month. One more mess like that, on a larger scale, and we lose more credibility than the money can compensate us for."

"You're backing out, then? Is that what you're saying? If it's so, let me tell you this: come what may, we're going to lift Pangolin one week from tomorrow, and if you don't want to buy we'll find someone who will."

"There is no one else," Diaz said flatly. "Since we are the only possible customers, we are able to make conditions."

"What conditions?"

Neither Major Wen, to the left of Diaz, nor the man called Mohammed Tariq, on the other side, had yet said a word. Baxter had assumed they did not speak English. But now the Chinese leaned to one side to whisper incomprehensibly into Diaz's ear. The Moro nodded,

134

scraped his chair back on the raw floorboards and stood up. He walked round the table to stand behind Baxter.

"Listen, my friend. I said your project had a flaw in it. That does not make it unsound as a whole. It has many merits. Its greatest recommendation is your choice of target: Pangolin. I think, as you do, that the Americans will do almost anything to get him back. They will pay the ransom. They will override any objections the police and others may have. On all these points you are correct. The details of the actual operation also seem sound enough, and the method by which payment is to be effected is clever. The flaw, from our point of view, is that we have no control over it. You are asking us to take public responsibility for a series of events that will be out of our hands from beginning to end. That is what we cannot accept."

Baxter stared down at the tabletop. "You couldn't do it yourselves. Not in Hong Kong."

"No," Diaz admitted. "We have not the resources."

"What's the answer, then?"

Diaz circled the table again, returning to stand behind his own chair. He grasped the back of it and leaned forward, watching Baxter closely. "It seems to me that this operation, like all similar ones, falls naturally into two phases. First, the kidnapping, removal and safe concealment of the target. Second, the waiting phase, ending in payment of the ransom and release of the target. What I propose is this: you carry out the first phase next Monday, exactly as you have planned it. Prove to me that it has been successful in every respect and then, only then, will you get our backing."

"In other words," Baxter said, "you support us if we succeed, you disown us if we fail."

"I have told you, and I repeat: we cannot risk a failure."

"Even for five million dollars?"

"When we have the money in our hands, we will count it."

"So, all right, we do the thing next Monday and you'll have your proof almost at once. It'll be in the news, on the radio. . . ."

"Not necessarily. The Americans may succeed in keeping it quiet. Even if they don't, I will want better proof than a news broadcast. I want an observer present from our side, to report back to me."

"For Christ's sake, we're not playing a bloody war game, we're—"

"You'll find it's far from being a game, Baxter, once you get started." The Moro jerked back his chair abruptly and sat down. "This observer: he will not take part in the operation, but he will be present

135

afterwards to ensure that everything has gone according to plan. He will then notify us here. There need not be more than a couple of hours' delay. He will have to be someone who can move in and out of Hong Kong freely and legally. I suggest Osman Khan here."

Khan looked surprised for a moment but then nodded thoughtfully. "I could also alert the Chief Minister, prepare him for his next move."

"Well," Baxter said with a sigh. "I can't say I like it: it only complicates things further. But I'll take it back and see what the others say."

"Good. All future communication between us will be carried out through Osman. And now, with that out of the way for the moment, I must tell you that there is one other condition."

Insects buzzed. A cockroach climbed out of the pot of rice, scuttled across the stove and fell to the floor with a plop.

"What condition?" Baxter said.

"As I told you, our objection to the plan was lack of control over it. That objection is not met simply by withholding our support from phase one until it is concluded. We require some supervision of phase two as well. We want you to move it from Hong Kong to the Philippines. We want you to bring Pangolin to us."

17

Canny got home from work late on Monday evening. It had been a tiring day at the surgery, with accounts to check over and send out as well as the normal busy routine of being receptionist in a partnership of five doctors. And the weather at this time of year, the unrelenting damp heat which didn't let up even late at night among the crowded, baking apartment blocks of Causeway Bay, was enough to exhaust anyone. Even Seymour, who had nothing better to do all day than go to the movies and hang about the apartment, got irritable. Seymour. Hell, she thought, as she rode to the ninth floor, things had got steadily worse between them. Back in April, when he had told her he was going to jump ship and come to live with her, the prospect had had an air of illicit excitement. Beyond that, there'd been the promise of rescue from the trap of grinding semi-poverty she had always known. When she and her family had fled from Foochow in 1962, Hong Kong had seemed like a promised land—the Golden Mountain, it was called in the mythology of the time, its glamour and glitter standing in stark contrast to the drab, repressive authoritarianism of the People's Republic. Her father was a well-off peasant whose few acres of land had been seized and communalized at the end of the civil war. He spent his life savings to get himself, his wife and his four children smuggled out in the hold of a cargo junk.

Once there, they discovered that the mountain was not quite so golden as it had been painted. To start with, they were only six out of hundreds of thousands of refugees with no jobs and no roof over their heads. They lived in the great squatter camp at Shek Kip Mei for two years, surviving on government charity and the odd bits of money that her father could earn as an occasional coolie labourer in the docks. Eventually he settled into regular work—making plastic toys on an assembly line, a job he was still holding down now, at a thousand Hong Kong dollars a month—and the family were allocated a room, ten feet by twelve, in a resettlement block with communal standpipes and lavatories down the corridor. Canny's parents did not find this degrading, but she did. At elementary and middle school, learning English and something of the world outside the great Middle Kingdom of Chinese culture, she began to understand the nature of the trap they were in. She had seen the chauffeur-driven Rolls-Royce that took the owner of her father's factory home from its gate; she saw the doctors arriving at the surgery every morning in their Mercedes and Mustangs, and when she phoned them at home she reached them through a succession of querulous amahs and houseboys. Her feelings were not revolutionary, not even resentful—merely hopeful, with the angry Chinese optimism that kept people working in sweatshops for sixty hours a week, as her father did, in the certain belief that one day they would be riding that Rolls out of the factory gates themselves.

Seymour had seemed, at first, a key to the fulfilment of some undefined ambition. Seymour, in the United States Navy, had been earning three times what her father pulled in, yet could talk about it disparagingly as "liberty bread," spending it freely on girls and booze, supplementing it with his profitable deals in White Dragon Pearl. He got free chow, free lodgings, and yet was able to take them so much for granted that he could desert with the knowledge that something better was waiting for him—someplace, sometime. It was this optimism, born of the inherent wealth of his country, that had excited Canny, had made

137

her believe in the possibilities of escaping from her trap. The disillusionment had taken a long time to sink in.

She found the burglarproofing trellis outside the door unlocked, which meant he was at home. She opened the door and smelt the appetizing odour of frying chicken. Seymour rarely cooked anything, even for himself, but she saw as she entered the room a panful of chicken pieces sizzling on one of the gas rings. On another, a pot of noodles was coming to the boil. Quinn turned to her with a smile. "Hi! Thought you might like a little home cooking."

She put down her handbag and stood looking at him. "What's the occasion?"

"No occasion, baby. Just me being domesticated for once. Appreciate it while it lasts. There's some wine over there. Help yourself."

Canny found the bottle of Australian claret standing with two glasses on a table beside the bed. She filled both glasses and carried one over to him.

"I said, what's the occasion?"

"And I said no occasion. All right, I got a good little deal going, if it comes off. I'm celebrating in advance, okay? Just be grateful for a dinner you didn't have to cook."

"What's the deal? Something to do with that new friend of yours? The Englishman?"

Seymour Quinn prodded with a fork at the chicken pieces. "Listen, chick. You ask no questions, you get told no lies. That's what my Irish grandmother used to say. Now let's eat."

They had dinner at a small, battered card table that stood at the foot of the bed. Quinn, who normally ate in single-minded silence, was unusually talkative and polite, filling up her glass whenever the level of the wine sank. The chicken was half raw but she was grateful for his gesture, lulled by the attention he was paying her. At the end of the meal, with the dirty dishes still on the table, they shared a rolled joint of Number Three mixed with tobacco.

"Listen," he said. "Remember you got me those spikes from the surgery a few months ago? You figure you could get some more?"

Canny stiffened. The disappearance of a dozen disposable hypodermic syringes back in May had caused a problem—not because such small and inexpensive items would normally have been missed from the surgery's storeroom, but because their usual suppliers had suddenly run out of stock and Dr. Yang, the senior partner, had fussily insisted that he had seen with his own eyes a box full of them on their usual shelf

138

only two days before. The argument had ended inconclusively but had left Canny unnerved. She said, warily, "Why d'you want more?"

"Well, I know this punk kid, shooting amphetamines, can't find enough spikes because all the guys in the drugstores are wise to him by now. Just trying to do him a favour."

"Last time there was trouble."

"It was bad luck they were missed. That wouldn't happen again."

"That's easy for you to say, Seymour. It's not your job that would be at risk."

"Okay, forget it. It's not important."

But later, when they were undressed and lying side by side in the narrow bed, he returned to the subject.

"This kid is in a bad way, Canny. Next thing, he'll wind up with blood poisoning or something, using the shitty needles he's got there. It wouldn't have to be a whole dozen this time. Just three, maybe four."

"And then? When he's used the three or four, is his problem solved? He'll be back asking for more."

"He'll find another source. It's just to see him right for a few days."

"All right, Seymour," she said with a sigh. "I'll see what I can do. But I don't promise anything. I will not take chances."

"Thanks, kid." He gave her an affectionate kiss. "By the way, you heard of some stuff called Pentothal?"

"Sure." She looked at him in puzzlement. "It's a short-acting barbiturate. Why?"

"Can you get me some?"

"But what—what the hell for?" Canny was not a trained nurse, but working at the surgery she'd become familiar with the uses of many drugs. "You got the right name, Seymour?"

"Pentothal, the guy says. This guy I know, he wants some."

"It's a general anaesthetic, Seymour. It's what they use for knocking people out before operating on them. You can't get high on it. Maybe if you diluted it down a lot it would make you drowsy, that's all."

"So maybe the guy wants to knock himself out. How the hell do I know? You gonna get me some?"

"You're crazy, Seymour."

18

"They want *what?*" Pritchard said in a fierce, explosive whisper. Baxter gave an unhappy shrug.

"They say it's that or nothing. And this Diaz, he's pretty stubborn."

"But why, God damn it? What's the point?"

"I can't be sure. Partly a matter of pride, I think; if the job is going to be pinned on them they want a bigger part in it than we were ready to give them. And Diaz is an idealist, you see: a committed revolutionary. I don't think he likes the idea of being used for mercenary motives. In effect, he's turning what was supposed to be a hoax into the real thing —a genuine political kidnapping."

"Jesus-Christ-all-fucking-mighty," Pritchard muttered. "Less than a week to go and we've got to find a way to get him to the Philippines—and for no bloody good reason whatever."

He took a hard pull at his whisky. They were sitting at a quiet end of the bar counter in the Quill. Baxter had got in from Zamboanga, via Manila, at nine that evening and had phoned Pritchard and arranged to meet him at once. He was sweaty, travel-weary, despondent at the news he had to bring. Pritchard had been in a buoyant mood after a third successful day of practice runs through the tunnel with Quinn and Fong. Now his expression was bleak.

"We'll have to call it off, that's all. I just can't see a way round it."

"Maybe if we all think very hard. . . ."

"Did these cunts have any helpful suggestions about how to get him there?"

"They mentioned the junk." Baxter stopped; Pritchard looked puzzled.

"Go on."

"They said, since we were using the junk to take him to Basalt Island, why didn't we just keep going and head for the north coast of Luzon?"

"Well? Would that be feasible?"

"Alan," said Baxter patiently, "that would be a trip of over four hundred miles across open sea. And this is the typhoon season."

"Just say we didn't run into any typhoons."

"You're as crazy as they are, you know that? You just can't take the chance at this time of year."

"Listen, Bax, this is an emergency. Be honest, now: we don't get typhoon warnings more than once every few weeks, do we? Even in the height of the season? Assuming the weather was okay—"

"You can't assume that!" Baxter said excitedly. "Those tropical storms come up from nowhere. Do you have any idea what they'd do to a boat that size? She'd be smashed to matchwood!"

"Assuming it was okay," Pritchard repeated patiently, "could the junk make it or couldn't she?"

"Well, sure, she's a seagoing boat, as seaworthy as they come. She'd take twice as much punishment as any Western boat the same size. But a typhoon—"

"Listen," Pritchard said quietly, and his expression was more intense and serious than Baxter had ever seen it. It reduced him to silence. "I've put everything I've got, and everything I am, into the Project. I'm at the end of the line now, and I'm living on nothing except the thought of making it work. If the Moros insist on having our man delivered to the Philippines, then I'll find a way of doing it, believe me. Right now, your junk seems like the only way of making it work. But there must be other ways. If you want to call quits, okay, I'll cut you out now. I'm going to do it, Bax, with or without you. What do you say?"

Baxter stared morosely into his empty glass. "What about the others? Fong? Quinn?"

"I need them, of course. I'll gamble on getting them to go along. Right now it's you I'm concerned with, you and the *Lady Belinda.*"

"Well, it's quite possible, physically. Matter of fact, last year I thought of taking a trip down there—not at this time of year, of course. November or December, perhaps. You could do it in forty-eight hours or so."

"What would we need?"

"A hell of a load of extra fuel. The tanks aren't big enough to give more than twelve hours' straight steaming. Then there'd be charts, life jackets, pyrotechnics, as well as extra stores: food and water, mostly. She's okay for navigational equipment: there's a decent compass, radar, echo sounder, direction finder, marine-band radio with longwave for weather forecasts. But look—"

"Look nothing, Bax. You want a million and a half or don't you?"

"Well, of course, but . . . we can't just change the plan like that and take off for the Philippines with him."

"Not right away, no. Partly because once the balloon goes up, they're going to do their best to intercept every boat leaving Hong Kong; partly because you and I have got to be around when question time begins. But if we follow the plan, take him to the island for just a couple of days, till the immediate heat is off, then slip away in the dark. . . . In fact, what you ought to do right this minute is decide that you're going to do that trip to Luzon that you were thinking of taking last year, and invite me along. We'll tell a few people we're planning it, prepare the ground. That'll give us the excuse to load up supplies later this week."

"Liz won't understand. She's suspicious of me as it is, taking all the time off work that I have been, and the trip to Simpang—"

"You'll have to make her understand," Pritchard said, his voice hard-edged. There were times when Baxter's snivelling infuriated him. "Now listen. You say they mentioned the junk. Did they suggest any arrangements?"

"They said, if we agreed, to contact them through this Osman Khan fellow. They would suggest a place to make a landfall on the north coast of Luzon, and we'd tell them when to expect us. They'd make sure it was safe. We'd have to come in by night, and they'd set up lights to guide us in."

"All right. Then let's do it, Bax."

"But—"

"Let's phone this man Khan, now."

19

The taxi driver had loaded Ailsa's baggage and stood holding the door of the cab open for her. In the doorway of the apartment she turned to face her husband. The gap between them had never seemed wider. She was talking to him across a million miles.

"Well?"

"Well, what?"

"For the last time, are you going to follow me to Sydney?"

142

He had been reading papers from an unmarked file cover, which he was still holding as he came out of the living room into the hallway, preoccupied even as she prepared to depart.

"I've tried to explain that it'll be difficult, honey. There was a hell of a backlog of work waiting when I got back from Wash—"

"There's always a backlog, Rod. Always has been, always will be. One day you'll have to learn to live with it. I've warned you, though; don't expect me to stick around until then."

"There's also a date I can't break, on September third."

"Every date is unbreakable, isn't it?"

"This one really is."

"What's more important to you, Rod? Some lousy meeting or your marriage? Go on, be honest."

He looked at her steadily for several seconds, with the cool blue eyes that never grew angry. Then he said, "Ailsa, I know you find my job difficult to live with. But I don't have it any too easy myself. What you call some lousy meeting happens to be absolutely vital. I shouldn't tell you this, but perhaps it will help convince you. We have an asset in China, a very highly placed agent who sends important material out to us by personal courier. I am running this agent myself; both he and the courier refuse to deal through anyone else. I have a meeting with the courier the first week of every month, when he comes back from Peking. It's him that I'm seeing on the third."

Ailsa was unmoved. "That may be true, Rod. Then again, it may not be. You live in a world of deceit, and I guess even I am not immune to it. You haven't answered my question. Which is more important, it or me?"

"I don't want to have to answer that, Ailsa."

Without another word she turned and walked out of the apartment.

On Friday they took out the *Lady Belinda*—just Pritchard and Baxter; the other two stayed at home. They had the twin excuse of loading the stores they had bought over the past few days and taking her out to sea to run a check on the instruments. When they arrived at Hebe Haven, Baxter spoke to the boatboy, Ah Leung.

"My friend and I are taking her on a cruise—Tuesday or Wednesday of next week."

"This time of year?" Ah Leung asked doubtfully.

"We'll only be at sea forty-eight hours. If there's a typhoon warning we'll have plenty of time to get back." Baxter spoke somewhat unconvincingly, but the boatboy made no further comment. He helped them unload their stores from the car and ferry them out on his sampan: the chemical toilet, crated in cardboard so that it might have been anything (he couldn't read the English labels on the sides anyway), the camp beds and sleeping bags, similarly boxed, the crates of food and jerrycans of water. If he thought there was a lot of equipment for two men on a short trip, he did not remark on it. They, in turn, relied on his studied lack of interest in the affairs of *gwai-los*. When they had loaded everything aboard, Baxter tipped him a hundred dollars Hong Kong and asked him to look out for the oil company lighter that would later be delivering their supply of reserve fuel. Then they set out for Basalt Island.

They dropped anchor off the beach shortly before midday and rowed ashore in the rubber dinghy. Pritchard was relieved to find it had not been visited in their absence. Rain and tides had obliterated footprints on the sand and other signs of their earlier visit, but otherwise nothing had changed. The same rusted beer can lay in the same corner of the pillbox; the footprints on the sandy floor were their own. They returned to the junk and carried the supplies for the pillbox ashore, stacking the crates in one corner of the building. There would be plenty of time for Quinn and Fong to unpack them once they were here. Indeed, there would be little else for them to do. One item, however, Pritchard fished out of the top crate before they left: a six-foot length of heavy chain with a big anchor shackle on one end; he pulled the other end over towards the wall, produced a strong padlock from his trouser pocket, and fastened the end link of the chain to one of the rusted brackets which had once held the vertical mountings of a heavy machine gun. He tested its strength by lying down with his feet against the wall and hauling on the chain with all his weight and strength. The bracket gave no sign of budging. He stood up again, red-faced with exertion, grinning.

"That'll hold him. That's one facility that needs to be in place for him on arrival."

"Do we really have to do that to him?" Baxter asked.

"Bax, there are going to be spotter planes out over these islands soon after his disappearance—or so we have to assume. The last thing we need is to have him running out there waving at them."

When they got back to the jetty the diesel fuel they had ordered was waiting for them—six forty-four-gallon drums which they hoisted aboard with the block and tackle mounted on the *Lady Belinda*'s stout little boom. They manhandled them aft and lashed them separately, upright on the deck, to the stern rail. Then they took the junk back to her mooring. In the sampan, going ashore, Baxter said to Ah Leung, "We'll have to come back on Monday, to check the compass again."

"Monday I'm not here."

"That's all right. Just leave the sampan, like you said."

20

Sunday morning, twenty-four hours before target time, arrived hot and damp, the heat lying over the colony like a thick, choking blanket. In the built-up areas that faced each other across the harbour it was specially intense, with the air trapped in the canyons between apartment blocks and tenements, and residents flooding out to enjoy their weekly day of leisure. Those who had cars, or could at any rate afford bus, minibus and taxi fares, headed out of town towards the beaches or the rural New Territories, but that still left enough of them behind to crowd the sidewalks and markets, the parks and open spaces of the residential zones.

The little town of Aberdeen was busy, bustling with women in black pyjamas who haggled over the price of fish at the market stalls, and merchants setting up displays of cheap plastic toys and children's clothes and rattan ware. Along the dockside, where the vast city of floating junks began, the boat people were exhorting anyone who looked like a visitor to pay ten dollars for a sampan ride. A few streets back from the waterfront, however, where the tenements of the old fishing port gave way to featureless factory buildings, godowns and lumber yards, it was much quieter. On a corner here stood the local post office, closed today. Just behind it, off the narrow, deserted street to one side of the building, was an alley that led to a pair of corrugated-iron gates. Seymour Quinn, carrying a canvas grip, paused in the entrance to the alley and glanced around. No one was in sight. He slipped quickly through the opening and within a couple of seconds was squatting by the gates, opening the grip.

He took out a pair of rubber dishwashing gloves, which he pulled on. Then he fished out the heavy steel bolt cutters that Pritchard had

supplied him with, clamping their jaws round the shackle of the padlock on the gates. Another quick look round, then sharp, strong pressure on the arms of the cutters and the shackle snapped. He slipped the
broken lock into his pocket and opened the gates wide, revealing a small
yard behind the post office. During the week mail vans were loaded
here, from a small bay at the rear of the building, and today it was
where they were parked—four shiny red Ford Transit one-and-a-half
tonners, with closed sides and double doors at the rear, the sides decorated with a crown and the title Royal Mail. Like taxis and minibuses,
they were seen everywhere in Hong Kong—ubiquitous and anonymous, with no one questioning their right to go wherever they happened
to be. They were working, obviously so; if they were parked somewhere
illegally for a while, or travelling at a shade over the speed limit, it was
out of necessity, and no one, not even a cop, was going to get fussed
about it.

Another beauty of them, Quinn thought, as he opened the door of
the leading van and tossed the bag and the bolt cutters inside, was that
they were so easy to rip off. Any one van might be used by several
drivers working in shifts, so to avoid the complications of individual
ignition locks they all had a common switch, turned by a simple metal
key. Simple, too, to find a copy of one at a junk-metal stall in Cat Street.

He switched on the engine and it fired first time, with a good,
throaty roar. He eased the van out through the gates, stopped, went
back and closed them. He took out a new padlock, removed the key,
slid the shackle through the ring of the door bolt and snapped it shut.
That would puzzle them, for starters. They wouldn't know that the van
was missing till eight thirty tomorrow morning; by then it would be too
late to matter.

He drove out into the streets of Aberdeen. This Pritchard dude had
his shit together, he had to admit that. The research, the preparation,
the thought that had gone into every tiny detail of the Project—all that
stuff had taken some doing. For the first time since they had met, Quinn
found himself thinking of Pritchard with a certain respect.

He had told himself that it was the last car he would ever hire. It
was a Datsun with a tinted windscreen, behind which he sat in a bay
on the first floor of a private multi-storey car park opposite the Hong
Kong–Macau ferry terminal. From the cubicle of the *shroff,* the cash-
ier, he was invisible. He, on the other hand, could watch the comings
and goings of the *shroff,* a harassed young Cantonese who had to act

146

as a parking attendant as well as take money. It was the practice of wealthy Chinese to leave their cars here before catching the hydrofoil to Macau for a day or two's gambling. Sunday was the most popular day for such an excursion, and the *shroff* danced attendance on his customers in the hope of good tips. He had barely glanced at the small Datsun, and had certainly not taken any notice of its driver, before waving it into a bay. Pritchard had taken the lift down to the ground floor, then climbed back up by the concrete stairway in the rear, surreptitiously to re-enter his car. Now, after an hour's wait, it was time to move.

He had watched the first-floor parking bays gradually fill up; he had seen later arrivals directed up the ramps to the second and third levels. Some did not want to be directed; the drivers of Lincolns and Rolls-Royces and Cadillacs got out and handed their keys to the *shroff*, who took their cars up to the higher levels and came back to stick the keys on hooks on a board behind him, to be collected when they returned.

Now Pritchard had selected his car, a black Mercedes 350 SE saloon with tinted windows all round, from which a fat Chinese in a tussore suit and a girl too young to be his wife had disembarked, leaving a servant to follow them with the baggage—enough baggage to show that they would spend at least one night away. The *shroff* took their car up the ramp and returned to hang the keys behind him.

When he left, six minutes later, to drive a Continental to the upper floors, Pritchard got out of his car and went to the open door of the cubicle. He took the keys of the Mercedes off their hook and walked back across the concrete floor to the stairway. He climbed to the third level and in less than a minute had found the car. He pulled on his cotton driving gloves, opened the door, started the engine and backed out of the bay.

At two o'clock, Fong strolled along the footpath beside the roller-skating rink in Victoria Park. He wore leather motorcycle gauntlets and carried a white crash helmet. He stood for a while in a crowd of several hundred people taking in the dank afternoon air, watching the antics of teenagers skating to the rhythm of synthetic Western dance music that blared from a speaker in one corner of the rink. Across the way, other kids were doing Tai Chi exercises and playing soccer, basketball and badminton. It reminded him of his own childhood, the energy of youth spilling out of the cramped tenements to fill any available empty space. Casually he made his way along the fence, past the smoothly caroming bodies of the teenagers circling the concrete, away from the clacking of the skates into the motorcycle park that adjoined the rink. There were at least three hundred bikes and motor scooters in there, and probably half the bikes were Hondas. He was relieved to find he was not alone; a group of four or five incipient motorcycle freaks were there, pawing and stroking the bikes, comparing them, straddling them on their stands. Fong latched vaguely onto them, glad to dilute his own presence, moving from one bike to another and surreptitiously testing out the key of his own—the one Pritchard had bought, that was to say—in the ignition locks of the Hondas as he passed.

He tried perhaps twenty before he found one that the key fitted. It was a black model with a high, curved windshield, parked at the far end of the enclosure away from the skating rink. Casually he pulled on the crash helmet with its dark visor. He straddled the bike and started the motor. He heaved it off its stand and, without looking back, rode it out into Causeway Road.

Thirty minutes later, wearing new licence plates, it was parked in a back street off Nathan Road on the Kowloon side, close to the apartment building where Fong lived in a room the size of a cupboard.

At six thirty Osman Khan, personal assistant to Chief Minister Salim, walked out of the customs hall into the arrivals area of Kai Tak Airport. He had flown first-class, direct from Simpang. He wore a lightweight suit with an expensive silk shirt and tie and carried an attaché case and an overnight bag. He looked what he very largely was, a successful, progressive young Asian businessman, briefly in town to finalize a deal. Baxter was there to meet him, looking worried and furtive.

"Where are you staying?"

"I have a booking at the Hilton."

"I'd offer you a lift, only we oughtn't to risk being seen together."

"Don't worry. I'm collecting a hire car here."

"Ask them to lend you a road map. Be at a village called Pak Sha Wan, in the New Territories, at eight thirty in the morning. There's a turnoff that leads to a jetty. There shouldn't be anyone else around, but in case there is just act like a sightseer."

"Very well, Mr. Baxter."

"And have the documents with you."

"Of course."

At eight o'clock Seymour Quinn was lying back on the bed in Canny's apartment, drinking San Miguel out of a can and watching an American police serial on the Pearl channel of HK-TVB. He'd seen the episode before—and in colour—on the closed-circuit service on board ship. Canny had cleared the dinner dishes and was sitting in the opposite corner in a sullen silence. She had wanted to see some Cantonese soap opera on the Chinese channel; he had nixed it on the grounds that she understood English whereas he didn't know a word of Chink.

The commercials came on: Johnny Walker, Marlboro, Cathay Pacific Airlines. On a channel aimed at a European audience, the theme was often of a white guy making out with a Chinese chick. They ought to be told, he thought, about these sulky evenings with the Chinese chick who really wanted to be a suburban Stateside housewife. Shit on that; as of tomorrow there would be no tomorrow, at least not for Miss Chan. Everything he was taking along was already in the mail van; everything was ready for lighting-out time.

His musing was interrupted by Canny.

"Someone at the door."

He hadn't heard the knocking over the sound from the set, but now he made it out, a repeated, cautious rat-tat, like a signal. It was a signal he knew. He rolled off the bed to his feet, went to the door and opened it. A lanky black man stood on the threshold, wearing white denims and a bright red cotton shirt with the buttons open all the way down to his waist. There was a gold chain round his neck holding a huge enamelled Rastafarian pendant against his hairless chest.

"Blow Job!" Quinn exclaimed. "What the hell!"

"How do, Seymour."

"Blow Job Johnson, what the hell!" he repeated. "I didn't think the Fleet was in town."

"It ain't. Just our flotilla, got in this afternoon. First thing Tuesday we're headin' on back to the World. I got a liberty till midnight."

"Well, Jesus, come on in," Quinn said, stepping aside and showing the black man through. He closed the door behind him. "Canny, we got a guest, switch that TV off. Blow Job, I guess you never met Canny?"

149

"How do," said Blow Job. The girl gave him the faintest of nods, her face expressionless.

"Blow Job's an old buddy of mine. We were on the *Kitty Hawk* together, before he switched to destroyers. How'd you find out where the hell I was? Hey, Canny, at least turn that goddam racket down, will you? And get the man a beer."

Sulkily she got to her feet and turned down the volume. Then she moved through to the kitchen. "Take a seat," Quinn said, and the visitor eased his long, narrow frame down in the chair Canny had left. Blow Job had a waist of maybe twenty-six, and a reputation among his soul brothers for being the only man in the Navy long and lithe enough to suck himself off. He came from Birmingham and his accent was a slow, liquid, Alabama drawl.

"Great to see you," Quinn said, sitting down on the end of the bed. "How'd you find me?"

"You got quite a reputation in the Fleet, you know that?"

"Well, I appreciate your trouble, looking me up."

"Ain't strictly a social call," Blow Job said. "I got your address off a guy—" He broke off as Canny returned and gracelessly shoved a can of beer into his hand. He raised his eyebrows; Quinn signalled back with a nod. He could talk in front of the girl. She had turned ostentatiously back to the TV.

"This guy, he knew where you lived, you got some stuff for him after you jumped ship."

"What stuff?" Quinn asked cautiously You had to be careful, even with someone you knew as well as Blow Job. "What guy?"

Blow Job pulled the seal off the can and took a slow sip of San Mig. "Raffinetti, used to be on the *Kitty*. Told me you might be able to get ahold of some smack. Number Four, they call it here."

"Hell, I ain't into that strong stuff now. Don't tell me you're doing dope, Blow Job?"

"No, sir. I'm talking about bulk buying. Raffinetti said you could get it in bulk, if anybody could." Blow Job leaned to his left and pulled a roll of money out of the back pocket of his denims. It was a thick wad, which he unfolded and counted out silently into his lap. The bills were U.S. dollars: four hundreds, ten fifties, five twenties. He folded the money and stacked it into a roll which he clutched in his right fist.

"One thousand bucks," he said. "What do you figure that would buy?"

"You mean right now? I don't keep a stock of that stuff, I—"

150

"I mean by tomorrow night, latest."

"Tomorrow I won't be around." Quinn glanced uneasily at Canny; she gave no sign that she was listening.

"Then what about tonight? See, Seymour, I figure on quitting the service, end of my tour next year, and this is the only stake I got. Now this stake I can turn into three times as much, maybe four times, getting this good stuff into Frisco, which is where we're heading Tuesday. Guy I know there will take as much as I can give him. What do you say, Seymour? How much will this get me?"

Quinn had already done a quick calculation. The price that good Chinese heroin could command Stateside, even from a big wholesaler, was at least five times as high as he would pay for it in Hong Kong. And it *was* good, guaranteed ninety-five per cent pure, not like the watered-down shit that the zips had peddled to the poor mothers in 'Nam. That meant he could probably get enough for three or four hundred to satisfy Blow Job, leaving him six or seven profit. Two thoughts made him hesitate: he wouldn't be around tomorrow to set it up, and he had promised Pritchard, for the sake of the security of the Project, not to do any more dealing. He said, "Look, Blow Job, like I said, I ain't too far into Number Four."

"You mean you can't produce? Man, you're the only contact I got."

"Well, I mean, it ain't that easy." Quinn was torn between the risk and the profit. He was strongly conscious of the warning Pritchard had given him: if he fucked up now he stood to lose a million. Yet the million was still in his imagination; here was a thousand bucks, for real, clutched in Blow Job Johnson's skinny black fist. It was a long time since he'd seen that much money all at once.

"You jiving me, Seymour? Tell me you gotta eat and I'll understand, man. You gotta make something out of it, that's fine by me. Figure on taking your cut and then tell me how much this roll will get me."

"I guess around a hundred twenty grams. That's about a quarter pound, and the purest snow you'll ever see."

"Ain't bad," Blow Job conceded.

"Ain't bad? You got any idea what that much stuff would be worth on the street in Frisco?"

"Well, can you get it for me or can't you?"

Quinn hesitated only a second more. "I can try," he said, the decision taken. "I can go see a man I know. If anyone can supply that

151

much without notice he's the one. You stay here. I'll be back in an hour." He held out his hand for the money.

Blow Job suddenly got suspicious. "Wait, man. You want me to just sit here while you walk outta that door with my thousand bucks?"

"You can't come along. This guy doesn't open his door to strangers, specially foreign-devil strangers. Just rely on me, okay? I'm too smart to double-cross anybody, it doesn't pay."

Blow Job surrendered his bankroll reluctantly. "But hurry it up, man."

"Sure. There's more beer in the icebox. Canny, can I trust you with this man for a while?"

She turned briefly from the TV set to give him a look of withering contempt.

"She's great company," he informed Blow Job. "Specially when she doesn't open her trap. So long."

By a quarter to nine Pritchard had finished running through the final checklist of things to be done and equipment to be stowed. Everything was in place, every last detail had been taken care of—right down to winding the stopwatch. Even so, it was impossible to stop worrying that he might have overlooked something, some unaccountable weakness in the Project that could be used to destroy it.

Quinn and Fong had both called to report that they'd procured their vehicles successfully, and Baxter had phoned to say he had met Osman Khan at the airport. Pritchard didn't like the Osman Khan arrangement one little bit—that, if anything, was a potential weakness —but there had been no way around the Moros' insistence on his presence.

Pritchard took ten milligrams of Valium and went to bed. No booze tonight—this must be the first day since his crackup that he'd done without a drink. He read for a while, and soon the tranquillizer began to ease the ache of nervous anticipation in his stomach and the tension in his muscles. The rendezvous was at seven the next morning.

21

Mr. Yau, a squat, tubby man in striped pyjamas, bowed Seymour Quinn with a gold-toothed smile out of his twelfth-floor apartment. Then he slammed the steel trellis across the doorway and locked it. He closed the heavy teak door and Quinn heard the bolts being driven home. There were two bolts on the door as well as a deadlock and a peephole. Mr. Yau was security-conscious, though it was not against robbers that he took these precautions.

Quinn turned away and hurried along the open balcony to the elevator. It took about two minutes to arrive and he stood champing with impatience, feeling his heart thump with a mixture of triumph and anxiety. For four hundred bucks he had bought from Mr. Yau what Blow Job Johnson was willing to pay a thousand for. All he had to do now was get away from this dingy North Point apartment block back to Canny's place and deliver, get the stuff off his ass. It felt already as though it were burning a hole in his pocket. Pritchard would go ape if he knew where he was right now, but there was no reason why he need ever know. For six hundred bucks a guy had to be ready to face a few small risks.

The elevator went all the way down without stopping. Quinn stepped out into the lobby and stood for a moment blinking into the gloom. The overhead light wasn't working, a fact he'd been grateful for when he arrived, since this was not an area where Westerners were often seen, and he did not want to be remembered.

It was in that moment that a voice to his right said, "Hold it there, sonny."

It was a European voice, strongly accented: some kind of limey, his brain registered stupidly, having nothing else to get hold of in the dark. He turned his head, seeing now a shape dimly outlined against the near-black opening of a stairwell to the basement, a figure that moved slowly towards him as he watched.

"Just stand still, sonny," the man said. The voice was hard with authority. "That's right, nice and easy. I want a little talk."

"What is this?" Quinn asked numbly. "Who are you?" But something told him he already knew, something that had begun sending an urgent signal of fear from the pit of his guts to every corner of his body.

"The name is Lewis. Detective Inspector Lewis, Narcotics Bureau,

Royal Hong Kong Police. Stay right there and answer a simple question for me: who were you visiting on the twelfth floor?"

Quinn stood exposed in the light from the rectangular opening in the elevator door, while Lewis, still masked by darkness, began to circle behind him. If he was going to make a run for it, he thought, this was the moment; but as if the thought had flashed across the gap between them, the policeman said, "I don't advise you to try running, sonny. Listen."

Quinn heard a metallic click that echoed round the empty lobby: the unmistakable sound of an automatic pistol being cocked.

"Come on now," the cop said, "who did you see on the twelfth floor? I'm betting on my old pal Johnny Yau, the Shithead's Friend."

"No. . . . No, I don't know anybody by that name."

"Who, then? Forgotten already?"

Quinn's mind bobbed helplessly in a vortex of confusion. He said nothing. Lewis paced back and forth behind him in tight little semicircles, like an animal in too small a cage. Suddenly he stopped and jabbed the muzzle of his gun painfully into Quinn's spine.

"Get over there!" he grated. "Next to the wall. Hands against it, legs spread out."

Quinn obeyed like an automaton. He walked to the right-hand wall of the lobby; there was more light here, filtering in from the street through the glass front doors of the building. He pressed his palms against the wall and leant on them.

"I said spread those fucking legs!" the narc said fiercely from behind him, and he shuffled backwards and moved his feet a yard apart. The gun was stuck into his back again. With his free hand, Lewis frisked him expertly, patting up and down his torso and legs. Within a few seconds he had located the package of Number Four, tightly wrapped in an envelope, in the right-hand pants pocket. Quinn felt him tug it gently out, heard him sniff at it.

"Mister Yau's Special Brew," he said with satisfaction. "I've waited a long time for this, sonny, you know that? Mister Yau is going to go down for a long, long time, and you're going to help me send him there. Turn around. Make it slow."

The American swung round and backed up against the wall, smelling the rankness of his own nervous sweat. He got his first proper look at Lewis now, in the half-light from the street. He was on the small side, maybe five-eight, with heavy shoulders, a short neck and a square, crop-haired head set at an aggressive angle. He was pointing the auto-

154

matic at Quinn's middle from a professional distance. With his other hand he was tucking the package of smack into the pocket of his sport coat.

The cop's eyes glittered colourlessly. "Well, sonny, you're in a load of shit, you know that?"

"I guess I do."

"You're a Yank, eh? Off a ship?"

"Yeah," Quinn lied swiftly.

"We'll go into the details later. Right now I'll tell you what I want. I don't give a fuck if the whole bloody U.S. Navy poisons itself with this stuff. I'm here to stop people like Yau from selling it to you, that's all. I want that Chink down for ten years. Help me do that, sonny, and I'll see you get off lightly. Say no, and you won't see daylight for five."

Quinn was breathing more easily now. "What do I have to do?"

"It's simple. Yau trusts you, eh? You go back up to his flat and hit the bell. You make up a story that'll get you inside. Tell him you put some more bread together and you want a second batch. Tell him anything that'll make him open the goddam door—and I will be right there beside you, sonnyboy, out of range of his goddam peephole, ready to take him out the moment the trellis is open. Got it? That's how I like to operate, alone, my own style. I could get a search warrant any day of the week and stand banging on that door and sure, he'd let me in eventually, once he'd flushed all the evidence down the shithouse. This way I get him in it up to his elbows. Got it?"

"I guess so." He was calm. He had reached a decision. He did not believe what Lewis had said about getting him off the hook. Narcs were the same everywhere; if they could grind their heels in the face of a pusher, they would. Once he had helped to nail Yau, Lewis wouldn't owe him any favours. He had to get the cop off his guard—by co-operating, playing it his way. He said, "I guess I don't have much choice."

"You guess right. Let's go and pay our friend a visit, then. And remember—you do or say anything to warn him, whether it's deliberate or accidental, anything at all, and you are right back where you started, stepping out of that lift." He jerked the gun, indicating that Quinn should move.

Quinn pushed himself off the wall and walked, with a conscious effort to keep steady, towards the elevator. Lewis kept two yards behind, ordering him to open the door and step in, then following quickly

155

and pressing himself into a rear corner, the automatic constantly trained on the American's middle.

Quinn pressed the button and they rode up in silence. On the twelfth floor they stepped out and turned down the long balcony towards Yau's apartment. Reaching the door, Lewis flattened himself against the wall beside it. He signalled to Quinn to press the bell.

Rubber sandals padded towards him and he felt himself scrutinized through the peephole. Yau spoke from behind the door, his voice muffled.

"What now?"

"I came back for more."

"So soon?"

"This guy I was getting it for—he's in a car just across the street. That stuff I got from you, he liked it so much he said did you have any more. I said I thought so. He told me to go get it. He gave me the bread."

"You show, please."

That had been a sudden inspiration of Quinn's. He pulled out the rest of Blow Job's roll and held it up to be inspected through the peephole. "Six hundred dollars," he said, conscious, without needing to glance sideways, of Lewis's tense face a few feet to his right, of the gun still pointing at him.

It was the money that clinched it. After a few seconds' hesitation Mr. Yau unlocked the door and undid the bolts. The door swung open. He plucked a key from the pocket of his pyjama top and turned it in the trellis lock. As he drew back the squeaky contraption Lewis shoved himself off the wall, very fast, and bobbed up in the doorway next to Quinn. The pistol was trained on Yau; for the first time, it pointed away from Quinn.

"Back up, sunshine," Lewis said. "Go on, move! Back inside, nice and slow."

Yau's face was a travesty of shock and anger. Emotion had stiffened the muscles into a sort of grin, a fierce baring of gold teeth as his gaze went from the gun muzzle to Quinn's face.

"I couldn't help it," Quinn said. "He got me on the way out."

"Shut up!" Lewis commanded. "Get inside with this creep."

The cop had to back out on the balcony to let Quinn squeeze past into the doorway. It was then that the big man seized his moment. He stepped in front of Lewis, as if about to go through the door, and lunged at the hand holding the gun. One big fist closed round the wrist and

156

smashed it against the door jamb. The pistol fell to the floor. Still gripping the wrist, Quinn swung the cop round to face him and drove a left into his guts. Lewis doubled over and went reeling back against the low balcony wall, making a retching noise. Yau began to gibber hysterically.

Lewis was a rugged little man and by no means finished. He straightened up and bounded off the wall, swinging a right at Quinn's head. The American parried automatically with his left before realizing, almost too late, that the move had been a feint. Lewis, small and nimble, had ducked to the left and flung himself full-length on the floor, scrabbling for the gun which still lay in the doorway. He had got his fingers on the butt before Quinn stamped on them, a crushing downward jab with the hard leather heel of his boot that made Lewis cry out sharply in pain. Quinn bent swiftly and scooped up the gun. He pointed it down at the cop, who lay on his side now, the fingers of his right hand tightly clenched in the other fist, his face white with pain as he stared up at the American.

Quinn glanced swiftly at Mr. Yau. He had stopped yammering but still stood there, rigid with disbelief; he hadn't even had the presence of mind to lock himself inside his apartment.

"Get up," Quinn said, aiming the gun at Lewis's head. "On your hands and knees."

Lewis obeyed, getting clumsily onto all fours, crouching like a baby. The fingers of his right hand were already swollen and discoloured. Quinn was trembling slightly in the aftermath of the struggle, but he was in command of himself.

"Crawl, motherfucker," he said. "Into the apartment."

The cop crept on his hands and knees through the doorway.

"All the way down," Quinn ordered, following him with the gun, and Lewis kept moving down the hallway towards the living room. Quinn stepped into the doorway, yanked the key from the trellis lock and put it back in from the outside. He pulled the trellis shut, locked it, and took out the key.

"You two can cool it together for a while," he said.

Lewis had quit crawling. He sat up, several yards down the hall, nursing his injured hand, facing Quinn. "You think you'll get away with this?" he said thickly.

"I'll take the chance."

"You'll make it harder on yourself."

"Then maybe I should make it easier by wasting you bastards right

157

now." That shut him up. "What are you complaining about, Lewis? You got your man, don't you? Search the apartment for your evidence; it should help you pass the time till someone comes to let you out. So long."

He stuck the gun in the waistband of his jeans and pulled the flap of his shirt out to conceal it. Without pausing again, he turned and walked to the elevator. Down in the lobby he hesitated for several seconds, peering about in the gloom. Lewis might have been lying about working alone; there could be a partner down here someplace. But there was no sign of anyone who might have been a cop, either inside the lobby or out on the sidewalk.

He walked the mile and a half back to Causeway Bay, not risking the possibility of being seen and remembered by a cabdriver or even a conductor on a crowded streetcar. He avoided the busy King's Road and chose a parallel route along the narrow, ill-lit streets close to the docks. In a trash can in Electric Road he disposed of Yau's key. He thought of getting rid of the gun the same way but decided not to. Now that he was really deep in the shit, he found its presence kind of comforting.

As he walked, he tried to calculate how the odds were stacked. He'd been busted walking out of a wholesaler's place with a quarter pound of heroin, okay, but he'd gotten away from it. That narc, Lewis, had a pretty good idea of his size and shape, but in the half-light of the lobby and the balcony up on the twelfth floor he hadn't got a really good look at his kisser. Also, Lewis had jumped to the conclusion that he was a sailor off one of the Fleet units in port, which would send him off on the wrong scent once he got out of his cage back there. The one thing he didn't have was an identity: he didn't know that the guy who had jumped him was Seymour Quinn, Gunner's Mate Third, presently resident in the apartment of Miss Chan Chuk-yan in Causeway Bay. And after tomorrow morning it couldn't matter whether they identified him or not.

The scene wasn't too heavy, then. All the same, he decided he'd better not tell Pritchard about it. Pritchard had enough problems. Besides, he had trouble too, figuring out how to explain to Blow Job.

"You expect me to believe this—this jive? Jesus, man, you are one crazy honky!"

"Stay cool, man," Quinn said. "What I'm saying is true."

They were in the bathroom, Quinn sitting wearily on the lid of the

158

john, Blow Job standing in front of him, gesticulating with long pink palms like a bad actor against a backdrop of plastic shower curtain. Outside, in the living room, Canny was still glued to the TV.

"It's true, Blow Job. What the fuck, you're lucky I didn't stay caught and lose the other six C's."

"Lucky?" Blow Job's eyes were wide and white, his voice was high with agitation. "Man, you walk outta here with a grand, you come back ninety minutes later shy four hundred—*my* four hundred—with nothing to show for it, and you tell me I'm *lucky?*"

"I got this to show for it." Quinn tapped his waistband, indicating the pistol that he had shown the black man earlier. It had turned out to be a Walther PPK, 7.65, fully loaded. "Where the fuck would I get a piece like this? That's my proof. I don't like it any more than you do. But I'll tell you what: for that four hundred I'll give you my I.O.U."

"What the fuck good is your I.O.U., man? I told you, we goin' back to the World; Tuesday morning."

"For Christ's sake stop yelling and listen." Quinn spoke evenly, keeping his voice low. "I'll be back in the World myself soon. I dunno, maybe three, four weeks' time. Don't say anything to Canny; she doesn't know. I'll be back there, and with a stake—bigger stake than I ever had before. I'll mail the money to you, maybe even bring it to you myself."

"How much skag the man give you for them four C's anyway?" Blow Job asked suspiciously.

"About two ounces," Seymour lied. "That was all he had. Listen, you're just gonna have to *trust* me, okay?"

PART TWO

22

Benjamin Chin was nearing the end of his two-year tour of duty in Hong Kong, and he couldn't say he was sorry to be going. He had nothing against the place in itself—for a bachelor of twenty-six it had a lot to recommend it—and his job, as an officer in the State Department Security Service responsible for guarding American diplomats abroad, had been more enjoyable here than in his previous posting in Ottawa. It was simply that Hong Kong heightened his cultural confusion.

Some well-meaning soul in Personnel, on examining his file and seeing that he was a full-blooded Chinese, had no doubt thought Hong Kong would be the perfect posting for him. This was far from so. Racially he was Chinese, but as a fourth-generation Californian he had as little in common with others of his race as a Harlem black might have with a tribal African. Language was the big problem. Wherever he went —in stores and restaurants, streetcars and taxicabs—he was addressed in Cantonese by people who were mystified at his failure to understand. After a while he had begun to feel as though there was a doppelgänger at large, some throwback to his own ancestry for whom he was always being mistaken.

So it would be a relief to get out. Within a couple of weeks he expected to hear from Horace Stanley, the consulate security chief, about his next posting. Two months after that he would be gone. Meanwhile his duties in Hong Kong followed their humdrum routine. His first job every day was to drive Vice-Consul Kiley to the office.

It was hot and still this morning, about as hot as it had been all summer, real tropical-storm weather. The Plymouth's air conditioning was on but even that didn't quite eliminate the humidity. The collar of his uniform shirt was damp and the gun that he wore—a five-shot Smith and Wesson Airweight .38 revolver in a leather shoulder holster —made an uncomfortable lump in his armpit.

Heavy Monday-morning traffic in the tunnel and up Chatham

Road had made him a minute or two late today. He swung into the driveway of the apartment block on Quarry Hill and stopped to show his ID card to the guard. The man waved him through. He parked under the canopy outside the front entrance of the building, picked up the handset of the VHF and briefly reported his arrival to the duty man in the security office. Leaving the engine idling, he reached down to press the lever beside the steering column that unlocked the doors. He got out and opened the heavy, armour-plated rear door just in time to turn and greet Kiley as he came tripping down the steps with his attaché case.

"Morning, Benjy."

"Morning, sir."

"Hot as hell again."

"Sure is."

Kiley slipped into the rear seat. Chin shut him in and went round to his own door. He climbed in, re-locked all the doors, engaged the automatic transmission and slid smoothly away. As he swung out onto Quarry Hill Road he spoke into the radio handset again.

"Pangolin. Okay, we're on our way."

"Roger," said the man at base.

Chin glanced in the driving mirror at the man seated behind him. As usual he had immediately opened, with his own key, the locked dispatch box that Chin brought out to him every morning and had begun to read the papers it contained. Chin had no idea what they were —overnight cables, perhaps, nothing very secret if they were allowed out of the Annex, but something that had to be waded through before Kiley began his day. Chin had guessed that Kiley was some kind of bigwig in the Annex. It wasn't his business to speculate on how big, but the fact was that out of the entire consular staff only he and the Consul General rated a chauffeur-bodyguard. Which had to mean that he was somebody a lot more important than his official rank of vice-consul suggested.

The car sped down through the twists and turns of Quarry Hill towards the Chatham Road junction. Chin thought about his next posting. London? Paris? He'd requested Europe, though Horace Stanley had mentioned the possibility of Latin America. Rio or B.A. would be okay, he guessed, cosmopolitan and lively, but what if he wound up somewhere like Guadeloupe? Anyplace out there, of course, in this job you really started earning your bread. More American diplomats got killed or kidnapped in Latin America than anywhere else, not to mention what had happened to a few incautious bodyguards. This job, by comparison, was a pushover.

While he daydreamed, another part of Chin's mind was constantly at work. His eyes moved ahead, left, right, into the rear-view mirror, and his brain analysed and stored what he saw. Behind the Plymouth was a black Mercedes that must have come out of a crossroad higher up the hill. Two occupants: through the tinted windshield they looked male and European, though he couldn't be sure. Businessmen on their way to the office, probably. Ahead was a familiar small vegetable truck: a farmer from the New Territories who hawked his provisions door to door.

Seymour Quinn, at the wheel of the Mercedes, kept it a safe distance behind the Plymouth. Pritchard sat beside him. Both of them wore gloves and light overalls over their street clothes. Two motorcycle crash helmets, similar to Fong's, with black plastic visors, lay on the back seat. Pritchard picked up the walkie-talkie transceiver. He pressed the transmitter button and said, "Unit One to Two."

"Two receiving," came Fong's voice after a moment, crackling with static.

"We're on target. About a minute behind schedule, just approaching Chatham Road."

"Roger."

"Unit Three, receiving?"

Baxter's voice was clearer than Fong's, carrying smoothly across the harbour from where he sat in the mail-van, in the temporary car park off Waterfront Road. "Receiving you, Number One. All's well this end."

"Pangolin," said Benjamin Chin. "We're in Chatham Road now."

"Roger."

"How's Mrs. Kiley, sir?" he asked the man in the back.

"Hm?" Kiley sounded slightly peeved at the interruption. "Oh, she's in Australia right now, visiting with her mother."

"So you're alone at home? Living on jelly sandwiches, I bet."

Kiley grunted. He had the Monday-morning grumps, Chin decided, resolving not to make any more jokes.

In Chatham Road, Quinn let the Mercedes drop behind and switched lanes. In the course of their dummy runs last week they'd learned that it was quite easy to tail a car down this long, straight road without sticking too close behind it.

Pritchard spoke on the walkie-talkie again. "One to Two. We're just approaching the Fat Kwong Street flyover. With you in about two minutes."

"Roger."

Baxter could not believe what his eyes told him. He fumbled for his transceiver and pressed the transmitter button. His voice came out in a strangled cry. "Alan!"

"No names, idiot!" Pritchard replied in a fierce whisper.

"There's a police car, stopping on Waterfront Road, right opposite me!"

Pritchard felt his entire body go rigid, as though the blood had suddenly solidified in his veins. It was perhaps three seconds before he could speak.

"What are they doing?"

"My God, they're getting out!"

"They're looking for stolen cars, probably. Sit tight."

"But the mail van—"

"It hasn't been reported stolen yet. Just sit tight."

"They're coming this way. I can't let them see me using this thing. Over and out."

Pritchard turned and looked wildly at Quinn. "We've got about three minutes before we hit the tunnel and lose radio contact."

"If the fuzz hasn't moved on by then we'll have to abort."

"Call it off? No. We're going through with it. There won't be another chance."

They stopped at a traffic light, two cars behind the Plymouth. Quinn said in a measured tone, "I ain't walking into a shootout with no cops, man."

"You'll do exactly what I tell you!" Pritchard said savagely. He made a grab at the door of the glove compartment, fumbling with the catch. Quinn dipped his right hand swiftly into the map pocket on his door and scooped something out.

"Don't do it, man."

Pritchard turned in disbelief. The American was holding a pistol across his chest, the muzzle pointed at Pritchard's head.

The light was still red. Pedestrians streamed across the road, be-

166

hind and in front of the car. "Where . . . where did you get that?"
Pritchard asked numbly.

"It's a long story. Let's just say it makes me feel better to have it.
Now you'll listen to me, mister. Unless Baxter radios that the cops have
moved off before we get to the tunnel, we're calling it off. Right now
you better call up Fong before we overshoot."

Pritchard watched him with hot malevolence in his eyes. Then the
light changed and Quinn eased the car forward, steering with one hand.
Pritchard grabbed the walkie-talkie.

"Unit Two, Unit Two. Roll it."

"Roger."

Fong must have heard the exchange with Baxter, but he sounded
as imperturbable as ever.

Benjamin Chin spotted the black motorcycle coming out of a side
street near the Cable and Wireless compound. It cut recklessly across
Chatham Road in front of the northbound traffic, and he had to brake
slightly as it forced its way into the southbound stream in front of him.
Goddam awful Chinese drivers, he thought, with no sense of irony.
There was never a cop in sight, either, when that sort of thing happened.

He glanced in his mirror, signalled, waited for a gap and then
switched lanes to the left, preparing to take the tunnel approach. The
motorcycle rider had done the same, but without showing any consider-
ation for other motorists. He looked like a typical cowboy, in a light,
one-piece racing suit, gauntlets and a black-visored helmet. He honked
his horn impatiently at a slow taxi in front of him as he swung onto
the flyover leading to the tunnel. Chin, twenty yards behind, checked
his mirror: a minibus behind, the taxi and the motorcycle up front. He
fished in his jacket pocket for money for the toll. The he lifted the radio
handset and said, "Pangolin. Going into the tunnel about one minute
from now."

Baxter sat very still in the cab of the mail van, pouring sweat,
watching the two Chinese policemen from the patrol car. Pritchard had
been right: they'd strolled, at an infuriating pace, around the strip of
waste ground between Waterfront Road and the construction site,
checking the cars parked there and comparing them with a duplicated
list they had with them. Half a minute ago they had gone back to their
car. Then, nothing. They hadn't moved. They might have been check-

ing that list again, or making a radio call. If they had stopped for a smoke break he'd had it; the whole bloody Project would have had it. Perhaps it was already too late: he glanced at his watch. Not quite, perhaps half a minute more. He still dared not use the transceiver, which he had shoved hastily under his seat.

The Mercedes was behind the minibus, as they went up the ramp, and neatly shielded by it from the rear-view mirror of the Plymouth. Where the road widened out, Pritchard and Quinn could see ahead to the queues at the toll booths. Kiley's car had gone, as usual, to the left-hand one; Fong's motorbike had headed for the one on the right but then slowed down to let the Mercedes catch up and overtake. That was bang-on, with everyone in the right position, but what the hell was going to happen?

"I figure we've lost out," Quinn said, as they stopped to join the queue. His pistol was still trained on Pritchard even though his eyes had been on the road ahead.

"All right, all right," Pritchard snapped. "You've made your point. Now put that bloody gun away, you can't go past the toll booth with it."

The American slid the Walther back into the map pocket. The cars edged forward, a few yards at a time. Pritchard saw the Plymouth pass the barrier and accelerate towards the mouth of the tunnel perhaps ten seconds before Quinn thrust his five dollars into the attendant's hand and let the Mercedes glide forward down the ramp. The tunnel gaped before them. There were only seconds to spare when Baxter's voice shrieked hysterically from the walkie-talkie in Pritchard's lap.

"Alan! They're going! It's all clear, they're go—"

The voice faded to a hum as they roared into the tunnel. Pritchard and Quinn exchanged an incredulous look.

"Get ready, man!" Quinn yelled, flattening his foot on the gas pedal. "We're back in business!"

The light in the tunnel was too dim to read by and Benjamin Chin noticed that Kiley, as usual, had started re-packing the papers in the dispatch box in preparation for their arrival at the Annex about five minutes from now. He never seemed to waste a minute; Chin envied him for not having to hang around, as he did himself, awaiting other people's orders.

He glanced in his mirror. A big Mercedes was creeping up to

168

overtake him in the fast lane on the right. Behind that was a motorcyclist—the same impatient one he'd seen earlier; must have fallen behind at the toll gates—and this time it was the Mercedes that wasn't moving fast enough for him. He was riding right on its tail, honking furiously. Chin shook his head; he sometimes thought people should be made to take a personality test before they were allowed to drive.

The Mercedes, moving not much faster than the Plymouth, was roughly alongside now. The Hong Kong exit was visible as a rectangle of bright light a couple of hundred yards ahead. Suddenly, over the dull roar of the tunnel he was aware of a new noise, the snarl of an engine close, dangerously close, on his right, and of a shape, a blur, moving in fast from the edge of his vision. With disbelief he realized that the crazy bastard was trying to cut between the two cars, was riding the white lines to force his way at speed through a gap that must have been four feet at the most.

His first, instinctive, reaction was to widen the gap, to pull the Plymouth to the left. But in the tenth of a second of conscious thought that accompanied it he knew that an accident was inevitable.

Quite what happened, Benjamin Chin never found out. The motorcyclist drew level with the front wheels of the two cars. Then either he lurched to the right or the driver of the Mercedes unwittingly drifted to the left. The result was that he bumped the rear end of the motorcycle lightly with his fender and the bike cannoned off the side of the Plymouth. It was only a glancing blow, with a faint crunch of metal, but it sent the bike out of control.

Chin stood on his brakes. Kiley was thrown forward in a welter of paper. The bike, still moving faster than the car, shot through the gap, wobbling crazily, then began to jackknife from side to side, tilting at wider and wider angles as it slowed like a figure skater reaching a finale, the rider fighting to control it. The tunnel was suddenly filled with the sound of squealing brakes and protesting tyres. The minibus behind the Plymouth slid forward several yards on locked wheels to slam gently into the back of the car. Chin felt his head whipped back and then forward by the impact, recovering in time to see the motorcycle slide through one complete circle and then, with its front brakes locked, upend itself like a bucking horse to tip its rider into the road. It left him sprawled on his side across the left lane; the bike spun one more time before it collapsed, blocking the right side of the carriageway. From behind came the continuing shriek of brakes, punctuated by honking horns and the crunching of metal and glass as cars that had been travelling too close ploughed into one another.

"Stupid Chinese son of a bitch!" Chin screamed, grabbing at the lever that unlocked the doors.

"Benjy, what the hell—?" Kiley had been knocked forward against the front seats and then back against the rear window; his reactions were seconds behind his bodyguard's. As Chin opened his door, scrambled out and began to run forward he shouted, "Benjy, no! . . ."

The rest was lost against the cacophany of horns and shouts and the thunder of traffic still pouring in from the Kowloon side. Chin ran towards the motorcyclist, lying where he had fallen twenty yards ahead of the Plymouth. He was conscious that the Mercedes had stopped too, aware of doors opening, but all his attention was on the prone form, his mood a mixture of anger and concern.

He reached the man and knelt beside him. He could see almost nothing of the face behind the dark visor, just the mouth below it, teeth bared in a grimace of pain. There was no visible injury, but the fall he'd taken had looked pretty severe.

"You all right? Where are you hurt?"

The man groaned and muttered in Cantonese. Chin felt a familiar sense of helplessness. He stood up and turned, seeking assistance, and what he saw made his skin prickle with horror.

Two men had jumped out of the Mercedes. They were both wearing overalls and crash helmets like the motorcyclist's. One was running to the Plymouth, and even as Chin watched he dived through the open door into the front seat. The other was coming towards him.

Kiley hadn't moved, hadn't had a chance to. It was less than ten seconds after the Plymouth had stopped that the helmeted man flung himself into the car, faceless like some alien being in a science-fiction movie. He leaned over the backrest of the front seat to thrust the muzzle of a huge revolver into Kiley's neck. With the other gloved hand he shoved something at him: a small gunnysack.

"Put that on. Over your head—quick!"

Training, instinct, the sudden awareness of the trap he'd been drawn into, combined to make Chin move very fast. He jerked his revolver from its holster, cocking it and dropping to one knee at the same time, drawing down on the man who ran towards him. As he squeezed the trigger, something hit him on the back of the head. The gun jerked up. The sound of the shot boomed off the walls; the bullet smacked harmlessly into the concrete roof of the tunnel as Chin sprawled face down on the road. He managed to land on his elbows and roll to the right. The motorcyclist, whose helmeted head had butted him, tried to dive on top of him and missed, hitting the tarmac hard on knees and elbows.

Chin had held onto his revolver. He rolled to his feet in a low squat, realizing that the running man was almost on top of him. Realizing, too late, that he had a gun as well.

Chin fired blindly, too quickly, knowing it even as he pulled the trigger, the lessons of his training momentarily lost in panic, in a swelling sense of failure.

The shot went wild. Seymour Quinn did not flinch. From a distance of eight feet he fired twice. The first bullet took Chin in the throat, knocking him back against the wall of the tunnel. The second hit him in the forehead just below the hairline, blowing a chunk out of the back of his head. Mouth slack, eyes wide with incredulity, he began to slide slowly down the wall, smearing it with blood that gleamed fiercely in the glare of the floodlights.

Screams were echoing off the walls, piercing through the drumming of engines. Two solid lines of vehicles stretched back along the tunnel for a hundred yards or more behind the Mercedes and the Plymouth. Some of their occupants had got out and stood in a small knot; they scattered as Quinn and Fong ran back towards them.

"*Di, di, di!*" Quinn yelled after them, waving his gun. "Fuck off, rubbernecks!"

They tumbled into the Plymouth, Fong in the driving seat, Quinn in the rear next to Kiley. The driver had left the engine running and they were moving even before the doors were closed, pulling away with a shriek of tyres towards the rectangle of daylight. Pritchard turned the black blankness of his visor to Quinn. Despair was in his voice. "What have you done?"

"It was him or me, man."

"But you've killed him. You bloody maniac, you didn't have to *kill* him!"

Kiley, sitting rigid in his corner, the gunnysack covering his head and Pritchard's Webley still digging into his throat, spoke for the first time. There was a slight quake in his voice.

"Have you killed my driver?"

"You shut up," Quinn snapped. He had put down his gun and was shaking the hypodermic syringe, already loaded, out of its protective wrapping.

171

"Answer me. I heard shooting. Did you kill my driver?"

"I said shut the fuck up!" Quinn shouted. "And keep still." He grabbed Kiley's left wrist, held the arm rigid and jabbed the needle brutally into his triceps, right through the thin material of his jacket and shirt, making him yelp with pain. At that moment, their speed up to seventy, they burst into daylight at the Hong Kong end of the tunnel.

A Tunnel Patrol Land Rover was already nosing cautiously down the ramp, its orange emergency lamp flashing. Further on, two uniformed patrolmen ran out into the road, trying to wave the Plymouth to a stop. Fong drove straight at them and they leapt aside.

"There wasn't supposed to be any shooting," Pritchard said, his voice pitched high with tension.

"And there ain't supposed to be any talking," Quinn said, "not until this motherfucker is asleep. How we doing for time?"

"One minute and twenty seconds," Pritchard said, consulting the stopwatch he had set going as they leapt from the Mercedes. "We're right on schedule."

They were touching ninety by the time Fong swung the car left onto the Waterfront Road filter. Quinn squeezed the last of the Pentothal into Kiley's arm. Almost as soon as he had withdrawn the needle, the victim slumped back on his seat. Quinn pulled the sack off his head and studied his face to be sure he wasn't shamming.

One minute and fifty seconds after the crash, the Plymouth slithered to a halt on the waste ground beside Waterfront Road, where Baxter was waiting in the mail van. The engine was running and the double doors at the rear were open. It took them fifteen seconds to drag Kiley's body out of the car and dump it on the cargo deck of the Transit, and another ten to check over the Plymouth, making sure they were leaving nothing behind. Walkie-talkies, the hypodermic, even the gunnysack went into the mail van. They couldn't eradicate all the clues, but the fewer they left behind the better. Fong, Quinn and Pritchard scrambled in after the victim, closing the doors behind them as the van bumped over the broken kerbstones onto Waterfront Road.

The four Chinese patrolmen in the Land Rover were the first official arrivals on the scene. Their television monitors had shown this to be no ordinary accident, but the full scope of it eluded them even for the first couple of minutes they were down there—particularly since

172

they had over a hundred near-hysterical people as well as a monumental traffic problem to deal with.

The electronic cameras had been designed and positioned for traffic control, not to show fine detail on a human scale; the picture they had shown, therefore, had been somewhat confusing. A motorcyclist had taken a spill and fallen in such a way as to block both traffic lanes. People had got out of the two leading cars in the line and run to his assistance. For some reason a scuffle had followed, and at least one of the men had threatened another with a gun; the cameras did not transmit sound, so the shots had not been heard. Finally, one of the leading cars had driven off very fast.

The patrol leader wasted no time speculating. There would be plenty of opportunity later to work out what had happened. He sent one of his men to examine the man lying against the left-hand wall and told the other two to move down the lines of cars, to assess injuries and damage and calm the people down. From what he had seen already, though, he knew what would have to be done.

He ran to the nearest emergency telephone and was connected instantly to the control centre at Hung Hom.

"We will need the heavy towing equipment," he said. "There is no hope of getting it through on this side. The other tunnel will have to be closed. Did your monitor pick up the car that drove away? Better notify RHKP at once. . . . Hold on." He covered the mouthpiece with his hand and listened to what his breathless subordinate had run up to tell him. Then he spoke into the phone again.

"Better tell the police something else, too. Somebody's been shot. Yes, dead."

"You killed the bodyguard?" Baxter wailed. "Oh, my God!" Involuntarily he turned his head and the Transit lurched across the road. He corrected hastily.

"Yeah, yeah, you heard right," Quinn said irritably, from the rear of the mail van, undoing the chinstrap of his crash helmet and pulling it off. "I had no choice."

"It should never have happened," Pritchard said. It had taken only a minute's breathing space for the recriminations to break out anew. "It didn't need to happen. You were supposed to get there in time to overpower and disarm him."

"Yeah, well, I didn't. He was faster than we expected, any of us." Quinn unbuttoned his overalls and shrugged himself out of them.

"What would you have done, wise-ass, if some guy was drawing down on you and you had a gun in your hand? Baxter, for Christ's sake can't you drive any faster?"

"Not can't, won't."

"If they close the tunnel on us we're in Shit City, man."

"If we get stopped for speeding it'll be even worse."

From the pickup point Baxter had driven them half a mile east on Waterfront Road; there, at the corner of Victoria Park, he had gone up and over on the cloverleaf junction to reverse their direction. The traffic was heavy and fast, the hotels and apartment blocks of the Causeway Bay waterfront blurring by on the left, junks and sampans moored on the bright blue water to the right.

"Three and a half minutes," Pritchard said, intent on the stop-watch. "You've got thirty seconds to get us into the tunnel."

Baxter took the left-hand filter into the Causeway Bay interchange at sixty. A few seconds later the mail van was up on the flyover that arced over the waterfront and spiralled down to the tunnel entrance.

"How is he?" Baxter asked anxiously.

"Seems okay," Fong called from the back of the van, where he crouched beside Kiley. The American lay on his back. His breathing was shallow and harsh and his skin had turned pale, but these were natural reactions to the anaesthetic, as Pritchard had warned. Pritchard had researched the subject in medical books. The main danger was that he might vomit and choke, but he showed no signs of doing so.

"Right, everybody lie down," Pritchard said, and the three of them in the rear flattened themselves across the deck behind the driver's seat, beside the unconscious Kiley, where they could not be seen. From somewhere a police siren began to bray.

There was a direct red-telephone link from the Hung Hom tunnel control room to Hong Kong Island District Control of the Royal Hong Kong Police. The policewoman who fielded the Hung Hom call was, coincidentally, the same one who had taken one a minute before from the security officer at the American Consulate General. After entering it in the message book, timed at 0821, she buzzed the control-room superintendent on the intercom.

"There's been an accident in the Cross-Harbour Tunnel, sir. They're closing it off in both directions."

"Have they put the alarm through to Traffic?"

"Yes, sir. But they called us to say there's also been some kind of shooting down there. One fatality."

"You can blow that up to CID. It's all happening in the tunnel today, obviously. I take it you've got someone on the way?"

"But for a different reason. The American consulate say one of their diplomats who's in radio contact with them drove into the tunnel a few minutes ago and hasn't come out."

"I expect he's involved in the accident. Christ, what a way to start Monday!"

Baxter's heart sank as they approached the mouth of the tunnel.

"They're switching the lights to red. I think we're too late!"

A patrol car was already drawn across the left lane of the northbound carriageway, blocking it off, and the bank of lights above it was red. The lights on the right were still green, but even as the Transit came down the ramp a uniformed man stepped into the opening, obviously preparing to wave away oncoming traffic.

"They've let the last car through!"

"I *said* you were driving too fucking slowly," Quinn muttered savagely from his prone position in the rear.

"What am I going to *do?*" Baxter moaned, his voice near to panic.

"Crash through," said Quinn.

"Don't be mad. Talk your way past," Pritchard called urgently.

But neither expedient proved necessary. Any other vehicle would have been turned away. The patrolman glanced at the Royal Mail livery of the van, stepped aside and waved it into the tunnel. The lights turned red at the moment it passed them.

Pritchard heaved a gigantic sigh of relief. He sat up and mopped the sweat off his face with the arm of his discarded overalls. The others sat up as well, backs against the sides of the van, breathing deeply and more easily.

"That's the trickiest bit over," Pritchard said, "but it doesn't mean we can relax. From this moment on we are the most wanted men in Hong Kong, and they'll be setting up a manhunt second to none. One slip-up on our part and it could all be over. Thanks to you, Quinn, we will be wanted for murder as well as kidnapping."

His tone was hard. The huge revolver was in his hand, resting lightly in his lap. Quinn looked uncomfortable.

"You gonna spend the rest of the day talking about that?"

"If I have to."

"Look, you saw what happened—some of it, anyway. If I hadn'ta shot the guy he'd have shot me. And then Fong. And where would you have been then, Genius?"

"Where did you get that gun, Quinn?"

"Off a cop."

"You *what?*"

Quinn shrugged, as if to trivialize what he had to say. "Narcotics dick. Prick got hold of me last night, in an apartment block over to North Point. I got his piece off him and locked him in an apartment. Don't worry, he doesn't even know who I am. Thinks I'm off a ship in harbour."

"Christ, give me strength," Pritchard said, through teeth tightly clenched. "What were you doing in North Point to get nicked by a narcotics cop the night before the Project got under way?"

"I was buying a little smack. Trying to do a friend a favour. Okay, it was stupid, but shitting me out won't change anything."

"Why in God's name didn't you tell me this had happened?"

"Because you'da gone bananas. You're going bananas now."

"You think they're not going to be able to trace that gun, Quinn? To work out that the guy who stole it and the guy who shot the bodyguard are one and the same?"

"That's as far as they can take it, believe me. The guy doesn't know me from a hole in his sock."

"I hope you're right," Pritchard said evenly. "Because if they get onto us because of you, Quinn, it's you who'll have to answer to the rest of us."

23

By eight forty-five the southbound carriageway of the tunnel was swarming with police from a dozen different branches.

Communications and Transport had provided a command vehicle, mounted on a bus chassis and equipped with radio-telephones to serve as a temporary headquarters. It was parked on the ramp beside the exit portal, next to the Tunnel Company's emergency trucks, which had been rushed over from the Kowloon side only to be forced by the police to wait before they towed out the damaged vehicles.

Land Rovers from the Police Tactical Unit, which had happened to be in the Causeway Bay area at the time of the accident and had responded to an emergency call on the radio, had ferried the injured to hospital. There were eight casualties of various pile-ups, mostly the victims of neck whiplash and bumps sustained through banging foreheads into steering wheels or dashboards.

In the tunnel itself, a team of Chinese CID men were conducting brief interviews with the uninjured occupants of the trapped cars. Those who had seen or heard anything that might be useful in determining exactly what had happened were escorted out to the command vehicle to have their statements taken.

Two photographers were taking shots of the scene from every angle. Two scene-of-crime teams from the Identification Bureau, a total of six men, were engaged in a variety of jobs: taking blood scrapings from the wall, searching for footprints in the oil patches on the road, lifting fingerprints from the motorcycle and the Mercedes. One was giving the inside of the car a thorough vacuum cleaning. The two cartridge cases which had been found on the road had been bagged and labelled and rushed to Ballistics.

At ten to nine, the superintendent from Hong Kong Island District Control escorted Horace Stanley, the security officer from the American Consulate General, into the tunnel. Stanley informally identified the dead Chinese-American as Benjamin Chin, a bodyguard who had worked for the State Department Security Service. It was only then that Stanley proved willing to divulge the name of the diplomat Chin had been protecting, and who was now, all too obviously, missing.

The car park at Kai Tak Airport was three quarters empty at this time of day. Baxter had no difficulty in finding a bay for the mail van right opposite the one where his own Range Rover had been parked since seven that morning. He got out of the van, went to the Range Rover, unlocked the rear door, and took out one of the two cylindrical canvas sail bags in which the batwing sails of the *Lady Belinda* were normally stowed. It was seven feet long and two feet in section, and it fastened up the side by means of a cord passing through double rows of brass eyes. The other bag contained a sail and was already done up.

He passed it through the front door of the Transit to Pritchard in the rear, who spread it out flat on the cargo deck. He and Quinn rolled the limp form of Kiley onto it, squaring him up till he lay on his back in the middle of the rectangle. He moaned gently but lay still, mouth

177

slightly open, breathing stertorously. Pritchard began rapidly to reeve the rope through the eyes, turning the bag into a sausage-shaped bundle that would close at both ends.

"He going to be all right?" Fong asked anxiously. "Will he get enough air?"

"If we bundle him up loosely. He'll start coming round from his first shot about half an hour from now. Then we give him a second one."

When Kiley was securely wrapped up, they slid him to the rear of the mail van and opened the double doors. Quinn got out and picked up the bundle, grunting as he humped it over one shoulder in a fireman's lift. He carried it to the open door of the Range Rover, lowered it in among the other sailing gear and slammed the door shut.

They all climbed out of the Transit. They took their overalls, helmets, guns and walkie-talkies. The only things they discarded were their gloves, throwing them into the van before Pritchard nudged the doors closed with his shoulder.

Then Quinn and Fong left the other two, going out separately through the airport terminal and walking several blocks in opposite directions before hailing a taxi each to take them to Hebe Haven.

Pritchard and Baxter drove out of the car park. The *shroff* barely glanced up when Baxter paid him. As the Range Rover nosed through the traffic up Prince Edward Road, towards the New Territories, Pritchard tore up the ticket from the machine at the entry boom that showed the arrival time of the mail van and scattered the pieces along the road.

By this time the superintendent in charge of Traffic Control had arrived at the temporary HQ, agitating to re-open the southbound section of the tunnel. He had a good case. Apart from the fact that there was a one-mile tailback of vehicles on the Kowloon side, Traffic were the only people, so far, to have made any progress in the investigation. Their computer had revealed the number plates on the Honda motorcycle to be false; the engine number showed it to have been stolen the previous day in Victoria Park. The Mercedes had not been reported stolen but had been left, around noon on Sunday, in a private car park.

Also, within the last three minutes, a traffic cop on a motorcycle had found the consular Plymouth abandoned on a piece of waste ground beside Waterfront Road, less than a quarter mile from the Hong Kong exit of the tunnel.

———

178

It was only when this news reached the head of Hong Kong Island CID, Chief Superintendent Gordon Boyd, at four minutes past nine, that he knew for certain he had a diplomatic kidnapping, in addition to a murder, on his hands.

Boyd was a dark, square-jawed New Zealander, approaching fifty, whose talents would have qualified him for higher rank before now if it were not for an outspoken and uncompromising manner. His bluntness worried his superiors; he lacked the flexibility of mind that was required in the topmost echelon of a police force, they said. But everyone, from the Commissioner down, would readily agree that he was one of the finest investigating officers they had ever had. It was he who would be in charge of the case.

From his office on the eighth floor of the police headquarters building in Wanchai, Boyd put through a direct internal call to his immediate superior, the Director of Criminal Investigation. He had already alerted the Director of the potential seriousness of the incident, and now he sketched in the latest available details.

The Director passed this information to the Commissioner of Police. Within five minutes the Governor of Hong Kong, Sir William Wilkie, G.B.E., K.C.V.O., was taking a call from the Commissioner in the privacy of his study at Government House.

Wilkie, a shrewd, dryly humorous Scot, had been Governor for the past five years and had handled the job—the crowning achievement of a long career in the British Colonial Service—with tact and flair. One of his gifts was the ability to think like a politician as well as a civil servant, and it was his political instinct, as he listened to what the Commissioner said, that gave him an understanding of the scope of the crisis. Crisis was the right word; it was quite different from anything he had had to handle before.

When the Commissioner, Basil Young, had finished his explanation of what had happened, Wilkie said, "Does the Consul General know?"

"Not officially, sir. We've been dealing with their security people, of course, but I thought the formal word was best left to you."

"Quite right, Young. I'll be on to them at once. Is it too soon to ask whether you have any theories about who may be responsible?"

"We can only speculate. The first thought is that the motive must be political. I've got Special Branch working on that angle—oh, and by the way, they've informed me of a complication. They think this man Kiley is no simple diplomat but someone fairly big in the CIA. Only

179

we're not supposed to know that, and the Americans will want to keep it quiet."

"Yes, that does rather complicate things," Wilkie said thoughtfully. "What action are you taking on the ground?"

"Roadblocks and vehicle searches on all major roads, initially, and a special watch on airport and dock departures. I'm throwing in as many men as we can possibly spare, but you'll appreciate, sir, that they can't all be mobilized at once. For the moment we're concentrating on the Island side. And, of course, the whole incident was recorded on videotape; that may give us some valuable leads."

"You realize the Americans are going to want a say in the way this thing is handled?"

"Well, he's their man, of course," Young said defensively. "But we're the only people capable of finding him."

"It may not be quite that simple." The Governor chose his words carefully. Young was a good policeman, but like most policemen he was jealous of his own authority; for that reason he would find it difficult to appreciate the pressures that Wilkie knew were inevitable. "Tell me, are you quite confident that you can handle this without outside help? I'm not thinking of the Americans, but from the UK: Scotland Yard, military intelligence?"

"They wouldn't know where to begin," the Commissioner said decisively. "We've got the men and the resources, and we know our own territory. If we can't do it, nobody can."

"Good. I think I can persuade the army to lend you some men, if you need them. In the meantime I'll be speaking to the Under-Secretary in London. If they can hold off the State Department from that direction, I don't think we need worry too much about pressure at this end. Depending on who claims responsibility for this business, though, there may be some inclination to play along with them."

"You mean submit to a ransom demand?" Young asked stonily.

"Something like that, perhaps."

"There's never been a crime like this here before, sir. It's very important to ensure that it doesn't work the first time."

"I know what you mean, Young. Well, what we've got to do now is inspire confidence in the Americans. And that means taking them into our confidence. I suggest a meeting later this morning between you, me and the American Consul General. All the available information can be pooled. I'll ask him to bring along the appropriate advisers.

180

Perhaps you'd bring a few people as well: heads of departments directly involved, perhaps, three or four at the most. I want to reassure the Americans. And impress them, of course."

When Wilkie had put down the phone he buzzed his personal secretary in her office in the executive wing of the building.

"Sophie, please get me the United States Consul General, then—"

"Actually, he's already called you, Your Excellency. His office is waiting for you on my line."

"Fine. While I'm talking to him, try and raise the Under-Secretary of State for the Colonies."

"In London, sir?" Wilkie sensed an eyebrow being raised. "It's after one in the morning over there."

"I know that, Sophie."

In the few seconds while he waited for the Consul General to be put through, the Governor thought about his situation. He did not, oddly enough, feel unfamiliar in it. He had often considered the possibility of something like this happening in his territory, and wondered what his responses would be. He had rehearsed his performance, in a sense, and thought out some of the moves.

The phone crackled in his ear. "Your Excellency?"

"Ah, Mr. Kirschmann. Good morning. First let me say how shocked and dismayed I am at this deplorable incident. . . ."

They encountered only one roadblock on the way to Hebe Haven, and they were prepared for it. Halfway out along Clear Water Bay Road, a pair of overworked young police constables were desperately trying to cope with an ever-lengthening queue of cars. Baxter and Pritchard had to wait nearly ten minutes for their turn to be searched.

"Open your rear door, please."

"What's this all about?" Pritchard asked curiously, hopping out of the car to join Baxter. "You're holding up our sailing."

"A man has been kidnapped."

"Is *that* so?"

Baxter opened the door to the cargo deck. The policeman looked dubiously at the two sausage-shaped bundles of canvas lying among lengths of rope, life jackets, and old boating shoes. "What are those?"

"Sails," Baxter said. "We're taking them out to my junk, at Hebe Haven. Want to see?"

The cop nodded. It took Baxter nearly two minutes to undo the cord on the first sail bag and open it out to show the folds of stiff red canvas.

"Do I *have* to open the other one? They're a devil of a job to do up again."

The policeman glanced despairingly at the line of cars, then at the two men. They were so obviously what they claimed to be, a pair of Europeans off on a sailing jaunt, that he could not help thinking he would be wasting his time.

"Carry on," he said, and moved to the next car.

Twenty minutes later the four of them had reassembled on the jetty at Hebe Haven. They had also met up with Osman Khan, who had parked his hired car on the track that led off the road through Pak Sha Wan and, with his road map and his camera, looked the part of a solitary sightseer taking in the view. The bay was deserted, with Ah Leung off on his weekly opium binge, and as peaceful as one of those willow-framed scenes on an old Chinese scroll, with junks riding at their moorings on water flat as glass.

They unloaded the prone form of Kiley, still in the sail bag, and laid him across the centre thwarts of the boatboy's sampan. The rest of them crowded into the small boat and Fong propelled them, energetically waggling the oar fixed to the stern, out to the *Lady Belinda*.

They tied the sampan to the stern of the junk so that it would run behind them; that would save time launching the rubber dinghy. Then they pulled the sampan alongside, and Baxter scrambled aboard and lowered the aluminium ladder. Fong, Pritchard and Osman Khan followed him. Quinn got the limp canvas package with some difficulty over his shoulder in the rocking little boat and heaved the top end up to the level of the junk's rail. Pritchard, Fong and Baxter got a grip on the criss-crossed cord and heaved the dead weight inboard, dropping it on the deck until Quinn could clamber up the ladder and help them lug it across to the companionway that led down to the saloon.

"Everybody out of sight now except Baxter and me," Pritchard said. "There are supposed to be only two of us on board."

Leaving the others to take Kiley below deck, Pritchard went to the cockpit and started the engines. Baxter had already gone forward to release the junk from its moorings.

At exactly ten o'clock, the *Lady Belinda* moved gracefully out through the lines of other boats and into the channel towards open water.

24

Once every four weeks Gavin McNair, a chief inspector in the Special Branch, had a long weekend off. It was strictly an unofficial long weekend. He had managed to arrange his shift pattern so as to take the Friday off regularly in return for a day's work the previous weekend, and to begin his one week in four of night duty the following Monday. This meant he was free from late on Thursday afternoon until ten on Monday night. Strictly speaking, the officers' duty roster should not have favoured him in this way, but McNair regarded it as one of the perks of seniority. If you couldn't work a small point like that after twelve years' service, you'd be a pretty poor policeman, after all.

As often as they could he and his wife, Siu, would go away somewhere over these weekends: by hydrofoil to Macau for Portuguese food and some modest gambling or—when they could afford it—by plane to Baguio in the cool mountains of the northern Philippines. They both believed that the best way to enjoy life in Hong Kong was to get away from it occasionally.

This weekend, though, they had stayed at home; one of McNair's fellow-officers had got married on the Saturday and they had attended the wedding. On Sunday they had considered going out somewhere, had thought about the heat and the jammed roads and the horribly overcrowded beaches and had finally just stayed indoors, reading the papers and listening to music. Their flat, on the twelfth floor of a tower block in Mid-Levels on the Island, was small—McNair had lived in it as a bachelor until they'd got married two years ago—but comfortable enough and blessed with good air conditioning.

This morning, Monday, they planned to drive to Fanling. McNair would play eighteen holes of golf while Siu went riding from the stables adjoining the Royal Hong Kong Golf Club. Afterwards they would meet for a late lunch, and possibly a swim in the club pool.

They had actually closed the door of the flat behind them when the telephone rang.

"Hell," McNair said.

"Let it ring," Siu said quickly. But that was a thing he found difficult to do. For a few moments he stood undecided, listening to the repeated double ring, half hoping it would stop of its own accord. Then he swung the golf bag resignedly off his shoulder, unlocked the door and stepped over to the telephone.

"Mac? John Nightingale. I'd almost given you up."

"I was on my way out," McNair said uneasily. Nightingale was the day desk officer at branch headquarters. "What is it, John?"

"A flap, I'm afraid. The boss wants you."

"Has the boss looked at the roster? I'm on nights this week."

"This is an emergency, Mac."

"Isn't there anyone else?"

"He'll accept no substitutes, like the ad says. You're not the only one who's been called in, if that's any comfort."

"Just what is the flap, John?"

"Who tells me anything? This isn't our baby, we're just helping CID out. But the word is that some Yankee diplomat's been abducted, his bodyguard shot. Now, can you meet the boss at ten thirty? Not here, at Government House. Chance to polish your marble, if nothing else. The Commissioner and the Governor himself will be there for a confab. They'll be expecting you. Sorry to drop you in it."

He put down the phone, the immediate vexation he had felt at the prospect of his leisure being spoilt giving way to that gut-sinking sensation of excitement that came from being assigned to a big case. But he tried to disguise the feeling as he turned to face Siu in the doorway.

"It's the office," he said. "I'm afraid they want me."

"I gathered." She gave him the set, expressionless Chinese look that denoted anger. "I told you to let it ring. If we had left a minute earlier—"

"But we didn't, darling. This is something big. You know they wouldn't break into my weekend if it wasn't." He fished for his car keys and held them out to her. "I'll take a taxi," he said. "You go to Fanling and ride."

"It would be no fun going on my own."

"Hell, you'd have been on your own while I played golf! Look, go on out there. It could be I'll only be needed for an hour; perhaps we can still meet for lunch after all."

"The last time you were called out I didn't see you for two days, Gavin. Go on, you'd better go. I'll call the stables and cancel my horse."

"Have it your way." He pecked her on the cheek; she was stiff, unresponsive. "I don't like to think of you cooping yourself up here just because I can't be with you, that's all. I'll phone later, let you know how I'm placed."

He left the flat and walked to the lifts, angry with himself and with her, torn between guilt and exasperation. Guilt, because he enjoyed his work too much to mind upsetting their domestic arrangements, annoyance because when she was unhappy she managed silently to make him feel responsible for it. Damn. There were times when he wondered if he'd made a mistake getting married—not because he didn't love Siu, hell, no, he couldn't imagine being without her now—but because cops ought perhaps to resign themselves to not marrying at all. Compromise between the demands of the job and a reasonable home life was rarely possible, and he and Siu made the best of it, nothing more.

Both feelings, the guilt and the resentment, diminished as he rode downstairs to the basement and went to his car, a three-year-old Lancia 2000. It wasn't as if he and Siu didn't have a lot going for them, after all, not least the victory over double-edged prejudice that their marriage represented. There was beautiful irony in the fact that his family— respectable Dumfriesshire shopkeepers—had been as quietly aghast over his marrying a Chinese as Siu's father—a wealthy textile merchant from Shanghai who had decamped to Hong Kong with two trunkfuls of gold bars, one jump ahead of the Communists, in 1948—had been scandalized at his daughter's choice of an impecunious European for a husband. A policeman at that, who had shown no interest in the offer —redeeming for McNair, as it would be face-saving for his father-in-law—to join the family business. The powerful tentacles of the Chinese family had for once failed to clutch an outsider in their embrace. Relations with his in-laws these days were restricted to a ritual fortnightly Sunday supper and polite exchange of pleasantries at the mansion on the Peak.

He reached Government House in less than ten minutes. The classical white mansion that had once dominated the settlement below was now overlooked by thirty-storey apartment blocks, but it had retained some elegance even from the rear, where the tall iron palings were camouflaged by tropical shrubbery and the open gateway was guarded by Gurkhas with knife-edge trouser creases and gleaming bayonets. This morning there were also a couple of uniformed European traffic officers on duty. McNair swung into the approach to the gates, pulled out his warrant card and showed it to one of them. The man recognized his face.

"I'm expected at the feast," he said.

"Okay, pull in wherever you can."

The car park, built to accommodate a fleet of limousines for receptions and balls, had room to spare for his Lancia. As he got out and walked to the main entrance he noticed the American Consul General's Cadillac and a couple of other cars with CD plates as well as the Police Commissioner's Humber and the personal, permanently filthy Volvo Estate that belonged to his immediate superior, Chief Superintendent Arthur Leggo.

He went up the steps, across the porticoed veranda and through the door. The big lobby was empty except for one of the Governor's military aides in a white tunic and a couple of Chinese servants who blended into the oak-panelled background.

"Your name, sir?" said the lieutenant, stepping forward.

"McNair, Special Branch."

The soldier pulled a clipboard from under one arm and inspected a sheet of paper attached to it. "Come this way, please."

He led McNair to a door that opened directly off the lobby, rapped on it twice and opened it. He showed the policeman into a long room dominated by a single huge table of polished mahogany: a table built to accommodate perhaps twenty dinner guests, so that the seven men who sat clustered at the far end of it looked oddly insignificant. The table was bare but for a jug of iced water and drinking glasses; there were portraits of former governors in gilt frames on the walls. McNair felt slightly ill at ease as the lieutenant closed the door and left him to plod across a thick-piled carpet towards the group at the table.

From one side of it, Chief Superintendent Leggo stood up. "Hello, Mac," he said, waving him to the chair beside his own. "I think this completes the party."

McNair made gratefully for the proffered seat and stood behind it. Leggo said to the others, "I'd like to introduce Chief Inspector McNair. Mac, we're not wasting time with handshakes, so I'll just quickly introduce everyone. His Excellency, of course"—the Governor smiled and nodded at him absently from the head of the table—"and the Commissioner, and of course Chief Superintendent Boyd of CID. The American Consul General, Mr. Kirschmann; Vice-Consul Koch; and Mr. Stanley, their chief of security." Leggo waved towards the three Americans who sat in a close group at one side of the table, as though they were a threatened minority. The Consul General looked grey and harassed; the two who flanked him were both crew-cut and sharp-eyed and darted appraising looks at the newcomer.

"Do sit down, Chief Inspector," said the Governor, indicating the

186

chair behind which McNair still hovered. "Mr. Young was about to give us an up-to-date summary of the incident which has led to this meeting."

McNair sat down. The Commissioner of Police cleared his throat. He crossed his arms on the edge of the table and began speaking, without notes, the facts all committed to memory. "Your Excellency, gentlemen, just to sum up what some of you know already and some of you don't, the facts we have so far are these. At eight seventeen this morning, a car carrying a diplomat attached to the American Consulate General was stopped by a carefully contrived accident in the southbound carriageway of the Cross-Harbour Tunnel. The diplomat, Mr. Roderick Neill Kiley, was abducted and his chauffeur-bodyguard was shot and killed. . . ."

It took the Commissioner two succinct minutes to depict the crime in general outline. He told them the police had not yet issued a statement on it, but reporters were besieging the press office at headquarters and wild rumours had begun flying about. He thought it would be advisable to make a full official announcement immediately after the meeting. The Consul General had confirmed that the victims' next-of-kin had been notified: the driver's parents in San Francisco and Mrs. Kiley, who was on a visit to Australia and was making arrangements to fly back at once.

Finally, the Commissioner said that he would personally supervise the overall operation that was being mounted to capture the kidnappers and free their victim. Immediate follow-up work on the crime, however, was in the hands of Mr. Boyd, who would sum up for them the lines of inquiry that were being pursued.

Gordon Boyd was in an unco-operative frame of mind. He hadn't wanted to attend this meeting, regarding it as an unnecessary distraction and an unforgivable waste of time. At the insistence of the Commissioner, however, he had reluctantly left his desk in the new Incident Centre they were setting up for him at headquarters, swearing to his deputy that he would be back inside half an hour.

He told the meeting what was being done in operational terms: roadblocks had been set up on all main roads, and a search of premises and systematic questioning of people was being conducted within a steadily increasing radius of the scene of the crime. Meanwhile, full priority had been given to forensic examination of all clues and traces found on the scene. Until there were some positive results from these tests and inquiries it would be impossible, he said bluntly, to state what progress, if any, the investigation had made.

The Consul General had been growing impatient. He said, "Just how long is it going to take you to form some idea who the kidnappers are and what they want, Mr. Boyd?"

"That may very well depend on how soon they choose to communicate with us—or with you. This shows all the hallmarks of a well-planned operation, carried out probably with a political motive. That means we must expect a ransom demand of some kind fairly soon. All we can do in the meantime is go through normal investigation procedures. We're doing that as rapidly as possible, but it still doesn't mean we'll be able to identify the kidnappers before they choose to identify themselves."

"If you think there's a political motive," the Consul General said, "then surely you can hazard a guess as to who might be responsible?"

"I'm a policeman, sir. I don't deal in guesswork, I'm interested in evi—"

"All right, Gordon, thank you," the Commissioner interrupted smoothly. They could do without putting the Americans' backs up this early. "Guesswork isn't usually a very reliable method to use in police work, gentlemen, but there's one of our departments that does deal in a certain amount of it. That's why I've asked Arthur Leggo along. Politics is Special Branch's baby, so if anyone is qualified to guess it's him. Arthur?"

"Yes, sir." McNair's chief was a tall, gangling man with a schoolmaster's air. He peered over his spectacles at the Americans opposite him. McNair had been studying them too. The Consul General looked like a small-town Rotarian, a conventional, middle-rung career diplomat, probably out of his depth in this situation and blustering to hide his helplessness. No doubt someone more senior would be flying in to handle their end of the crisis. Stanley, the security man, was thick-set and heavy-jowled, in his mid-fifties —pensioned off, at a guess, by the FBI or a big-city police department before being hired by State, and probably as worried about his own future as about Kiley's. Then there was Koch, his role undefined, his feelings masked. A slight, academic-looking man with rimless glasses and short black hair peppered with grey, he was dressed in Ivy League style—button-down collar and striped tie, on the narrow side, and a lightweight blazer with patch pockets. He watched the speakers intently, each in turn.

"Well," Leggo said, "for a long time it has been British Government policy not to encourage political activity of any kind here. Hong Kong survives partly by being politically neuter, by giving offence to no one, and a good part of our job in Special Branch is to maintain that position. Not an easy job, when you consider that forty per cent of our population can be classed as immigrants or refugees—not just from mainland China but from Macau and Taiwan and in recent years from Korea, Vietnam, Indonesia and the Philippines. Among these people there have inevitably been political activists. We've admitted them on condition they cease to be activists, but of course sometimes that condition hasn't been kept. You've all read about the occasional bomb going off in a Communist newspaper office, or Nationalist Chinese factions settling scores with knives or hatchets. What you don't read about is the hundred or so people a year that we arrange to have quietly deported before they can cause any trouble."

The Consul General stirred again. "I don't quite see where this is taking us, Mr. Leggo."

"I hope you will in a moment, sir. First let me ask you a question. You invite us to have a guess at who the kidnappers are. Very well. Are we to narrow the field down to political movements with an anti-American bias? Or should we include those that might have more specific grudges?"

The Consul General looked blank. "Meaning what?"

"Meaning those who might be hostile towards Mr. Kiley himself. Or towards the CIA as a whole."

All three Americans stiffened. Leggo watched them closely. He and the Commissioner and the Governor had planned this moment carefully, before the consular party arrived.

"I don't get it," the Consul General snapped.

"Perhaps you might tell us why an ordinary political vice-consul had to live in a guarded compound on Quarry Hill? Or why he needed an armed bodyguard and an armour-plated car with a radio link to your office?"

"Your department, Horace," said the Consul General grimly, passing the buck to his security man.

"Well—we assign guard duties according to priorities." Horace Stanley, flustered, was clutching phrases from the air. "The Consul General here has a permanent guard, and so do certain other personnel—"

"Why did Mr. Kiley need a bodyguard?"

Stanley flashed a significant, desperate glance at Vice-Consul Koch. "I'm not sure I'm qualified to answer that. Anyway, I didn't come here expecting to be put through the third degree."

Leggo looked shocked. It was the exaggerated shock of a schoolmaster towards a pupil who has misunderstood. He said, "I'm not here to interrogate you, Mr. Stanley. Perhaps Mr. Koch can answer the question. You see, we can't conduct an efficient investigation without having all the facts to hand. And I don't think you've given us all the relevant facts about Mr. Kiley."

Koch spoke for the first time. He ignored Leggo and addressed the Governor directly.

"Your Excellency, Mr. Kiley happens to have a particularly sensitive job in our consulate. I'm sure that the nature of that job can have no bearing on the reasons for this crime."

"I have confidence in these police officers," Wilkie replied mildly. "If they think the information is important, then they ought to have it."

Koch turned back to Leggo. "Just what do you feel you need to know?"

"Exactly what that sensitive job of Kiley's involved. And who else might know about it."

"I'm afraid I simply can't comment."

"Then let me remind you, Mr. Koch, of the agreement that your government has with all friendly countries on the question of posting intelligence officers to diplomatic missions under State Department cover."

"What agreement is that?" Boyd asked.

"When that happens," said the Consul General uncomfortably, "and God knows it happens often enough—people like me have no idea what they're doing ninety per cent of the time—then it's tacitly understood that the government of the host country is notified."

"In this case," Koch said, "that means the Foreign Office in London. The agreement does not extend to the Hong Kong police force."

"That being so," said Leggo, "we have had to work a few things out for ourselves. It's one of our jobs in Special Branch to know who's who on the diplomatic circuit. Part of that is guesswork, but since we seem to be in a guessing mood, let me tell you what we think. We think that Kiley is number one in the CIA pecking order here. And that you, Mr. Koch, are number two. We do know a little about what goes on in the Annex, you see."

190

Koch glared at him, quietly angry behind the rimless glasses. "You can do all the guessing you like, Mr. Leggo."

"But why do I have to guess? Why the hell can't you people drop your guard for once and co-operate?"

"Gentlemen!" The Governor's voice was stern. "We are here to cope with an emergency, and we'll not get anywhere by squabbling. What is your point, Mr. Leggo?"

"Just this, sir. The kidnappers chose Kiley for one of two reasons. He's an American diplomat—but there are a hundred other people in the consulate who would make softer targets. The second reason, the only conceivable one, is the fact that he's a senior CIA officer."

"How would anyone know that?" Koch demanded.

"How would I know it? These things are not impossible to work out."

"Mr. Koch," said the Governor, turning to the American, "it wouldn't compromise your rules of secrecy, would it, if you were to concede that this kidnapping has implications for your intelligence service as well as the State Department? If you would just admit that much, on the understanding that it will never be repeated outside this room, that would give these policemen a better grasp of the dimensions of the problem. In return, I think I might persuade them not to take too close an interest in the details of Mr. Kiley's work."

It was a face-saving formula, perhaps the only possible one. Koch shrugged and said, "Very well, Your Excellency. Mr. Leggo's assessment was correct. Rod Kiley is the agency's Chief of Station here, which makes him the most senior man in the Far East. It's an ultra-sensitive post. Only three people in the consulate, and not more than a dozen in the Annex itself, know that he holds it; I find it difficult to believe that some group of outsiders has penetrated his diplomatic cover."

"I think you're going to have to believe it," Leggo said. "And that brings me to the reason I invited McNair here. He's a specialist on the subject of those clandestine organizations I mentioned. He's closely in touch with their activities and his working methods are all his own. Mac, would you give us your thoughts, run through a few possibilities for us? What potential political terrorists do we have on our hands here?"

McNair had understood the reason for calling him to the meeting as soon as he had heard the Commissioner's opening remarks, and he had been turning things over in his mind ever since. The result was a degree of puzzlement. "We may as well start with the biggest outfits," he said, "Chinese Communists and Nationalists—and I'm talking about underground factions, not legitimate ones. Between them they're the biggest headache we've got. The Nats—sometimes with official help from the government in Taiwan, sometimes not—are always smuggling in shiploads of arms and explosives. They use Hong Kong as a forward base for all sorts of crazy operations on the mainland. As for the CTs, they're less obvious but often just as troublesome." He glanced from the Governor to the American trio. "It's hard to see, frankly, just what either of those parties would stand to gain from kidnapping an American. On the other hand, I suppose it's possible that some small group from either side has acted on its own initiative.

"As for the rest, they tend to be small ethnic groups, engaged in conventional crime as often as not, who spout political slogans when it suits them. For instance, there's a crowd of ex-South Vietnamese soldiers who fled from the Communists in 'seventy-five and got themselves smuggled in here. They're the hard core of a movement that's vaguely dedicated to overthrowing the Hanoi government. Until that happens they're happy enough running protection rackets. The Viets are a tough lot, quite capable of a kidnapping like this, I'd say, and they don't have much love for the Americans these days. So they're a possibility to be borne in mind.

"Then there are Indonesians. It's hard to tell where they stand, because half of them are anti-Communists who fled from Sukarno and the other half are Communists chased out by Suharto. They're another possibility, but a less likely one; they're badly organized and their discipline is nil. That covers just about everyone we handle." McNair paused. "Of course, if Mr. Koch could tell us whether Mr. Kiley ever had any contact with any of those people, that might narrow the field down."

Koch gave a small, indulgent smile. "Obviously you aren't familiar with intelligence work at that level, Mr. McNair. Mr. Kiley's function was purely administrative."

"You mean he had no personal contact with agents?"

"If he did, I would certainly not be free to divulge the fact."

"That's not very helpful," Boyd said flatly.

"I think, Gordon," said the Commissioner, stepping swiftly into the breach again, "that it would be an excellent idea to have McNair here seconded to your team."

192

"I was going to suggest that, sir," Leggo said. "It'll save a lot of to-ing and fro-ing if he can report direct to the Incident Centre. You can start making the rounds of your contacts, Mac, find out which if any of our friends might have an interest in this job. In fact, if you left us right now you could get some useful work done before the story breaks in the press."

"Suits me," McNair said, "if the Chief Super is agreeable?"

"Certainly," said Boyd. "And if you think you can excuse me as well, there's a lot of work waiting down at HQ."

They left the room together and went out through the lobby to the car park. McNair said, "At this stage you'll find even negative info useful, won't you?"

"You mean like who didn't do it? Right now, I'd kiss your arse for any information at all."

"I'll phone anything I get straight through to your desk. It won't be attributable, of course."

"Don't tell me," Boyd said sourly. "You've got sources to protect just like those CIA johnnies. Their attitude is about as helpful as a kick in the crotch. You know what I think? I think they're going to give us trouble before the day is out. You wait and see. The minute we get a ransom demand they're going to go behind our backs. They'll try to negotiate direct with the kidnappers, perhaps do a deal with them to get Kiley back. I don't want that to happen, and the only way to stop it will be to get to him first." He paused. "You going to help me, Mac?"

25

The stockless anchor of the *Lady Belinda* dropped with a resounding splash into the smooth blue water off the coast of Basalt Island. On the deck of the junk, Kiley, released from the sail bag, lay unconscious in the shade of a canvas awning.

"Well, there's your man," Pritchard said to Osman Khan. "There is ten million dollars' worth."

The Malay nodded, staring down at the American. The two of them stood with Fong and Pritchard in a semicircle around him. Baxter, after dropping the anchor and making sure it had held, was coming back to cut the engines. As the junk came round to head into the wind, the bleak grey landscape of the island faced them. Apart from that, nothing could be seen in any direction but sea and haze.

Kiley stirred uneasily. The facial muscles round his eyes twitched, as though he were in the last stages of a dream before wakening.

"Hit him with more Pentothal," Pritchard said to Quinn.

"A third dose? Listen, I told you what Canny said about that stuff. It's dangerous."

"We can't risk having him come round too soon. He is never to see our faces, remember? He is never to see my face in particular, because he would recognize it."

"Then why don't you hit him? I already wasted one guy today."

"Let's just do things the way they were planned, can we?"

Quinn went below, grumbling still, but he was back shortly with the third loaded syringe. They had taken Kiley's jacket off and rolled up his shirt sleeves. Quinn chose the left arm this time, inserted the hypo, found a vein and sent the drug flooding into the American's system. In half a minute he had settled down again, his breathing becoming stertorous and uneven once more.

"Let's go," Pritchard said.

Fong pulled the sampan up alongside the swimming steps and climbed down into it, followed by Pritchard. Quinn picked up Kiley's limp form, humped it over his shoulder, backed up to the rail above the steps and carefully lowered the bundle over it until the other two had a firm grasp of it. The sampan rocked crazily until they managed, gasping, to settle Kiley in the bottom. Then Quinn, Baxter and Osman Khan clambered down to squeeze into the boat. Fong untied the painter and began to row towards the beach.

They grounded the sampan and swung it broadside-on in the sand, within a couple of feet of the water's edge. Their shoes and socks were already off, their trousers rolled up. They waded ashore, pulled the boat higher up the beach and, between them, dragged Kiley out and laid him on the sand. While Osman Khan looked on, the other four, taking hold of a limb each, lifted Kiley and staggered across the sand with him towards the pillbox.

At 11 A.M. the first statement on the kidnapping was issued jointly by the Hong Kong Government Information Service and the United States Consulate General. It was fed out on the internal telex system to all major Hong Kong newspapers, and within a few minutes the international wire services had picked it up.

194

The Associated Press was the first of these off the mark. Their flash read:

HONG KONG, AUG. 21 (AP). A U.S. DIPLOMAT WAS KIDNAPPED AT GUNPOINT HERE THIS MORNING AS HE DROVE TO HIS OFFICE. HIS CHAUFFEUR WAS SHOT DEAD.

The second take of the story came over a minute later:

HONG KONG, AUG. 21 (AP). THE DIPLOMAT WAS NAMED AS RODERICK N. KILEY, 48, POLITICAL VICE-CONSUL AT THE U.S. CONSULATE GENERAL HERE. UNIDENTIFIED GUNMEN FORCED HIS CAR TO A HALT IN A TUNNEL UNDER HONG KONG'S HARBOUR. THEY ABDUCTED HIM AFTER TWICE SHOOTING THE CHAUFFEUR, BENJAMIN CHIN, 26, A NATIVE OF SAN FRANCISCO.

In the barrackslike building in Happy Valley that housed the Hong Kong offices of Hsin Hua, the New China News Agency, together with the living quarters of its staff, the first two takes of the AP message were torn off the teleprinter and clipped together by a taperoom *foki,* who then carried them to the duty editor at his small, paper-strewn desk. The duty editor read the story and dismissed the *foki.* He left his desk, climbed a flight of stairs and walked to the end of a long corridor. He knocked on a door and was admitted to the presence of Kao Ling, third assistant editor of the Hong Kong Bureau of the NCNA and a member of the Central Committee of the Communist Party of China.

Kao was a Party veteran of long standing. As a boy of fourteen he had joined Mao Tse-tung's Long March and later fought in the Eighth Route Army against both the Japanese invaders and the Kuomintang. He was the type of follower beloved of all political leaders, a party workhorse with limited personal ambitions. In his late fifties now, he was lean and grey-haired, mild of appearance and manner. He wore Western clothes, spoke excellent English and had a fondness for good French brandy. Politically he was a moderate who had escaped purging during the Cultural Revolution only by keeping his views strictly to himself. He had occupied his humble position in the NCNA's Hong Kong Bureau for eight years. For six of those years he had also directed China's espionage activities in the colony.

For the Chinese secret service—the T'e Wu or Ministry of Public Security, with headquarters at Fragrant Hill Park on the western outskirts of Peking—Hong Kong had always been the main gateway to the rest of the world. Through here they smuggled their agents, many of them posing as refugees and settling in the colony until they had acquired Hong Kong identity cards, then applying for visas to other countries. Through here, too, the bulk of secret intelligence flowing into Peking was channelled—partly through a vast, overlapping courier system, partly through the NCNA, which was not a wire service in the conventional sense but an arm of the Party and the State. To its workers, the collecting of secret information was as much a part of their duty as the dissemination of conventional news.

Kao Ling was one of the T'e Wu's most important employees outside China itself. His orders came direct from Party Vice-Chairman Wang Tung-hsing, Chairman Mao's former personal bodyguard, who was also chief of the security department of the Party's Military Affairs Commission—in effect, the head of intelligence and secret police services.

He broke off studying overnight dispatches from Peking to read through the two short takes of the AP message that the duty editor handed him. Then he adjusted his glasses and read them again, giving himself time to think. It was the duty editor who finally broke the silence.

"I thought you would want to see that at once, Comrade."

"Yes. Thank you."

"It was the name: Kiley. I recalled filing a report on him, perhaps six months ago, classifying him as a possible CIA official."

"The file should be updated. The CIA connection is confirmed. Bring me the rest of this as it comes in, please."

"Do you wish me to relay it to Peking?"

"Only on the open news circuit. Cut down the content drastically and delay it for an hour, to make it seem as though we are treating it without urgency. I do not want the British monitors to think we have any special interest. I shall alert the Ministry myself."

"Then we do have an interest?"

Kao struck the teleprinter message with the flat of his hand. "This is a matter of great concern to us."

"Do you have some idea who might have kidnapped him?"

"No. But we must try to find out. Speak to the head of Investigation for me. His men must learn whatever they can about the progress of police inquiries."

When the duty editor had left, Kao Ling stood up and went to a filing cabinet in the corner. He pulled the top drawer open and took out a bottle of Rémy Martin and a tumbler. His hands shook slightly with nerves as he poured half a glass of brandy and downed it in one swallow.

Then he felt his breath coming more easily, the knot of tension loosening in his stomach. The duty editor could not be expected to guess how strong his interest was. Nobody in the building but Kao Ling himself knew that.

He put away the brandy and the glass and made his way up to the top floor of the building, to the room housing the secure radio-telephone that would connect him directly with Peking.

The big joke in the Narcotics Bureau that morning was how Ted Lewis had had his piece taken off him by a pusher and got himself locked in with Johnny Yau, the wholesaler he'd been trying to nail all this time. Even the injuries to the hand that had been stamped on didn't merit quite enough sympathy to offset the teasing: one finger was broken and in a splint, the others were bruised and swollen. Privately some of the narcs thought Lewis had got what was coming to him for being such a wise-ass one-man band. The only ones who didn't find it funny were Lewis himself and the head of the Bureau, who was carpeting him for the second time that day.

"Sit down, you're not facing a court-martial. Not yet, anyway. I've spoken to the Deputy Commissioner, put in as good a word for you as I could. It'll be a while before I know what'll happen—they've all got their hands full with this kidnapping now—but you'll be lucky to get away with a stiff suspension."

"I see."

"It was a bloody daft thing to do," the superintendent said. "I've warned you before about trying to tackle these things single-handed."

"I cocked it up," Lewis admitted, "and I've learned a lesson. I underestimated this Yank, didn't expect a fight. Anyway, I did nail Yau: there was enough Number Four in his place to keep the Seventh Fleet high for a month."

"You also lost your pistol," his chief pointed out tartly. "There's never, ever, an excuse for that. We have tight gun laws in this colony for precisely one reason: to keep firearms out of the hands of criminals. I just hope for everyone's sake that this doesn't get into the papers."

"How are we doing at tracing this sailor, anyway? Did we get any dabs?"

"A few good prints, from in and around the apartment, but they don't match up with anything in Identification's records. Not surprising: if his ship just calls occasionally he'd hardly have a criminal record

197

here. Our best bet is a comb-out among all the American sailors who were on liberty last night, but that's taking time to arrange. There's a flotilla of destroyers and a couple of fleet-support vessels in harbour; there were about seven hundred matelots on the streets last night. If you'd taken the elementary precaution, Ted, of asking for his name and his ship before you took him upstairs . . ."

"I was anxious to get going, sir. I thought all that could wait until—"

The superintendent's telephone rang. He snatched at the receiver and spoke his name crisply into the mouthpiece.

"Why, yes," he said, in a tone of slight surprise, and glanced across the desk at Lewis. "He's in my office at this moment, in fact."

The detective half rose to his feet, making a gesture at the door, but the bureau chief waved him back into his chair. For a minute he continued to listen to the voice on the phone, his brow crinkled in concentration. Finally he said, "I'll send him up to you at once." He replaced the receiver, folded his arms and looked at Lewis. His gaze was hard and significant.

"I thought you were in enough trouble already," he said.

"What do you mean, sir?"

"That gun of yours. It's made a return appearance."

"I don't follow."

"It's been *used,* man. This diplomat who was kidnapped this morning: his car was ambushed, his driver shot dead. Shot with your gun, Ted."

Lewis was on his feet, staring incredulously down into his chief's face. "It can't have been!"

"Ballistics say so, Ted."

"Christ!" Lewis exclaimed. "But . . . look, it was just last night that I lost it. And the kidnap was just this morning—what, ten, twelve hours later? These jokers must have been planning for months: how would they get hold of my shooter at the last minute? Anyway, they're politicos of some kind, aren't they? This guy was a Yank sailor, I swear it."

"He might have sold it to somebody." The superintendent shrugged. "Anyway, how they got hold of it is not so important, any longer, as finding out who they are. You may have a lead for the CID."

"What's Ballistics' story, anyway?"

"They've got a trace on your Walther. The one shot you ever fired in anger, remember?"

Lewis remembered. Three years ago, the bust on a heroin factory

198

in a farmhouse near Tsuen Wan. The chemist who'd been cooking the stuff up in the bathroom went off his nut and came screaming at the narc, wielding a meat cleaver. He'd fired in pure self-defence, and the shot had gone through the chemist's shoulder. Lewis had never admitted that he'd been aiming at his head.

"It was a nice clean flesh wound," the superintendent said, "and a nice clean undistorted seven-sixty-five half-jacketed bullet was recovered. The lads in Ballistics put it in an envelope and filed it away. When the bullet was dug out of this diplomat's driver a couple of hours ago, your old slug was one of the unmatched ones their computer told them to compare it with. They matched up, Ted. Exactly."

Lewis nodded gloomily. Experience had taught him that Ballistics officers were just about the only policemen who were always right. Every firearm ever made carried an individual "signature" which it stamped on the bullet passing through its barrel. Even two otherwise identical guns, their rifling cut with the same dies, showed microscopic differences because the dies became slightly more worn with each barrel that was bored.

"What now, sir?" he asked.

"I'm seconding you to Boyd's CID staff. You're going straight up there to help them in every way you can."

Walking through the Walled City, Mr. Tan sensed eyes watching him. They watched from the open-fronted rooms at street level where whole families lived and small merchants and handymen plied their trades, and from the first-floor windows where prostitutes and pushers plied theirs. There were always watching eyes in the Walled City—eyes glazed with opium, rheumy with age, sharp with suspicion—peering through the permanent twilight of the crooked little alleys that were the only thoroughfares in this rabbit warren of a slum.

They watched Mr. Tan with curiosity rather than suspicion, for he was known and respected here. Not *feared,* as a Sunday newspaper had once claimed in a sensational so-called exposé, simply respected. Mr. Tan was Red Stick, a member of the inner council of the 14-K Triad, the secret society that ran the Walled City. Red Stick was far removed from the strong-arm men who extorted "tea money" from shopkeepers, the pimps who controlled child prostitutes, the drug peddlers and debt collectors who served the Triad. There was no need to fear Mr. Tan; he could even afford to be affable, like a general among private soldiers, the task of coercion left to his subordinates.

199

The Walled City was a six-acre enclave on the Kowloon Peninsula, the subject of an old territorial dispute between Britain and China which had left it for fifty years without effective administration or policing. Vice and violence, disease and defilement had flourished, to the point where now the criminals and their victims lived in a symbiosis of total dependence on each other: protectors and protected, addicts and pushers, pimps and whores. Mr. Tan, at home like a rat in his domain of subterranean alleyways, moved surefooted to an appointment with his dentist.

Along the street that formed the northern boundary of the ghetto, a point beyond which no stranger could venture unnoticed, was a row of dental parlours with sets of false teeth grinning hideously from their windows. In the middle of the row was one shop with a particularly gruesome display of dentures gleaming in the jaws of skulls. Mr. Tan entered it. The dentist was slumped in his chair, smoking and reading a newspaper; an ancient, immensely complicated drilling machine was suspended above him, like the skeleton of some extinct flying reptile. The dentist, like the others in the row, was neither qualified nor licensed to practise, but in the Walled City that did not matter. He folded his paper and sat up promptly.

"Is he here?" the visitor asked, without preamble.

"He is waiting."

"See that we are not disturbed."

Mr. Tan passed through the room, which was more like a scruffy, one-man barber shop than a surgery, to a peeling lacquered screen that shielded a doorway at the rear. Round the screen and through the door was a narrow, windowless storeroom with shelves from floor to ceiling, crammed with cardboard boxes, glass jars full of pills, bottles with anonymous potions encrusted at their necks, nightmarish dental instruments and a few more skulls. There was about twelve square feet of floor space, half of it occupied by Chief Inspector McNair, sitting on a beer crate. In the tiny, airless room he had been perspiring; the smell of European sweat offended Mr. Tan's nostrils.

"What you want?"

"The usual. A little help."

"Only last week I help. I give you plenty help."

"This is different. And urgent."

"About hotel business I know nothing new. I told everything."

"It's not about that. Just relax and listen."

The Chinese glanced uneasily around him, looking for somewhere to sit. There was nowhere; he leaned against the shelves. The relationship McNair had formed with him would have been difficult to explain to a policeman outside the Special Branch. It was based on opportunism rather than trust; in fact, McNair disliked Mr. Tan and guessed that the feeling was reciprocated. Tan was not a police informer in the conventional sense. He betrayed no confidences and accepted no money. Whatever information he gave McNair came with the approval of his brethren in the Triad. The 14-K, in spite of their rapaciously capitalist instincts, in fact had strong connections with the Communist underground. It was a uniquely Chinese sort of compromise. Their thugs had helped to fan the flames of the Cultural Revolution riots in 1967 in exchange for a free hand in the looting that followed. More important, from McNair's point of view, was the fact that they had a well-equipped intelligence service that monitored the activities of the rival pro-Nationalist gangs. It was with the object of damaging these that Mr. Tan, when it suited him, co-operated with Special Branch.

The hotel business, as he described it, was a good example of the mutually beneficial nature of the relationship. Only last week, a decorator who was a member of the Triad and who had been working on a new Taiwanese-owned hotel, had reported the arrival of some suspicious-looking crates of furnishings shipped from Taipei. After Tan had reported this to McNair, a surreptitious Special Branch examination of the packing cases had shown them to contain arms and explosives destined for delivery to Nationalist cells. The stuff was confiscated. Responsibility was pinned down to the hotel manager and three employees, all of whom were deported quietly; it was the sort of thing that rarely got into the newspapers.

Clearly, though, Mr. Tan thought he was about to be pressured. "I told you to relax," McNair said. "This is something quite different. Something between you and me. Tell the Triad, if you like; it's none of my business. But you could turn a little personal profit on it."

Mr. Tan mirrored blank suspicion from the lenses of his dark glasses. "I am not *ma chai,*" he said. "Not informer."

"I'm not asking you to be one. This is something different, important to us. You heard this morning's news?"

Tan paused for a few seconds, merely out of the habit of never answering a question immediately. "I hear," he said.

"About the American who's been kidnapped?"

"Yes."

"Got any ideas?"

McNair watched Tan's face closely, but not because he expected any reaction from the wooden features. This kind of thing wasn't the Triads' form. They worked within the Chinese community, preferring not to court trouble from the long-nosed foreigners. Again, there was the ritual few seconds' hesitation.

"No ideas."

"Take a guess, then."

"No guess."

"Look, I don't expect hard information, just helpful thoughts. You think the kidnappers could be Kuomintang?"

"Not them. This man who is kidnap, he is *May gok yun,* yes?" Mr. Tan used the Cantonese slang for American. "You look for white man, not Chinese."

"We don't know what race they are yet. Chinese or not, if anyone starts asking questions around the Walled City, you'll hear about it— and the questions won't be from us. I want to know who's asking. You think the kidnappers could be CT?"

This time it was police slang, with which Mr. Tan was equally at home. "Communist? I don't think. Not their way."

"Then who? Just listen around, is all I'm asking."

Mr. Tan's face was expressionless. He said, "You mention money."

McNair took out his wallet and counted out five hundred-dollar bills. He folded them once and held them out between two fingers to the Chinese.

"That's for your trouble this morning. There's a lot more available for a good lead."

Tan pushed himself off the shelves and stood upright. He reached out, took the money, and thrust it into the breast pocket of his shirt.

"What I can, I do."

"That's fine. Now, I'm getting out of this steam bath and I want you to wait fifteen minutes before you move."

Tan hesitated for the last time. "One thing I can tell. You are follow."

"Followed? By whom?"

"Two men. I don't know. Chinese men, in blue car. Strangers. I look-see." Mr. Tan tapped the edge of one eye sagely.

26

In the Incident Centre, up on the thirteenth floor, they were preparing to run the videotape of the kidnapping for perhaps the twentieth time that morning. The tunnel company had rushed it across from their control room in Hung Hom, complete with a portable viewing apparatus and a technician to operate it. The machine was installed in one corner of the big open-plan office. Half a dozen policemen stood in a semicircle facing the screen, waiting for the operator to rewind the tape. It was there that Ted Lewis from Narcotics found Chief Superintendent Boyd.

"So you're the fellow they got the shooter from, eh?"

"It looks that way, sir."

Boyd had an intimidating way of tilting his head forward when he spoke to people, so that he appeared to be glowering at them through his shaggy black eyebrows. "I don't think I'd care to be in your shoes this morning."

"It isn't pleasant," the detective said, preparing for another blast of sarcasm. Instead he was grateful for Boyd's next remark.

"It's bad luck, that's all. We've all made cock-ups in our time. If they hadn't got hold of your gun they'd have had another from somewhere else. As things turned out, it's given us a lead—we hope. I want you to take a look at this."

The technician had lined up the tape once more. He pressed a switch and the screen flickered to life: a static, monochrome view of twin streams of cars passing through the tunnel. They seemed to be moving very fast, their speed exaggerated by the angle at which the electronic camera was mounted, high up on the right-hand wall. The vehicles entered the picture from the top right corner and disappeared at bottom left.

"Watch carefully," Boyd said to Lewis, "and see if this tells you anything."

Two cars approached the camera side by side in the lanes, at about the same speed. One had the distinctive rectangular grille of a Mercedes, the other was some American job. Suddenly, as if from nowhere, something came racing up between them: a motorbike, right on the white lines and moving very fast. Just as it was about to pull ahead of the cars, something happened—it was impossible to see exactly what

—to make the bike bump against both the Mercedes and the other car. It began to sway and slide until it vanished from the frame of the picture. The cars slowed suddenly and stopped. A man jumped out of the American car and ran forward. Two figures carrying guns emerged from the Mercedes, ghostly creatures under the tunnel floodlights, in one-piece overalls, gloves, and helmets which hid their faces. One ran to the American car; the other loped forward towards where the motor-cycle rider must obviously have fallen.

"Hold it!" Lewis said. "Can we have that bit again?"

The technician stopped the tape, wound it back a few feet and ran the sequence once more.

"That one—the big one."

"What about him?" Boyd asked.

"In size and shape he's very similar to the palooka who slugged me last night."

"Keep looking. There's more of him in a minute."

Lewis watched to the end, to the point where the helmeted figures scrambled into the car and it took off, leaving a line of trapped and wrecked vehicles behind it. Without a sound-track, without any camera movement, the event seemed to lack both drama and dimension. It was like something witnessed through a keyhole; you saw only what came into your line of sight and were unable to relate it to a whole.

"Well?" said Boyd.

"Without seeing his face I couldn't swear to a thing," Lewis said, "but in build that big bugger matches my sailor, all right. It's the way he moves, too: he's fast and agile for a man his size."

"We need very badly to turn up that sailor. Even if he's not the one who took part in the snatch, he's the one who took your gun. Find him, and we'll start breaking down a few doors."

Boyd turned away and began to walk back to his desk across the room. Lewis went at his side. "There's been an alert out ever since your tangle with him last night, of course, but now that he's a definite suspect in the kidnapping we've got the Americans to hurry things up. There were seven hundred men on shore leave last night, and every one who comes close to matching the description you've given is being questioned. That includes officers up to the rank of lieutenant-commander, but excludes obvious non-starters such as blacks and men under five-feet-ten. Everyone who can't give a full and convincing account of his movements last night is going on a separate list. I'll want you to attend a lineup just as soon as they've got all the suspects in one place."

Boyd paused and studied Lewis from under his eyebrows. "There's one thing that bothers me. Whoever did this job has been planning it for weeks, if not months. How did a sailor getting an occasional leave in Hong Kong have the opportunity to get mixed up in it? How sure are you that he was a sailor?"

"I must admit," Lewis said uncomfortably, "that I started out with an assumption. You see, in Narcotics we have more trouble with Yankee sailors than any other foreigners when it comes to buying stuff off wholesalers. Well, when I heard his accent I did rather put words in his mouth. I said, *Are you off a ship?* and he said yes. But then this was just after I'd collared him, and it takes a pretty cool villain to produce a spontaneous lie right at that moment. And this one wasn't cool; he was sweating like a pig. Also, my friend Johnny Yau, the wholesaler, has always understood him to be a sailor."

"How much did you get out of Yau?"

"I was locked up with him for an hour before they came to let me out," Lewis said with a sour grin. "I didn't waste the time, sir."

"Where is he now?"

"On remand in Stanley Prison."

They walked on, to a U-shaped set of desks in the middle of the room from which Boyd ran his Incident Centre. It occupied half a floor of the headquarters building, from which the civilian employees of the Criminal Records Office had been summarily evicted. Boyd's seat in the centre of the U was flanked by six aides whose telephones were constantly ringing. Facing him was a phalanx of desks occupied by others in the hastily formed command structure: the chief of operations, the head of Criminal Intelligence, a press officer and a young army captain appointed to act as liaison officer with the military command. Two battalions of troops had been pulled off normal duties and were formed up at Stanley Fort, awaiting orders to join the search just as soon as someone could tell them where they ought to go. There was also, waiting expectantly by the main desk, a Chinese civilian in a white laboratory coat. Lewis recognized him as one of the senior technicians from the Identification Bureau. He was clutching a sheaf of printed forms.

"Your fingerprint report?" Boyd said. "All right, tell me the worst."

"Sorry, sir. Plenty of dabs on the cars and the motorbike, but none of them matches up with anything in our collection."

Boyd grunted. "Hardly surprising, since they were wearing gloves.

And if they're foreign politicos we'd have no records on them anyway. What about the prints from Yau's place in North Point?"

"Again, nothing traceable. The problem is, we are only allowed to hold the prints of people with criminal convictions. We have nearly four hundred thousand of those, but if we could just gain access to the other three million in the Registration of Persons Department: everyone who has ever applied for an identity card—"

"In a case this serious they'll bend the rules for us," Boyd assured him. "But you know damn well that their usefulness is limited. Our system is geared to tracing suspects through their prints; theirs is for confirming identities. Give them a name and they'll find you a print—but they can't do it the other way round. And so far we don't have any names. All right, thank you."

Boyd dismissed the technician and then sat down at his desk and spoke to Lewis.

"I'll be frank with you. The only thing we've got resembling a lead is this fellow who mashed your fingers last night, and who may or may not have taken part in the job this morning. And the only people who know him by sight are you and this Johnny Yau character. Why don't you go out to Stanley and soften him up a little?"

"Believe me, sir, I did plenty of softening while we were locked in that flat together. I'm sure he's told me everything he knows—and on the subject of the sailor he knows almost nothing. He takes customers on personal recommendation only and makes a point of not finding out their names and addresses."

"You can usually prod a little extra out of someone's memory, if you keep at it. Besides, things have changed for Mr. Yau."

"Changed? Why?"

Boyd crossed his arms and looked steadily at Lewis. "Because now we have bigger fish to fry. You could offer him a little hope, for when he goes to trial. A word in the prosecutor's ear: co-operation on another, bigger, case; no insistence on maximum sentence."

"Bloody hell!" Lewis exploded. "I've spent months trying to nail that bastard! I'm not going to chuck up the chance of sending him down the line—and I mean all the way!"

"I know how you feel." Boyd had spent fifteen years on the ground as a detective himself and had felt the same sort of indignation at the thought of trading off a prime villain. "But, as I said, there are bigger things at stake. Suddenly Yau has the chance to get himself off the hook, partly anyway, by fingering someone who's more important to

206

us than he is. As for you, it wouldn't do your track record any harm to come up with something useful. Might even wipe out the bad marks you scored last night."

Gavin McNair appeared at the desk. He'd had to pass by HQ on his way back from meeting Mr. Tan, and dropping in was easier than phoning.

"Progress?" Boyd asked.

"At the moment I'm just laying groundbait. What I've picked up so far suggests the Triads know nothing about it. Blank looks all round —and they seem genuine to me."

"Keep it warm. What next?"

"I'm going to see a man out at Shek O."

"Mind dropping me at Stanley?" Lewis asked.

They headed together for the lift. McNair knew Lewis as a hard-drinking bachelor in the officers' mess and as a hard-assed loner in the Narcotics Bureau. On the way up to the Incident Centre he had also heard, in a heartily exaggerated form, the story about his being rolled by a pusher the night before. It was all around the building by now, and a glance at the injured hand confirmed at least the substance of the story. On the way down he paused in his office to phone Siu. He told her he couldn't say when he'd be home. Her tone was one of resentful resignation, I-told-you-so in all but the use of the phrase. On the way down to the car park he was silent, his mouth set in an angry line.

"Wife kicking up?" Lewis asked. "They all do, sooner or later."

"What would you know?" McNair asked acidly.

"Only what I hear from the other poor buggers. I'm a friendly bachelor ear, they pour it all out to me. You're out at all hours, you ruin their dinner parties. Above all, you give them no status, no face. That's the important thing, face. Everybody knows what a copper earns, and if he's living better than he ought to then he must be on the take. Is that the problem in a nutshell, Mac?"

"I don't have to answer that," McNair said. They had reached his Lancia in its numbered bay. "I don't need any friendly ears. Why don't you tell me how you got your gun taken off you last night?"

He grinned at Lewis as the narc climbed into the seat beside him. Lewis slammed the door harder than he needed to, and winced as he banged his injured knuckles against the handle.

Roderick Kiley came to the surface slowly, conscious at first only of the blackness behind his eyelids softening to grey. Then he became aware that he was lying on his side, his right shoulder pressing down into some pliable, gritty substance. The air around him was cool and dank, the atmosphere of a cave. His thoughts were woolly, his sensations confused. Suddenly his memory flickered fitfully to life, throwing up disjointed images from his last moments of consciousness: the crash with the motorcycle, the dark-helmeted man thrusting a gun at him. In a panic he sat up. At once he felt nauseated and a terrible bitter taste rose in his throat. He lowered his head and retched, several times, face to the ground.

"Take it easy," said a man's voice. It came from nowhere and everywhere, echoing off the surfaces around him. A cave? It seemed like a cave when he raised his head and looked around at the blank stone walls. He was sitting on sand, he realized. The man was standing in a doorway to his left, wearing jeans and a T-shirt and a blank, black-visored helmet that he recognized with a sudden feeling of horror.

"What is this?" he asked thickly. "Who are you?"

"Just take it easy," the man said. "This is a safe place. Safe for us, safe for you. So safe you can yell your lungs out and nobody's gonna hear you."

Kiley became aware of several points of pain in his body. There were the places in his upper arms where needles had been stuck into him, and which now felt bruised and swollen, and there was a rawness and heaviness around his right ankle. He raised his head to look up at it: it was chained and padlocked to the wall.

"We got you chained up like a puppy dog," said the man in the helmet, "to keep you out of trouble. You want to piss, you piss in the sand. You want to shit, you call us and we take you outside. We got to spend the night in here with you, we don't want to sleep in no shit."

"You've kidnapped me. Why?"

"You'll find out, in time. We got plenty of time."

"Does my wife know?"

"I guess they'll have told her by now."

There was something puzzling about the man in the helmet. "You . . . you're American, aren't you?" Kiley said.

"Don't you worry about what I am, man. And quit asking questions. Just relax."

Kiley sagged back onto the sand. Yes, it really was sand—soft, fine and cool, as it was on a shady beach or in a riverbed. Gazing round him, he realized his prison was not a cave: the walls were too regular, and at eye-level there were horizontal slits in them, through which he could see bands of blue sky. He jerked his shackled foot and felt the chain tauten immediately; it had been carefully positioned to prevent him from reaching and seeing through the slits.

The room—bunker, dugout, whatever it was—oppressed him like a form of blindness. Already, after a minute's groggy wakefulness, he was asserting the instincts of a blind man, gauging his surroundings by touch, sound, smell. The smell was of damp sand and—was it the sea? There was a faintly salt tang in the air. As he listened he heard a crunch of footsteps behind the helmeted man, heavy-heeled as though coming down a flight of steps. Another man appeared in the doorway, another helmet with its anonymous black visor. The newcomer was smaller and slighter than the first man. He said, "How is he?"

"Awake."

"Is he okay?"

"He's dandy."

"That's good." There was something like relief in the smaller man's tone. His voice was higher, gentler, more diffident than the other's. From the accent Kiley thought he was Chinese, or at least Asian, whereas he was more than ever convinced that the big one was American. He had begun to assemble his thoughts more coherently now, but they didn't make much sense. He'd lived for years with the thought of kidnap in the back of his mind, but it had always seemed as though there would be a clear reason, immediately recognizable. Who were these people, what the hell did they want? Suddenly another memory struck him and he struggled up onto his elbow.

"You're the one who shot my driver, aren't you?"

"I said no more questions."

"Aren't you?" Kiley insisted. "You killed him, didn't you? Are you afraid to admit it?"

"You'd better shut your trap, mister."

"You murdering son of a bitch, I'm going to see that you pay for that!"

Kiley spoke with the vehemence of blind rage. Then he was aware of the big man lunging towards him and he felt a kick in the chest that knocked him onto his back and sent him rolling across the ground until the chain round his ankle pulled him up short. He lay face down, spitting out sand.

"You give me any more of your lip and you'll go the same way as that fucking driver." The American towered above him, his breathing harsh with anger. Then Kiley felt a hard, cold rod of steel pressed into the back of his neck. It bored into him, pushing his face down into the sand until he was gasping for air, squirming with pain. Just as suddenly it was released and he rolled onto his back, panting. The big man hefted the pistol in his hand.

"This is what took your driver out," he said, "and it'll do the same for you if you start acting like a wise-ass. It don't matter to us, man, whether you're alive or dead when they get to you, because those motherfuckers are going to pay for your ass, sight unseen. Remember that, Mr. CIA man."

The American turned and went out through the doorway. The small man followed him. Kiley lay spitting sand from his lips, feeling a muddy mixture of grit and saliva dribble down his chin. Suddenly he was overwhelmed by a violent wave of despair.

The junk was back at her mooring at Hebe Haven shortly after midday. Pritchard and Baxter, in the Range Rover, and Osman Khan, in his hired Granada, drove separately to Central. There were more roadblocks out now, but the tunnel had been cleared and reopened in both directions, so there was little delay. Baxter dropped Pritchard in Chater Road and drove on to his office. Pritchard and Osman Khan met up in the Cable and Wireless office.

Khan wrote out two telegrams and showed them to Pritchard before handing them in. The first was addressed to Sulu Enterprises, 29 Madrid Street, Zamboanga, the Philippines, and read:

> YOUR CONSIGNMENT DELIVERED HERE ON SCHEDULE STOP SHIPPER NOW AWAITS VERBAL CONFIRMATION YOUR EARLIER INSTRUCTIONS FOR RE-EXPORT REGARDS KHALID.

That was the alert to the Moro National Liberation Front, telling them that the kidnapping had been successful. Sulu Enterprises was a Muslim-owned company that handled the Moros' external communications for them. The other was addressed to the Chartered Bank of Brunei. It read:

> PLEASE ADVISE YOUR ACCOUNT HOLDER NO. 0029443 HIS BILL OF EXCHANGE IN FAVOUR HONG KONG PROJECT GROUP HANDED OVER TODAY KHALID.

That was to tell Chief Minister Salim that everything was going as planned. He signed both forms in the name of R. N. Khalid and gave his address as the Excelsior Hotel, Hong Kong.

210

There was no reason in the world for anyone to attach suspicion to the cables: they were just two of the thousands of business messages that flowed out of the colony each day and were not couched in any mysterious code. It was even less likely that anyone would check whether there had been a man named Khalid staying at the Excelsior Hotel.

Khan paid urgent rates for both telegrams. Then he produced two documents from his briefcase. One was a bill of exchange drawn on the Chartered Bank of Brunei and signed by Salim and a fellow-director of the corporate front that he used to mask his private financial dealings. It accepted liability for payment to the bearer, one week from today, on August 28, of the sum of five million United States dollars. Since the bill was a negotiable instrument which could not be cancelled and which Pritchard—in theory, at least—could sell at a discount before the due date, Salim had to have a safeguard against the possibility of not receiving the ten-million-dollar ransom by then. This was provided by the second document, a promissory note drawn up and ready for notarization by a lawyer in Brunei, in terms of which Pritchard promised, on the same date, August 28, to pay five million dollars to Salim's fronting company. Standing with Khan at one of the writing counters in the Cable and Wireless office, Pritchard read through the note before signing it and handing it back. Each side to the bargain now held a legal instrument which could cancel out the other. If for any reason the ransom did not arrive they would simply exchange documents, destroy them and be none the worse off. Assuming it did arrive, Salim would return the promissory note, leaving Pritchard free to cash in his bill of exchange. Since he would have to go to Brunei to do this, and since both documents had equal validity under the legal code of the Sultanate, there was no possibility of either side doublecrossing the other. The arrangement also avoided the messy complications of trying to pick up the ransom in cash.

Pritchard tucked the bill of exchange into his jacket pocket. Khan returned the signed promissory note to his briefcase and then, after shaking hands, left to return to the Hilton and prepare for his flight home that evening: a businessman with another good deal under his belt.

Pritchard walked out of the Cable and Wireless office into Connaught Road. In a sudden release of the hours and days of nervous tension he laughed out loud—a long guffaw, half doubling him over on the pavement, making Chinese pedestrians skirt nervously round him, unused to such displays of emotion, before he regained his control and straightened up. It was a matter of waiting now, and that might be the hardest part of all. He needed a drink. It would be the best drink he'd ever tasted. He composed himself and set off for Gloucester Building and the Quill Club.

27

In a room in the administration block of Stanley Prison specially set aside for their interview, Detective Inspector Lewis and Mr. Yau faced each other across a formica-topped table. They had been talking for twenty minutes. Rather, Lewis had talked and Yau had given an appearance of listening, his face utterly blank. Lewis had encountered this Chinese recalcitrance a thousand times before, but always reached a point where he lost patience with it.

"Well?" he demanded. "Is it a deal?"

Yau wiped the palms of his hands for the umpteenth time on the legs of his striped pyjamas. It was the only sign of nervousness he had shown. It wasn't that he had anything to lose by grassing on a foreign-devil sailor who in any case had helped the police to bust him; the problem was the drug dealer's code of total non-co-operation. Lewis was asking him to go against his instincts; a thousand devils would torment him if he talked.

"What you want to know?" he asked.

"Everything. We need this sailor badly. With your help we may be able to find him. That means active help, not just saying yes and no to my questions. You want a remission, you've got to work for it."

"What can I tell? All I know, I tell already."

"All right," Lewis said resignedly. "Let's start by going through what you've told me, see if you can expand on it. He first came to you about two years ago, you think. You're sure he was a sailor?"

"Sure."

"Ever see him in uniform?"

"No." That wasn't surprising. Enlisted men had been going ashore in civilian clothes for many years now.

"How do you know, then?"

"He had to have introduction. Other sailor bring him."

"This other sailor: you didn't know his name either?"

"I deal with face, not name."

"Since you first met him, how many times has he been to your place?"

"Twenty, maybe twenty-five."

"Can you not remember just one single date?"

"No."

"You kept no written record of any of your transactions?"

"No."

"Did he come regularly at the same time of day?"

Yau shook his head. Lewis sighed. Willing to help or not, the wholesaler had a block in his memory, put there by his own secretive nature.

Lewis tried a different tack. "How did he pay you?"

"Always U.S. dollar."

"What sort of amounts?"

"One, two, three hundred."

"And you think he was selling the stuff to other sailors?"

"I never ask what happen to it. . . ." Yau paused and looked uneasily around the room, from the barred window to the shelves stacked with records to the polished brown linoleum on the floor. Lewis sensed a decision being made.

"There is way to know dates," the Chinese said. "I change U.S. dollar to Hong Kong always at same money changer. Lo Mong-hwa, Java Road."

"And he'll have records!" Lewis thumped the table with his fist. "Now we're starting to get somewhere!"

After dropping Lewis at Stanley, McNair had turned back onto the Tai Tam Road and driven along the scenic, tortuous coastal route towards the southeast corner of Hong Kong Island. He kept the Lancia down to forty as he negotiated the sharp twists and turns of the road across the cliff face above Tai Tam, where the yachts and junks at their moorings formed tiny shadows against a vast, blinding sheen of reflected sunlight. It was only after he had descended from the hills to the coast, deliberately missing a turning and doubling back from the cul-de-sac at Big Wave Bay, that he was certain that Mr. Tan had been right. He was being followed.

He passed the blue Datsun 180 halfway back to the turnoff, slowing for long enough to note the registration number and the fact that there were two occupants, Chinese, male. Then he gunned the Lancia hard, through the junction and on towards the little Chinese beach resort of Shek O.

He was nearing eighty miles an hour as he approached the village. Four hundred yards short of it he braked and swung off the road onto a paved driveway that went steeply up the hill to the right. Praying absently that nothing was coming the other way, he slammed down into second gear and raced the car round three hairpin bends. Then it bumped onto a patch of level ground and he skidded to a stop in the shade of the villa that stood at the top of the little knoll, overlooking the village. He got out, walked to the edge of the terrace and saw the Datsun racing on towards Shek O. Then he turned and went back to the house.

It was of classical Chinese design, with a crenellated roof that turned up at the corners, and doors and windows protected by wrought-iron burglar bars got up to look like bamboo screens. Pictures of a pair of door gods—fierce, bearded warriors with armour and battleaxes— were pasted to the glass panels of the front entrance, and at one end of the veranda was an alcove for burning joss sticks. The owner of the house, Lieutenant-General Fang Sze-yuen, had good reason to propitiate his gods: in the thirty years he had lived in Hong Kong, he had survived four attempts to assassinate him. The last, admittedly, had been more than ten years ago, but he could never quite be sure that someone would not try again.

Having seen McNair's arrival, and somehow guessing the reason for the manner of it, General Fang stood in the doorway with an ancient pair of field glasses clamped to his eyes, watching the progress of the Datsun. In Shek O, too, the road ended in a cul-de-sac, a small parking lot which the car circled in confusion. Then it turned and began to retrace its route.

"You know them?" McNair asked.

"So-called journalists from the New China News Agency. In fact, Peking spies," said the General contemptuously, lowering the glasses. "They often watch my house."

"But it was me they were following."

"Probably they have nothing better to do. They know you, the work that you do. You must expect them to take an interest in you."

"But why today?"

"Come in, Mr. McNair."

Fang was a short, fat, bald man, rarely seen wearing anything but

214

a dark business suit. His broad face, with its wide, thin-lipped mouth and pouched, heavy-lidded eyes, gave him the look of an ancient, sagacious toad. He had been a close friend of Chiang Kai-shek as well as one of his senior commanders in the Chinese civil war; after fleeing from the victorious Communists he had been appointed unofficial representative of the generalissimo in Hong Kong. One of his functions was to run the Nationalist intelligence service in the colony, and the government tolerated him on two conditions: that he did not involve himself in any illegal enterprise, and that he gave them information when they asked for it.

He led McNair into his parlour—a ramshackle room with pieces of Ming porcelain dotted about among the worn furniture—and waved him to a chair. He sank into the corner of a couch opposite the policeman and clapped his hands sharply. A woman servant appeared and hovered.

"Whisky, Mr. McNair?" The General glanced at his watch. "You don't have the excuse, this time, that it is too early for you."

"Today I could use one."

Fang rapped out an order to the woman, who vanished to the back of the house. Then he hunched himself forward, elbows on knees, watching McNair intently.

"I have expected a visit since I heard, this morning, the news of this American. You want to know if I have information. I have not."

"Tell me your thoughts, then. It couldn't have been someone on your side? The wilder shores of the Kuomintang?"

"Absolutely not. If any of them had been planning such a thing I could not have failed to hear of it. And I would have stopped it. It could do us nothing but harm."

"Who, then? Communists?"

"It is possible."

"Only possible?"

"Yes. But perhaps not for the obvious reasons."

McNair was impatient, today, with this oriental obliquity. He said, "Come on, tell me what you think. You don't usually miss an opportunity to blame the Communists."

"There is a difference between propaganda and intelligence, Mr. McNair. Both are effective in their own ways, but it is important not to allow them to overlap." General Fang opened an ornately carved ivory cigarette box that stood on the low coffee table between them. He offered it to McNair, who shook his head. Fang took a cigarette, tapped

215

it on the table and lit it, keeping his toadlike gaze on the detective's face. "We have our usual understanding?" he asked.

"Nothing you say will be attributable."

"I ask because what I have to say is especially confidential. It must not go beyond you. We—my government, that is—have a particular interest in seeing that this Kiley man comes back safely. I have already been on the phone to Taipei." The General exhaled smoke with his mouth wide open. "I owe you a few small favours, Mr. McNair. If what I tell you will help, in any way, to secure the return of Kiley, both of us will benefit."

"Go ahead," McNair said.

"The news reports I have heard on the radio call him a diplomat. I think you and I both know better. He is a very important intelligence officer, but important for a different reason than even you may think. Different than the Americans would be prepared to tell—"

He broke off as the servant arrived with a tray. There was whisky in a cut-glass decanter, two heavy crystal glasses, an ice bucket, soda syphon, water jug. The General dismissed the woman and began preparing the drinks himself.

"There is a great deal of co-operation between us and the Americans, including the CIA. More, probably, than they are willing to talk about to the British. They depend heavily on us for intelligence on Peking: the sort of ground-level stuff that only our agents can provide. The mood of the people, the contents of the wall newspapers, who is in favour and who is not, the location of army units. In turn, we receive the sort of intelligence that only the Americans can get: missile bases and large troop movements, observed by their satellites. In the last few months we have had some details—extraordinarily specific details—about their missile programme. Ice? Soda?"

"Yes. Thank you," McNair said, feeling a tightening in his stomach.

"The CIA have not divulged their source, of course. But we have our own sources, and our own thoughts. It was soon after this man Kiley came to Hong Kong that this very detailed information began to surface. Now, we know things about Kiley's background that you would not be in a position to know. There was a man he knew back in the fifties, a Chinese-American called Ch'ien Hsue-shen. Ch'ien was a brilliant physicist. He went to America from Shanghai in nineteen thirty-five and got some degrees in aeronautical engineering. During

216

World War Two he became Director of Rocket Research for the National Defence Scientific Board. After the war, he was accused by the McCarthyites of being a Communist. He was persecuted by the FBI. Eventually, in 'fifty-five, he took his family back to China. Kiley was one of the people—assigned to his case, in those days, as a junior CIA officer—who tried to persuade him not to go."

The General sipped delicately at his drink. "Dr. Ch'ien, today, is not only director of missile development in the Peking nuclear weapons programme. He is also an alternate member of the Central Committee of the Chinese Communist Party."

"Well?" said McNair, still slightly puzzled.

"What we have been getting from the CIA suggests a leak from a very high-level source," said General Fang. "A source as high, perhaps, as Dr. Ch'ien himself. Perhaps."

"You're suggesting," said McNair incredulously, "that Ch'ien is spying for the CIA? That he's what they call an asset?"

"Perhaps," Fang repeated judiciously. "There is no way of being sure. There is no way, either, of getting the Americans to admit it. The point is that the coincidence is remarkable. If Ch'ien is helping the CIA, then it is probable that Kiley is running him. That is why it is important to get Kiley back. That is why I am telling you this."

"Jesus Christ," McNair breathed. "I wonder whether those people who kidnapped him realize what the hell they've done?"

There was no television set in the Quill Club, but somebody had brought in a transistor radio and a group of men were huddling around it at a corner table to hear the one o'clock news on the English service of Radio Hong Kong. Pritchard moved casually across from the bar counter to listen.

"... *troops from Stanley Fort and helicopters from Twenty-eight Squadron of the Royal Air Force have joined police in the biggest manhunt in the colony's history. No one has yet claimed responsibility for the murder and kidnapping, but a police spokesman said that a ransom demand could probably be expected soon. The Governor, Sir William Wilkie, has sent personal messages of regret to the parents of the dead chauffeur and to Mr. Kiley's wife, who is now on her way back here from Australia. ...*"

Pritchard smiled a secret smile and walked back to the bar to order another drink. He missed the next item on the news bulletin, which was

217

about a tropical depression centred three hundred miles east of the Philippines and moving steadily northwestwards.

When McNair phoned his information in to the Incident Centre, Boyd told him he might as well take some time off to eat. Since he had to pass close to his own flat on the way back to headquarters, he stopped in and found Siu preparing herself a salad for lunch. Expecting to find her sulking, he was pleasantly surprised by her greeting.

"Gavin! You can't be finished work?"

"Just for half an hour or so."

"You can join me for lunch, then."

"Just what I had in mind. I'll have a shower first."

He went to the bathroom, stripped off his clothes and stepped under the shower, washing away the grime and sweat that had accumulated with just one morning's running around. When he had dried himself down, he dressed in slacks and sport shirt and went through to the living room to find Siu had poured him a drink.

"It's the kidnapping of this diplomat you're working on, isn't it? I've been hearing about it on the radio. Sorry I was so peevish this morning."

"Sorry your day was spoilt. What did you do this morning, anyway?"

Amends made on both sides, they sat down together. "Oh, I got a few chores out of the way. Paid some bills. And finally managed to go down to the magistracy and apply for a new identity card. What a performance! Forms, fingerprints, photographs—"

"I don't know why you bother." Siu had not, until now, got round to applying for a card in her married name. "You're a British subject by marriage now, you don't really need one of those things."

"Technically I'm also a citizen of China. I could use that card to cross the border, did you know that? One day it may come in useful. What is it, Gavin?"

He was staring past her, a sudden frown creasing his brow. "Just a wild thought. What's the non-Chinese population of Hong Kong?"

"About forty thousand, isn't it?"

"Of whom I suppose at least half must be women and children. And then, if you eliminate men below a certain height, you'd be left with a few thousand at most. . . ."

"What *are* you talking about?"

"We've got some fingerprints that may very well belong to one of

218

the men who took part in this caper this morning. But we don't have an identity to match them. We think he's an American sailor. If we're wrong, we've had it—unless, by any chance, the suspect has ever applied for a Hong Kong identity card. In which case his prints shouldn't take too much finding. Hold on while I make a phone call."

Chief Super Boyd was sceptical. "I was explaining to Lewis just this morning that the Registration of Persons files don't work that way. You can't go to them with a print and get them to match it to a name. They have three million or more people on their records; it would take months—"

"But only forty thousand of those are non-Chinese, sir, don't you see? And of those only half are men. If we went through the identity card applications of all European males in the colony—"

"And made a visual comparison of prints? Even that might take days."

"So what else have Fingerprints got to do?"

At five minutes to three that afternoon, in the radio monitoring room at Clark Air Force Base fifty miles northwest of Manila, a bored United States Air Force sergeant warmed up his powerful shortwave receiver, switched on the tape recorder that stood on the table beside it and made sure it was plugged in to the radio. He ran a few feet of the tape to test it, then turned the recorder back to start and checked to see that the receiver was tuned to the right wavelength. In spite of its audio-frequency controls and fine-tuning devices, it often took a good deal of juggling to record a coherent signal from the low-powered transmitter that came on the air from somewhere in the jungles of southern Mindanao every day at this time. Today, though, listening with an experienced ear to the low level of static, he guessed the reception would be fairly clear. The barometer was falling with the approach of the tropical depression; low pressure improved the signal.

The sergeant put on his headphones, settled comfortably in his chair and lit a cigarette. At exactly three o'clock, when the martial strains of the familiar anthem burst onto the airwaves, he pressed the *record* button on the tape machine. Then he made a small adjustment to the tuning knob and sat listening absently to the remainder of the forty seconds of music, which sounded something like a cross between "The East Is Red" and the Triumphal March from *Aida.* At the end of it the voice of the usual announcer came on, speaking American-accented English.

"This is Radio Free Moro, the voice of the Moro National Liberation Front, broadcasting to the world from the liberated zone of Mindanao in the Philippines."

To the world indeed, thought the sergeant wearily. Apart from him, that bunch of slopeheads would be lucky if they had an audience within a hundred miles of their transmitter, and then three quarters of them wouldn't understand English.

"Here is a special bulletin," said the announcer. *"The Military High Command of the Moro National Liberation Front announce the capture of an important agent of the American military establishment. The operation was carried out this morning in Hong Kong by an active service unit of the MNLF, who have now returned with their prisoner to the liberated area of Mindanao."*

The sergeant stiffened in his chair. He stubbed his cigarette out and turned up the volume.

"The agent is Roderick N. Kiley, who has admitted under interrogation to being a senior officer of the American Central Intelligence Agency. For many years the CIA has actively assisted the Manila regime in their campaign of repression against the Muslim people of the southern Philippines. Kiley is therefore not a prisoner of war. The MNLF would be fully justified in trying him as an enemy agent; if found guilty, he could be executed according to accepted international practice."

The sergeant had seized a pencil and pad and was scribbling incoherent notes.

"However," the announcer continued, *"since we have no wish to expend life unnecessarily, we are willing to release Kiley unharmed in exchange for the freedom of certain of our own patriots being held as political prisoners by the Manila regime. Responsibility for the safety of the agent Kiley now rests squarely with the Philippines Government and their American supporters."*

"Captain!" the sergeant shouted, spotting his officer passing by the doorway. "Come in here, please!"

"Details of the time, place and circumstances for the release of the prisoners will be announced in due course," the announcer concluded. As the captain approached his table, the sergeant heard the martial music break in again for a few seconds, followed by the start of a conventional "news" bulletin about atrocities committed against the Muslim people.

Ten minutes later the tape was being played to the commanding officer of the base. Twenty minutes after that a transcript of it was being read over the phone by his senior intelligence officer to the Air Force attaché at the U.S. Embassy on Roxas Boulevard in Manila, for the attention of the Ambassador, the State Department and the CIA Chief of Station. The tape itself was already on its way by motorcycle dispatch rider to the embassy.

The Ambassador read through the handwritten copy of the transcript just once before sending it to be typed up. Then he asked his secretary to call the Philippines Department of Foreign Affairs with a request for an urgent interview with the Secretary of State.

28

By four o'clock, the only new development Boyd could claim as a breakthrough was the discovery, in the airport car park, of a mail van that the post office had reported stolen at nine o'clock that morning. Members of a police patrol crew remembered seeing it earlier, a few minutes before the crime was committed, parked at the spot where Kiley's Plymouth was later found. They had been looking for stolen vehicles, had paid no attention to the van and couldn't recall whether there was anyone in it. A check on the tunnel company's videotape showed that it had been driven through to the Kowloon side in the last moments before the northbound carriageway was closed.

"The scene-of-crime lads are giving the van a good going-over," the young officer from traffic said hopefully. "They may come up with something."

"Not the way our luck is going." Though not yet desperate, Boyd had begun to feel anxious. There was another meeting of the emergency committee scheduled in an hour's time, and he would have to face those damned Yanks with no positive news. He didn't want to go to the meeting at all, but the Commissioner had again insisted that he be there to make a progress report. Some progress! Much of his faith was now pinned on the young narcotics cop, Lewis, who at this moment was attending an identity parade, arranged by the U.S. naval authorities, of twenty possible suspects on the deck of a destroyer.

One of his aides was waiting to speak to him, one hand over the mouthpiece of a telephone receiver. "Excuse me, sir. It's the chap in charge of that fingerprint squad that you sent down to the magistracy. He says they've got a possible match for you."

"They've *what?*" Boyd shouted incredulously, diving for the telephone.

"That's right, chief," said the technician at the other end laconically. "Can't be certain till we get her back to the shop, but there was one good latent right thumbprint off the wall at that address in North Point, and I'm pretty sure it tallies with the one on this application. Bit of luck, really, that we started on the most recently issued ones—"

"Give me a name, man! A name and an address!"

"Lindsay. Patrick Weir Lindsay, British subject, the Healthy Guest House, Nathan Road, Tsimshatsui."

"Right. Bring that stuff back here as fast as possible." Boyd slammed down the phone and said to the aide, "Get two squad cars to that address one minute ago. Tell them not to let anyone leave. Tell them to go in hard, expecting shooting!"

Ted Lewis was back at the Incident Centre by ten to five, utterly despondent. He found Boyd standing behind his desk in the middle of the room, looking dark and grim, clutching a sheaf of papers.

"Nothing, Lewis?"

"Nothing, sir. God damn it, I was so sure I'd find him among those matelots. I—"

"I'm not surprised, not any more. Take a look at this. Is he your man?"

Boyd tossed the papers on the desk for Lewis to examine. They were white printed forms with blank spaces filled in ink; there was a signature, rubber stamps, fingerprints. There was a small, clear photograph of a man clipped to the corner of the top sheet. Boyd saw recognition start into the narc's eyes.

"Christ, yes! That's him, Chief, no question! Where'd you . . . ?"

"If that's him, then how do you explain that he left Hong Kong three months ago and hasn't been back since?"

"Impossible!"

"Not according to Immigration. Not according to the records at the guesthouse where he was dossing, either. That's an application for a Hong Kong identity card. He put it in back in May—the ninth of May —and the very next day he flew to London on a charter flight."

"Strange."

"What's even stranger is that the card was collected from the magistracy just last Saturday, the twelfth of August."

"Who the hell by?"

"Good question. Some sort of switch has been made, damned if I know how. But if you're certain that's your man in that picture—your sailor, as you called him, though now he obviously isn't—then I think we can be just as sure that his name isn't Lindsay."

"Where does that leave us, Chief?"

"With a face, nothing more. A face with no name to put to it. And now I've got to go up to another gab session at Government House. You can take a break, if you like."

"I want to check out this money changer that Yau told me about first. The dates when this character bought his supplies of heroin may shed some light on something."

"We need all the light we can get." Boyd turned back to his aide again. "Put a call through to London, Scotland Yard. Ask them as an urgent priority to try and trace this Lindsay person for us—the real Lindsay, assuming he actually exists. We've got a name, a passport number and a date of arrival in London, nothing more. Not even a description."

"No one at the guesthouse remembered him?"

"No one. They carry a floating population of kids: freaks, hippies, whatever they call themselves these days. The bugger could be anywhere by now."

The meeting of the emergency committee began promptly at five o'clock, with some changes in its membership. The Governor presided, flanked once more by the Police Commissioner and Boyd. Chief Superintendent Leggo had said McNair might as well deputize for him. On the American side Stanley, the security officer, had been replaced by the Ambassador from Bangkok, newly arrived, under whose authority the consulate in Hong Kong fell. The Consul General looked more ill-at-ease than before. Howard Koch, Kiley's CIA deputy, had his usual thoughtful, self-contained air.

The Governor introduced the Ambassador, who told them he had been given authority "at a very high level" from Washington to act on behalf of the CIA as well as the State Department. Then he broke the news from Manila: responsibility for the kidnapping had been claimed by the Moro National Liberation Front.

For several seconds there was a stunned silence on the British side

223

of the table. Then Boyd said, "May I ask how long you've known about this?"

"I believe the Moros announced it at three P.M. It was in a bulletin that we monitored on their clandestine radio service."

Boyd was very angry. "Don't you think, sir," he said, "that it might have been helpful to let us know a little earlier?"

"Gordon!" the Commissioner cautioned him.

"We wanted to make some inquiries of our own," the Ambassador replied imperturbably. "The Moros have asked for the release of certain political prisoners in the Philippines in exchange for freeing Mr. Kiley. We have already approached the government of the Philippines, informally, to ask whether they would agree to such an exchange. They refuse the demand categorically."

"What right have—?" Boyd began. The Commissioner interrupted him.

"That's certainly dramatic news from your end, Ambassador. I think it would be useful for you now to hear a report on the progress of the investigation. Gordon?"

With an ill grace, Boyd brought them up to date with developments: the finding of the mail van, the matching of the fingerprints to a suspect whose photograph they had but whom they could not, otherwise, identify yet. The American Ambassador, in his turn, grew impatient. Finally he said, "Hasn't all this become a little irrelevant, gentlemen? Since Mr. Kiley appears to have been abducted to the Philippines—"

"With respect, sir," said Boyd, "you have only the Moros' word for that."

"You say you found this vehicle at the airport. Doesn't that imply he was flown out?"

"That may be exactly what they wanted us to think. It isn't easy to force someone aboard an aircraft, particularly with the security arrangements and weapons checks we have at Kai Tak. Besides, there was a full alert out."

"Are you suggesting the Moros are bluffing?"

"I suppose they wouldn't claim to be the kidnappers if they weren't," Boyd admitted. "On the other hand, they didn't have to do the job themselves. What we know about this suspect I mentioned— he's probably the man who killed the bodyguard—suggests that he was an American. A mercenary, perhaps: it wouldn't be the first time terrorists have used them. But if they're claiming to have got Kiley out of Hong Kong to their own territory already, then, yes, I think there's

224

a chance they're bluffing. That's why it's important to keep up the pressure at this end. I think I have your support in that, don't I, sir?"

Boyd turned to the Commissioner, who nodded thoughtfully and then spoke to McNair. "These Moros were one group you didn't mention when you were running through your list of suspect organizations this morning. What do you know about them?"

"Frankly, sir, almost nothing. We've never had any reason to suspect they were operating here. Either we have slipped up badly or they did this job almost entirely from outside. In other words, their target just happened to be here and they worked without any local backup."

"Is that possible?" the Governor asked.

"Anything is *possible*. It certainly wouldn't be easy. I think I can say with some confidence that if Moro dissidents had been in business here for any length of time then we would know something about them."

"May I return to the point I started out with?" the Ambassador asked. He was a professional politician and knew the right moment in a debate at which to assert himself, even to the point of taking the chair without seeming to. He paused at the interruption of the Governor's aide, the white-uniformed lieutenant, who entered the room, walked round the table and handed a sheet of paper to Sir William.

"Carry on, Ambassador," the Governor said, fishing for his reading glasses.

"Now that the Moros have claimed to be the kidnappers, it is our duty at least to talk with them. I'm not saying your inquiries at this end are no longer relevant, gentlemen, simply that the United States Government must assume a direct responsibility for the safety of one of its employees. I must tell you that I have a specific mandate from both the Secretary of State and the Director of the Central Intelligence Agency to do everything necessary to secure the safe release of Mr. Kiley."

"Would that include paying a ransom?" asked the Commissioner.

"That is conceivable, in the light of the Filipinos' refusal to hand over prisoners. We may consider trying to talk to the guerrillas themselves, offering them some alternative . . . compensation."

"Paying money to criminals is a sellout, in my book," said Boyd. "If these maniacs are still on our territory—"

"What makes you think they may be?" the Ambassador asked coolly.

"Just a hunch."

"A hunch?" the Ambassador pulled back his coat sleeve and deliberately studied his watch. "After nine hours of investigation, is that the best you can come up with? A hunch?"

Boyd, inarticulate with anger, turned to the Commissioner with a half-strangled appeal. "Sir! There is no excuse for—"

"Gentlemen, I have some news," the Governor interrupted. He was studying the paper that had been brought to him, a strip of tape off a teleprinter, serrated at the bottom where it had been hastily torn off the roll.

"This is a telex to me from Dato Abu Bakr Salim, Chief Minister of Simpang State, in Malaysia. Is any of you familiar with the name?"

Howard Koch nodded. Elsewhere around the table, uneasy glances were exchanged. Only Boyd admitted his ignorance.

"Can't say I've ever heard of him, sir."

"It seems he has heard of the Moros' claim to be the kidnappers. He is offering to act as a mediator to secure Mr. Kiley's release."

"Well," said the Ambassador, slightly taken back, "I'll be grateful for anyone who can use his good offices. But how does this Mr. Salim stand in relation to the Moros?"

"He's an outspoken supporter of theirs." That was Koch, entering the discussion for the first time. "We know for a fact that he has supplied them with arms and training facilities."

"If he has influence with them he'll be the ideal go-between. He must have some way of communicating directly with them, Howard?"

"Pretty certainly."

"Then let's talk with him right away." The Ambassador paused and addressed the Governor. "If that's all right with you, Your Excellency? The message was addressed to you, but now the ball seems to be in our court. One other thing," he added, not looking at anyone now. "If we do get to the stage of active negotiation, it could be a little embarrassing if . . . well, if anything happened at this end that upset the Moros' plans, got them flustered. Could we be kept informed of developments and perhaps be consulted before any new moves are made?"

Sir William had removed his glasses and was squinting shrewdly at the Americans. "I'll agree to that, Mr. Ambassador, as long as you'll accept that consultation does not give you a share in the making of decisions. Outside my jurisdiction you can do whatever you want, make any deals you please. Within it, a murder and a kidnapping have happened. These police officers have a right, as well as a duty, to follow it all the way through."

"Damn right," Gordon Boyd muttered, just loud enough for everyone to hear.

They had brought a camp bed into the pillbox for him to lie on. Several times he had dozed off on it, only to start awake within a few minutes to a new awareness of discomfort and despondency. His ankle was starting to chafe from the steel ring around it. His thoughts wandered obsessively from his own predicament to Ailsa. Trial separation: she had actually used the phrase, the morning she set off for the airport, and the truth was that they didn't have much going for each other any longer. All the same, he sensed an anguish which he knew she must be sharing. There was no torment in his mind, just an increasing detachment from reality, half awake, half asleep, in the timeless gloom of the pillbox. From somewhere just outside he heard desultory talk and the tinny squawking of a radio.

Somewhere towards dusk, the time guessed at by the dimming of light in the horizontal gun slits (they had taken his wristwatch away), he fell asleep again. When he awoke it was with a sense of alarm. The two men were scrambling down the steps, helmets jammed on to mask their faces. The big one, the American, had a small transistor set clutched in one hand.

"Chopper coming," he said to Kiley. "You just lay still and shut up."

The two of them sat down against the wall opposite him, tense, expectant. In half a minute he heard the helicopter approaching, the familiar whine of a turbojet engine, the thick, swift smacking of the rotor blades, faint at first and then rising to a fierce crescendo as the chopper passed over the pillbox, so close that he wanted to leap to his feet and scream in the insane hope of being heard. The sound faded, resurged briefly as the pilot circled the barren ellipse of the island, then died away. Hope went with it, leaving Kiley more desolate than before.

The big man released a breath. "Looking for you," he said. "You're pretty big stuff, huh? Wanna hear some news on the radio? That'll be about you as well."

He set the transistor set down on the sand, switched it on and raised the volume to compensate for the poor reception in the pillbox. Kiley had his accent pinned down now: it was working-class Boston, familiar to him from his time at Harvard.

The radio crackled. The pips of a time signal came over. The six-o'clock news on Radio Hong Kong was announced.

"Responsibility for the kidnapping of the American diplomat, Roderick Kiley, has been claimed by the Filipino separatist group, the Moro National Liberation Front. They say he is now being held in Moro-controlled territory in the Philippines. In another development in the last hour, a Malaysian politician has offered to mediate for his release . . ."

Kiley started to his feet, throwing his hands apart in a gesture of astonishment, moving towards the big man until he was jerked back by the restraining force of the chain.

"That isn't—"

"Can it! Listen."

Kiley sank back on the camp bed, bewildered all over again. He had missed a few seconds of the bulletin. *". . . have demanded the release of a group of Muslim prisoners from jail in Manila. The Filipinos are believed to have rejected this demand. The offer to act as mediator has come from Dato Salim, Chief Minister of the Malaysian state of Simpang, who is a supporter of the MNLF. Meanwhile, here in Hong Kong, police supported by army and air force units are continuing their search for—"*

The big American snapped the radio off. He turned the black visor of his helmet towards Kiley.

"How about that, man?"

"Who do you think you're fooling? You aren't the Moro National Liberation Front."

"You want to see our membership cards?"

"You're American. And this isn't the Philippines. You haven't had time to get me there. That helicopter—"

"Who cares, wise-ass? It don't make no difference where you are, long as the rest of the world believes that shit. Including the CIA, who are gonna pay to get your ass back. And they'll pay plenty, believe me. Right now it's chow time, soup and sandwiches. You gonna eat or not?"

The Governor's meeting broke up as early as it could, everyone having urgent business to get back to. McNair caught up with Howard Koch in the lobby on the way out.

"Can you spare a minute?"

There was caution on the CIA man's face. He had been conscious, during the meeting, of the policeman's scrutiny. "What is it?"

"I'd like a word, in private."

Koch glanced with contrived impatience at his watch. "I really don't think I have the time right now, Mr. McNair."

228

"Can I give you a lift back to the consulate?"

"I was intending to walk."

"Then let me walk with you. That can't cost you any time."

Bereft of excuses, Koch shrugged. They set out together down Upper Albert Road, the setting sun throwing a golden sheen on the harbour below them. The heat was still sticky but the walking was easy, all downhill. A couple of Horace Stanley's security men kept pace with them at a discreet distance, one ahead, one behind.

"This man of yours, Kiley. In the course of asking around today, I learned something about him. Something that isn't really my business."

"What sort of something?" Koch asked.

"Probably nothing to do with what's happened, but who knows? He's running Dr. Ch'ien, isn't he?"

McNair threw the name out casually, groundbait. It stopped Koch in his tracks. He stared down at the sidewalk for several seconds. Then he said, "Where did you hear that?"

"If I thought I could tell you that, I'd have brought it up at the meeting. I thought it was best kept between us. It's only a guess, Mr. Koch, but I'm not the only one who's guessing. If you care to take a casual glance over your shoulder, you'll see that a blue Datsun is kerb-crawling behind us. They've been following me all day. They're legmen for the T'e Wu, the Communist secret service."

It took an effort of will on Koch's part, but he didn't look back. He started walking again, and McNair kept pace with him.

"I don't want to pry. I don't need to, except insofar as prying touches on the investigation. These people just happen to be my department. It makes me interested."

Koch stopped again and this time faced him, eyes serious behind the glasses. "Mr. McNair, we're on the same side, right? Allies have to respect the need not to know too much about one another."

"We're not holding anything back from you on this case."

"You can accept my assurance that Mr. Kiley's relationship with Dr. Ch'ien has no bearing on the kidnapping."

"How can you be certain of that?"

"I'll tell you this much, and no more, on the understanding that it gets no further. Ch'ien sent a message to us, four or five months ago. He wants to re-defect, return to the States. He made the approach through a friend in Hong Kong, a trustworthy source. To prove his sincerity he has been letting us have information on the Chinese missile programme. It's a very hot number indeed, and Rod Kiley was handling it personally. Ch'ien—and the friend, who acts as his courier—will deal with no one else. Now perhaps you'll understand quite how badly we want him back."

Koch turned and headed down the hill once more, towards the Annex. This time McNair didn't follow.

29

Things had quietened down somewhat on the thirteenth floor. There was the usual battery of people manning desks and telephones, and Boyd sat at the centre of them once more like a queen bee returned to the hive. But the pace was less frenetic than before. Whatever they all said—and thought—about the principle of continuing to hunt down the kidnappers from this end, they knew that the initiative had passed largely out of their hands. The Americans were going to negotiate to get their man back, and nothing the cops did was going to stop them. Nothing, unless they got the breakthrough they had been working towards and could start dictating terms of their own.

Boyd called to McNair as soon as he entered the room.

"You're free now, aren't you, Mac? Mrs. Kiley's just flown in. Thought you might go and have a word with her. I spoke to her myself this morning, on the buzzer to Sydney: no joy there, but a personal chat is always more useful than a phone call. The Americans are trying to keep her under wraps, but you'll know how to fight your way through."

It took him twenty minutes to reach the apartment in Quarry Hill, and by then it was fully dark. He waved his police warrant card at the guard on the gate and left the Lancia in one of the parking bays reserved for visitors. The apartment door was opened by a stocky man in a striped shirt with his tie pulled loose.

"You Press? Sorry, Mrs. Kiley isn't giving any inter—"

"Police," McNair said, flashing the card again.

"You get permission from the consulate?"

"I don't need permission from anybody to knock on doors around here."

"Look, buddy." The man's tone became wheedling. "She's had a pretty bad day, a long flight. Can't you leave her be, at least till—?"

230

"It's all right, Mr. Albach." She was there herself, in the hallway just behind the stocky man, a tall, squarely built blonde in a cotton trouser suit. "Let him in, please. Would you excuse us?"

With a grunt of disapproval the man called Albach stepped outside. "Thanks, Mrs. Kiley," McNair said, closing the door on him. "I promise not to keep you more than a few minutes."

"Are you the man I spoke with this morning?" she asked, leading the way into a big, sparsely furnished living room.

"That was my boss," McNair said, and took the seat that she waved him into. She sat down opposite and placed her hands in her lap, composed but tense, lines of strain showing round the mouth and the pale blue eyes.

"What can I do for you?"

"I'll be as brief as possible. I know you've had a very bad time."

"Would you like a drink?"

"No, thank you." The offer had been automatic, and she did not argue against his refusal. "As you can imagine, one of our major concerns has been to establish just why the kidnappers should pick on your husband. I mean—beyond the obvious reason, that he was *what* he was. We'd like to find out how they knew that. Frankly, we haven't got very far."

Ailsa Kiley groped on the couch beside her for a packet of cigarettes and a lighter. McNair tried to take the lighter from her, but she had already used it and blew out a stream of smoke. "How can I help?"

"Well, in order to kidnap him, these people must have been keeping him under observation for some time—noting his routine, particularly the time he left for work each morning. Have you noticed anything unusual in the neighbourhood lately? Strangers hanging around? Strange cars?"

"The other man on the phone asked me that this morning. I said no. I've had eight hours in a plane to think some more about it, and it's still no."

"Very well. What about changes in otherwise routine visits? I mean you haven't suddenly had a new man round to read the gas meter, for instance? Or a new postman?"

She thought for a few moments and shook her head. She was only confirming what the amah had already told them this morning.

"On a rather more personal basis, what about your social life? You've been here—what, seven or eight months? Who have you mixed with?"

She gave a small, tight-lipped smile. "Almost nobody. A few people from the consulate, occasionally. It's been rather claustrophobic."

McNair hesitated, choosing his words, before he spoke again. "Mrs. Kiley," he said, "we know exactly what your husband's job is, in the Annex. It's part of our business to know."

"I'm not supposed to talk about that," she said uneasily.

"I'm not asking you to. I'd like to know how many other people have some knowledge—or even just an inkling—of what it involves."

"Rod once told me that no more than half a dozen of his colleagues in any one posting knew."

"And outside the consulate?"

"Nobody."

"But the kidnappers knew. That means there had to be a leak somewhere."

"Mr. McNair, are you suggesting that *I* leaked information?"

"Not at all. I'm just hunting for possibilities. These things can happen unconsciously. Can you think of anyone, anyone at all outside the consulate, who had some knowledge of what your husband's job entailed?"

"Nobody. Nobody in Hong Kong, anyway. Unless—" She gave a slightly embarrassed laugh. "There's Alan, but he's quite harmless."

"Alan?"

"I'd really rather not drag him into it." Her manner had changed; she was flustered, nervously twisting the wedding ring on her finger. "It could be awkward. And he really couldn't be involved in anything like this."

"Who is he, Mrs. Kiley?"

"Do you have to know?"

"I think I'd better."

She mashed out her half-smoked cigarette suddenly in an ashtray on the coffee table, then faced him with a frank look in her wide blue eyes. "How far will this go?"

"Only as far as it needs to."

"You mean you wouldn't have to tell the Company? The CIA, I mean."

"Possibly not, if this man is as innocuous as you say."

"All right. His name is Alan Pritchard. He's a journalist, he works for the *Cathay Star*. Years ago, before I was married, he and I were ... lovers. It was in Saigon. When I got married he dropped out of my life, until a few weeks ago when I bumped into him here in Hong Kong. I've seen him a couple of times since."

232

"Do you know where he lives?"

"Man Won Building, Happy Valley. If he's not at home you'll probably find him in a place called the Quill Club."

Her quick familiarity with the address told McNair most of what he needed to know. He said, "Your husband didn't know you were meeting him?"

"No."

"It's nothing to me, but the Company would take a pretty dim view."

"I'm past caring what the Company thinks, frankly. Anyway, I haven't been indiscreet. I didn't talk to Alan about Rod's work because I don't know anything to tell."

"He's simply aware of the CIA connection, is that it?"

"From the Vietnam days, yes. Several journalists knew, or guessed, at the job he had behind the diplomatic cover. It didn't seem to matter so much then; there wasn't this total obsession with secrecy."

"I'm afraid I'll have to talk to Mr. Pritchard. I'll be as tactful as I can." McNair stood up. Mrs. Kiley sat watching him with a small smile.

"You're probably thinking I'm not behaving very guiltily. I don't feel guilty. My husband and I were just about finished; I wouldn't have come back here if it wasn't for this business. It's upset me, of course, but I don't think it'll change anything—assuming he comes through it alive. The Alan thing was a little adventure, something I needed to get out of my system."

"You mean it's over, between you and him?"

"I think so. He was starting to take it too seriously."

"It makes no bloody sense," said Ted Lewis, pacing back and forth in frustration in front of Boyd's desk. "Yau and this money changer he put me on to: between them I've got seven definite dates pinned down over the first six months of this year when Yau changed American dollars given to him by this sailor. And only on the first three dates were there American ships in port."

"Then either Yau is lying," said the Chief Superintendent, "or the first three dates were just coincidences and the man we want isn't a sailor."

"Yau has no reason to lie. He's seen the light. And he insists that this man was a sailor."

Boyd was silent for several seconds. The sailor business was getting on his wick. It was the best lead they had, yet they couldn't follow it without constantly losing it. It should have been the easiest thing in the world to find a fugitive foreigner in a place like Hong Kong, but they'd got nowhere. There had to be a factor somewhere that they were not taking account of. No matter how experienced an investigator you were, you still occasionally found you had overlooked something that was as obvious as a slap in the face when eventually you saw it.

A telephone rang on the desk to Boyd's right. One of his Chinese assistants answered it, then clamped a hand over the mouthpiece. "It's Cable and Wireless, sir. They want to know if we'll pay for a reverse-charge call from London. It's person-to-person, for you."

"Scotland Yard." Boyd, tired and strained after twelve frenetic hours of work, laughed out loud with a sudden sense of absurdity. "We've got a kidnapping on our hands and they're worried about their phone bill! All right, put 'em on."

A few seconds later he was listening to a young-sounding voice from eight thousand miles away, clear as a bell. "Chief Superintendent Boyd? I've been handling your query and it seemed easier to phone you back than telex. Can I go ahead?"

"Sure. It's our nickel."

"Sorry about that. Regulations, I'm afraid. There'd be a fuss if our accountants . . ."

"Just go ahead, would you?" said Boyd impatiently.

"Very well, sir. Well, we've got your suspect here—"

"Lindsay?" Boyd asked incredulously. "You've found him?"

"It wasn't that difficult. He's been out on bail for the last three weeks on a charge of possessing LSD, so our drugs people knew exactly where to find him. He's in the next room from me at the moment."

"Give me a quick description."

"The name's as you had it, Patrick Weir Lindsay. Age twenty-two, fair hair, height five-feet-ten. Weighs maybe nine stone if he's lucky."

"And he *was* in Hong Kong, earlier this year?"

"That's right. He dropped out of a social science course at Reading University, took a charter flight to Hong Kong, ran out of money and got stuck there. Looking for the big Eastern experience, I gather: you'd have a better idea what that means than I do."

"It means a big nothing. How did he get back to England?"

"That's a complicated story. You'd save time by talking to him yourself. He's in enough trouble as it is and he's anxious to help."

"Yes," breathed Boyd. "Yes, put him on. . . ."

Five minutes later, after listening on the phone and pencilling notes

234

intently on a scratch pad, he slammed down the receiver. His expression as he faced Lewis was a cross between triumph and exasperation.

"A deserter!" he shouted.

"Sir?"

"The sailor was a bloody *deserter!*" There was the possibility overlooked, the slap in the face. "Why in the course of twelve hours hasn't that thought once entered the head of any of us?" Boyd rapped the side of his skull with his knuckles. "This kid, Lindsay, while he was in Hong Kong, staying at that guesthouse, was buying drugs from a deserter from the U.S. Navy called Seymour."

"Is that a first name or a surname?"

"He doesn't know. The sailor offered to pay the kid's fare home in return for a favour. And you know what the favour was? Applying for an identity card in his own name, and letting this Seymour substitute *his* face and *his* dabs on the application form."

"Right," said Lewis. "So now we've got a bloke named Seymour Something or Something Seymour, we've got his pictures and a set of prints. We still haven't got the bloke."

"But we're a big step closer." Boyd turned to one of his clerks. "Get me a list of every American sailor and marine who's been posted as a deserter in Hong Kong in the past two years. Full description, too. While you're waiting for it, get hold of the duty officer at the consulate. Tell him we'll want to check our list against theirs, to make sure no names are missing. Lewis, we'll nail these bastards yet: you wait and see!"

At eight thirty, McNair found Alan Pritchard in the Quill Club, where he'd gone after getting no reply at the Happy Valley address. A waiter pointed him out—a man of middling height and build in light slacks and a checked madras cotton shirt, hair brownish, starting to grey, a nondescript face that turned in surprise as McNair spoke from beside him.

"Mr. Pritchard?"

"Yes?"

"Excuse me. I didn't mean to startle you. My name is McNair. I heard I might find you here."

"Heard? From whom?"

McNair hoisted himself onto the stool beside Pritchard's. He spoke quietly. "I've just been to see Mrs. Kiley, the wife of the kidnapped diplomat. She told me she was a friend of yours. I'm a police officer."

It was a technique he had often used, dropping the word *police*

235

suddenly, waiting to see the ripples. Pritchard watched him suspiciously, brown eyes veined, whisky on his breath. He must have been in here quite a while.

"Copper, eh?" he said. "What do you want from me?"

"It's strictly informal. I'm part of the team investigating the case. We're trying to cover every possible angle, speak to anyone who was even remotely connected with the victim, in the hope of learning something useful. That includes people who were friendly with his family."

"Friendly?" Pritchard snorted derisively. "Yes, I suppose that's one way of putting it. Matter of fact, I was wondering when you'd get round to me. Did Ailsa tell you all about us?"

"She told me you'd once been very friendly. Look, I'm not here to dig into your private life, it's not my concern. I'm only interested in any facts that may have a bearing on the case. Can I buy you a drink?"

"Not unless you're a member. Chits only."

"Then how about going across to the Hilton or somewhere?"

"Thanks, but I'm nicely settled here. Besides, you can't buy information from me. Let me get you one. I may be out of a job but I'm not that skint. Still Life!" Pritchard called, and the fat, hostile-looking barman came to take their orders.

"I gather," said McNair, when the drinks had arrived and Pritchard had scribbled his signature on a chit, "that you knew Kiley himself, back in Saigon?"

"Sure."

"And knew the nature of the work he was doing?"

"He was Chief Spook in the American Mission; quite a few people knew that."

"You must have guessed, after you met Mrs. Kiley again here in Hong Kong, that he was still in the same business? That he was probably in the same sort of job?"

"When I gave him any thought at all. This part of the world, these CIA buggers are coming in at the windows."

"Sure. I'm just wondering whether you might have suggested this fact to anyone else? Let it slip, maybe, to the man beside you at work, something like that?"

Pritchard laughed, a short, high-pitched cackle that stopped as suddenly as it began. "Look, the man just doesn't figure in my conversation. Let's get that straight, can we?"

McNair drank some whisky. "I have to ask you this. Since you met her again, a few weeks ago, have you had any feelings of jealousy?

236

Any feeling that you'd have liked to keep her?"

"I thought you weren't going to get personal," Pritchard said.

"We can't rule out the possibility that there might be some personal motive involved in this crime."

"Well, the answer is no. Ailsa is a back number for me. I've turned a few pages again recently, nothing more."

That, McNair thought, didn't square with Ailsa's view of his feelings. So who was fooling whom? There was something about Pritchard, a deep-down bitterness perhaps, that almost made you feel sorry for him.

"You say you're out of a job? I thought you worked for the *Cathay Star.*"

"I was made redundant. Unquote. Nothing else has turned up yet. Can't say I've been looking too hard."

"What are you living on?"

"Redundancy pay."

"You weren't at work this morning then, obviously."

"Obviously."

"Where were you?"

"What time this morning?"

"All morning."

"Listen, Jesus, you don't suspect me of . . . ?"

"I don't suspect you of anything," McNair said calmly. "The way we work is by eliminating non-starters. You can make yourself a non-starter by accounting for your movements from about eight o'clock this morning onwards."

"Well, about eight o'clock I was on my way out to Hebe Haven with a pal of mine. Matter of fact, the car was searched at a roadblock on the way. He's got a junk moored out there; we're planning a trip to the Philippines in a couple of days' time. We ran her a few miles out to sea to check the compass, then brought her back."

"What time was that?"

"Round twelve."

"And then?"

"My pal, Eddie Baxter, drove me back to town. I was in here by one, because I heard about the kidnapping on the one o'clock news. I've been here ever since; Still Life over there will confirm that."

"Where does this Mr. Baxter live?"

"Up the Peak Road. I forget the exact address, but he's in the phone book." Pritchard grinned at the policeman, a slightly malevolent grin. "You're wasting your time, Mac—McWhat?"

"McNair."

"Why don't you have another drink, McNair?"

"Oh, I couldn't do that."

"I told you, I'm not all that skint."

"It's not that. I have work to do." McNair got off the barstool. "All right, I think you've told me everything I needed to know. Sorry for the bother. And thanks for the drink."

He left the club, vaguely aware as he walked towards the door of the Englishman's dark, laughing stare following him. As he stood waiting for the lift he heard Pritchard shout, "Still Life!"

30

In the American Consulate General, the duty officer put the call from Boyd's aide at the Incident Centre through to the top-floor conference room, where a meeting was in progress, presided over by the Ambassador from Bangkok.

The Consul General picked up the phone himself. He listened for half a minute and said testily, "You'll have to wait," then lowered the receiver with a hand clamped over the mouthpiece. He and the rest of the men in the room—Koch, Stanley and three others—were listening tensely to one end of a conversation on another telephone, and the discussion was being recorded by a cassette machine. The Ambassador was talking to Chief Minister Salim of Simpang State.

He listened and replied, his own comments mostly monosyllabic grunts, for about two minutes before saying, "Well, thank you very much for that information, Chief Minister. Let me add that I and my government are more grateful than we can tell you for the time and trouble you are taking in this matter. I'll talk with you again soon."

He replaced the receiver and switched off the recorder. "So far, so good," he said, looking up at the others. "He seems to have talked the Moros around."

"They'll deal with us?" Koch asked.

"He thinks he has succeeded in convincing them that the Filipino Government means what it says—they're not about to release any prisoners in exchange for Kiley, and the Moros will have to negotiate with us."

238

"That means they'll take money instead of prisoners," said the Consul General. "What sort of money?"

"He thought he could persuade them to accept ten million dollars."

"Ten million! They really have some goddam nerve!"

"I don't believe we can afford to refuse. Howard, that money could be got over here from the Director's Contingency Fund, couldn't it? How long would it take?"

"A couple of days at most, depending on the method of payment."

"The Chief Minister had some suggestions there, to speed things along. He says we should arrange for a bank draft to be issued to him, payable on sight at a bank in Brunei; there are no restrictions on currency import or export there, which will simplify things. He will then arrange to have the money made available to the Moros whatever way they want it, at an agreed rendezvous. They will issue a receipt which he will pass on to us, together with notification of where and when Kiley can be picked up. It'll be all very correct," the Ambassador added sarcastically. "Just like buying a piece of real estate unseen. The ripoff is that it was our property in the first place."

"This Salim has a pretty unsavoury business reputation," Koch said. "The way he's arranging this exchange, he could be planning to pocket some of the money himself."

"I don't give a damn who gets it, frankly, as long as it buys Kiley back for us. Gentlemen, I don't think we have any choice but to go along with this plan. But no word of it is to get out until the exchange is complete."

"What do we tell the British authorities here?" asked the Consul General. "They know we're under pressure to pay the ransom."

"We stall them. Who's that on the phone?"

"Chief Superintendent Boyd's office. They think they can identify one of the men involved. They're asking for a list of deserters from the U.S. Navy, to check against their own records."

"You mean they still suspect there's an American involved somewhere? Well, okay, let them have the list. We have to give the appearance of co-operating. On the other hand, we have to be careful that the police don't do something that screws up our plans."

Baxter came very quickly to the door of his flat, almost as though he'd been sitting close by, waiting for the bell to ring. And his concerned, over-eager manner as he ushered McNair through to the living room made the policeman wonder whether Pritchard had phoned to warn his friend of the impending visit. Even innocent people sometimes did peculiar things when dealing with the police; the encounter made them anxious, self-conscious.

Baxter introduced his wife, a sharp-featured blonde who nodded at him distantly from a corner of the settee. She'd been reading a book and seemed to resent the interruption.

"Mr. McNair is investigating this Kiley business, darling. The kidnapping, you know."

"What on earth has that got to do with us?"

"Nothing at all, I'm sure," McNair said. "This is purely routine. We've questioned a great many people whose names just happen to crop up on the periphery of the case. Do you mind telling me, Mr. Baxter, what you were doing between about eight and nine this morning?"

"Why, sure. I was on my way out to Hebe Haven. I keep a junk out there. Arrived a little after nine, if I remember."

"That took you long enough," said his wife. "You left the flat well before seven, and it's only a fifty-minute drive."

"I had some things to do on the way—"

"In fact, I remember now, it was just after half past six when I woke up and you were gone already. What took you all that time?"

"I *said* I had things to do, Liz." Baxter looked flustered, and McNair felt a man's embarrassed sympathy for a henpecked husband. "And then there was Alan to collect at eight."

"Is that Alan Pritchard?"

"Yes. D'you know him? Look, what's all this about, anyway?"

"You and Mr. Pritchard spent the morning together then, just the two of you?"

"Out on the boat, yes."

"All right, Mr. Baxter," said McNair, standing up. "Thanks, and sorry to have bothered you." At the door he said, "I believe you're sailing to the Philippines soon. I envy you. Hope this tropical depression will keep away. You wouldn't want to go out into that."

The two lists of Navy deserters, one from the police files, one from the consulate, arrived on Boyd's desk together. It took him less than ten seconds of running his eye down them to find the name he wanted.

"There!" he said triumphantly to Lewis, stabbing his finger down at a point on the typed sheet. "Quinn, Seymour Kevin. Gunner's Mate

240

Third Class. Reported absent without leave from the USS *Kitty Hawk* after a liberty on April fifteenth *and still not traced.* Height six-two, weight a hundred and ninety, brown hair, brown eyes. That sound like your man?"

"It has to be!" Lewis said fiercely. "Damn it, how does a guy like that stay free for all that time?"

"By having good shelter. By having friends to protect him, providing board and lodging. A woman, perhaps: some girl he knew from his earlier stopovers here? Someone, anyway, who may have no idea of his involvement in this caper."

"So what do we do? Get on to Vice and have them check out all the whores on their books?"

"That would take days. Besides, we don't know that she's a hustler, or even that there's a woman involved at all. My idea is this: we make a direct public appeal—to anyone who may have seen him, to anyone who might know who's sheltering him, even to the people who are sheltering him themselves." Boyd glanced at his watch; it was nine thirty-five. "Listen. There's enough time to get a statement and copies of that picture out to the morning papers. With a real rush job we might make it in time for tonight's late television news, Cantonese and English. We'll lay it on thick: deserted American sailor, wanted for murder and kidnapping. It should shock a reaction out of someone."

Lewis looked uneasy. "Putting all your eggs in one basket, aren't you, Chief? We'll look bloody silly if nobody comes forward."

"We're looking silly right now, son. It's more than thirteen hours since the job was done, and this is still the only lead we've got."

The statement went out ten minutes later, in the form of a telex message simultaneously relayed to all media. Five minutes after that, blowups of the photograph of Seymour Quinn were on their way by motorcycle dispatch rider to Hong Kong's three television stations.

McNair was back in the Incident Centre by then and had reported briefly on his interviews with Mrs. Kiley and the two men.

"Pritchard is a queer party," he said. "Can't quite make him out: a chip on his shoulder, definitely, and I think he's jealous of the woman in spite of what he says. But on the whole I'd have to put him down as harmless. I checked out his movements, just as a precaution. Seems he spent the morning sailing out of Hebe Haven on a friend's junk. Pak Sha Wan station say they can't locate the local boatboy to confirm that, but the junk is back at its mooring. Pritchard has spent the rest of the day drinking in the Quill Club."

"Sounds like you can forget about him then," Boyd said. "Look, since you're on night duty anyway, how'd you feel about taking over the desk about midnight? I'd like to stick in here till then, to catch any flak once this sailor's picture hits the TV screens. Then I'll crash for a while on the camp bed they've put in my office. You want to go home and get a couple of hours' rest?"

Canny sat on the couch, her gaze fixed on the television screen without really seeing it, the flickering images of yet another interminable Chinese soap opera bypassing her brain but providing a focus for her attention, like flames in a fireplace. She was tired, as she was most nights by this time, but with the added fatigue of emotional exhaustion that had been building up for weeks. She had felt Seymour slipping away from her, gradually but steadily. She was used now to getting home from work and finding him not here; it happened several times a week. This morning he had left early and had evidently not been back all day. At one time there had been excuses—he had to "see a guy" or "set up a deal"—but he no longer bothered explaining, just went out whenever it suited him and never suggested when he might be home. When he was back, usually at night, he used her body selfishly, unsharingly. Deep down, she knew that one day Seymour would leave her, yet she clung to the hope that he wouldn't.

Ten thirty: part one of the soap opera ended on the hysterical note of a family quarrel, giving way to commercials and then the title shot of the late news programme. It was time she went to bed, but she felt too dazed with tiredness to move. Suddenly she was brought back to life by some urgent impression on her consciousness. It took her a few seconds to focus her full attention on the small screen, perhaps even longer to realize that it showed a photograph—a likeness, anyway—of him! The words of the Chinese commentary began to strike home: "... *deserted his ship, the USS Kitty Hawk, in April. Police are asking anyone who knows him or may have seen him to come forward with information. He is described as six feet two inches tall, powerfully built...*"

After a minute the picture changed. Canny's mind, in a blur, recorded something of what followed: film of helicopters taking off and hovering over barren rocks, a European police officer having his remarks translated into Cantonese: "*No, we can't say for certain that the diplomat is still being held here, but we must continue to search. If this*

242

man Quinn is innocent then he should come forward. . . ."

The rest was lost to her. She stood up and stumbled towards the kitchen and then turned helplessly back into the main room, not knowing what she was looking for. A clue, any clue, to what had happened. Something to negate that stuff on the TV. There must be some explanation, some mistake.

For a minute she stood clutching the edge of the worktop in the kitchenette, regaining control of herself. Then she went to the small closet at the side of the room. On the left, on top of the stack of shelves where he kept his clothes, was the spot where he hid any spare money he had. She groped among shirts, socks, underwear: there was nothing. Only last night, after the Negro had left, she had seen him put eight or nine hundred Hong Kong dollars in there. And as this realization settled into her, she was aware of another impression. The clothes: there were too few of them. What was left was old and threadbare. In particular she recalled four cotton shirts in pastel shades that he'd bought a couple of weeks ago. They were gone. So were his only good pair of trousers and his leather brogues.

She forced herself to look further. On the other side of the wardrobe, hidden by her dresses, had stood her small leather suitcase, the only luggage she possessed. That, too, was missing.

The facts were screaming at her now, but still she could not bring herself to face them fully. And she was confused: distracted from her shock and hurt and anger by what she had heard on the TV. The police wanted Seymour—what for? Deserting his ship, after all this time? Dealing in drugs? Was that why he'd gone on the run? No, there'd been some mention of this kidnapped diplomat. But what in God's name could Seymour have to do with that?

One thing she did understand, an inner quake, a sudden desperate need. She half ran, stumbling, to the bathroom and flung open the cabinet above the washbasin. The jar of Seconal shook in her hand as she split half a dozen capsules into the other palm. She swallowed them one by one, chasing them with gulps of water. Then, controlling her breathing carefully, she went back to the living room and sat down, waiting for the soothing caress of the drug.

Shortly after midnight McNair, refreshed by two hours' sleep, a shower and a hot meal, returned to take charge of the Incident Centre. Boyd brought him up to date: after the police statement and Quinn's picture had gone out on the television bulletins there'd been a brief flurry of activity. Five people claimed to have seen the suspect at one time or another, and all their stories had been checked. A teller in the foreign exchange department of the Hong Kong and Shanghai Bank thought the American had changed some English pounds into local currency last Thursday. There was no name attached to the transaction. A girl assistant at the Wing On department store thought she had sold him some shirts a couple of weeks ago. Again, he had paid cash and given no name. Two people claimed to have seen him at different times on the Star Ferry.

The most electrifying call came from the night clerk of a small hotel in Tsimshatsui, who whispered fiercely that the suspect was staying in a room on the second floor. A posse of police surrounded the building and armed detectives hammered on the door. It was opened by a terrified Canadian tourist who bore a marked but superficial resemblance to Quinn. In the double bed behind him an equally frightened Chinese boy sat blinking into the light. The policemen apologized for the intrusion, thanked the clerk for his vigilance and went away.

By now, the phones had practically stopped ringing. Boyd was clearly worried when he left to get some sleep in his office, and McNair understood why. On every front, the investigation was grinding to a halt. Quinn's identity was the only good card they had, and now they had shown it to everyone—including, perhaps, the kidnappers. There was a chance of fresh developments first thing in the morning, when the newspapers came out with the photograph. Meanwhile, there was a long night ahead.

31

Pritchard woke up with a start. He was sitting on the couch in his living room. On the television screen in the opposite corner, the weatherman was mouthing in front of a chart covered in a tracery of isobars. He looked fuzzily at his watch; it was twenty past twelve.

"Damn!" he muttered. He became conscious of a headache and a bad taste in his mouth. He had come home from the Quill just after ten o'clock with the intention of watching the late news, but had drunk more than he'd intended—drinking away his anxiety, blurring the tension and boredom of the long wait. He had made himself a crude sandwich of cheese and pickle and slumped down with it and another glass of whisky in front of the set. He must have fallen asleep soon after he had eaten.

He got up, went to the bathroom and took two aspirins for his headache. He'd have to wait for news now until the one-o'clock bulletin on the radio. He should be getting a decent night's sleep. He had done his drinking in a spasm of sheer nervous release—at the success of the Project, at the way the Moros' story and Salim's offer of intercession had obviously been swallowed whole, even at how his interview with the policeman, McNair, had gone. The talk among the reporters in the club that evening had been of the police investigation getting bogged down, and there was at least one rumour that the Americans were bracing themselves to pay for the diplomat's release.

When he came back to the living room and headed for the TV to turn it off, he saw that the weather report was over. Instead, Seymour Quinn's face stared at him.

"Jesus Christ!" he breathed. It was like seeing a ghost, a sensation of skin-tingling horror. He took a few involuntary paces backwards, collapsing onto the couch at the same moment as he began to absorb the words of the continuity announcer.

"*. . . a reminder before we say good night that this is the man the police want to interview in connection with the kidnapping of the American diplomat Roderick Kiley this morning. His name is Seymour Kevin Quinn, a deserter from the American Navy, and anyone who recognizes him is asked to contact the nearest police reporting centre. Well, that's all from us tonight. We hope you'll tune in again to—*"

Pritchard stood up, walked to the set, and snapped it savagely off. He went to the bathroom, ran cold water into the basin and splashed it on his face. Then he looked up into the mirror, into his own eyes, wild and red and unbelieving. His fevered mind ached with the need to concentrate, to think things out through the faint haze of alcohol.

It took a minute for him to calm down and straighten his mind out to the point where he could analyse the information. They'd identified Quinn. Somehow or other, they'd got onto Quinn. It could only be because the big ape had left some clue behind him: the tussle he'd had with the cop last night, the gun he'd taken off him, the fact that he had been wanted in the first place. Pritchard thought he'd been a fool to take Quinn into the Project. They'd traced him within—what was it?—sixteen hours. What else might they not find out before the ransom was paid?

Pritchard got himself a drink and began to calm down. The thing was not to panic, to work out the moves before he made them. What did that crap on the television mean? It meant they'd identified Quinn, yes, but the fact they were asking people who knew him to come forward meant they didn't know much beyond that. Or did they know more than they were telling? That was the most uncomfortable question of all.

Who might come forward? Who knew Seymour Quinn? Who might be willing to inform on him? One name sprang to Pritchard's mind.

Canny.

He had met her just once. She'd seemed a sullen little bitch, and her relationship with Quinn wasn't good. Since Quinn had now walked out on her, would she be keen to get her own back on him? Would her instinct be to protect or to condemn him? Either way, she was potentially very dangerous. Besides, she had met Pritchard himself, knew his first name, would be able to identify him. He decided he would have to pay Canny a visit.

The big Webley revolver was out at Basalt Island. He wished he had it with him but knew that the wish was not practical; one shot from that would wake up half of Causeway Bay.

Here was a challenge, he thought, as he left the flat and made his way down the stairs. Here was a test of how ruthless he could be. He had got the Project this far and was not going to see it fail through squeamishness. But what if he were too late already? The sign-off on the TV programme had been just a sequel to an earlier broadcast, which could mean that the police had two or even three hours' start on him. But he had to know, had to act.

The midnight atmosphere was still like an oven. He walked down to Hennessy Road and flagged down a half-full minibus going to Causeway Bay, got out at the Daimaru store terminus and walked the two blocks to Canny's apartment building. He waited a couple of minutes in the shadows outside to make sure the lobby was empty before he entered. He took the graffiti-scarred lift up to the eleventh floor, then walked down two flights of stairs, pausing carefully on the bottom step, looking and listening along the long open balcony of Floor Nine until he was satisfied that no police guards had been posted—outside the apartment, at least. This, after all, could have been the whole object of the TV broadcast. With Canny's co-operation already secured, they might be trying to lure Quinn's accomplices into a trap.

Heart pounding, he walked down the balcony. Like a halfhearted suicide, his reflexes tautened to pull him back from the ledge, he put his fist through the bars of the burglar trellis and rapped softly on the door. There was no response. He repeated it twice before he heard a creak of springs, a shuffling, stumbling noise as the door was approached.

"*Wei?*" The Cantonese query was slurred, as if she'd woken from a deep sleep. It reassured Pritchard; if she'd been expecting him she'd have spoken English. But there was suspicion in her tone.

"Canny?" he called.

"Yes?"

"This is Alan. Seymour's friend. Remember me?"

She hesitated, whether through uncertainty or sleepiness he couldn't tell. Eventually she said, "What you want?"

"I must talk to you. It's urgent."

"Seymour is not here."

"I know." Seizing on her anxiety, he said, "I've brought a message from him. Please let me in."

She paused only briefly before opening the door. She was still dressed but her eyes were heavy, dazed with sleep. She turned and groped her way back into the room, returning with a key which she inserted in the lock on the burglar guard. When she had turned it Pritchard pulled back the trellis and entered.

"Where is Seymour?" she demanded. "Staying with you?"

He closed the door before replying. "Did you see the news on television, Canny?"

"Police want him. Why?"

"He's safe. I can tell you that much."

Canny watched him with confused resentment. She was trembling slightly, and that gave him the clue: she'd been on pills, downers had put her to sleep. The behaviour of someone depressed, not angry.

"What is this thing he is mixed up in, Alan?"

"He's not. They've made a mistake. They're looking for the wrong man."

"He run out on me. Why?"

"He's scared of the police, Canny. Just because of what he is—a deserter. And he hasn't run out on you. He just had to leave in a hurry."

"He sent you to tell me that?"

"Yes."

Her face masked her feelings, but Pritchard sensed the relief in the way her body lost its tension. Christ, he thought: women and their capacity for self-delusion. She sat down on the couch.

"He could have said something to me. He doesn't trust me?"

"Of course he does," Pritchard said soothingly. "He had to leave without warning, that's all. He thought the police might trace him here and he didn't want you involved."

"How long can he run like this, Alan? It's better that he gives himself up."

"They'll lose interest in him once they find the right man. Till then he must lie low." Pritchard, standing over her, watched Canny's face closely. "That picture on the television: it was aimed at you, you know —or someone like you that they think has been sheltering Seymour. They wanted you to give him away."

"Yes."

"You didn't think of doing that, did you, Canny?"

She did not catch the menace in his tone. She said candidly, "I thought it, yes. I thought, He has left me, what do I owe him? Maybe police make trouble for me."

"What made you think he had left you?"

"He took clothes." She waved at the wardrobe. "And my suitcase. And all his money."

Pritchard went to the side of the room and opened one of the closet doors. Stupid berk, he thought; he could have done it without making it this obvious. What clothes he had left behind were obviously unwanted: worn jeans, some threadbare shirts and underwear, a black silk tie made shapeless by too much knotting. He took the tie off its rack and turned to Canny. She sat with her back to him, staring at the opposite wall.

"And now?" he asked. "Would you go to the police now?"

"No. If he is telling the truth, I will wait for him."

But for how long? Pritchard wondered. How long before the doubt hardened into a certainty and the hurt turned back to anger, sending her tripping up the steps of the Wanchai police station to tell everything she knew? It was an option Pritchard could not afford to allow her.

He moved slowly towards her, his gaze fixed on the back of her delicate neck, below the hairline. He raised his arms above her head, the tie held taut between his hands, eighteen inches apart. At that moment she turned her head.

Some sense of threat had reached her and she looked round quickly, startled, eyes widening with shock.

248

"Alan!" she exclaimed.

In an instant he had the tie over her head and round her neck and she was screaming, "Alan! No, no, Alan, no!" Then as he tightened the loop the scream was squeezed down to a gasp. Off-balance, she fell forward onto the floor, dragging Pritchard over the back of the couch after her. She landed on her back; he rolled on top of her, pinning her down, pulling the tie tighter. She struggled to push him off, squirming and twisting with surprising strength, but her hands were at her own throat, sharp nails tearing the skin as she frantically dragged at the tie, fighting to remove its growing pressure. Her face was twisted into an ugly mask of panic, mouth open, tongue beginning to protrude. The movements of her body beneath him, struggling convulsively, gave him a sudden perverse pang of excitement as he tightened the grip of the tie even further.

Whether logic overwhelmed instinct, whether in her last moments of consciousness some dimly remembered survival tactic surfaced in Canny's brain, it was impossible to say. Without warning, her hands left her throat and she was tearing with her long nails at Pritchard's eyes.

It was as if a frantic cat had sprung at his face, claws open. He felt a thumb thrust sickeningly into his right eye and a nail like a razor blade slash across his left. He reared back, letting go of the tie, releasing his hands to smack away the grasping claws. He made a grab, two-handed, at her throat; half blinded, he missed, and his hands clutched at nothing. The right eye couldn't focus, the left was filling with blood. He felt her roll to the left, lunged after her and missed again, and now his weight was off her and she was struggling to her feet. He reached out, grabbed her ankle, sent her sprawling, but lost his grip. Then she was up again, running towards the door. He rose and staggered after her. His vision in one eye was a red blank, in the other a painful blur like an out-of-focus film shot. She got to the doorway three seconds ahead of him, released the Yale catch, swung the door open and ran. Then she started screaming.

It was a wild, high, Chinese scream that echoed off the bare walls of the apartment block with a penetrating intensity: *"Gow man ah!"* Help! He ran after her, cannoning off the door-jamb as he left the flat and turned to follow her to the head of the stairs. Then she was running down them, three at a time, still shrieking.

He went after her, stumbling, vision fogged, filled with panic. Their footfalls and her screams reverberated off the walls as they moved in a nightmarish spiral down the dimly lit stairwell, round and round the lift shaft. Doors began to open above them, around them; faces appeared over the banister rail and voices were raised in confusion.

Pritchard was blinking through blood; he could feel it on his left cheek. But his sight was improving as he ran, and he was starting to catch up on Canny. By the time they were three or four floors down he was just a pace behind. He reached out to grab the collar of her dress but lost his footing and fell. She gained half a flight on him, tripping on down the stairs, still hysterically shrieking, *"Gow man ah, gow man ah!"*

They got to the ground floor of the building, nine storeys down from her apartment, before he caught up with her again. Leaping down the last flight and running after her across the empty lobby, he brought her down with a high flying tackle just by the doorway to the street. She banged her head hard against the wall as she went down. Then she rolled over once and lay limp and still, breathing harshly.

Pritchard stood up, panting. He turned Canny on her back, the filth of the floor clinging to her dress. Her head lolled, and there was a ring of bruising and swelling round her neck where he had tried to · strangle her.

She was unconscious, perhaps badly hurt, but she was still alive. He bent over her, hands going back to her throat. At the same moment he heard voices on the stairs and looked up; a crowd of Chinese men in shorts and pyjamas, tenants of the upstairs flats, was coming towards him, yammering at him in excited Cantonese, half menacing, half unsure of themselves. One was brandishing a meat axe. He lost his nerve, turned and ran from the building.

The night streets of Causeway Bay swallowed him. He ran just far enough to lose the few men who ventured out of the building after him, then slowed to a walk, getting his breath back. They'd been halfhearted in the first place, the rights and wrongs unclear to them: for all they knew Canny might have been a whore who'd robbed him and was getting what she deserved. But that wasn't going to help him once the police arrived. He knew he'd blown it this time—blown it about as wide as it would go, because if and when Canny regained consciousness she was going to identify her assailant and send them after him. But everything wasn't lost yet.

He walked on for about half a mile towards Central, not stopping till he reached the girlie-bar district of Wanchai, where, among the groups of late-strolling Westerners—tourists, American sailors, British

250

soldiers—he felt less conspicuous. His vision was almost back to normal now but both eyes hurt: the edge of the left one, the eyeball nicked by Canny's fingernail, was encrusted with blood; the right one felt bruised and swollen where she had dug her thumb into it.

He found a telephone booth hidden in shadow behind the China Fleet Club, entered it, and dialled Baxter's number. He fretted with impatience while it rang, half a dozen times. When Baxter finally answered, his voice was thick with sleep.

"Bax, there's an emergency," Pritchard said.

"What . . . ? Who's this?"

"Baxter, wake up, for Christ's sake! I said we've got an emergency on our hands. We're going to bring the programme forward by twenty-four hours plus. We're taking the boat out tonight."

"Tonight! But what's happen—?"

"I'll explain when I see you. Pick me up in Wanchai as soon as possible, twenty minutes at most." He gave Baxter the address. "Meanwhile, get a call through to Simpang and tell Osman Khan to bring the rendezvous forward by one full day. Got that?"

"But Alan," Baxter howled, "have you heard tonight's weather forecast? There's—"

"Bax, we have to go, weather or no weather. Understand? Now get moving."

"What'll I tell Liz?"

Pritchard didn't answer, but slammed down the phone and stepped out of the booth. Better walk round the block a few times, he thought; it would help calm his nerves as well as avoid drawing attention to himself. He rounded the corner into Arsenal Street to a view of a tall slender building, an office block with many of its windows still lit up, particularly those of one floor near the top where every light seemed to be blazing; a building that never closed up for the night. He realized uncomfortably that he was walking past the front entrance of police headquarters.

On the thirteenth floor of that building, McNair turned away from a window in the Incident Centre at the summons of an aide on the desk. He'd been daydreaming about taking Siu back to Scotland next summer; given the state of their finances, it was likely to remain a day-dream.

"Wanchai CID. They've got something they think we ought to know about."

251

McNair picked up the receiver and a moment later was listening to a youthful Australian voice.

"Hi, Chief. Look, if this sounds a load of bollocks to you, just go ahead and say so. I thought I'd offer it to you anyway. We've had an assault with intent on this patch in the last half-hour. Chinese girl in a ninth-floor room was attacked by a European man. Seems he tried to strangle her. She fought him off somehow, got out of the room, ran down the stairs. He caught her in the lobby and she took a hard crack on the head. Up in Queen Mary's now with concussion and shock. He got away. There's no way we'll get to talk to her in the next couple of hours, but meanwhile we've turned up a few other things. There were some men's clothes in her room—someone shacking up, obviously. Big sizes: shirts, size sixteen, a pair of American Levis, thirty-two waist, thirty-six inside leg. That's a big man, bigger than most Chinese I can think of. There was also an old white sweat shirt that one of my fellows says is U.S. Navy issue. It doesn't amount to much, but it made me think of this sailor you're looking for."

"No name tags, anything like that?"

"Nothing."

"Did you get a description of the man who attacked her?" ·

"Well, that's the bad news. I've got a dozen people who saw him quite clearly, and he doesn't match up with the stuff you put out on the sailor. He doesn't fit the clothes either. The witnesses put him at five-nine or -ten, medium build, brown hair, brown eyes."

"Neighbours know anything?" McNair asked.

"We're working our way through them. You know what it's like in these crowded blocks. The impression we've got so far is that, yes, the girl was living with a *gwai-lo,* but nobody seems to have caught a glimpse of him."

"Then all I can do for now is get a couple of our own fingerprint men down to check the place over for us. Meanwhile, perhaps you'd buzz me as soon as they're ready to let us talk to the girl."

32

The rain began just a few minutes before Pritchard and Baxter got to Hebe Haven. It did not announce itself with a few preliminary drops but fell out of the sky in a sudden blinding torrent, drumming on the roof of the car, sheeting across the windscreen. Baxter drove at five miles an hour, blinking worriedly past the slashing blades of the wipers as they approached Pak Sha Wan, searching for the turnoff to the jetty.

"Alan, I'm telling you this is crazy. This is the first sign, this rain. Then the wind will get up. It'll blow harder and harder. To go out in this is lunacy!"

"Would you rather wait for the cops to come knocking on our doors, picking us off one by one? We've still got one trump card: Kiley. We're going to hang on to him until we're ready to let him go. We're going to see the Project through, Bax."

"And get ourselves drowned while we're about it?"

"It's only a tropical storm, not a typhoon."

"At the moment. And it's moving parallel to our course to Luzon. Do you know what that means? Even if we don't get anywhere near the middle of it, it means winds of thirty or forty knots, waves fifteen feet high."

"You've said often enough that the junk is sturdy, that she'll take anything the weather throws at her."

"Yes, but can we take it? I'm nothing but a bloody weekend sailor. I wish I'd never let you talk me into this, Alan, I really do. You should have heard Liz kick up. She thinks I'm out of my mind. And I mean, hell, when am I going to see her and the kid again?"

"You can send for them, once things cool off."

"But where can we go, Alan? Who would have us, any of us, now?"

"You just wait till we get our five million bucks. That sort of money can buy a lot of protection in Asia."

They bumped off the road down the track—already turned into a mudslide by the rain—to the jetty. In the light from the headlamps they could see the boatboy's sampan, still tied up where they had left it on returning from Basalt Island the previous morning. That seemed an age ago now, in a time of tranquillity before this nightmare had descended.

Rain lashed down unrelentingly. Baxter doused his lights. They got out of the car and ran down the jetty and were sodden even before they scrambled into the sampan, unhitched the painter and began to row to the *Lady Belinda.*

On board the junk there was more shelter—the cockpit and its instruments were protected by glass screens and a coach roof that could be slid open in good weather—but before they could take advantage of it they had to secure the sampan, start the engines, and cast off the mooring lines. Before moving out of the harbour Baxter insisted on going down to the saloon and putting on his life jacket. He returned to the cockpit wearing it, his stout frame padded out so that he looked like a pouter pigeon, and busied himself with the controls and the instruments arrayed on a wide sill around the wheel of the junk. He got the engines running within a few seconds, then started up the rotating weather screen that would enable him to see through the driving rain. He switched on the echo sounder and the Decca 606 radar scanner, and finally the navigation lights.

"No lights," Pritchard said. "At least, not until we've cleared Hong Kong waters."

"It's a regulation, Alan. If the marine police get curious about us they'll stop us for sure."

"If the marine police have any sense they'll stay in harbour on a night like this."

"What if they pick us up on radar? I mean, it's going to look pretty curious, a vessel heading out into the teeth of a storm."

"We've left enough trouble behind us, Bax, don't go anticipating more. Anyway, I'm hoping we'll be well out to sea before anybody back there wakes up to the fact that we're missing."

The *Lady Belinda* picked her way slowly out between the other boats at their moorings. Baxter had been in and out of this harbour a hundred times, and with the weather screen to help him see through the rain, together with a little moonlight filtering through the cloud, he was able to negotiate a safe passage to the mouth of the bay. Once there, he set the junk on a course of 135 degrees, which would give her a clear run all the way to the southern tip of Basalt.

He punched the two throttle levers up to full speed and the *Lady Belinda* gradually gained momentum, ploughing on through the rain towards an utterly black horizon. There was still no wind to speak of. The time was two thirty-five in the morning.

At ten past three McNair got the call from the fingerprint section of the Identification Bureau that he'd been awaiting for nearly two hours. The delay was frustrating but understandable. The two finger-print men and the photographer he'd sent to the building where the girl had been attacked had been told to take a random sampling of prints found all around the room. In a domestic environment these ran into many thousands. The team had been dusting and photographing franti-cally; the exposed film had been sent back in relays to the fingerprint section to be developed, enlarged, examined and referred to the index-ing system.

"Chief?" said the lab technician. "I think we've finally got some-thing that matches. Two clear thumbprints, taken off a kettle in the kitchen and a door handle on a cupboard."

"Whose?" McNair hardly dared to ask.

"No one on our regular index. Someone whose name you sent us this afternoon. Someone called Lindsay, Patrick Lindsay."

"Quinn!" McNair exclaimed. "Seymour Bloody Quinn!"

"That's not the name we have here. It's Lindsay, L-I-N—"

"Thanks," said McNair, and banged down the phone. Boyd walked in at that moment, freshly washed, shaved and changed after three hours' sleep.

"What's doing, Mac?"

"Sounds like your public appeal might have worked after all, sir. Not quite the way we expected, but perhaps it's paid off all the same." He picked up the phone again, and while he dialled the Wanchai CID number and waited for a reply, he explained briefly what had happened.

"Looks as though the sailor was living with this girl, at least until recently," he concluded. "But judging by the description of the at-tacker, it wasn't Quinn who came back to do her in."

"Who, then?"

"Somebody close to him. Somebody who was afraid that the girl might respond to our appeal, that she'd come to us. This man has to be an accomplice. And that means your guess was right: they're still here in Hong Kong—some of them, at least."

The Australian detective came on the line. McNair said, "Ten out of ten for you, mate. The man who was living with the girl is the one we want. Any chance of talking to her yet?"

"I've got a man sitting outside her ward at the hospital, waiting to do just that. She's come round, partly anyway, but she's pretty shattered, very confused. Has no clear recollection of what happened tonight. That's normal in concussion cases, the doc up there tells me."

"We're figuring on the attacker being an accomplice of Quinn's. If she opened the door to him she had to know him. All I want is a name, one name."

The rain ceased, as abruptly as it had begun, at twenty to four, just as Baxter and Pritchard were nosing the *Lady Belinda* in towards the Basalt Island coast. The thunderous drumming on the hull suddenly stopped; the hiss of rain on the sea all around them, which had obliterated every other sound, gave way to the ominous surge and slap of choppy little waves. Now they could appreciate how the wind had got up in the last hour—from a heavy near-calm to a stiff southwesterly breeze, force four and steadily strengthening. They had passed through the rainy front—a mere shower compared with what could yet be expected—and were now poised on the very edge of the tropical storm itself, its epicentre still two hundred wind-torn miles away across the South China Sea.

"Lucky we set off when we did," Pritchard said. "In another hour we probably wouldn't be able to make a landing."

Baxter nodded absently, concentrating on the view ahead. Since they'd set off from Hebe Haven he had been growing steadily gloomier and more withdrawn. Afraid of the storm, Pritchard thought, and just plain worried about everything. Not that there wasn't good reason for them all to be worried: it was just that Baxter was the type who would give up and lie down under it. Luckily he hadn't been given the chance; it was too late to back out now. Like the rest of them, he was totally committed to the Project.

Taking advantage of the improved visibility now that the rain had stopped, Pritchard fetched Baxter's high-powered torch from the saloon, left the cockpit and made his way forward to the prow of the junk. Cirrus clouds, like tufts of windblown wool, were scudding very fast across the face of the moon, giving enough light at intervals to allow him to see the dark outline of the island ahead. The wind dragged at him as he stood at the rail and signalled with the torch: one short, two long, one short, the Morse sign for P, the emergency signal. P for Pangolin, Project, Pritchard, it didn't matter which as long as it was seen. A few minutes earlier Baxter had taken a fix from the radio beacons on Cape Collinson and High Island, which made the course they were steering now accurate to within a couple of hundred yards. But still they needed a visual signal to home in on if they were to run the junk straight into the little bay and avoid the risk of hitting a rock or going aground. Let's hope the buggers are keeping a proper lookout, Pritchard thought, signalling a second time. They were supposed to spell each other on watch, but after the exhausting day they had had, it would be all too easy for them both to fall asleep at once.

By the time he had given a third signal and got no response, he was getting anxious. The junk must be less than a quarter mile off the coast now, with the wind and the following seas pushing her rapidly towards the shore, and he could still not make out the beach. Fong and Quinn were not expecting them till the following night; clearly they had not prepared themselves for a possible emergency.

Then he saw the signal: a single short flash, repeated after five seconds, then repeated again—close ahead, startlingly close. He ran back along the slippery deck to the cockpit.

"Slow down!" he said to Baxter. "Watch the light."

The fat man throttled back to quarter speed. The junk slowed until the wind and the waves were doing most of the work, carrying her forward towards the lights. There were two of them now, one higher than the other, flashing on together at twenty-second intervals. Lining up on them, Baxter steered the junk gently into the very centre of the bay. Pritchard ran forward and let go the anchor. Baxter put the engines in reverse, letting the boat strain gently against the chain until he was sure the anchor was dug in. He cut the engines and the *Lady Belinda* came round sharply into the wind.

The two discs of torchlight had moved down from the high ground behind the pillbox onto the beach, and the beams were pointed out towards the junk.

"Switch those bloody things off!" Pritchard yelled, but his voice was lost to the wind. "Let's go," he said impatiently to Baxter.

"You take the sampan. I want to catch the four o'clock weather bulletin. And be quick, Alan: when we hit this storm I want to do it at sea, not inshore."

Pritchard lowered the swimming steps, pulled the little boat round to them and climbed awkwardly down into it. He rowed rapidly to the shore, and in less than a minute Fong and Quinn were dragging the prow up onto the beach.

"Man, what's happening?" the American demanded, even before Pritchard had hopped out onto the sand. "You got trouble?"

"We've all got trouble. We're getting out and taking Kiley with us. I'll explain later."

He turned to walk up the beach towards the pillbox. Quinn

reached out a big paw, seized him by the shirt front and spun him round, bringing his face close to Pritchard's.

"Don't hand me that shit. Bad news don't take long to tell, and you got bad news stuck all over you like barnacles. What happened?"

Quinn's face in the thin moonlight was set into hard, tired lines, his temper as frayed as Pritchard's by the tension of waiting. Pritchard recognized suddenly that a critical moment had arrived for all of them, a choice between conflict and conciliation. They were going to need each other; there was no advantage, any longer, in playing the heavy in charge. He reached out a hand and gripped Quinn's shoulder.

"All right, sailor, but let's make it quick. There's a storm out there, moving in fast, and we've got to sail out into it. We've got to go, believe me. We're rumbled. That's to say, you're rumbled, and the rest of us are going to follow soon."

"Rumbled?" The American did not understand.

"You haven't heard any news broadcasts lately?"

"I quit listening around ten. There was nothing new all day."

"Now there is. Your face has been all over the television screens. They've got you nabbed, and pretty soon they're going to trace the rest of us through you, if they haven't already. We've got to get out, and now. We haven't lost yet: as long as we can make it to our rendezvous in the Philippines we'll be okay. The Moros and Salim will protect us: they've got to, for their own sakes."

"How the fuck did they trace me?"

"I don't know." Pritchard had already decided he wouldn't mention the Canny business, not now anyway, with tempers so volatile. "The point is we have to go, and I mean this minute."

"Out into that? Why can't we hole up here for another day?"

"Because," said Pritchard, restraining the almost irresistible urge, even now, to be sarcastic, "because through you they are going to trace me and Bax, and pretty soon they are going to learn that Bax has a boat out at Hebe Haven, and they are going to check on that boat and find it's gone. And then, perhaps even with a storm going, provided it's not too severe, they can send out aerial reconnaissance, and how would you like them to find the junk riding at anchor out here, off an uninhabited island, and send the marine police boats in? If we can get just ten miles south of here, preferably before dawn, we'll be out of their territorial limits where they can't chase us."

The wind had veered slightly, perhaps momentarily, to the south, and it suddenly flung a gust of fine sand into their faces. Quinn at last

258

let go his grip on Pritchard's shirt front. He said, "They got a navy, don't they? They don't have to stick to territorial waters."

"They've got five patrol boats that are no more seaworthy than that junk. As long as we get a head start on them we're laughing."

Quinn turned uncertainly to Fong, who as usual was hovering on the fringe of the discussion, a few yards up the beach. "What do you think?"

Fong, characteristically, paused before committing himself. "I think," he said, "there is no choice. We must go."

"Okay," said Quinn. "What do we do?"

"Get Kiley out, that's all." Pritchard's role as leader reasserted itself without his needing to make the point. "We can abandon all the stuff here, as long as it's tucked away in the pillbox. There's no reason why it should ever be found. Not soon enough to matter, anyway. Just let's do it fast."

They trotted up to the pillbox together. Pritchard and Quinn gathered up the few bits of camping gear that were scattered outside, while Fong put on his motorcycle helmet and went inside. A minute later he reappeared, guiding Kiley. The American walked unsteadily, roused from an uncomfortable sleep, the chain that had been used to hold him now locked round his wrist, the gunnysack over his head again. Fong unbuttoned his helmet and tossed it aside.

"What the hell now?" Kiley mumbled, his words muffled by the sacking. He was still wearing the suit in which he'd been kidnapped, now rumpled and filthy.

"We're taking you on a little boat trip, is all," Quinn said. "Just you be good and you won't come to no harm."

"There's a storm brewing up out there, isn't there?" Kiley had heard and smelt the change in the weather from inside the pillbox. "Are you going to take a boat out in that?"

"Ain't none of your fucking business," Quinn said. "You just keep right on thinking how lucky you are to be alive, man."

Fong and Quinn, walking on either side of Kiley, led him down to the sampan while Pritchard carried into the pillbox the last of the gear that had been left outside, the things that might be spotted from the air: the chemical toilet, the gas stove, the coffee pot and plastic mugs. The last thing he did was dig down with his hands into the sand at one of the outside corners of the building and disinter the Webley revolver and its cartridges, still sealed intact in the oilskin. He had made sure, on the last visit here yesterday morning, that nobody had seen him bury the package. When it came to dictating terms—or, at worst, curbing rebellion—the man with authority was the man who held the weapon. He stood up, clutching the package, and ran down to the sampan.

From the darkness of the *Lady Belinda's* cockpit, Baxter watched the others—dimly silhouetted against the reflection of moonlight from the pale sand of the beach—pile into the boat and start paddling towards the junk. The radio receiver was on, tuned to the medium-wave transmission from Radio Hong Kong, and the half-hourly storm-warning bulletin at four o'clock had just told him what he had been dreading to hear. The tropical storm had been reclassified as a tropical cyclone, the official name for a typhoon. It had also been given a name.

"At three-thirty A.M.," said the detached voice of the announcer, running through the routine information once again, *"Tropical Cyclone Miranda was centred about one hundred and eighty miles south southeast of Hong Kong and was expected to move northwest at ten knots. For those of you who are plotting the course of the cyclone, its position at three thirty was twenty degrees, five minutes North, one hundred and sixteen degrees, twenty-five minutes East.*

"Strong Wind Signal Number Three has now been hoisted. Services on some bus routes and on ferries to outlying islands have been suspended. Window and door fastenings should be checked, and small boats secured—"

Baxter switched off the set. He went out on deck in time to grab the painter from the sampan and make it fast to the guardrail of the junk. Then he started helping the others aboard. Against the stiffening wind and the strengthening waves, the *Lady Belinda* had already begun to pitch and roll at her anchor. All right for them, he thought, setting off into the teeth of this thing with no one to consider but themselves. As for him, he knew now exactly what he was going to have to do.

"Miss Chan?"

The girl lay back among the folds of the hospital pillow, staring mistily up at McNair through glazed almond eyes. Whether she saw him was impossible to say; she gave no sign that she was aware of his presence.

"Miss Chan, I'm a police officer. I want you to try to answer a couple of very simple questions for me."

She blinked and continued to gaze at him vacantly.

260

"It's no good," said the agitated Chinese doctor from behind him. "She does not follow. You must understand, please: concussion prevents the higher centres of the brain from working. Trying to force them to work may retard her recovery."

"There's no risk of permanent damage?" McNair asked.

"She will be fully back to normal within twenty-four hours. If you could come back tomorrow morning—"

"That may be too late for us. Please let me have just two minutes alone with her, will you?"

The doctor sighed and departed fussily from the room. McNair pulled a chair up to the bedside, sat down and took one of the girl's hands in his. It was cool and limp. He began to speak, slowly and carefully: he didn't know how much English she understood, and it was no time to exercise his competent but rather limited Cantonese. He said, "Listen. You can't speak, not just yet, but you may be able to talk to me just the same. Do you hear me? Understand me? If you understand, squeeze my hand."

He waited, tense and expectant, hoping his anxiety would not communicate itself to her. She stared into his face, the incomprehension continuing. Then he felt a hesitant squeeze on his palm.

Trying to contain his excitement, he went on calmly talking. "You understood me? Good. Now, I'm going to ask you some questions, very easy questions. If the answer is yes, squeeze my hand once. If it's no, squeeze twice. Understand?"

He got another squeeze, firmer this time.

"Very good. Now, keep listening. You're in hospital. You're going to be all right soon, but for the moment it's best that you stay here. Do you remember anything about what happened last night, about what brought you to hospital?"

A few seconds' pause, then came two squeezes.

"No? All right. I'll try to remind you. A man came to your flat. You let him in, and he tried to strangle you. Right?"

She stirred uncomfortably and her free hand went up to the livid line of bruising on her throat. Otherwise she did not respond.

"Did you know the man?"

A squeeze.

"You've been living with Seymour Quinn. Was he a friend of Seymour's?"

After a few seconds of hesitation, with a troubled look on her face, she squeezed his hand again.

261

"Do you know his name?"

The glazed eyes remained fixed on him; he could sense the effort she was making to pierce through to her frozen memory cells. But no reply came.

"Do you know where he lives?"

She pulled her hand away, defeated by the attempt to remember. McNair was beaten too; for a moment he had felt himself on the brink of discovery. Then the doctor came in.

"Please, it is enough. You must leave her alone now."

McNair stood up and moved the chair back from the bed. "Thank you," he said. "Perhaps you'd let us know as soon as she's fit to—"

"Alan!" the girl cried suddenly, the name uttered in a choking sob. She was sitting up in bed, both hands clutched to her bruised throat. "Alan, no! No, no, Alan, no!"

McNair and the doctor exchanged a glance, then looked back at the girl. Possessed by some memory suddenly dredged up from her subconscious, she was sitting bolt upright, wide-eyed, tearing at an imaginary constriction round her throat. "Alan! No, no, no!" she screamed. The doctor moved swiftly to the bed to pacify her. McNair, after a moment's hesitation, went to the door, and as he walked out the name was still ringing with an urgent vibrancy in his ears. Alan: he'd heard the name spoken somewhere tonight—or last night, yesterday? Tiredness and the sheer overwhelming complexity of the investigation had compressed everything he had learned into a solid ball of information from which it was difficult to extract one single strand. The name battered at his brain the way it had been trying to get through to the girl's.

Outside, in the corridor, he found the wind howling at a window and the Chinese detective from Wanchai sitting patiently on a bench.

"Have you got a description of the man that's wanted in this case?"

"Yes, sir." The detective pulled a notebook from his pocket and consulted it. "European, five-feet-nine or -ten, brown eyes, brown hair, last seen wearing a checked shirt, open-necked, short-sleeved, dark trousers—"

He stopped in confusion as McNair turned and sprinted down the corridor. He had made the connection now: startling and almost unbelievable. He reached the floor porter's cubicle, flashed his warrant card and said, "Let me use that phone."

To get to it, he had to evict the hapless porter and occupy the cubicle itself. He seized the handset and dialled the code for an outside line, with his other hand paging hastily through his notebook for the number he wanted.

He let Alan Pritchard's phone ring for a full two minutes before giving up. He might, he thought, be making a bloody fool of himself. He had a pair of matching names and descriptions, nothing more. A coincidence? Perhaps, but one that was too neat for his liking. It had to be checked out, even at the cost of putting a few people's backs up.

He lifted the receiver again and dialled the number of Pritchard's friend, Baxter.

His wife answered. She did not sound as though she had been asleep.

"Mrs. Baxter? This is McNair. The policeman who was round to see you last evening, remember? I really must apologize for phoning at this—"

"Yes, yes," she interrupted sharply. "What's happened?"

"Happened?"

Now she sounded confused. "You mean you're not phoning to tell me that . . . something's happened? To my husband?"

"No. Why should you think that?"

"Because the crazy fool has gone out on the junk, that's why." Her familiar bitter tone had reasserted itself. "I'm sitting here waiting, just *waiting,* for a call to tell me he's dead."

McNair could hardly believe his ears. "In this weather? In the middle of the night?"

"If that's not the reason you're calling, what is?"

"I just wanted to ask your husband if he'd seen his friend Pritchard tonight."

"He certainly has. Pritchard's gone with him."

33

The five-o'clock weather bulletin gave the wind strength as force six on the Beaufort scale; the barometric pressure was falling dramatically. On the *Lady Belinda* they didn't need any telling. They were headed straight into the wind, cutting through waves six and eight feet high, the boat cresting them at regular intervals and then ploughing down with a shudder into the troughs. To the east, a feeble grey dawn had barely penetrated the storm clouds.

Baxter, standing at the wheel, switched off the radio. Pritchard was beside him in the cockpit. Fong was off being seasick somewhere and Quinn was down in the galley, making coffee. Kiley lay on a bunk in the main saloon, the gunnysack still over his head, his ankle chained to a support.

"What's the light?" Pritchard asked. It was visible intermittently above the waves, ahead and slightly to the right, giving two quick flashes once every ten or twelve seconds.

"Waglan Island lighthouse," Baxter said. "Once we're past that we'll be out of Hong Kong waters within a few minutes."

"And then? How much more bad weather?"

"Well, the typhoon is moving towards us at ten knots, and we're heading straight into it at about the same speed. We should reach the eye of the storm in nine hours or so. Then there'll be an interval of calm, with another six to twelve hours of rough stuff to follow."

Pritchard glanced at him curiously. "You're sounding more confident now, Bax. You reckon we're going to make it after all?"

"Let's say I'm resigned, Alan. We're in this together. I've just got to believe we're going to pull through."

"Good," said Pritchard encouragingly. But he knew there was something just a little too pat about the way Baxter had spoken. "I'll get you some coffee. Like a shot of brandy in it?"

"Hell, yes."

It was five minutes before Pritchard returned to the cockpit. He set a plastic cup of black coffee down on the sill in front of Baxter, moving in close enough to take a quick surreptitious glance at the heading on the compass. Apart from the bulb in the windowless galley, the dim binnacle lamp that lit up the compass was the only one burning. The regular flash of the lighthouse was much closer now as the boat lunged across the swell towards it. Pritchard moved to the rear of the cockpit and stood directly behind Baxter. He said, "Have you got the course plotted all the way to Luzon, Bax?"

"Yes."

"I've worked out a roster that'll give us all turns at steering, cooking and resting. And we'll all need the rest. I thought I might take over the wheel from you now."

"No!" said Baxter, suddenly agitated. "Wait till I've got us out of territorial waters. Past the light, anyway."

264

"What's so special about that light? Are you sure it's the Waglan lighthouse?"

"Of course I'm sure."

"What's your compass heading?"

"One-forty."

"That's a lie, Bax."

Baxter clung grimly to the wheel. He tried to turn his head in protest but felt a sudden pain in the back of his neck as something cold, hard and blunt was thrust into it.

"That was a lie, Bax, and this is a gun, Bax. It's my trusty old Webley, which is just aching to blow your head off your bloody shoulders. You're trying to bullshit me. You've got a book down in the saloon called the Admiralty List of Lights. I've just looked up that light ahead there, and it isn't the Waglan light. Besides, your course isn't one-forty, it's two-twenty. That's the Cape D'Aguilar light you're heading us for, Bax. You're trying to take us back to Hong Kong!"

"No!" The fat man's cry was strangled, fearful. "No, I'm taking us round the islands, that's all."

"Don't make it worse for yourself, Bax. What were you trying to do?"

"Worse? I don't get you."

"You're in trouble, friend. You were trying to screw up the Project. That was a very silly thing to do, after the work we've all put into it."

Baxter gulped and stared straight ahead, the muzzle of the gun still pressed into the back of his neck. Quinn came up the companionway from the saloon, blinked into the dimly lit cockpit and froze.

"Baxter here has made a horse's arse of himself," Pritchard told him. "Why don't you explain just what you were planning to do, Bax?"

"Alan, look, please, I . . . was doing it for all our sakes, not only mine. Going out into that typhoon . . . we might as well just commit suicide. I . . . I was going to run her aground, on the beach at Cape d'Aguilar."

There was silence for several seconds. "And then what?" Pritchard demanded harshly. "Then what would you have done, Bax? Made a run for it, on your own? Hope to get to the cops before we got to you? Rat on us, in exchange for protection?"

"No, Alan, no! I swear, none of those things."

"What, then?"

Quinn was peering ahead through the weather screen. "Hey," he said, "that light's getting pretty close."

"What?" Pritchard demanded, ignoring him. "What were you going to do, Bax?"

"I hadn't thought that far ahead. I wanted to get off the boat, that's—"

"And that ain't no fucking beach!" Quinn suddenly shouted. "That's rocks!"

Pritchard saw them then too, a huge pile of boulders, lashed by foaming breakers, at the foot of the Cape d'Aguilar cliff, looming out of the darkness no more than a hundred yards ahead. He gasped. It was Quinn who acted first, leaping across the cockpit, seizing Baxter and shoving him away from the wheel.

"Get this dumb fuck outta here!"

Baxter staggered back against the rear bulkhead. Quinn grabbed the controls, immediately slamming the throttle levers of both engines into full reverse. The boat began slowing, but its momentum still carried it helplessly forward, lunging like a stricken animal towards the rocks.

Pritchard gazed ahead, mesmerized, the revolver hanging forgotten at his side. Quinn was swearing steadily as he gripped the wheel and willed the junk to respond to the reverse thrust of its propellers. Baxter, unnoticed for the moment, moved stealthily to the left side of the cockpit. Then he opened the door and ran.

Pritchard went after him, the gun raised again, his whole being filled with a sudden burning hatred of Baxter. The fat man ran unsteadily across the heaving deck towards the stem of the boat as it closed on the boulders. It was moving ever more slowly but was only fifteen yards from the rocks, and then ten, and Baxter was climbing over the guardrail onto the coaming at the prow, preparing himself to jump.

Both the roaring headwind and the engines were working to drag the junk back from collision, but the gap was five yards of foaming water now and still slowly closing. Pritchard stopped running, rested the big revolver in a two-handed grip on the coach roof over the saloon, took careful aim at Baxter's broad back, and fired. At that moment the junk jarred against the rocks.

It wasn't a hard bump, just strong enough to jolt his arm and send the shot wild. A moment later Baxter leapt the gap onto the nearest boulder and began scrambling towards the shadow of the cliff. Pritchard ran to the prow. The boat was backing off from the rocks now, the

266

gap widening. He braced himself against the rail and took aim again. Baxter was scuttling up the seaward face of a boulder like a great overgrown crab. There was no cover for him among the rocks, and the luminous yellow plastic of the life jacket made him a perfect target, even in the half-light of the stormy dawn. Pritchard squeezed off one shot and heard it smack home.

Some convulsive action of Baxter's muscles kept him clinging to the rock face for several seconds. Then he dropped like a stone. He hit a lower ledge and rolled down into the foaming sea, where the life jacket set his body upright and kept it afloat. Pritchard's last view of him was of a head and a padded upper torso bobbing on the waves, the head lolling grotesquely, the face a pale blur.

He turned and made his way back to the cockpit, shaking with delayed reaction to the sudden violence. Quinn gave him a weak grin.

"That's one each now, man."

"Shut up. It isn't funny. How bad was that bump?"

"Not too bad, I hope. We were just about standing still when it happened. I'll go check below in a moment."

Quinn had backed the junk about fifty yards off the rocks. He spun the wheel sharply to the right, putting her broadside-on to the waves, and she bucketed violently for several seconds before he slammed the throttles down to full speed ahead and she came round and began making way with the wind behind her. Fong appeared at the head of the companionway to the saloon, where for the whole of the past hour, in between throwing up in the toilet, he'd lain groaning on the bunk opposite Kiley. He looked dreadful, ghostly pale, eyes watery and vacant.

"What happened?" he asked weakly.

"We hit some rocks and we wasted Baxter," Quinn said. "Apart from that, not a hell of a lot."

Fong stared at him for several seconds and then, with the utter indifference of the seasick to everything but personal misery, he nodded and went back to his bunk.

"That's one thing we didn't figure on," Quinn said. In between peering ahead through the weather screen, he was rummaging with one hand through the pile of charts Baxter had left on the table beside the controls. "With Bax gone and Fong out of it, it leaves us kinda short of hands."

"Fong will have to work, seasick or not."

"You kidding? Guy in that state, he'd rather die. I've seen it.

There's nothing you can do to make him. How you holding up your-self?"

"I've never been seasick. I'm not going to start now."

"Well, you and me got to take this scow to Luzon on our own. Long as she's still fit to get us there. Take the wheel while I go check for damage. Hold her on one-forty: that's near enough the original course, far as I can see. We'll correct once I can get bearings off the Seafix."

"You sound as if you know what you're talking about. I hope you do."

"I learned all this navigation shit when I was an inductee at San Diego. Besides, I pulled a six-month tour on a minesweeper, one time: you get to do everything on those mothers short of rowing them."

Pritchard took over the wheel while Quinn clattered down the steps to the saloon. The boat was pitching and rolling more heavily than ever, and as he strained to see through the weather screen it began to rain again, a few fat drops followed by a thunderous, obliterating down-pour, reducing the already limited visibility to nothing. The compass swung wildly with every movement of the boat, but he tried to keep the needle centred on 140 degrees. He was grateful for Quinn's presence—his expertise, his strength, his guts—but he could not rid himself of the knowledge that had rankled in him since midnight, the knowledge that this whole cock-up was the sailor's fault. It was he who had been traced; it was he whose conspicuous trail had probably, by now, led to the rest of them. Pritchard took one hand off the wheel and felt experimentally for the butt of the Webley sticking out of his waistband, a heavy, awkward, comforting presence.

Boyd and McNair travelled to Hebe Haven together in a police utility vehicle. Many country roads, already flooded by the typhoon rains, were in no condition to be used by private cars, and even the four-wheel-drive Land Rover with its low-transfer gearbox engaged had to crawl many times through axle-deep mud and water. The jour-ney took well over an hour.

Uniformed men from Pak Sha Wan had been down at the water's edge for some time. With great difficulty they had aroused the boatboy from his bed in the hut beside the jetty. He stank of opium. He had come home at midnight, he said; he had fallen deeply asleep and had seen and heard nothing since. But he was able to confirm that it was Baxter's Range Rover that was parked

268

there, and that Baxter's junk was the only one absent from its moorings.

They had also found another man in the village who, hurrying home from a late-night gambling session to take shelter from the typhoon, had seen the car turn down the track towards the bay at about two o'clock that morning.

"Four hours," said Boyd grimly, checking his watch. "They'll be out of our waters by now—if they haven't sunk already."

"I know our marine people aren't authorized to work outside our limits," McNair said, "but couldn't we send the Navy after them?"

"We could ask. They might say yes, but it would be sheer bravado. Their craft are designed for inshore patrol work, just like ours. Besides, they carry a crew of twenty, twenty-five. I wouldn't like to be responsible for risking that many lives, just for the sake of saving these maniacs. That's what it amounts to, now."

There was a lull between the cascades of rain. The two of them stood sheltering from the wind on the lee side of the Land Rover, looking out across the turbulent grey of the South China Sea to a dirty, leaden, early morning sky; that was about as much sunlight as they could expect all day.

"There's Kiley too, sir," McNair reminded Boyd. In his determination to get the perpetrators of the crime, the Chief Superintendent, not unnaturally, was inclined to overlook the victim.

"We don't even know that Kiley's still alive. He might be out on that junk with them, or he might be lying in a ditch somewhere with a bullet in his head. We got close enough to panic them, obviously; when that happens, you can never predict what a villain will do. One way or another, it looks as though we've lost him."

There was an uncharacteristic note of defeat in Boyd's tone. The tiredness that was etched into the lines on his face had also diminished his confidence. "Well, we'd better get back to Central before the weather really lands on us. We can't get planes up to look for the junk until the typhoon blows over, and we can't even pick it up with shore radar: the storm has blotted it out. In fact there's pretty well damn-all we can do except batten down the hatches and wait. Go straight home and get yourself some sleep. I'm going to report to the Commissioner and then do the same. And by the way, Mac—"

"Sir?"

"Thanks for everything you've done. We wouldn't have achieved half of what we did without you."

269

"Hell, I don't feel very proud of myself. To think that I actually interviewed both of those bastards last night, Pritchard and Baxter, and eliminated them as suspects!"

"Anyone would have done the same. The deception was carefully planned. Don't let it worry you, Mac, you can't win 'em all."

The words were lightly spoken but the set of Boyd's shoulders as he turned to climb back into the Land Rover suggested that this, the biggest one of all, was the one he would most have liked to win.

The bow of the *Lady Belinda* dipped sickeningly into another immense, grey-green swell, falling so fast and hard that it seemed impossible that the junk would ever stop, just go on diving straight to the bottom. Then the whole boat shuddered, the bow rising again in time for the next wave to break across it, sending a ton of foaming water racing back to smash against the weather screen, wash down the decks, and flood out through the scuppers. Pritchard, still at the wheel, had given up trying to see ahead through the foam and spray. He had enough work holding his balance and, as the boat smashed through waves that rose above the level of the cockpit roof, trying to keep steering somewhere close to the compass heading. The course didn't matter too much, Quinn had told him, provided it didn't vary by more than ten degrees either way. It would be badly distorted by the weather anyway, and they could correct later. What mattered most was to keep heading into the wind and to watch for any sudden change. A line squall taken broadside-on could knock the boat over like a ninepin.

Quinn had been out of the cockpit a long time. He'd spent thirty minutes down in the saloon and in the chain closet, right up in the bows, checking the outer skin of the junk for damage and lifting the deck-boards that opened into the bilge. Then, without any comment to Pritchard, he had gone down to the engine room, aft of the controls, and spent some time in there.

He returned in time to catch the seven-o'clock weather bulletin. It told them that the epicentre of Tropical Cyclone Miranda was now 145 miles south southeast of Hong Kong. He spent another couple of minutes studying the Admiralty chart of the South China Sea and pencilling some calculations in the margin. Finally he turned to face Pritchard.

"We're taking in water. Couple of timbers, way up in the bows, got knocked loose when we hit the rocks. In good weather it wouldn't matter much, the hole'd be above the waterline, but in this mother.

270

..." The junk lunged into another swell, dipping, shuddering, cresting. "Every time we hit one of them, we ship a few gallons more. The bilge pump can't keep up. We got two hand pumps as well. We're gonna have to man them, starting right now."

"Just the two of us? That's imposs—"

"We can work one at a time and spell each other at the wheel."

"No, Fong will have to work, that's all. There's at least another eighteen hours' sailing left. We can't possibly keep it up that long."

"The more water we ship, the slower we get, the longer it takes. Way I figure it, we don't have to go straight to Luzon. We can change course and head for here. Look." He seized the chart and shoved it in front of Pritchard's face, tapping with one finger at a point halfway across the South China Sea, a tiny blob at the centre of a scattering of depth soundings, a few degrees east of the course they were presently steering. "Pratas Island, about seven, eight hours' steaming from here."

"Can you get us there, in this weather?"

"Why not? The wind'll be pushing us that way anyhow. It says in the sailing directions there's an all-weather anchorage behind a reef on the south side. We can ride out the typhoon there and move on tomorrow."

"It's still asking a hell of a lot of ourselves."

"There's only one other choice, man. It ain't too late to turn back."

"Like hell!" said Pritchard, and braced himself to drive the junk into another swell.

During the night it had become clear—at least to the meteorologists at the Royal Observatory in Kowloon—that Hong Kong would escape the full fury of Miranda. The typhoon had altered course during the night, and when it struck land before dispersing, its epicentre would be further east along the China coast, halfway to Taiwan. Full precautions nonetheless remained in force. Aircraft were grounded; the typhoon shelters on both sides of the harbour were crammed to capacity with junks and sampans. With all shops, offices, factories, and schools closed, the colony's life virtually ground to a halt for the day. In the resettlement estates, families of ten and twelve huddled together in their tiny apartments, resigned to sitting out the storm, their windows plastered with typhoon tape to minimize the danger from shattering glass, buckets and mops ready to swab up the driving rain that would penetrate the smallest crack in a wall and flood through a window frame that was the tiniest bit loose. On the Peak, groups of Europeans, Ameri-

271

cans and Australians gathered in each other's flats, first to help roll up carpets and stack the furniture in corners, then to settle down with plenty of booze and enjoy the novelty of the situation.

At these typhoon parties, the main theme of conversation was the drama of the occasion itself. Sometimes it shifted back to the subject of the kidnapped diplomat, but there wasn't much new to talk about. No fresh developments had been announced since last evening. Some people—mostly the sort of men who had been airing their opinions of the case, just as Baxter would have been, in club bars the night before —made dark suggestions about a news blackout. A deal with the kidnappers was on the cards, they said, and the Americans didn't want anyone upsetting the applecart. A bloody shame, really, to let these Filipinos get away with a thing like that. After all, who might they not grab next?

In her own flat on the Peak, Liz Baxter sat staring through the big sheet-glass window at the rain. It was a modern, well-made building and there was little danger of water damage, but the wind howled down the access corridors and the whole block quivered occasionally under the impact of a particularly fierce gust. On the floor behind her the child played disconsolately with blocks. In a minute, she knew, he would get bored and come and cling to her, asking where Daddy was, seeking distraction. The amah had hurried off first thing that morning, to her relatives in Kowloon; Liz had never had to amuse the boy herself and found she hardly knew how.

She had stayed close to the telephone since four that morning, pacing past it warily, as if it were some small but dangerous animal that might suddenly leap at her. Three times, when it rang, she had curtly refused invitations from friends to typhoon parties. The friends were mystified: wasn't that the sort of thing Bax loved? Finally, at eight thirty, the policeman, McNair, had rung to confirm what she had still hardly dared to believe: Ed had quite certainly gone out on the *Lady Belinda* with Pritchard. Why? she had shrieked. Why, why?

"I don't like to add to your worries, Mrs. Baxter, but you've got to know this sooner or later: we think your husband was involved in this kidnapping. We have a definite suspect in his friend, Pritchard, and the fact that they've gone off together seems to confirm their guilt."

"But what . . . what's happening to him out there?"

"There's no way of knowing, Mrs. Baxter. I'm sorry. Can I also ask you, for your own sake as much as ours, not to talk about this to anyone for the moment? At least until we have more definite news."

272

He hadn't needed to ask. Her feelings were so confused between shame, anger and fear that she would not have thought of confiding in anyone. At an unprecedented hour of the morning she poured herself a stiff brandy and went and sat down to stare out at the rain-swept landscape of the Peak. Then she discovered, with guilty horror, that she already had a clear idea of what she would do. It was as if a plan had been filed away for years in her subconscious, a plan whose existence she now acknowledged for the first time. If she was parted from Ed— by death or desertion—she would pack her bags, take the child and get out. At once, without even bothering to sell up, she would take the first available flight to London and land on her parents. Anything to get away from this place, anything. She did not—could not—wish Ed dead or gone, but there was a terrible tremor of excitement at the challenge of managing her life without him.

"Can I fix you a sandwich or something, Mrs. Kiley?"

Ailsa started out of her reverie. Albach, the security man, had made himself at home in the kitchen of the apartment on Quarry Hill. Once every half-hour or so he came through to the living room on some pretext or other, apparently hoping each time to find her a little more cheerful. Her long, distracted silences seemed to embarrass him.

"Oh . . . no, thank you very much."

"You really ought to eat. You've done nothing but smoke cigarettes and drink black coffee since last night."

"I'm not hungry. You go ahead and make yourself something."

"Anything else I can do?"

"I don't think so."

He departed with a shrug, leaving her to stare again at nothing. She had had a good night's sleep—indecently good, it seemed, under the benign influence of a couple of pills—but as soon as she had wakened the anxiety had been with her, and all morning it had worsened. It was deeply ironic: she knew that she no longer loved Rod, yet the thought of his life being in danger was almost more than she could bear. She'd tried to divert herself—with a book, with a few chores, with unpacking from her trip—but found it impossible to summon up the slightest concentration.

She wished she could confide in someone, seek reassurance from just one close friend. Apart from her husband there was no one she knew well here except Alan, and she could hardly talk to him with Albach hanging around. Dear old Alan, she thought: destined as it often seemed to be one of life's losers, rejected as a lover, he might yet prove his worth as a friend. Perhaps he had been wanting to call her since the news about Rod had broken but had remembered her insistence that he should not phone her at home. Bloody security! She had lived for so long under its spell that she'd started making rules of her own.

She took another cigarette from her pack and lit it. Then the telephone rang and she pounced on it, snatching up the receiver.

"Mrs. Kiley? This is McNair. I have some news for you."

"About my husband?"

"About him, yes. And about your friend Mr. Pritchard. I think you'd better brace yourself for a shock."

The American Consulate General was closed for the day. The main building was manned by a skeleton staff, but in the Annex there was a fair amount of activity. Radio and telex links with Company headquarters in Langley, Virginia, and with other stations in the region remained open. Incoming messages had to be copied, decoded, read, replied to and filed as usual. Quite a few people had moved camp beds into their offices in case of having to spend the night there, among them Howard Koch, the acting Chief of Station.

Two clocks stood side by side on the wall opposite Koch's desk, one showing local time, the other permanently set to United States Eastern Standard Time, thirteen hours behind. It had been nine that morning, or eight o'clock Monday evening in Langley, when, after receiving a full and up-to-date report from the Commissioner of Police, he had dictated a long message addressed personally to the Director of the Agency. Two hours later the reply came. The Director must be working overtime too.

Koch read the message carefully, then left his office and walked down the corridor to the room they had found for the Ambassador from Bangkok. He was using his hours of enforced inactivity to catch up on reading some policy documents from the State Department. Koch knocked on the door, entered, and handed him the two sheets of printout from the decoder.

"It's about what we expected," he said. "He wants us to hang in there. As long as there's the remotest chance that Kiley is still alive, we're to proceed with arrangements for the exchange."

" 'Courier left here thirteen hundred hours Monday,' " said the Ambassador, reading aloud from the message, " 'carrying bank draft in

274

the sum of ten million. . . . ' Well, he'll be delayed by the typhoon, but with luck he'll be here tomorrow. Meanwhile, all we can do is keep the line open to Chief Minister Salim and wait for news."

"The next word on Kiley will come from that end, for sure. If there's going to be any word, that is. Frankly, I don't know what to think about this whole thing any longer. The Moros claim to have carried out the crime, but the suspects turn out to be a deserted American sailor and two local Europeans: a journalist and a businessman, for God's sake! They get flushed out of hiding and take off in a boat in the middle of a goddam typhoon. Maybe they have Kiley along with them, maybe they don't." He shook his head. "The whole thing is crazy."

"What's this bit here?" asked the Ambassador, still reading. " '. . . *imperative for the sake of saving Pangolin's personal special operation that every possible effort be made to secure his safe release.*' "

"That's Rod Kiley's pet project," Koch said. "An asset he's running in China. If Kiley goes, so does the asset—and he happens to be one of the best we've got."

Out of habit learned from her husband's weeks on night shift, Siu McNair tiptoed into the bedroom where he lay sleeping. Then she remembered the typhoon: anyone who could sleep through that could sleep through anything.

She parted the curtains just wide enough to make sure no water was getting in at the window. Through it, nothing was visible but the rain, nothing could be heard but the roar of the wind. She'd heard on the radio news a short while ago that several small boats had sunk at their moorings and that a landslip caused by flooding had sent an avalanche of mud down on the flimsy huts of a squatter settlement. A dozen people were feared killed. But this was tame compared to some typhoons she had experienced. Miranda's strongest gales had missed Hong Kong altogether and were starting to blow themselves out two hundred miles along the China coast. The forecast was good: by midnight the worst would be over.

For a minute she stood watching her husband as he slept. He had worked for almost twenty-four hours, with only a brief break last night, and his face was drawn with tiredness. He would be summoned back sometime later in the day, he had told her. She prayed that the telephone would not ring too soon.

34

Sometime between two thirty and three o'clock, the *Lady Belinda* passed by the eye of the typhoon, a hundred miles to the east. Soon after that the wind, spiralling constantly inward towards the centre of the storm, lost some of its strength and veered sharply to the northwest. Instead of resisting the junk's progress it now favoured it, chasing her faster down the long troughs of the waves and up to the foaming crests. The benefit was lost, however, as the boat ploughed ever more sluggishly forward. The hull was well down and the seas still came pounding over the bow and through the hole in the timbers. Tons of water slopped back and forth in the bilges and they could not work the pumps fast enough to shift it. They all knew that they were in trouble, and that the trouble was steadily getting worse.

Fong had done his best. In between spells at the wheel he had taken his turn at the hand pumps, their plunger handles set in the decking at either side of the cockpit. It was a back-breaking job, and even at the best of times Fong had been agile rather than strong. After a couple of minutes' pumping he would have to turn aside and retch; otherwise he would simply collapse on the soaking deck, lacking the sheer will to save himself. Then more time would be wasted guiding him down to his bunk to rest. Eventually they had to let him steer full-time, but after an hour even that had proved too much. Weakened by illness, he kept getting thrown to the deck and letting the junk drift dangerously across the wind. At midday Pritchard and Quinn had ordered him back below—he was more trouble than he was worth in the cockpit —and begun taking turns at the wheel. That meant that only one of the hand pumps could be worked at a time.

They hadn't had time to prepare food, or even a cup of coffee, all day. In spite of this and his lack of sleep, Pritchard had discovered unexpected reserves of strength in himself. They were steering and pumping alternately for half an hour at a time. Pumping meant squatting on the deck in the foaming water that ran back from the bow, dressed in underwear and life jacket, strapped into a harness suspended by a steel cable from the mast, watching the disheartening little squirt of water that shot through the outlet cock every time he plunged the handle down. He knew that with each dive into the waves the boat was taking in more than he could get rid of. He knew, too, that he was beginning to flag. His shoulders ached intolerably and the muscles of his arms had turned to quivering jelly.

He had grown both to admire and resent Quinn in these past few hours. The big man's strength did not seem to have diminished at all. He worked at the pumps with a furious, rhythmic energy; on his steering spells he also took radio bearings and did what he could to plot the junk's course as well as the typhoon's. With his physical power and sheer capability he had, effectively, taken command of the boat.

Fong emerged groggily from the saloon into the cockpit at three thirty. Quinn had just taken over the wheel.

"How you feeling?"

"Bit better now. I had some sleep."

"What about Kiley?"

"I don't know. Just lying there. What can I do to help?"

"Well, the fuel tanks are kinda low. Think you can manhandle one of them barrels from the stern to the inlet?" Fong nodded in reply. "Just ease it on its side and roll it. And be careful."

Fong stepped out of the cockpit on the port side. A wave burst over the bow and he clung hard to the coach roof until the water had washed over and past his legs. Then he clutched at the guardrail and held fast to it as he made his way astern. He realized he had forgotten to put on his life jacket; it was too late to turn back for it now.

"Hey!" Quinn yelled to Pritchard at the starboard pump. The American was leaning out of the cockpit, his face contorted into a snarl against the wind. "Hey, man, you want to hear the bad news?"

Pritchard stopped pumping. "What?"

"I just took some new bearings on the Seafix. Be another four hours before we hit Pratas Island, three and a half minimum. Way we're shipping water right now, we just ain't gonna make it."

"Thanks, that's bloody encouraging."

"I ain't shitting you. We got to work those pumps faster."

"I see Fong is back on his feet," Pritchard shouted. "Why don't you take the port pump and put him back on the wheel?"

"Sure, but how long will he last this time? You forgot something. We got a passenger down below, ain't done nothing to earn his keep yet."

"Kiley?" Pritchard was incredulous. "No, that's out of the question."

"Why?"

277

"In the first place, we can't force him to work."

"Convince him his ass'll get drowned if he don't. He'll work."

"He can't come up here without seeing our faces, remembering them. He'll probably recognize mine."

"What do you care about right now, your face or your goddam life?"

Quinn had been neglecting the wheel as he talked and the junk had veered slightly to take the swell on the starboard quarter. Suddenly, violently, she was slammed sideways by a huge wave. Pritchard saw a two-foot wall of water rushing across the foredeck and felt himself swung back in his harness against the rail. Quinn staggered and dived for the wheel.

Fong had just untied one of the row of six steel barrels full of diesel fuel that were lashed separately to the stern rail. He was braced against it, hauling down on the top end in an effort to lower it gently on its side. He lurched at the impact of the wave. The barrel toppled. He lost his footing on the slippery deck and fell on his back, and the barrel dropped onto him, the five-hundred-pound weight crushing his ribs and pressing the air out of his lungs. He gave a short scream. The junk pitched steeply into the trough and the barrel rolled off him, racing to the starboard rail, breaking and bending the stanchions before rebounding across the afterdeck, this time rolling right over him with a sickening crunch of breaking bones before it smashed through the port rail and dropped into the sea.

Pritchard had seen it all. He struggled out of his harness and ran, clutching the rail, to the stern. He was just in time to see Fong, eyes closed, pale blood bubbling from his mouth, lifted by the rushing water and dropped gently overboard through the gap in the rail. The moon face bobbed for a few seconds among the waves and then disappeared.

He ran back down the deck. "Quinn!" he screamed. "Fong is overboard!"

"I saw!" Quinn yelled back. "What the fuck can I do?"

"Turn back, pick him up!"

"Never happen!" In the cockpit he explained. "I try to turn through one-eighty, halfway through we're broadside-on and over. Besides, he was totalled soon as that barrel landed on him. Why spend half an hour hunting for a corpse?" Quinn had the boat back on course now, the wind following as it plunged through the seas.

"Now will you listen to me? With Fong and Baxter both gone, it

278

leaves just two of us running this mother. Unless we get Kiley up here to help with the pumps we'll go down inside an hour."

Pritchard hesitated only a second more. "All right," he said. "I'll take the wheel. Go and get him."

In spite of the pitching and rolling of the boat, Kiley had dozed uncomfortably on his bunk for much of the day, his brain taking refuge in sleep from the knowledge of his predicament. There was nothing else to occupy his mind, not even the slight visual stimulation he might have had if the sack were not still over his head. His hands were free and he could easily have undone the loosely knotted cord by which the sack was fastened round his neck. Several times he had considered doing so and rejected the thought as unwise. His kidnappers had taken elaborate precautions to make sure that he never saw their faces, no doubt with good reason. Was it because they feared he would know them?

He had racked his brain for some memory of the big American and come up with nothing. Likewise the small Chinese. It was he, Kiley had worked out, who had been seasick; he'd spent a lot of time somewhere in close proximity to the bunk, groaning and occasionally retching, and the stink of his vomit was still in the air. Then there were others—at least two others, to judge by the voices, one of which Kiley could almost swear he had heard before. That intensity of tone, that English colonial accent, almost but not quite like Ailsa's Australian one: it was the dimmest of memories, from a long time ago, and it would not come back to him.

Instinct told him—the instinct of a blind man, powerfully fortified by his other senses—that this boat and its crew, whoever they were, wherever they were going, were in trouble. It wasn't just the obvious violence of the storm they were sailing through and the increasing heaviness of the vessel's movement, but a feeling of growing desperation in the odd snatches of shouted conversation that he heard over the rush of water against the hull. They must have been pretty desperate to begin with, setting off in this. Did that mean the police had been close behind them?

His musing was interrupted by footfalls: someone descending the steps down which he'd been guided when they had first brought him aboard. He heard the man approach the bunk, sensed him standing over him.

"Sit up, Kiley."

It was the American. Kiley swung his legs over the edge of the

279

bunk, as far as the chain round his right ankle would permit, and straightened up.

"Now listen good," the man said. "I'm gonna take that chain off, that and the sack. There's work to be done, we need you up on deck. But we don't need you so bad that we won't waste you if we have to. There's two of us up there, both carrying. You try any funny shit, one of us'll blow your goddam head off."

To emphasize the point, the man took hold of the top of the gunnysack and, without untying the cord, ripped it straight off over his head, pulling at his neck muscles. Kiley, startled, found himself looking up at the face he had never seen—a young, coarse-featured face bisected by a black moustache, a face that managed to look intelligent and brutal at once. He was wearing only a life jacket, sneakers, and a pair of soaking jeans with the butt of a pistol sticking out of one pocket.

Kiley blinked against the half-light. The bunk he was sitting on, he now saw, was fixed against the starboard bulkhead of a comfortably furnished cabin. There was another bunk opposite him; that must have been where the seasick Chinese had been lying.

"This boat's in trouble," he said. "Am I right?"

"You'll never be righter in your life, mister." The big man had a key in his hand. He knelt quickly in front of Kiley, undid the padlock that held the chain fast round his ankle and slipped it off. "She's filling with water, and fast. We need you to help on the pumps."

"I don't owe you anything," Kiley said. "What if I say no?"

The big man went very still. When he looked up at Kiley his eyes were hard, glittering. "You ain't being offered a choice. This scow goes down, you go with it. Now move!"

Kiley didn't argue but got stiffly to his feet, aware, in a way that the big man obviously wasn't, of the irony of the situation: the kidnappers suddenly dependent on their victim, their own lives at risk unless he helped them. Perhaps they were even more afraid than he was by now. He had lived with fear for thirty hours; the prospect of drowning seemed like just one more risk, one of the less unpleasant of the options that faced him.

He walked ahead of the big man, between the bunks and up the short companionway that led to the cockpit of the boat. A man wearing jockey shorts and a life jacket stood at the wheel, a man whose face he knew but couldn't place. A big revolver was shoved down the front of the life jacket. He returned Kiley's stare curiously, with apprehension, as though expecting to be recognized, waiting to hear his name blurted out. Then he said, "Well, don't just stand there. Grab a life jacket and get weaving."

Kiley connected the voice and the face now, but recognition still eluded him. The memory reached out from many years ago: Saigon? Washington? Perhaps it would be best not to remember. He turned back to the big man, who had come up behind and was thrusting a life jacket at him.

"Get into that. Then come out on deck. I'll strap you in and you can start hitting the pump."

"Where are the others?" he asked, shrugging himself into the jacket.

"What others?" the man at the wheel demanded.

"There were more than two of you, when we started out."

"We've had a couple of accidents," the man said tersely.

"Just remember what I told you about behaving yourself," the big one said, "or the next accident will be to you. Move it!"

Kiley braced himself as he stepped out of the cockpit, but even so was unprepared for the force of the wind. It almost knocked him over as he scrambled down to the deck of the boat—a big seagoing junk, as he now realized. The sea all around it was a shifting, foam-streaked mass of grey, mountainous waves. The big man hopped down after him; within a minute he had strapped Kiley into the canvas harness and shown him how to work the pump.

"Just you keep right on going till I tell you to stop. I'm going aft to top up the fuel tanks, then I'll take over the starboard pump."

Suddenly he remembered. Kneeling on the deck with the handle of the pump in his hands, he looked up at the man in the cockpit and said involuntarily, "Pritchard!"

Pritchard could not hear his name spoken over the wind, but the big man standing beside Kiley did. "Right the first time," he said with contrived casualness. "That's Pritchard."

"Alan Pritchard! The newspaperman, from Saigon! He knew me there. Is all this *his* crazy idea?"

"I guess you could say it is."

"He knew my wife. He was—"

"I know. Fucking her before you came along. Matter of fact," he added with a snigger, "I don't think it stopped there, exactly."

"What do you mean?" Kiley's face was blank.

"I figure she's been putting a little action his way lately, back there in Hong Kong. Can't say I blame her. All that big high-powered work of yours, late nights at the office, trips outta town: the lady's pussy is bound to get a little twitchy."

"That's a dirty lie!" Kiley said, cold with anger.

"I didn't say it was gospel, just my opinion. Whyn't you ask her when you get back? Rate you're working right now, looks like you don't even want to get back! Hop to it, man!"

The big American grasped the guardrail and began to make his way aft. Kiley, filled with confusion and doubt, turned back to the pump. He depressed the plunger a couple of times, experimentally; then, bending over it, he began pushing down with all his weight, working with a ferocious, angry strength.

McNair surfaced from what he thought must have been the deepest sleep he had ever had and gradually became aware of several things. The first was that the light coming in through the window was paler than it had been when he had gone to bed; the second was that the howl of the typhoon had died to a murmur. He raised his left hand and gazed fuzzily at his watch. It was ten past five. Then he realized that he was not alone in the bed. Siu lay on her side, the sheet up to her neck, smiling at him. He reached out for her hand, missed it and found himself cupping a small, firm breast in his palm. Beneath the sheet she was naked. The smile became wider.

"What are you doing here?" he murmured.

"Best place to be, in a typhoon. What better way to pass the time?"

She moved across the bed to snuggle close to him, kissing his neck and chest, small hands caressing his naked stomach and moving down to his loins. Then she crawled on top of him, like a lithe, tiny-boned, determined little animal, her hardened nipples thrusting into his face, legs encircling his hips.

"You like Chinese girl?" she demanded, mimicking the Suzie Wong pidgin of the Wanchai bars as she began tugging off his pyjama pants. "Chinee girl make number one lovey-lovey for foreign devil policeman, okay?"

"Number one," he said, letting her straddle him and bear down with her pelvis until the moist warmth between her thighs was teasing his rapidly tumescent flesh. "Number one, can do."

Twenty minutes later, as they lay relaxing in the afterglow of passion, the telephone rang. McNair reached out and took the call on the bedside extension. His other arm was still around Siu's slender waist.

"Mac?" It was Boyd's voice. "Did I wake you?"

"Not exactly. What's new?"

"Nothing much, except that the typhoon is blowing itself out. The RAF will start sending out aerial reconnaissance for us at first light tomorrow. Civil air traffic and shipping will be back to normal by then as well, and all planes and vessels are being asked to keep a lookout for the junk. Between you and me, I doubt if anything will come of it all."

"You think they've sunk, do you?"

"Let's say I think their chances of survival are very slender. But we've got to keep looking. Good fairies have been at work while you and I were asleep, by the way: we've filled in a lot of background on Pritchard and Baxter and Quinn. We're fairly certain there was a Chinese involved as well: an ex-movie stuntman and ex-boyfriend of Quinn's mistress. They planned it incredibly well—but you can fill yourself in on the details later. The question that matters now, apart from the problem of whether they've survived or not, is, where have they gone? They had to be heading for somewhere when they left here this morning."

"The Philippines?"

"That's the best guess. If they've really got a deal of some kind to hand Kiley over to the Moro guerrillas, that's the logical place to meet up. Besides, apart from China and Taiwan, it's the nearest landfall from here. So let's assume for the moment that they have survived and that they're now halfway to Luzon. From tomorrow onwards, the centre of attention shifts from here to there. That brings me to the reason for this call."

Boyd paused. McNair waited. "The Americans have a lot of clout with the Filipinos. And it's the Americans who want to do a deal with the kidnappers. They'll be putting pressure on Manila not to act in haste, to go gently, because their first priority is to get Kiley back, whatever the price. It'll be the same kind of pressure they put on us, but across there it will be much more effective: they've got foreign-aid agreements and other carrots to dangle. As far as I'm concerned we've still got four villains to catch, a fact that'll get overlooked if we're not careful. I want a presence across there, in Manila. I've already spoken to a top man in their National Bureau of Investigation—they've been making inquiries of their own, of course, ever since the Moros first claimed responsibility—and they're willing to have us send one officer over to act as liaison. I'd like you to go, Mac."

"Well, sure, but you'd carry more weight than I would. Don't you want to go yourself?"

"Not unless we get definite word that they've reached the islands. Besides, there are a lot of loose ends to be tied up here. We'll get you out on the first flight tomorrow. Spend some time chatting their people up, getting to know them. You'll have established your presence, then, if the crunch comes."

"Where to now?" asked Siu, steely-eyed, when he put down the phone.

"Manila. Not for long, I think. And not till tomorrow morning." With the arm that was around her waist he drew her small naked body to his. "That's a long time from now," he said.

As the wind slackened and the waves lost some of their power, the afternoon gradually brightened. There were still heavy, scudding clouds and occasional flurries of rain, but after the leaden gloom that had prevailed when the *Lady Belinda* was closest to the heart of the typhoon, the sky by six thirty was lighter than it had been all day. Then it began to darken again with the approach of night. It was in that brief interval of clarity that they caught sight of Pratas Island, dead ahead.

There seemed no logic to the existence of the place, a single, low, scrub-covered mound standing alone in the middle of the South China Sea, two hundred miles from the nearest land. It was little more than a shoal surrounded by a jagged, rocky reef, but to the depleted crew of the junk it represented salvation. Pritchard and Quinn were close to the limits of their endurance. Kiley had done less physical work, but emotional strain was proving just as debilitating. Withdrawn into himself, he knelt on the deck and worked his pump steadily, saying nothing to the others.

Quinn took over the wheel from Pritchard as they neared the island thirty minutes later, altering course to circle to the south, searching anxiously for the gap in the reef that the book of sailing directions had mentioned. The light was fading fast now; they would have to get through the reef within the next few minutes or not at all.

He turned the boat to run her parallel to the south coast of the island, keeping a hundred yards clear of the wall of spiky rocks, watching them carefully as the wind-driven waves broke and surged around them. There were several narrow breaks in the line, but the light was already so bad it was hard to tell whether they were actually gaps or simply places where the rock was submerged. With her bilges full, the

Lady Belinda was drawing six or seven feet of water; there was no room for a mistake.

He nosed the junk closer to the reef, getting to within forty yards before he came round to continue riding parallel with it. It was a perilously close distance, with considerable danger from hidden rocks and rises of the seabed, but he could not afford to miss finding the gap. Suddenly he remembered the echo sounder.

It was bolted down to a shelf on his right, a modern, inshore type that worked on an ultrasonic frequency. He switched it on and at once got a flash against the four-fathom mark on the depth scale. Twenty-four feet of water beneath the bottom of the hull: that was comfortable.

"Hey! Quinn! Have you lost your bloody bearings?"

That was Pritchard, pausing in his pumping to yell up at him from the deck. The fact that he could hear the shout was proof of how much the wind had gone down. He ignored the Englishman and continued gazing hard out to the left. In the rapidly fading tropical twilight the reef was no more than an uneven black line with the sea creaming and boiling over it.

"Quinn, are you taking us to that anchorage or not?"

"Shut the fuck up!" the American yelled, twisting his head round irritably to snarl down at Pritchard. Then, as he turned back to face the port side, he noticed an alarming thing. The depth shown on the lighted scale of the echo sounder had fallen from four fathoms to two. And as he watched, mesmerized, it dropped fast, to one and a half and then one. At half a fathom he acted. With only three feet of water under the junk's hull he swung her as hard as he could to starboard, across the wind, heading for deeper water. She moved sluggishly, pitching hard into the waves and then rolling, knocking the two men at the pumps off balance. He heard Pritchard cursing. He saw, for just a moment on the port quarter, as the swell subsided with a sudden rush, the crest of the undersea ridge they had nearly slammed into. Then, shaking in a cold sweat of shock, he was steering her into rapidly deepening water: five fathoms, eight, fifteen.

Pritchard was yelling obscenities at him while he righted himself in his harness. Kiley looked numb and afraid as he tackled the pump again, still not moved to say anything.

Quinn righted the boat and steered her back on her earlier course. Almost at once the echo sounder began to show shallower water again: twelve fathoms, nine, seven. He threw a glance at the reef and caught a glimpse of an opening that ran diagonally southeastwards, invisible

285

till now but wider than anything he had yet seen. Within a moment he had lost sight of it behind the next outcrop of rock, but now he was desperate enough to trust nothing but instinct. Instinct told him the junk had just crossed a deep channel in the seabed. If the channel led into the gap, there was at least a chance that the opening was deep enough to take the boat. The twilight was dwindling rapidly into night. He would take the chance.

He called to Pritchard through the starboard window of the cockpit. "Hey! I'm gonna put her about!" To Kiley on the other side he shouted, "Brace yourself, cocksucker!" Then he swung the *Lady Belinda* through 180 degrees, right against the swell, bucking violently and shipping water over both rails in turn. He came round in a tight circle, driving her against the wind, heading for the almost invisible gap in the reef, his concentration darting second by second between the heading of the boat and the echo sounder. They were pushing fast up the channel now, the readings going down, fourteen fathoms, eleven, nine, the opening between the rocks approaching like a pair of hungry jaws, the sea slavering between them. Seven fathoms, five, four. The gap was twenty feet wide, he reckoned, and with the junk's twelve-foot beam that left them four feet on either side to play with.

The swell rose as it funnelled into the gap. It flung the boat hard to the left, almost onto the jagged teeth of the reef before the backwash sucked it violently in the other direction. The echo sounder veered wildly from four fathoms to one. There was a ridge of rock underwater across the gap, maybe deep enough to cross, maybe not. It was too late to choose. The junk breasted the rocks and Quinn steered between them. A huge sea lifted the boat then and, like a horse reluctant to take a jump, it was pushed over the ridge and dropped precipitately into the shallow water of the lagoon behind the reef.

Pritchard unhooked himself from the harness and made his way unsteadily up the steps to the cockpit. He found Quinn slumped forward over the wheel, arms dangling, eyes glassy with shock and exhaustion. In the light swell behind the reef, the gentle rolling of the boat felt strange—like stepping onto land.

"Bloody well done, sailor. I'll take over here if you want to go and throw out the anchor."

Quinn nodded absently and went, wobbly-legged, down the steps to the deck. Pritchard brought the throttles back to quarter speed and the boat chugged steadily across the lagoon towards a strip of beach, its white coral sand gleaming in the gathering dusk against the dark

286

scrub behind. By the time Quinn had dropped the anchor and Pritchard had cut the engines to let the junk come round into the wind, night had fallen on the island, deep and dark, faintly menacing.

They took off their life jackets and assembled in the forward saloon. Quinn sat heavily down at the table and buried his face in his hands, speechless with tiredness. Kiley slumped back on the bunk he had occupied earlier, his silent, questioning gaze going from Quinn to Pritchard, who stood in the doorway. Both of them still carried their guns in their pants; they hadn't discarded them for a second, even at the height of the storm. There'd been several occasions during Kiley's hours of relative freedom on the boat when he might have been able to snatch one or other of the weapons, but each time he had rejected the thought. To get hold of one gun would, at best, only balance the scales. At worst it would lead to a violent, self-destructive showdown. The only way to tip the balance in his favour would be somehow to seize both weapons at once, and no opportunity of doing that seemed likely to arise. Besides, they all still needed each other too badly.

"Did you get a look at the hole in the bow?" Pritchard asked. Quinn nodded and spoke through his fingers.

"It's okay. Way above the waterline now."

"Then we can leave the electric pump to clear the bilges once we're under way again tomorrow. Now, the sooner we eat and get to sleep the better. Weather permitting, I want to be out of here by dawn."

"I'm too bushed to eat," Quinn said.

"You have to. You've had no food for twenty-four hours. There's a long way to go yet and we've got to keep our strength up."

Pritchard squeezed past the table, heading for the galley. Quinn groaned but stood up and followed him, too fatigued to notice that the Englishman was already, subtly, reasserting the authority he had relinquished during the typhoon.

It took Pritchard only ten minutes to find some cans of beef stew and baked beans in the ship's stores—jumbled but miraculously still packed in a locker beside the gas stove—and to open the cans, stir the contents together in a saucepan, and heat them through. Quinn made coffee and buttered some bread. Then they took the food through to the saloon. They gave a plateful to Kiley, who accepted it with a nod. They sat down and ate hungrily, in silence, Kiley's gaze going back constantly to the faces of the other two, particularly Pritchard's. It was a curious, watchful, wary gaze that effectively masked whatever he was thinking.

When they had finished, Quinn belched and sighed and lay back across the bunk he'd been sitting on. Pritchard collected the plates and dumped them in the galley. He came back holding a full bottle of Scotch. He unscrewed the metal top, raised the bottle and took a long swallow. Then he offered the bottle to Quinn. Already half asleep, he shook his head and murmured, "No."

Pritchard held the bottle out to Kiley. The American looked slightly startled.

"Go on," Pritchard urged him. "You've earned it."

Kiley reached for the whisky hesitantly, as if afraid that Pritchard would snatch it away and laugh at him. Once he had hold of the bottle he put it to his lips and drank deeply, gratefully, before handing it back.

"Thanks," he said.

Then Pritchard did laugh, a brief, humourless chuckle, before turning to Quinn.

"Aren't you forgetting something, Seymour?"

"Wha's that?" Quinn muttered sleepily.

"This."

Pritchard reached under the table. He lifted the length of chain which had earlier been round Kiley's ankle, one end of it still fastened to the iron support of his bunk. He rattled the chain aganst the metal, loudly and suddenly enough to make Quinn's eyes pop open.

"You're forgetting that our friend here is still our prisoner. He's starting to forget it too. He helped us save the boat and he thinks that gives him a new status, softens us up. What he's thinking right now is that he'll start playing on that; he'll get around us by being friendly while he waits for a chance to knife us in the back. I think we'd better nip that thought in the bud right now, don't you?"

"Listen, Pritchard." Kiley had little to lose now by asking the question that had worried him all afternoon. "That man there said you'd been seeing my wife in Hong Kong."

"Did he, now?"

"Is it true?"

Pritchard made a show of thinking about it. "Well, as a matter of fact, yes." He grinned. "*Seeing* is the polite term for it. Just like the old Saigon days, eh? But with the boot on the other foot. You don't have much claim on her any longer, Kiley."

"If you've arranged this whole crazy business just to get back at me for taking her away from you, I—"

"Don't flatter yourself, Super Spook. I'm in this for the money. All the same, when it's all over Ailsa's going to come back to me."

"You're fooling yourself. We may quarrel from time to time but she'll stick by me. She's my wife."

"Let's wait and see about that. Seymour, give me the key."

35

The typhoon blew itself out as expected during the night, dispersing over mainland China two hundred miles east of Hong Kong. A few minutes after dawn an elderly Shackleton Mark III long-range maritime reconnaissance aircraft lumbered into the air from RAF Kai Tak to begin searching for the junk. It levelled out at two thousand feet and headed almost due southeast on a course that would take it to the northwestern tip of Luzon. There it would turn northeastwards for twenty miles before turning again to double back to Hong Kong on a flight path parallel to the first. Employing this block-sector search technique, its crew in the course of the five-hour sortie would have visual and radar coverage of some twenty thousand square miles of water. At intervals throughout the day, other aircraft would fly similar parallelogram search patterns over different areas. It sounded impressive, but no one knew better than the air crews themselves the difficulties of trying to single out one among the hundreds of junks that fished and traded in the South China Sea. Added to which, the *Lady Belinda* had twenty-four hours' start, was on no known course and might be anywhere within a radius of three hundred miles of Hong Kong. She might also—which seemed the likeliest possibility—have been sunk by the typhoon.

Across in the civil terminal at Kai Tak, things were busier than usual that morning, with flights delayed and diverted by the storm coming in at intervals between the usual crop of intercontinental arrivals. Siu McNair dropped her husband at the entrance to the departure hall at nine forty. Equipped with an overnight bag, five hundred U.S. dollars in advance expenses, and a ticket for the first plane to Manila, a Philippines Airlines flight scheduled to leave at ten thirty, he checked in and learned that the departure had been delayed by half an hour. Resignedly he went across to the cafeteria, bought a cup of coffee, sat down at a table and started reading the *South China Morning Post*. Two stories dominated the front page: the aftermath of the typhoon and the

Kiley case. NEWS BLACKOUT BY POLICE ON DIPLOMAT KIDNAP, said the main headline. The report went on to suggest that the inquiry had reached a dead end, that the kidnappers and their victims were already outside the jurisdiction of the Hong Kong police and that the Americans were planning to deal in private with the Moros to secure Kiley's release.

Most of which, he thought, was substantially true. Happily, Boyd had managed so far to keep news of the breakthrough in the investigation and the escape of the junk out of the newspapers, but at some cost to his own reputation.

An announcement came over the PA, in English first, then in adenoidal Cantonese. McNair listened in case they were announcing the departure of his plane. They weren't. It was the arrival of Pan Am's flight 001, from New York via London and Delhi, delayed in Bangkok since yesterday afternoon. Halfway through the announcement he heard several chairs scrape back simultaneously. He glanced over his newspaper and saw Horace Stanley, the security officer from the American consulate, and two other men getting up from an adjacent table. Stanley hadn't seen McNair, perhaps wouldn't even remember him if he did. He had a restless, preoccupied air. The other two were nondescript heavies who followed Stanley out of the cafeteria, heading for the stairs that led down to the arrivals hall.

McNair folded his paper, picked up his grip and went after them, more out of an ingrained curiosity than in the hope of learning anything that mattered. They went down the stairs and crossed the narrow, crowded hall towards the barrier that separated the public area from customs and immigration controls. McNair stationed himself at the rear of the hall, mingling with hotel and taxi touts, and watched the Americans.

They stood fidgeting about, eyeing the doors in the barrier, passing desultory remarks to each other. It was fifteen minutes before the first, hand-baggage-only passengers from Pan Am 001 began coming through.

McNair picked out the courier at once, a youngish man carrying a small bag in one hand, an attaché case in the other. Too formally dressed to be a tourist but lacking the self-assurance of a businessman, he had civil servant all over him. Anxious to be met, he was looking round him as he walked down the trolley ramp. Stanley pushed forward through the crowd, spoke to him and discreetly flashed a card. The newcomer searched in a jacket pocket for his own identification. The two heavies moved in behind him. Stanley offered to take the attaché case; the courier shook his head and said something.

McNair got close behind the group as they made their way to the exit. He heard the courier say, ". . . the delay. There was just no way to avoid it."

"Sure, sure," Stanley muttered uneasily. "It's just that we were getting kind of antsy, thinking of you hanging around airports and hotel lobbies, with *that*."

"Well, it's here now."

Then they were out of the door and McNair was listening to his flight being called. There was time for a quick phone call to Boyd. He described what he had seen and said, "Any betting there was ten million dollars in that attaché case?"

"In cash?"

"Probably not. That's quite a lot of paper. Letters of credit, perhaps, or a bank-guaranteed cheque."

"Looks as though they're all geared up to do the deal, then. It all depends on whether Kiley is still alive."

"Maybe they know more about that than we do. It might be a good idea to check the passenger list on the next flight to Simpang. I've got to go now."

"Good luck, Mac."

"Chief Inspector McNair?"

"That's right."

"Special Agent Antonio Mendez. Tony to my friends. I was sent to meet you. Welcome to Manila."

Mendez, a short, thick-set Filipino, stood beside the cubicle where an immigration officer was scrutinizing McNair's passport. He was wearing a cheap Panama hat, a loudly patterned batik sport shirt, cream denims and sandals. The butt of a .38 Police Positive stuck out prominently from a holster on his left hip. For a special agent of the National Bureau of Investigation—the Filipino equivalent of the FBI—he could hardly be called inconspicuous. However, since gaudy clothes were part of the Filipino style and half the population went about armed, he probably did not cut a particularly noteworthy figure. He was about Mc-Nair's age and had a cocky, engaging grin. When the visitor had retrieved his passport Mendez took his arm and guided him through to customs.

"They give you lunch on the plane?" he asked in his Spanish-American accent.

"No."

"Then let's go eat. I'll take you to my favourite seafood place. You like shark steaks? Abalone? Clams?"

"Shouldn't I check in at your headquarters first?"

"What for?" Mendez said with a careless wave. "Nobody there can tell you anything more than I can. We're keeping a lookout along the north coast for the missing junk. Until it turns up, what can you and I do? We might as well have a good lunch while we're waiting."

"All right," McNair said, pleasantly resigned. Things moved at their own pace in the Philippines, and there was no way of hurrying them along.

"We're kind of interested in one of your fellow-passengers, by the way. You recognize him?"

"Which one?"

Mendez stopped and gripped his upper arm more tightly. "Up ahead there."

There was only one man at the customs bench ten yards in front of them, a grey-haired, bespectacled Chinese, stooping over the bag he was opening for inspection by the Filipino customs officer. Then, as he straightened up, McNair realized his face was familiar from photographs in one of the Special Branch files. The name eluded him for a second.

"Hold on, that's . . ."

"Kao Ling," said Mendez. "Works for the New China News Agency bureau in Hong Kong."

"Which means he also doubles as an intelligence officer. Does he come here often?"

"He's been a few times, always with a legitimate excuse. We have no reason to deny him entry. We wondered if you might have some idea what brings him this time."

"Not a clue. All I can tell you is that his people have had a pair of legmen following me about for the last couple of days. I doubt if they learned very much. We can't work out why the Chinese should be interested in the Kiley case."

"Well, we suspect they give a certain amount of aid to the Moros. Maybe they helped plan this thing."

"Maybe," said McNair thoughtfully, watching Kao Ling fasten his bag, pick it up and walk out into the arrivals hall. Then Tony Mendez steered him through customs without stopping, waving genially at the uniformed man behind the bench.

———

At five o'clock that afternoon the Shackleton flying the last reconnaissance sortie of the day turned back from the coast of Luzon and headed on a northwesterly course for Hong Kong. When it was seventy miles out to sea the flight sergeant manning the Mark 21 ASC radar caught a blip on the edge of his screen, a vessel about twelve miles to the east, steaming towards the Philippines.

The pilot altered course. Four minutes later the air electronics officer in the nose compartment sighted the junk and the captain took the Shackleton down to two hundred feet to circle it. It was the twelfth boat the crew had checked out on this trip alone. What excited their interest, distinguishing this junk from the others, was the lack of clutter on deck. Fishing and trading boats were usually packed to the gunwales with cargo or nets; children swarmed all over them and would wave up at the aircraft. This one had plenty of clear deck space and looked decidedly underpopulated.

The plane banked and circled the junk from the rear. It flew no flag. There was a name printed across the stern but the crew were not close enough to read it. The signaller in the starboard blister window got the best view of the boat as they cut across its bows. There was a single deckhouse, a coach roof forward of it, a short boom fixed to the mast. That matched the description the police had put out, but it still wasn't firm evidence. Then, for perhaps half a second, the signaller got a glimpse of the man standing at the wheel behind the weather screen, the only person visible on the boat. He was ready to swear that the man was European.

He reported what he had seen to the flight deck. The tactical navigator logged the junk's position and course. The radio operator relayed the information over his high-frequency side-band set to Kai Tak.

Lunch at the comfortable, air-conditioned restaurant overlooking Manila Bay had been a leisurely feast, fit for a Filipino saint's day. Tony Mendez, an unrepentant gourmand, had ordered for both of them: curried shrimps, dressed crab, red snapper baked with peppers and a whole grilled crayfish each, all washed down with prodigal quantities of Californian Dry Graves. It was followed by a fruit salad consisting mostly of rum and papaya, then coffee, liqueurs and Havana cigars. They were getting on famously.

At four o'clock, arriving somewhat unsteadily at the NBI's modern, four-storeyed headquarters off Taft Avenue in central Manila, they had been given an up-to-date briefing by Mendez's superior, the officer in charge of the case. A special alert was in force in northern Luzon, he said; police, coast guards and army and navy units were all on the lookout for the appearance of the junk or the fugitives. McNair acknowledged that the little man had been right: there was nothing any of them could do but wait.

Mendez had dropped him at the Bayview Hotel, where a room was reserved for him. After putting a call through to Boyd in Hong Kong he'd collapsed on the bed from a surfeit of food and drink, and fallen into a deep sleep.

He awoke with a headache and a dry mouth, to hear the telephone at his bedside ringing. The light had faded considerably. He looked at his watch: it was twenty past six.

"Mac?" The caller was Mendez. "I got news. We just heard from Hong Kong. One of your planes sighted a junk heading for Luzon a little over an hour ago. It's not a hundred per cent certain, but it looks very much like our number."

"They survived the storm, then," McNair breathed incredulously. "What happens now?"

"Well, we've asked our air force to get a plane up and do a second check on position and course. That will give us an idea of the boat's speed and where she's heading for. One problem is that it'll be dark inside an hour, and they're obviously planning to make a landfall by night. But with radar and patrol boats in the area, we stand a pretty good chance of making an intercept."

"They must be expecting the Moros to meet them. What if they do slip past the boats and make contact?"

"Roadblocks should take care of that. To get Kiley back to their own territory they have to travel hundreds of miles south with him, remember. Now listen, Mac. I'm about to drive up north myself, to around Bangui, where we hope they'll make the landing. You want to come along yourself, get a little closer to the action?"

"You bet!"

"Okay. I'll pick you up fifteen minutes from now."

On the junk, in the last few minutes of daylight, Seymour Quinn scrambled down the wooden mast, his feet braced against it, lowering himself hand over hand down the rope he had thrown over the short yard near the top and secured at the bottom to a bollard amidships. He dropped lightly onto the coach roof and then sprang down to the deck.

294

He picked up the radar reflector, a foot-wide aluminum dish, which he had unbolted from the masthead and flung down on the deck, and prepared to throw it overboard.

"Wait!" Pritchard shouted from the cockpit.

"What is it?" Quinn appeared irritably at the door, the reflector in his hands.

"I've been thinking. I've got an idea. Just wait a minute till I sort things out."

He had been thinking hard, in fact, ever since the RAF Shackleton had circled them more than two hours earlier. Since then, not more than half an hour ago, a Cessna reconnaissance spotter with Philippines Air Force markings had done the same thing. It was pretty obvious that they'd been identified and that their course was marked out. Even with the cover that darkness would give, it would not be hard for the Filipinos to detect and intercept them off the coast.

It had been Quinn's idea to take down the reflector. It would reduce by at least seventy-five per cent, he said, the likelihood of being picked up on the naval radar scanners. But Pritchard had been carrying the idea further.

"Listen. You say the patrol boats will be depending on that thing for their target signal?"

"Not entirely. This amplifies the signal, is all. Could be we'll still get to make a blip on the screen."

"But a smaller blip, right? What if we manage to keep the reflector afloat and separate from us, like a decoy? They go after the big dot and forget about us."

"Never happen. They track us because this mother is up at the masthead, twenty feet above sea level."

"But suppose we can get it up to something approaching that height? We've got a rubber dinghy back there, doing nothing, with a step for an emergency mast. You can make a mast by lashing two oars together and tying the radar reflector to the top. As soon as we get near the coast, we release the dinghy, let it run with the tidal stream and go our own way."

"I suppose I heard of a worse idea once," said Quinn, resignedly, "but right now I can't think of a better one."

Driving north out of Manila was a long, slow haul for the first hour. The road passed through a succession of dusty *barrios* and chaotic little villages that had fused together into a gigantic urban sprawl of clapboard shacks, ugly modern churches and ramshackle stores with metal signboards advertising root beer and Coke. The road was cluttered with jeepneys, trucks, bicycles, rattling country buses and aged American cars, lopsided and down on their springs. Once in a while there would be a queue of vehicles waiting to overtake a cart being pulled at a leisurely pace by a water buffalo. There was military traffic too, going to and from the great American air and naval bases at Clark Field and Subic Bay.

Once they had passed the town of San Fernando, however, the traffic thinned out and Tony Mendez was able to push his Chevrolet up to a hundred kilometres an hour along Route Three, towards the northwest coast of Luzon. Night had fallen; the headlights probed far ahead along the road as it twisted between fields of dry rice and pineapple, coffee and coconut plantations.

"Heard anything from the American end?" McNair asked.

"Not yet. The bureau was about to bring the Ambassador up to date just as I was leaving. You can guess the result, though: pressure on us not to do anything that might endanger Kiley. I can see their point: the one thing we don't want to wind up with is a siege or a shootout. By the way, I thought we might stop for dinner in Rosario. There's a nice little place there, open late. . . ."

36

At twenty minutes past midnight, the *Lady Belinda* slowly entered Bangui Bay, on the northwestern tip of Luzon island. She showed no lights and her diesel engines, down to a quarter speed, sent out only a muffled thudding. Pritchard and Quinn stood tensely, side by side, in the cockpit. Earlier a half-moon had been shining, but fortunately it had now set behind the vast bulk of the volcanic Ilocos Mountains that reared above the shoreline ahead of them, steep and black, almost threatening.

Both of them strained to see through the darkness ahead. The rendezvous point was the wharf of a small sawmill adjacent to a fishing village called Estancia, close to the centre of the bay and about five kilometres east of the lighthouse at Negra Point. They were just a couple of miles offshore now, with the lighthouse well to their right, the glow of Bangui town coming from the far end of the bay. They were listening hard as well, alert for the giveaway grumble of a patrol boat's engines. Just fifteen minutes ago, soon after they had launched the rubber dinghy with the radar reflector on the top of its makeshift mast, a boat had come nosing towards them from the west. It must have got within half a mile of the junk before it turned away, perhaps distracted by the reflector, perhaps not.

"Isn't that our landmark?" Quinn demanded suddenly, pointing out across the port quarter. "Three lights in a row, right?"

In a moment Pritchard saw them too. Among the thinly scattered points of light in the villages between coastline and mountains they were unmistakable, though not conspicuous enough to look like a signal: three lamps in a vertical row, mounted perhaps on a gantry like floodlights in a stadium.

He turned the boat towards them, only just able to resist the temptation to put on speed. His heart was pounding with anticipation, excitement. The journey was almost over, the Project entering its final phase. They had had many close calls, had endured treachery and danger, but still they were winning. They had what they had set out to get—Kiley; once they linked up with the Moros it would be merely a matter of staying in hiding and waiting till the ransom turned up.

The lights drew steadily closer across the still, dark water of the bay. The mountains towered above them now. They made out the fishing village, Estancia; a couple of minutes later they saw the big square shape of an unlit building a hundred yards further along the water's edge. The sawmill. Still aiming straight for the lights, they spotted the small jetty beside the mill where—as Osman Khan had explained to Pritchard when relaying the Moros' instructions—small inter-island cargo boats tied up to be loaded with cut timber. It was the ideal berth for the junk.

Quinn left the cockpit and walked up to the bow. He picked up the coiled head rope and stood ready to jump ashore with it. Pritchard, when he estimated he was fifty yards short of the jetty, lined up the *Lady Belinda* to run in next to it and put the engines in neutral.

The boat coasted smoothly in until it was alongside the jetty. Quinn hopped off the bow and put a turn of the rope around a bollard. A minute later the boat was tied up, the engines were silent and the two of them stood on the jetty, staring into the inland darkness. There was little to see. The row of lights that had guided them in shone from some distance behind the sawmill, up a low slope densely covered with jungle.

Beyond that was nothing but the blackness of farmland and more jungle, clinging to the sides of the Ilocos Mountains until they became too steep to support any soil. The night was warm and still, full of unfamiliar insect noises.

"You figure they know we're here?" Quinn asked uneasily after a minute.

"They'd better know. They're supposed to have a lookout posted right through the night."

Suddenly the row of lights up the hill went out. At the same moment Pritchard saw a movement at the side of the sawmill and tensed, reaching for the butt of his revolver. In a few seconds a figure emerged from the shadows beside the building and came quickly down the jetty towards them.

He was a small, dark Filipino in shorts and a singlet, with a sweat scarf tied round his head and a submachine gun clutched in one hand. His feet bare, he walked with an uncanny silence. He stopped in front of Pritchard and said quietly, without preamble, "You have the prisoner?"

"In the boat."

"Where are the others? There are supposed to be four of you."

"Two are dead."

The Moro showed neither surprise nor puzzlement. He said, "Bring the prisoner—gagged and blindfolded. And hurry. We are breaking curfew. Patrols are everywhere."

They went back aboard the *Lady Belinda* and down to the saloon. Kiley was sitting on the edge of his bunk in the dark.

"Where are you taking me now?" he asked.

"For once I can give you a straightforward answer," Pritchard said. "I don't have a bloody clue. But wherever it is, they don't want you to see it."

They found a pair of tea cloths in the galley and tied them tightly across Kiley's mouth and eyes before taking the chain off his ankle. Quinn padlocked it to his right wrist instead and held onto the free end, wrapping it a couple of times around his hand. They led him up on deck and across the rail onto the jetty. Without a word the Moro turned and walked away, leaving them to follow.

Beside the sawmill was a narrow path that led up the slope through the jungle. Although it seemed quite well defined, in the dark under the canopy of interlocking tree branches and foliage it was difficult to follow without stumbling over roots or getting limbs entangled in the

298

trailing, thorny branches of rattan. Kiley's blindfold didn't help their progress; he had to be steered or pulled almost every step of the way up the short, steep hillside, while their guide paused every few yards, waiting impatiently for them to catch up.

It took five minutes of sweating, uphill struggle before the Moro made a final stop and gave a soft whistle. The signal was returned from higher up the hill. The guide waved at them to hurry and they stumbled out suddenly into a small clearing in the jungle.

It was roughly square in shape, and the opening in the overhead canopy let in just enough starlight to give Pritchard a fairly clear view of the scene. The cover of nipa palms, creepers and undergrowth had been recently cut down and thrown on a pile in one corner. The clearing was dominated by the big, bulky shape of a truck that had been backed into it down a track that entered from the south side. Most of the rest of the space was taken by Moros bivouacked under blankets on the ground, stirring now at the whispered command of a tall, lean man who moved swiftly among them.

Pritchard and Quinn, with Kiley between them and the guide to one side, halted at the edge of the clearing. The thin man approached them, stopped and then shone the beam of a hooded torch into each of their faces in turn. His own was in shadow.

"Only two of you?" His accent was Chabakano, with a trace of American. "Where is Baxter?"

"Dead," said Quinn.

"How?"

"He tried to chicken out," Pritchard said. "He would have betrayed us, ruined everything."

"So you killed him?"

"Yes. And we lost our other partner in the typhoon."

The Moro turned the torch back to Pritchard's face and scrutinized him for several seconds. Then he laughed, quietly, unexpectedly.

"I had a feeling that Baxter would turn out to be the soft grape in your bunch. So you plucked him off. And now we are left with the hard ones, yes? Pritchard. And the sailor."

He swung the beam to Quinn. The American blinked irritably at the light and said, "Let's cut the crap. Who the hell are you, anyway?"

The Moro lifted the torch to shine vertically on his own face, showing a predatory nose and gleaming brown eyes. "I am Mustapha Diaz, military leader of the Moro National Liberation Front."

"You're running this thing yourself?" Pritchard said. "Isn't that taking a risk, this far from your home ground?"

"Some risks are worth taking." He turned the dim light onto Kiley's gagged and blinded face. "Here is a property worth ten million dollars. That's not something I would like to leave to subordinates."

He spoke quietly. He flicked the torch away and circled its beam round the clearing. Apart from the guide and the sentry, there were six other men who had been roused from sleep and who were now carrying their blankets, weapons and other gear to the back of the truck, casting covertly curious glances at the newcomers. Four of them were raggedly dressed in jeans and T-shirts; the other two, smartly turned out in Filipino army fatigues, field caps and boots, were dismantling and loading up the gantry and the small petrol-driven generator that had provided the light to guide the junk to its rendezvous.

Diaz snapped off the torch. "Let me explain the procedure. I want no mistakes. There is a curfew in force until six in the morning. Only military vehicles and others with special permission are allowed on the roads. We captured this truck from the army tonight, together with the uniforms of its crew and the papers authorizing it to travel east of here, to Santa Ana. We turn off the coast road just a few kilometres from here, but there is at least one roadblock to pass before that. The men in uniform will be in the cab, the rest of us in the rear, under the canopy. The truck is supposed to be empty; there is no reason why anyone should look under the canvas, but if they do then we come out shooting. Is that clear?"

Pritchard nodded. Quinn said, "Where we going, anyhow?"

"To a temporary base, up in the mountains. That junk will be found soon, and the search in this area will quickly intensify." Diaz paused. "We take charge of the prisoner now."

In the darkness, Pritchard exchanged the ghost of a glance with Quinn. "No," he said. "We'll hang on to him—at least until we've seen our slice of the ransom. As you said, he's valuable property."

The Moro seemed about to object. But then he shrugged, turned away and led them to the truck. It was an olive-drab Chevrolet six-by-six. Apart from the men in army uniform, the rest of the guerrillas had already climbed on the cargo deck and were squatting beneath the canvas canopy. Quinn hopped up to join them and, still clutching the free end of the chain, steered Kiley up the steps in the tailboard. Pritchard followed. Diaz was the last to go. He closed the flaps of the canopy and began lacing them together while the men in the captured fatigues raised and secured the tailboard.

300

"By the way," Pritchard said, "what happened to the real crew of this thing?"

Mustapha Diaz turned and gave him a brief, penetrating stare. Then he lifted a corner of one flap, picked up the torch that he had set down on the deck and shone it across the clearing. Beside the pile of felled palms and dying creepers, two figures in khaki shorts and undershirts lay side by side with their faces to the ground. Their hands were tied behind them; the backs of their heads were mashed to a bloody, gleaming pulp.

"Christ!" Pritchard turned away, sickened. "Did you have to do that?"

"An enemy spared today kills tomorrow. It is easy for you to be squeamish; tomorrow you will be gone. Tomorrow, next week, next year, we will still be fighting. And as I told your friend Baxter, guerrilla war is not a game."

In the darkness of the truck, Pritchard could not see the Moro leader's fierce brown eyes, but he sensed the intensity of his gaze. He disguised a shudder. Then the truck started up with a roar and moved down the track.

Within a minute it was out of the jungle and turning left onto Route Three, the main highway across the narrow coastal plain of northern Luzon. The time was ten minutes to one.

At two fifteen a naval patrol craft, homing in on a weak radar signal three miles off the coast, came upon the *Lady Belinda*'s rubber dinghy with the reflector lashed to its mast. At once, all vessels in the area were ordered to proceed to Bangui Bay and intensify their search —but in fact it was an army foot patrol moving from village to village that first found the junk tied up at the jetty beside the sawmill.

"Well, they did it," said McNair to Mendez.

"I'll admit that," the NBI man said. "They did all the things I said they wouldn't. They avoided the intercept. Since then they must have met up with the Moros. And if they're not on foot then they must also have managed to slip through the roadblocks."

"Well, what next?"

Mendez stood up with a sigh, carrying his plastic cup of coffee, and walked across to the large-scale wall map of north Luzon. Pasted onto a hardboard backing, it was a permanent fixture in the office of the lieutenant-colonel commanding the Ilocos Norte military region, at whose headquarters they had arrived an hour earlier. The colonel himself was out, supervising the positioning of roadblocks and the dispatch of patrols, and had abandoned his office to the special agent and the visiting police officer.

"Here," said Mendez, tapping at the map with his ballpoint, "is Route Three, the way we came in. It's virtually the only usable road running east–west along this coast, and it has roadblocks every few kilometres along it. If they've managed to evade them it can only mean one thing: they've turned inland." He swung his pen to describe a wide arc south of the road. "In here. The Ilocos range, an offshoot of the Cordillera Central, with mountains rising to five thousand feet. Volcanic mountains, some of them still active, the jungle around them nearly uninhabited."

"Could they get in there, by road?"

"In and out, with the right kind of vehicle: something with enough ground clearance is all they'd need. There are plenty of tracks to follow, some of them not even marked on our maps. What we'll have to do is get some choppers up at first light and take a look in there—"

The telephone rang. Mendez answered it. He listened at some length and said just a few words in Tagalog before replacing the receiver. When he faced McNair his mouth was set in a tight, angry line.

"That was the colonel. They hijacked an army truck, killed the driver and his buddy. The bodies have just been found. They could be anywhere within a radius of a hundred k's by now."

The air had grown steadily cooler as the truck climbed into the mountains. By dawn, Quinn and Pritchard in their short-sleeved shirts and thin trousers were positively cold. The Moros, similarly dressed, did not seem to notice the change in temperature; most of them were dozing on the long metal benches at either side of the cargo deck, oblivious of the violent rocking, swaying and gear-clashing of the truck as it ground its way up a succession of tortuous tracks towards the mountainous interior of Luzon. Kiley, too, his gag now removed but the blindfold still in place, had fallen into an uneasy, open-mouthed sleep where he sat between Pritchard and Quinn. They were the only ones wholly awake, apart from Mustapha Diaz, who sat opposite them holding an M3 in his lap, a faint smile playing occasionally across his face.

There had been two roadblocks on Route Three before they had turned off onto this series of steadily deteriorating mountain tracks. While the soldiers checked the papers carried by the two uniformed men in the cab, the tension in the back had been almost unbearable. Waiting for the rear flaps of the canopy to be flung open, the Moros had sat with their weapons cocked, safety catches off. Pritchard had expected someone to loose off a burst of shots in a sheer release of nervous strain. But the guns had stayed silent and the canopy closed. Now, in the comparative safety of the uplands, Diaz had rolled back the canvas to show a succession of spectacular views: north and west, the South China Sea stretching mistily to the horizon; to the east, dawn breaking over the dark, jagged peaks of the Cordillera Central. They had left the coastal jungle far behind and risen through successive belts of bare mountainside and pine forest. Suddenly, after passing a final line of trees, the truck rolled onto more level ground. The track was running across a vast, empty plateau, totally covered by a thick layer of what looked like jagged, grey-black cinders.

"Lava clinker," explained Diaz, seeing the frown on Pritchard's brow. "We are close to the summit of Mount Lambayo. An active volcano, four and a half thousand feet high."

"What in God's name . . . ?"

"Wait. You will see."

In the thin, clear mountain air, the lava field seemed to stretch to eternity. The clinker had obliterated whatever vegetation might once have grown on the slope. As the truck lurched through a hairpin bend, Pritchard got a glimpse of the cone of the volcano, a wide, truncated peak of barren rock towering perhaps a thousand feet above them. Then he caught a sudden sharp smell of sulphur.

Diaz laughed at Pritchard's expression. "Don't worry. It last erupted in nineteen twenty. Gas escapes from the fissures sometimes, that's all."

A minute later the truck jerked to a halt and the engine was cut. Mustapha Diaz, still clutching the M3, jumped over the tailboard and backed off to let the two men from the cab lower it. The sleepy Moros yawned and stretched. Quinn jerked the chain fastened round Kiley's wrist to waken him, then guided him down and out of the truck. Pritchard followed.

For a moment, the sight of his surroundings bewildered him. The newly risen sun, slanting in blindingly across the mountain peaks to the east, showed that the truck was parked within a complex of ruined buildings. It stood, in fact, inside part of the structure, between two high walls with a few sheets of rusted corrugated-iron roofing still clinging to them, so that the vehicle was quite effectively hidden from both the ground and the air. The rest of the buildings, standing in eerie isolation in the middle of the lava field, consisted of a square of single-storeyed adobe surrounding a courtyard that was covered in clinker. Three sides of this had once been overlooked by a colonnaded walkway or veranda; on the fourth side stood the Spanish-baroque facade and bell tower of a church or chapel, its roof caved in. Two other sides of the square were collapsed and partly submerged by the clinker. The fourth was nearly intact.

The place seemed deserted. After the noise inside the truck the silence of the lifeless plateau was uncanny, almost oppressive. He turned to Diaz.

"The Monastery of San Roberto de Molesmes," the Moro supplied. "It was built by Cistercian monks, seeking seclusion to meditate. This was supposed to be the safe side of the volcano, away from the lava channels. Their God was not very grateful for their prayers: He opened a new fissure and fried them in lava." Diaz's face wore a mocking smile. "Their ghosts are supposed to be here still; at night they walk the colonnades, chanting prayers."

The ruins made sense to Pritchard now: the raised walkways around the quadrangle had been the monastery's cloisters, built to connect the church, the centre of its existence, with the other buildings. He said, "Why have you brought us here?"

"To lie low for the day. We move south at dusk—before the ghosts walk. But you are not superstitious, surely?"

"It's pretty exposed, isn't it?"

"It is inaccessible. And safe. What few people live hereabouts fear it. No Christian ever comes near."

"I wasn't thinking of the locals. There'll be choppers out looking for us. They could land troops here."

"No. Helicopters cannot land on the clinker; it would not support their weight. And the track is too steep. They may come to look, perhaps, but there will be no sign that we are here. We hide in the cells of the monks. We are safe. Come."

Diaz turned away. Without waiting for them to follow he walked across the courtyard, feet crunching on the clinker, towards the north end of the monastery, the part that was least badly damaged.

Pritchard hesitated, glancing at Quinn. The American seemed unsure of himself as well. Maybe the unnerving quality of the place had got through to him, or perhaps its isolation had brought home to him, as it had to Pritchard, how alone they now were, how dependent on

304

Diaz. Then he visibly shook off the feeling and said, "You don't believe in ghosts, do you?"

"Not usually."

"C'mon, then."

Quinn tugged at Kiley's chain and led him across the quadrangle, the blindfolded man stumbling over the clinker. After a second Pritchard followed, and the guerrillas came shambling behind. On the north side of the square there were four or five steps leading up between two thick pillars to the colonnade, which had a row of gaping doorways leading off it into dim little rooms: the monks' cells. Diaz was already up there, standing in the nearest of the jagged openings and beckoning to them.

Quinn started up the steps, pausing as Kiley tripped over the first one and then began to pick his way up on all fours. Pritchard, at the bottom, paused again. He did not know why, beyond sensing some falseness in Diaz's gesture, some sudden tension in his manner.

He stood and watched the other two, Quinn now stopping on the second step from the top, waiting for Kiley at the end of the chain to scramble clumsily up behind him. Then, to their left, he saw a shadow: a human shape sharply outlined against the adobe wall behind the colonnade, elongated by the hard slanting sunlight from the right. The shadow moved.

Some faint distrust of his own perception—the talk of ghosts, an awareness of the tricks that fear and fatigue play on the mind—made him hesitate a fraction of a second more before acting. But suddenly his instincts were screaming at him; he knew something terrible was going to happen. He shouted, "Quinn! Watch it!"

The American spun round, startled; then, checking himself as he realized the danger could only lie the other way, he whirled back, releasing Kiley's chain, dropping to his knees on the step and whipping the pistol from his pocket in one swift movement. The man who had been standing behind the pillar on the left stepped into the open, raising his machine pistol to level it calmly at Quinn's head. Too calmly. Quinn shot him in the stomach before he could pull the trigger. The man grunted and fell on his behind, dropping the gun with a clatter. Quinn swung his pistol towards Diaz in the doorway, but already he was too late. The second ambusher had moved out from behind the right-hand pillar, his machine pistol held at the hip.

The stairway seemed to explode around Quinn. The brief, thunderous burst of automatic fire, rebounding amplified from the walls, came

305

out across the courtyard with a force like high explosive, carrying Quinn with it. Blown off his knees by the full clipful of bullets that tore into him, he cartwheeled down the steps, knocking Kiley down with him. The two of them landed at the bottom in a tangle of limbs.

Pritchard had his own revolver out. He fired point-blank at the second gunman and saw him lurch back across the colonnade. His mind reeling with the knowledge of treachery, he dived at the two men on the ground. With some notion of using Kiley as a shield, he seized the American's collar with his free hand and tried to drag him out from under Quinn's weight. Something smashed down on his wrist, breaking his grip: a numbing blow from the barrel of one of the Moros' submachine guns. He tried to turn the Webley on the man but another guerrilla was behind him, throwing an arm round his neck and seizing the hand with the gun in it. He pulled the trigger, loosing off a useless shot. Two or three of the Moros had hold of him now, jabbering excitedly and dragging at him like wild dogs as he staggered about the courtyard, cursing and trying to fight them off. He felt the revolver wrenched from his grasp. Then he collapsed under their weight and was pinned down.

Lying with his face half buried in the rough clinker, he could see nothing. Someone was sitting on his back; others were milling about in his vicinity, shouting at each other in Chabakano. After a minute or so the Moro got off his back and he was hauled to his feet.

He stood facing the steps again. The guerrillas had formed a semicircle around him and were holding their weapons at the ready. Quinn's body lay where it had fallen at the foot of the blood-spattered stairway, but Kiley had been taken away. Up on the colonnade Diaz still stood, flanked by a couple of guards. This time there was another man with him, a lean and ugly Chinese in a cotton drill suit.

"Put your hands on your head," Diaz ordered.

Pritchard obeyed like an automaton.

"I am sorry about your friend," said the voice from the colonnade. "There was no other way. If you had agreed to hand the prisoner over to us, this would not have been necessary. Obviously you were determined not to. You would have used him as a hostage, with a gun at his head. This was the only sure way of getting him safely into our hands."

"*Your* hands?" Pritchard spoke thickly, dazedly. "We're supposed to be in this together."

"No longer."

Pritchard's gaze was drawn back to Quinn's shattered, blood-

306

soaked body. He had taken all the shots in the torso and they had almost blown him in two, the score of bullet holes across his chest and midriff running together into one vast open wound.

"What good do you think it'll do you, double-crossing us? Salim's bill of exchange names me as the bearer. It's worthless to you. Half the ransom is still mine."

"No longer." Diaz paused. "New arrangements have been made. Come up here. Slowly."

There seemed no point in arguing. Keeping his hands on his head, Pritchard walked awkwardly across the clinker. He stepped over Quinn's body and mounted the steps to the colonnade. There was lots more blood on the stone floor here, but the dead or wounded gunmen had been removed—presumably to the cells. Inexplicably, some fleeting memory of them, some blurred impression that their appearance had made on his subconscious in the mad moment of the ambush, drew his stare past Diaz to the ratlike features of the Chinese stranger, seeking a comparison. And he knew that his impression was right: the killers had been Chinese, too.

From another broken doorway further along the colonnade, two men had emerged and were walking towards them. One was yet another unfamiliar Chinese, short, grey-haired, bespectacled, and incongruously dressed in a rather shabby business suit. The other, dapper in a smart, well-pressed safari jacket, was Osman Khan. Looking from them back to Diaz, Pritchard felt the first real shock of betrayal, a sense of being overwhelmed by all the corruption and venality of Asia.

The two men stopped in front of them. Diaz spoke to Khan.

"Tell Pritchard, here, about the new arrangements."

"To begin with," said Khan seriously, "the bill of exchange that I gave you is no longer encashable."

"What does that mean? Speak plain English, will you?" Pritchard was suddenly irritable, tiredness burning behind his eyes, the shock of the ambush receding behind a flood of bitterness.

Diaz replied. He had no need to explain, but to judge by his smile he was enjoying it. "In plain English, we will take Kiley to the south and hand him over to the Americans, just as you envisaged. They will pay Chief Minister Salim ten million dollars, and he will give it to us —all of it. He has no need of it himself, and he has never seen any good reason for giving half of it to you. In a nutshell, the political fiction which you invented to cover your crime, we have turned into fact. The deception has become the reality."

Pritchard nodded wearily; no longer angry, he felt merely jaded by the knowledge of what a bloody fool he'd been. He glanced at the two politely silent Chinese again and said, without much interest, "So where do they come in?"

"You have not, of course, met Major Wen or Mr. Kao Ling."

The rat-faced one was Wen. Baxter had mentioned him. He'd been present at that first meeting with the Moros in Zamboanga, an adviser sent to them by the Chinese Communists. The name Kao Ling meant nothing.

"We have friends apart from the Chief Minister," said Diaz. "And we have responsibilities to them. In the case of Kiley, our plan happened to coincide with their interests. The Chinese People's Liberation Army has helped us for many years to arm and train our freedom fighters. Major Wen is their liaison officer. As a matter of routine he reported your plan to his superiors. Word came back that they wanted it prevented at all costs. But by then it was too late to stop you. We did the next best thing: we undertook to ensure the safe return of Kiley."

"He'd have been safe enough as it was."

"There was no guarantee of that."

"Perhaps I can explain." A new voice spoke, a gentle voice, that of the middle-aged Chinese called Kao Ling. He was watching Pritchard with what might almost have been concern, an expression suggesting eagerness to please. "I believe I am the only one here who can answer your question."

Pritchard's hands were still clasped together on top of his head. Now he lowered them slowly to his sides. Nobody objected. He looked at the other three men in turn, then spoke to Kao Ling.

"Well, I know about the others now. You might as well tell me what instrument you play in the quartet."

"You and I have been colleagues of a sort, Mr. Pritchard, in Hong Kong." Kao spoke English with a smooth, fluent authority. "I work for the New China News Agency. I also have a certain security function."

"You mean your wire-service job is a cover for secret service work? All right, I'll buy that."

To Pritchard's surprise, Kao stepped forward and took him by the arm. "Mr. Pritchard, let us talk privately for a moment."

He turned Pritchard and walked him down the steps, past Quinn's body, into the courtyard. The pressure of the small hand on his arm was gentle, almost friendly. The armed guerrillas ringed them as they walked across the clinker to the centre of the quadrangle, now baking in the early sun. Once they were out of the Moros' earshot the Chinese stopped and turned to face Pritchard. He spoke earnestly.

"These men do not need to know any of this. Nor want to, for that matter. Their war is parochial; their world is small. You are different. I knew your work when you were with the Federated Press. I have a high professional regard for you. You deserve to understand what is happening here."

"You can cut out the bloody flattery. It doesn't take much to understand a stab in the back."

"There is more to it than that," Kao said. "Much more. When I heard of Kiley's kidnapping I was dismayed. Dismayed and frightened. To explain why I must first tell you that many years ago, when he worked in the United States, he became friendly with a Chinese rocket scientist working there, a man named Ch'ien Hsue-shen. Ch'ien was persecuted during the McCarthy era and made plans to go back to China. Kiley tried to persuade him to stay, but failed."

"I remember the name," Pritchard said. "He ended up as head of the missile research programme at Lop Nor."

"He also became a good friend of mine. Several months ago, when I learned that Kiley had been transferred to Hong Kong, I arranged to make a personal approach to him. I told him that Ch'ien wished to return to America, to re-defect. Kiley was mistrustful. He asked that Ch'ien should prove his good faith, by supplying the CIA with some secret information connected with his work. Ever since then Kiley has been receiving, at monthly intervals, copies of top-secret drawings and other technical data. Some of these documents have been quite startling. They show our nuclear capability to be much greater than the Americans had believed. We have cruise missiles already stockpiled and a neutron warhead in the production stage."

Kao Ling paused, watching Pritchard carefully.

"I am the courier who has brought out this information, Mr. Pritchard. Every month I meet Kiley. Every month I renew Ch'ien's plea for help in escaping. Always Kiley procrastinates. He would rather have him stay, as what they call an asset. Of course, the arrangement breaks all the CIA's ground rules. It is one thing their computers cannot evaluate: a relationship based on personal trust. So perhaps you can see, now, how you upset that relationship by kidnapping him. And how important it is to me to see that he is safely returned to Hong Kong."

"I don't understand why you're telling me all this," Pritchard said, confused. After a lifetime in Asia, its unfathomable gaze still perplexed him. What motive could this grey little man have for confessing treachery? "If Ch'ien is a CIA asset, that must be one of the biggest intelligence scoops in years. It—"

"Yes. But not for the CIA." Kao Ling paused. "The information that I supply to Kiley is false: sketch plans made to look like working drawings, reports on the development of weapons that in fact have got no further than the drawing board, engineering schedules for nonexistent projects, and of course many small truths that help to mask several big lies. There is one objective to all this: to make our nuclear development programme seem twenty years ahead of the stage it has reached, and thus increase the value of our deterrent. The plan has worked, beyond our wildest expectations. The CIA believe that Ch'ien is their asset. In point of fact Kiley, without knowing it, is our asset. We intend him to remain so."

"Then you are really . . .?"

"A servant of my country," Kao said modestly.

"And Ch'ien?"

"Dr. Ch'ien has been dead for two years." Kao Ling smiled faintly. "He would think his memory well served. When we resurrected him and told the Americans that he wished to defect, we gambled on their response. When I first met Kiley he told me he distrusted people who came offering him things. He was offered Ch'ien's defection and he did not believe it. But he did not question the authenticity of what he thought he had got by his own cleverness—the documents that Ch'ien apparently, and with reluctance, agreed to supply. A large doubt overshadowed a lesser one. So you see, Mr. Pritchard, what murky waters you have stirred. As an amateur meddling in a dangerous profession, I can only say you have been foolish and—"

Suddenly there was a shout of alarm. Both of them turned. One of the Moros, posted as a lookout on the ruined east colonnade, was racing back across the clinker, calling out to Diaz. Pritchard caught only one word in the stream of dialect: *Helicóptero!*

The Chinese faced him again, suddenly tense. "They are coming to look, nothing more. They cannot know we are here."

"I want you to tell me one thing," Pritchard said. "Why have you said all this to me?"

"I told you, you deserve to know." Kao looked troubled again. "Also, as things stand now, you are something of an embarrassment."

310

The Moros were shouting to each other and running from all directions towards the colonnade that led to the cells. Two of them were dragging Quinn's body up the steps to get it out of sight. Kao said, "We cannot linger here, in the open."

"The helicopter can't make a landing."

"But it will see us."

"What do you mean, an embarrassment?"

"To the world at large, Mr. Pritchard, this whole business will seem to be what you pretended it was, something conceived and carried out by the Moros. It is unfortunate for you that you know otherwise."

They could hear the helicopter now, the whipping of its blades and the high-pitched hum of its engine coming from somewhere beyond the rim of the plateau. Most of the Moros had vanished into the monastery cells, but Diaz still stood in the colonnade, by the steps. He was shouting at them to get out of the courtyard.

"Wait." Pritchard seized Kao by the shoulder. "Just what is it you're telling me?"

"That a man has a right to know why he must die." The Chinese looked steadily into his eyes. "It must happen—if not now, then soon. The choice is yours, Mr. Pritchard."

Terror, like a startled snake, uncoiled itself swiftly within Pritchard. In disbelief he watched Kao Ling turn and walk away. Then he was aware of standing there alone and terribly exposed, the blood screaming in his head, his heart pounding fast enough to hurt. Yet his thoughts were still blindingly clear. His alternatives were reduced to two: he could stand, or he could run. The helicopter was drawing closer. There was a chance in a thousand that he could draw its pilot's attention to the monastery, betray the Moros, destroy the monster he had created.

He caught a movement from the colonnade: Diaz, standing alone with a submachine gun in his hands, raising it. He turned and ran.

He ran awkwardly, stumbling over the clinker, to the eastern edge of the courtyard. Through the broken masonry of its pillars he got a glimpse of the helicopter, a dark speck moving close to the ground, still more than a mile across the lava field. He stopped and raised his arms.

He felt three violent blows at once: two on the back, one in the base of his skull. Something seemed to explode with a gigantic white flash inside his head and suddenly he was on the ground, face down among the clinker, hearing the echo of the burst of shots merge into a single brief bark. He had fallen into a hollow beside the colonnade. He knew he would have to stand up to be seen, but his limbs refused to move. He smelled sulphur from the volcano and tasted blood in his mouth. His consciousness flickered like a guttering candle, flaring briefly to an intense awareness of the fierce red glow of the sun over the mountaintops. The last things he heard were the slashing of the helicopter's blades and the scream of its engine as it approached the ruins. It circled them for only half a minute before turning away.

37

Tony Mendez drove McNair to Manila International Airport on Saturday morning. They parted promising to look each other up again and knowing they wouldn't. They had nothing in common but a failure, and they would never want to reminisce about it. They said good-bye at the passport barrier with a degree of mutual relief.

In the departure lounge as he waited for his flight to be called, the failure shrieked at him from the headlines of the *Manila Times:* ENVOY GOES FREE AS KIDNAP MOB SCOOP $10M. At eight o'clock the night before, Roderick Kiley had walked into a police station in the Manila suburb of San Juan del Monte, after being pushed blindfolded out of a moving car. An hour earlier, the ransom taken to Simpang by the American courier had been paid over in cash by Chief Minister Salim to a representative of the Moro National Liberation Front at an undisclosed rendezvous. "We are profoundly grateful to Mr. Salim for his humanitarian intercession," the American Secretary of State was quoted as saying. "It was nothing, my dear fellow," Salim had told a reporter. "When a life is at stake, it is only natural to try to save it."

The flight was announced—Cathay Pacific 114 to Hong Kong, departing on schedule—and McNair folded his newspaper and stood up. Then he recognized the elderly Chinese who rose from the chair opposite him: Kao Ling, the journalist and suspected Communist agent who'd come in on the same flight as he had last Wednesday. McNair hadn't given him a thought since.

He would add a note to Kao's file when he got back, he thought. But that would have to wait until he'd written his report for Boyd and the Kiley case could be closed. Meanwhile, he still had the best part of the weekend to spend with Siu.

312

Driscoll,
Pangolin

55540

DATE			

8-79   1986